The Adventures of Ryushin

The Adventures of Ryushin
Two Hearts

By
Derric Euperio

E-BookTime, LLC
Montgomery, Alabama

The Adventures of Ryushin
Two Hearts

Copyright © 2007 by Derric Euperio

All rights reserved. No part of this book may be reproduced or transmitted in any form or by any means, electronic or mechanical, including photocopying, recording, or by any information storage and retrieval system, without permission in writing from the copyright owner.

This is a work of fiction. Names, characters, places and incidents either are the product of the author's imagination or are used fictitiously, and any resemblance to any actual persons, living or dead, events, or locales is entirely coincidental.

Library of Congress Control Number: 2007927498

ISBN: 978-1-59824-519-6

First Edition
Published May 2007
E-BookTime, LLC
6598 Pumpkin Road
Montgomery, AL 36108
www.e-booktime.com

Dedications

Dedicated to my friends, my family, the ones I love
- to Marlene B. Euperio

Love,
      Her Son- Derric Euperio

Contents

One	Mysterious Occurrence	25
Two	One Year's Time	46
Three	The Other Girl	67
Four	Ahz-Bovan	81
Five	The Great Divide	102
Six	The Elven and the Troll	115
Seven	The Fallen Kingdom	142
Eight	Kyugen, the Great Escape	156
Nine	More than just a Past	175
Ten	The Windfields of Garuda	186
Eleven	The Dragon and the Snake	196
Twelve	Bandits of the Southsands	210
Thirteen	The Secret of Ifrit's Ring	227
Fourteen	First Love	243
Fifteen	Path of Memories	264
Sixteen	Last Minute Tactics	270
Seventeen	Battle For Destati	288
Eighteen	The Dragon's Den	339
Nineteen	Far Worse than a Gisuru	356
Twenty	Resigning of the Prince	363

Characters

Aeric

Characters

Aida

Characters

Onry

Characters

Rheaa

Characters

Rhyona

Characters

Ryushin

Characters

Valen

Characters

Xamnesces

Characters

Yoichi

Characters

Zandaris

Characters

Kitsune

Characters

Dracolyte

Characters

Kṣama

Chapter One
Mysterious Occurrence

I was walking along a plain of empty space. There was no texture or anything in around me, but I could feel it, the surface was there. The only sound that echoed around me was the light thud from my footsteps.

The words, *'Are you ready?'* flew across the empty space, one word at a time.

"Ready for what?" I tried to ask. I was muted, not a word would fall out of my mouth. I grabbed my throat with my hands, trying to squeeze it out but nothing budged.

'Ready for your adventure...?' the words continued to appear slowly.

There wasn't much I could do. I started running straight ahead... but to what? Nothing was here for me. Where would running get me? Nowhere...

The further I ran ahead, the more scenery would fall into place.

I was standing on a dark field, the sky filled with the night and the moon showered its light all over the lands. I had no idea where I was or why I was here, but all I knew was I wasn't home anymore.

"I've been waiting for you."

I turned around, meeting face to face with a boy, masked away by his dark blue hood. He held a staff in his right hand, overlapping his height by about a foot.

"Who are you?" I asked.

"Funny, I expected someone beefier," he said, ignoring my question. "Do you remember who you are?" I thought for a moment thinking about whom I am or rather who I was. "Maybe He's right. This will be a great test for you."

"Look, I know who I am, so I'll pass on the test."

"You do? Then tell me, what is your name?"

His question struck major confusion into my head. "My name is…" I repeated back and forth. The more I thought of it, the more I've seemed to blank out.

"So, you don't know," he chuckled. "He better know what He's doing, putting His trust into someone like you."

"What's that suppose to mean?"

"It is time."

The boy faded into the dark, leaving behind a sword resting on top of a mound. I walked to the sword to retrieve it. As I continued to move closer, the area began to fade back to the black empty space. Soon, the mound faded away from underneath the sword. It was strange at first, the sword floating in mid air, but it was quite interesting to see.

I gripped the sword by the handle and tugged on it, breaking it free from its levitation. As soon as I unsheathed the sword, I was swarmed by demon looking creatures. I panicked, dropping the sword.

"Wait, I don't want the sword. Take it back!" The demons were disfigured, winged creatures with a rough built shape. They had no texture, shining very little light in their eyes and their claws were gigantic, so were their feet.

The demons leaped into the air all together, ready to attack. I closed my eyes, crouched to my knees and defended myself powerless with my hands.

"It is time." A voice echoed.

I opened my eyes, finding myself drenched in my sweat, back in my bedroom. I wiped it off my forehead with my arm, relieved that it was only a dream.

"What the hell was that?"

I jumped out of bed and sat into one of the chairs by my computer desk. I turned on my computer to see who was online for chatting. Unfortunately, there was no one on. I turned around, knocking some papers off the desk with my arm. I crouched down to pick them up.

Under one of the papers was a picture of me and my ex girlfriend.

The Adventures of Ryushin

"How did we ever go wrong?" I asked myself.

Her name is Ayaka. She was the first love of my life and now that she's gone, I felt so lifeless inside. We've been together for almost three years and I actually came to the conclusion of wanting to commit to her, but I was only fooling myself. It's been almost a year since I last saw her, and still to these days I worry all too much. I wonder about how she's doing without me... we did almost everything together.

In the picture, Ayaka and I were dressed formally, her wearing a beautiful pink dress and I in black tuxedo with a blue vest and tie. I took the picture, stashing it away into my wallet for safe keeping.

Underneath the rest of the papers laid a picture of my family- my brother, sister, father and my mother. At first we were a dysfunctional family, no cooperation whatsoever. That was until my mother had passed away three years ago. Watching her go was one of the worst experiences in my life and I hope to never feel that kind of pain again.

I got ready for the day, putting on some cargo khaki shorts and a red short shirt, covering a black long sleeve shirt underneath. I styled my hair with hair gel, spiking it on the left, curving it with style on the right. I slipped on some black socks all the way up to my knees, strapping on my black and white shoes over it.

I live in a nice quiet area called Ladera Ranch with my family, somewhat hidden in Southern Orange County in California. My family was never home though because we all work. Since the tragedy that befell my family, all we've been doing is working so damn much. My mom left us at a good time, however, a time where we were experienced in life just enough that we could take care of ourselves.

I'm a high school graduate from Tesoro High School's class of 2004. I guess that's all I can really say about myself right now. I'm Filipino, so I have a lot of Asian friends. They've all been really busy with their own lives lately and I don't blame them. The definition of life after high school was work, at least, to us. It's been almost two months since I last saw them. I even find it hard enough to find time to spend time with my younger brother.

I walked out of the house and into my truck, driving off toward Mission Viejo Mall, relaxing for the most part of the day. But I ended up sitting in traffic for a good half hour.

"Damn it."

I pulled out my cell phone and surfed through my phone book.

I hated being alone. I would call up anybody, asking them to hang out for even a little while. Everyone's so busy with their girlfriends and boyfriends, it made me feel left out, knowing that I had no partner to associate myself with.

"Come on, the mall is right there!" I yelled, honking my horn.

The explanation of the hold up was the result of a car incident. The car was torn to shreds and the owners of the car stood on the sidewalk in disbelief. The police tried to solve the problem but they looked just as confused as the owners. On the torn up car were scratch marks, looked more like slashes from claws up close.

In the distance on top of the hill, stood a boy covered in a dark hood with his arms crossed. He looked just like the boy from my dream. He turned around, vanishing behind the hill. I looked straight forward frightened a bit, pulling into the mall.

Once I stepped foot inside the mall, my heart beat began to relax. I couldn't help but wonder about the boy on the hill. There had to be a similarity from the strange character from my dream. I walked passed the clothing stores on the second floor and went down to the first floor on the escalator.

"Hey Derric!"

I looked behind to find Alex, an old friend of mine from high school.

"Alex! Long time no see!" I greeted cheerfully, giving him a hug.

A girl popped out from behind with a smile.

The Adventures of Ryushin

"Hey! You remember Eliza, right?" Alex asked.

I chuckled shaking her hand, "There's no way I could forget the first girlfriend of Alex."

Alex wore a white short sleeved shirt with Army camouflaged pants and converse sneakers. He was a lot bigger than the last time I saw him, more bulky in definition. Eliza wore a white top with jean Capri's and white sandals to match with him.

"So what are you doing here?" he asked.

"Just looking around. I'm actually here to grab a bite," I smiled, "I haven't eaten all morning. My stomach has been practically growling nonstop."

"Why don't you come join us for lunch?" Eliza asked. "We're here to eat too, and shop of course."

"You guys don't mind?" I asked.

"Of course not, let's go to the food court," Alex said, leading the way.

Off in the distance, the water fountain splashed remarkably with a creative design, located center of the mall. A long time pal of mine stood alongside of the fountain, tossing in coins. He had this wandering look on his face and I could sense that everything was alright with him.

"Ralph," I called.

He looked up surprised. He wore a semi big black shirt with some jeans. His hair spiked straight up on all sides. I laughed joyfully as he walked up to us, "Where the hell have you been man?"

"I've been busy lately with some things," he answered.

"Like what, throwing some coins into the water fountain?" I asked, "If I remember right, only little kids do that."

He was overjoyed, greeting Alex and Eliza.

"How's Kyra?" Alex asked.

"She's fine, somewhere shopping around here," he laughed.

"Why don't you come eat with us?" I asked.

"Nah, not right now. It's our anniversary today so I'm spending time with her. She'll be leaving early though, so maybe I'll catch up to you then," Ralph replied.

"Sounds like a plan," I said. Ralph walked away.

We sat down at the table with our food, yummy teriyaki chicken and rice, talking about our lives after high school. Alex and Eliza attend Cal State Fullerton and both met one another there, where as I have been unemployed for the last year.

"So what do you do on your free time?" Alex asked.

"I, uh, well... I usually just sit around home trying to find things to do," I answered, scrunching food between my teeth.

"No girlfriend yet?" he asked. "You still haven't gotten over Her, have you?"

"Who? Ayaka?" I asked. I began to burst into laughter, "What makes you think I'm not over her?"

"Well... you just sit around home, so and so quote. Derric, she's been with her new boyfriend for almost a year. Shouldn't you consider moving on?" He asked.

"Are you kidding me? I don't need a girlfriend. I'm doing just fine without one, right? Look at me. I don't have to worry about anyone but myself. As far as Ayaka goes, I don't give a damn if she's been with her boyfriend for a year," I said.

I became aggravated.

"Okay, okay, sheesh," he said, "I shouldn't have mentioned anything."

"What does it matter anyway? Maybe I'm not ready to have a new girlfriend, ever consider that?" I asked.

"Calm down man, I'm sorry," he apologized. Eliza sat there quietly. "I just don't like to see you alone. You were just so full of life when you were with her."

I glared at him evilly and walked off.

Every time one of my friends brings up the subject of my past relationship, I explode. Everything I did in life always bounced back to her, as if I can't do anything without her. Pacing my tracks around the mall was the only thing that could help me blow off steam.

I entered the Apple Imac store, touching one of their computers. As I moved the mouse to remove the screen saver from the computer, the boy in the hood appeared on the screen. I flinched back into a table, staring at the screen.

"It is time."

Shocked to see him on the screen, I ran out of the store and back to the middle of the mall.

Ralph caught me by surprise.

"Hey, where's Kyra?" I asked.

"She had to take off. Family business ya know?" He said. He then asked, "You want to get out of here?"

"Sure, where do you want to go?"

"Heard Justin and Jeice are at the spectrum. Let's head over there and see what they're up to."

I nodded.

Ralph and I left the mall, heading toward the Irvine Spectrum, a big outlet in the center of Irvine, California. It was the main attraction, the sort of place people of all ages would gather to hang out. To us, it was more like a refuge place for us when we wanted to get away from the silence and long hours of thinking.

There, we ran into my younger, eighteen year old brother, Justin, who was hanging out with our friend, Jeice, the youngest of us five. They're tall thin guys, reaching six feet. Justin wore a collared white polo shirt with some baggy jeans. Jeice wore a black long sleeved dress shirt with black dress pants. Justin's hair was shaved and Jeice's was sort of spiked into a Mohawk.

"What are you guys up to?" Ralph asked.

"Just here watching a movie and looking around at shoes," Justin answered. "How about you guys?"

"Eh, just came from the mall," I said, "Nothing really exciting going on." I walked forward as they trailed closely behind me.

Several cute girls passed by, smiling at me.

"Hey! Let's go get you a girlfriend Derric," Jeice said.

"No thanks, I'll pass on that one," I said.

"Why not? You're always complaining about having no one to hang out with and besides, it'll be good for you," he explained.

"Okay you're done now, shut up please," I said, irritated.

I examined the distance ahead into the crowd and there she was. Ayaka was standing next to window store, looking at clothes from a manikin. Around the corner came her boyfriend to hold her hand.

Ayaka was wearing a light, baby blue top to cover her silky-smooth Japanese skin, with jeans to match at the bottom. Whenever I see her, I crumble at the knees and I fall so quickly for her. Her hair was held up by some chopsticks and a blue purse hung from her right side. Her boyfriend wore a green and white thin sweater with a white shirt underneath. He, too, also wore jeans.

"You know, we don't have to stand here, let's keep moving," Ralph said.

They turned around and I began to follow.

The instant that I saw her here, all I could ever think of is running into her. All I wanted was to say 'hi' and have a brief moment with her.

We passed through the movie theater and passed the Cheesecake Factory over to the first water fountain.

"Check that out," Justin said.

Up ahead by the merry-go-round was a show. We gathered together, joining the other people watching. It was a medieval-ish kind of event with a support cast of knights and dragons.

"Alright you youngins out there on this wonderful bright evening of ours, are there any volunteers that would like to try and slay the evil dragon that has cursed us all upon our beloved land?" the host asked loudly.

No one volunteered and stayed silent out there.

"Come on brave lads, we need a hero to save us all!"

Ayaka and her boyfriend showed up on the other side to watch.

"How about you young sir?" he said looking down at me.

"I, uh, I don't know…" I said shyly.

"The world is counting on you sir! You can do it!" he cheered.

"Yeah, Derric!" Jeice yelled.

I punched him on the arm angrily and snorted, "What the hell are you doing?"

"Ah, so your name is Derric," he said, raising up his voice. "Everyone! We have a hero!"

"You ass," I said to Jeice.

"Everyone give a round of applaud to Sir Derric!"

The crowd started to clap and cheer in my direction, waiting for me to go up on stage. They flashed a high beam on me, nearly blinding my eyes.

"Are you ready?"

I looked around at everyone watching. I was so clueless to what I'm supposed to do, they didn't tell me anything. "Ready for what?"

"Just play along kid," he whispered.

I hesitated, dropping sweat faster than a shower could spray water. They handed me a sword and shield, strapping iron armor around my entire body, making me into a knight.

"What the hell are you guys doing?"

Out from under the stage came out a mechanical head of a dragon. You could tell it was a poor mechanical machine by the horrible design they put on it. And the poisonous gas it would breathe out was pretty poisonous, worse than spoiled milk.

Ralph jumped onto stage really quick and whispered, "Hey, just to let you know, Ayaka is in the crowd watching. So, don't try to look to bad."

"Hey, you think I don't know that?" I said as they finished putting on the armor.

Ralph jumped off the stage along with the host and stage crew.

"Are you all ready for the hero to slay the evil dragon?" he asked the crowd with a dramatic cry in his voice.

"Are you ready, Ryushin?"

I turned around to look and there he was, the boy in the hood.

"Oh no…" I gasped.

"Tsuikai."

He palmed his hand toward me and fired a light energy ball. I dodged to the side. The ball of energy struck the mechanical dragon. In a blink of an eye, the mechanical dragon turned into a real one and the ground underneath began to quake. All the people faded in their places and only I was left with the dragon.

The dark, green dragon roared with vigor, pushing me back a bit with its force. Its wings spread out about eight feet each, its muscles ripped tightly under its rough skin. The dragon's sharp teeth didn't look to friendly either.

"Why are you doing this to me?" I asked.

"This is what He wants," he answered.

"Who is HE, damn it!"

"You will see Him soon enough. He is testing your ability and your heart. He needs you more than ever."

"What does He want from me?" I asked, gripping the sword and shielding myself with the shield. "Tell me you little punk!"

"Forget everything in your past," the boy said, "You have to believe in yourself, just as He believes in you. You don't have to look back anymore. The path ahead is more than enough for you.

The dragon darted into the air and flapped its wings fiercely, knocking me onto my back with great force. I stood up and held my ground. The dragon ducked its head inward. It swung its fierce claws breaking the shield with one swipe. I tried my best to defend against it but it knocked my sword out of my hands.

I ran away from the dragon, looking for a place to hide. It hovered over me, striking my armor loose from my body. Now that I have no armor, the dragon was going to cut me up into pieces.

"Every hit you take means nothing anymore. You must face the challenges that lie before you, cast away your sorrow, your pain, your despair."

I dodged the dragon's next attack rolling to the side.

"Rise to the occasion and be that somebody that everyone sees in you."

The dragon took one deep breath, spilling a cloud of poisonous gas all around me. I turned my back, shielding my face from the gas. It was so strong, I was beginning to choke.

"Don't be afraid to accept yourself as a failure, because when you fail, you build your courage to stand up once more."

I fell to my knees, hazily looking up at the dragon. My sight was starting to go. I placed my hand on the ground to hold myself up. I swayed my free hand back and forth on the ground, finding my sword. I gripped a handle, listening to the blade grind up against the ground.

"Are you ready, Ryushin?"

"Shut up!" I yelled, hurling the sword toward the dragon. I closed my eyes, shielding them from the rest of the gas. All I could hear was the roar of the dragon in pain.

"Do you understand what I am trying to say?" he asked.

"Why do you keep calling me Ryushin?" I asked, but there was no reply.

I opened my eyes, finding myself back on the stage with the show crew at the Irvine Spectrum. I looked over at the mechanical dragon. The sword I hurled was pierced right into the heart.

"Yeah Derric!" Jeice cheered loudly. The crowd jumped into an uproar of cheers. I stood up and smiled.

"Let's give it up for the hero!" the host cried.

I scratched my head embarrassed. I looked over at Ayaka's direction to see her smiling, so I smiled in return watching her walk away from the show.

"How the hell did you pull that off?" my brother asked.

"Pull what off?" I asked.

"Don't you remember what you did?" Justin asked, confused. "Dude, you got knocked off the stage but you still managed to throw the sword right at the dragon's heart."

I laughed, "Oh yeah, I guess I got lucky."

My friends and I sat around a dinner table at the Cheesecake Factory, talking and exchanging stories of our past and current lives. All of them would talk about their girlfriends of course, and I felt stupid, not having any stories to share with them. But I did bring up some memories I had with Ayaka to tell. They would give me the 'raised eyebrow' look, then continue talking about their stories as if I didn't say anything at all. Then the subject about weird dreams came up. This time I had a story to tell.

"Speaking of dreams," I cut in, "I've been having this weird one."

"Oh really, what about?" Ralph asked.

"Well, it's about this boy who keeps following me… sort of like, he's haunting me and stuff, ya know?" I said.

"Dude, you dream about little boys?" Jeice asked. "That's the kind of dream I wouldn't want to share."

All of them started cracking up in laughter.

"I'm being serious," I said. "Watch, don't be surprised if you find me missing the next morning." They still continued to burst in laughter. With my spirit low, I just ducked my head downward and swallowed my tongue.

The rest of that night, I sat around the water fountain, minding my own business. My friends were off looking at stuff from a kiosk, just taking a look around. I caught Ayaka in the corner of my eye, checking out the movie list. I turned my head just before she caught me looking, pretending I never saw her.

The Adventures of Ryushin

She told her boyfriend to wait there for a moment, and then made her way over to my direction. Frightened about what might happen, I suddenly stood up for no reason, looking around for something to make it look like I was busy.

"Hey," she said.

I couldn't help but put a lousy act on for her. My face broke out into a 'too cool for you' look, opening my eyes wide as my way of responding to her. With a hard push, my voice finally opened up to, "What's up?"

"What are you doing here?"

"Oh..." I paused my response, looking around for my friends, "...I'm just here with some friends."

She smiled, "Having an all guys night, huh?"

"Yea, I guess," I answered, scratching the back of my head. I didn't know what else to say.

"Well, I gotta run. You take care okay?" she said, walking away. She looked back once more with a smile, leaving me completely breathless.

My friends huddled around me, staring deep within my eyes. Snapping their fingers in front of my face, I smiled, taking a seat next to the fountain again.

"What just happened?" Ralph asked. I didn't say a word. I was still amazed at that moment and I stayed that way the rest of the evening.

That night, I thought about what the boy had said to me during that fight. It was strange. Every little thing he said had to do with the dragon's attacks. He was right. If I bottle myself up so much, sooner or later I'm going to explode. I have to take courage to my heart, be the person I want to be and what everyone sees.

Recalling everything that I had learned in life, every lesson that I had followed, it all came down to this decision. Somehow, I had a feeling I was going to have to do this whether I wanted to or not. But if didn't listen to my heart, then I wouldn't go anywhere at all. I wanted to be somewhere, some place where no one knew who I was. I wanted to start all over again, to start fresh without any worry. If I stayed here with my friends and family, lock myself up at home, and then it wasn't going to happen. Maybe, just maybe, this boy can help me find what I'm looking for.

I sat quietly on one of the chairs on my porch, thinking endlessly of what I should do. The time on my watch read midnight. My heart was beating rapidly, like I forgot to do something. The thought of Ayaka raced through my mind, seeing her smile at me continuously as she drifted further away from me. I wanted to see her, I had to, just to say goodbye.

Deeper into the night, I parked my vehicle on the side of the road, having to continue on foot due to the night security at the gate and the patrol that watches the streets. That was the city of Coto de Caza, a giant city that stretched for miles of giant high rising hills, filled with houses and twirling roads. Ayaka's house wasn't too far from the security gate.

There I was, after a long year, standing on Ayaka's driveway, looking up at her dark window. She must be asleep already. Not wanting to wake her parents, I reached for my cell phone and dialed her number.

It was ringing, but no answer. Going straight to her voice mail, I hung up and redialed her number. After several tries, she finally picked up.

"What do you want? I'm sleeping," her tired voice said.

"Ayaka, come outside," I requested.

"What's outside?" she asked.

After a few seconds, she raised her blinds and shot a hysterical look down toward me. "Are you crazy? It's passed midnight. How did you get in here anyway?"

"Just come outside and I'll tell you."

She took her time, keeping me out in the cold for about ten minutes. She finally came out, wrapped in a big blanket.

"Well, what is it? You have to be quick, otherwise, if my parents find out you're here, we'll both be in big trouble."

"Come walk with me," I said, walking down the pavement. I paced myself quite slowly, attempting to make this last as long as it can. She walked by my side, faced straight forward, wrapping the blanket tight.

"Are you going to tell me?" she finally asked, breaking her patience.

We stopped walking, halting at a children's playground. I sat down on one of the swings, she on the other. The moon was large and bright tonight. Light showered onto her face, brightening her beautiful face. A puzzled distraught face expressed her motions of the moment.

I looked at her, frowning and disturbed.

"It is time," I said.

Those were the words that came from my heart.

Her puzzled face grew more confused. "What are you talking about? It is time? Time for what?"

"I don't exactly know, but I won't be here anymore."

She closed her eyes, dropping her head in disappointment. "You always say that. You've always act like you're leaving but end up staying anyway. Derric, I don't want a part of this anymore."

"I know I know, just hear me out. This time I'm telling you the truth."

She looked back up at me with a frown, believing I was lying again.

"Fine, where are you going?"

As soon as she asked that question, dark looking creatures emerged from the ground around us. They were bold, muscular looking things, small ripped wings on their back, giant hands with sharp nails, pure black skin and giant feet with long talons.

I hopped off the swing, defending Ayaka.

"Ayaka, stay close."

Frightened at these figures, Ayaka quickly wrapped her arms around my left arm. There were four of them. What was I going to do?

"We are not foxes, we are Kitsunes," the Kitsune said. "How dare you."

The Kitsune had soft orange fur with black tipped ears and a pointed snout. They were pretty cute; fuzzy looking creatures. So adorable, I could squeeze them tighter than a pillow.

Aida walked up to the Kitsune and apologized, "Please excuse him. He's new to the kingdom. I think he's new to this world actually. Sounds funny, but I'm here to ask Penyae for some help.

"Aida," the Kitsune saluted, "I am very sorry. Penyae should be in his laboratory. I don't think he'd mind if you walked right in. It is an honor helping you."

Aida smiled, "Thank you very much."

"I'm sorry," I said, bowing to the little Kitsune.

"Come on Ryushin," Aida said.

We continued to walk down the block, passed all the machinery. At our feet rose a fairly tall and fairly wide building with many windows. The first room we walked into was packed with a lot of hi-tech software and little Kitsunes operating them. In the center of the room was a wide screen. It turned on by itself and a Kitsune appeared on the screen.

"Aida," the Kitsune said surprised, "What brings you here? It's been so long."

"Hello Penyae," she smiled, "It's wonderful to see you again as well." She looked over at me and then back up at the screen. "I need to ask a favor of you. May we come up? I have a friend I want to introduce to you."

"Give me just a moment and I'll have you ported up in a sec." Penyae said.

The screen turned off.

"Please show your best manners, Ryushin," Aida said, "He is a dear friend of mine."

"I'll do my best," I said.

The words, *'use the sword'*, raced through the sky in bold white letters. Lying down on the ground was a sword in a sheath. I grabbed it by the handle and gripped it tight.

"Ayaka, you gotta give me my left arm," I said.

She let go, still very close to me. I grabbed the sheath with my left hand and slashed the sword out and held it down to my right.

The demons charged one at a time.

I pushed Ayaka out of the way, taking the tackle from one of the demons. Before we hit the ground, I locked its head under my left arm, driving it head first into the ground. I rolled to the side, getting back to my feet. Another demon slammed its closed fist into my stomach, grabbed my shirt and tossed me off to the side.

"Ayaka… get out of here," I grudged. I stood up once more, facing the four demons. She couldn't move. She was too afraid. "Ayaka, they're not after you, get going now!"

One of the demons looked over at her. Drool dripped from its mouth. I quickly ran to Ayaka as so did the demon. I lunged into the demon, lowering my shoulder into its body. The other demons were on the move. I swung my sword slowly, missing the first one. With an uppercut to my stomach, I was knocked into the air. The second demon delivered a knee, knocking me even higher. I felt a sharp pain in my back, as the third demon was slamming the sharp of its heel into my spine. I dove straight down, bouncing off the ground and onto my back next to Ayaka.

She knelt next to me holding me up. "You're hurt…"

I could feel the blood drip from my mouth caused by the blows to my stomach. I could barely feel my body. I've never endured this much pain before.

"Ayaka… you gotta get out of here…"

"I'm not leaving you," she said, tears falling from her eyes. I looked up at the night sky as the demons were coming toward us.

The Adventures of Ryushin

The words again appeared in the sky. *'I am here with you, together we can do it'.*

I can see him. He was there, floating down toward me. He wore a red and black hat with a feather sticking out of it. A dark red tunic with a black cape wrapped around his shoulders, covering his body. He wore black, somewhat baggy pants with a strong pair of red and black boots. He placed his hand onto my chest, creating a light.

I yelled in pain, closing my eyes.

Ayaka cried, "Don't leave me!"

He transferred himself into my body, renewing my wounds. I felt him there by my side, giving my strength, courage, spirit, and the heart to fight. Opening my eyes, I palmed my left hand at the demons.

"Kagayaku Hikari!" I cried.

A bright light formed into a ball in the palm of my hand. It exploded into a giant ray of energy, destroying the demons on contact. The light faded in the night sky, leaving the two of us alone.

Still crying, she held me closer in her arms. I smiled, wiping her tears from her red cheeks.

"Ayaka, I can't breathe," I chuckled a bit, but still a little sore.

"I'm scared," she cried.

I smiled again. "Don't worry, I'm here. I won't let anyone hurt you, I promise."

Unable to walk on my own, Ayaka carried me around her shoulders back to her house. She opened the door slowly and helped me up the stairs. I rested onto one of the sofas in her guest room, letting the pain sink in a bit. She left the room in a hurry.

"So he chose you after all."

Over in the corner was the boy in the hood.

"Did you send those demons after me?" I asked. He answered no with a nod. "What were those things?"

"Those are demons from the other world, they were after you," he answered.

"They're from another world? What world is that?" I asked.

"You will learn about it soon. Just have a little patience."

I tossed the sword at his feet. "Who was that guy?"

"It was Him, which is now you," he answered picking up the sword. "Everything is happening according to what He said. I'll give you the rest of this night. I'll be waiting on top of the hill near your home at dawn. If you don't show, I will be coming after you."

"Shut up already," I grieved. "I will be there."

Ayaka walked into the room with a cup of tea. "Were you talking to someone?"

I looked over to the corner, he was gone.

I replied, "No one, just myself."

Ayaka sat onto her other sofa across from me, wrapping herself in her blanket again. She sighed, looking straight at me while I sipped the tea slowly.

"Kagayaku Hikari… I remember you asking me about it two years ago when we were in class…" she said. "It means Shining Light in Japanese, do you remember?"

I continued to sip my tea, listening to her talk. There was a moment of silence between us. I guessed that recalling memories of the past might be too painful for both of us, especially for her.

"I…"

"Look," I interrupted her, "I gotta go."

I stood up, placing the cup of tea aside. She grabbed my hand as I walked by slowly. "Will you stay with me tonight?"

"Ayaka… this is just too much. I just wanted to come and say goodbye. I don't know when I'll be coming back… I don't even know if I'm coming back and…"

"Please…?" she asked, regardless of what I just said. "I don't want to be alone…"

Tears continued to fall from her eyes. I gave a long drawn out sigh, looking away from her eyes. She hasn't held my hand for so long... I could feel the sharp pain from the past build up in my heart.

"Only for a while," I answered.

The rest of the night, Ayaka and I sat up against the couch on the floor, talking about the fun we used to have back when we were together. I was sad for the most part, yet very happy I could able to spend my last night with her. I couldn't tell how she was feeling, maybe a little distant, but was still glad I was around to keep her company.

"Here," she said, holding her closed fist over my open palm. She dropped a golden heart shaped locket into my hand. Inside the locket were two pictures of her and her friends.

"What's with the locket?"

"Don't you remember? You gave that to me for my eighteenth birthday," she said.

"Oh yeah," I nodded, "I wanted you to have it because I wanted you to always remember where you were from."

"And now, I want you to have it. So that if you're ever stuck in a bind, wherever you go, I will be there for you."

"Thanks, but I really think you should hold onto it."

She crossed her arms and looked away.

"Take it or I'll trash it."

"Okay, sheesh," I said, putting it in my pocket.

"Don't forget it! Don't forget me, promise?"

I chuckled, "What makes you think I'd forget you?"

"Just don't or I'll be very mad." She frowned at me. "Stay strong, right here..." She rested her hand upon my chest where my heart was. "If you're strong here, then you will never forget."

Tired as she was, she hazily rested her head on my chest, tucking herself wrapped in her blanket under my arm and up against my side. I was afraid at first, but not letting this moment go to waste, I closed my arms around her keeping her warm. One tear slowly trailed down the side of my cheek, one for happiness.

I woke up close to dawn with Ayaka still in my arms. Without waking her up, I carried her back to her room and gently laid her to rest on her bed. I sat there next to her side, just watching her for a moment. She was so beautiful, even in her sleep. I pulled out the picture in my wallet of us and placed it on her drawer next to her bed.

"Goodbye, Ayaka," I said, kissing her gently on the cheek.

She looked up at me, still half asleep, shuffling her head in her pillow.

I left the house quietly, finding my way back to my truck.

Just like the boy said, he'd be there waiting near home for me on top of a hill.

"I've been waiting for you," the boy said.

"Yeah, yeah. Why do you wait for me so much? Why don't you go watch some cartoons or something?" I said sarcastically.

"Are you ready?"

I thought for a second before answering.

"Not really. I don't know what I'm supposed to be ready for."

"You'll see," he chuckled.

"What is it with children having to be so scary?" I asked myself.

He raised his hands up, opening a gate in mid air. "I wish you luck on your journey, Ryushin."

I raised my hand, stopping him from doing anything further. I wanted to know from him, why this is happening to me and no one else.

"What will happen to me when I cross through that gate? Will everything change? What will happen to me in this world?"

"You will forget everything you leave behind here," he answered. "As far as yourself missing from this world, the world will continue to move on without you."

"So you're saying I'm gonna be dead?"

"Pretty much. Just think of the reactions you'll get from your friends and families when you come back… if you come back."

Everything I loved and cared for stood before me in spirit with a smile. I, opposite of them, smiled back. They were there with me, Ayaka, my friends, my family. A sudden tear escaped my eye, leaving me very emotional. It was as if I was never going to see them again. But somewhere in my heart, this had to be done. I'll come back to them, back to her… I promise. I walked through the gate with poise…

Chapter Two
One Year's Time

I opened my eyes slowly, finding myself in a dark enclosed forest. I rubbed my blurry eyed visions, bringing back my sight.

"Where am I?"

"You're here."

I looked to my side. There was a girl in shining armor sitting next to me. I stood up quickly, a little shaken up.

"You look just like …"

"Like who?" she asked.

My head was a bit woozy from the boy's energy ball.

"Damn it, what's her name? You look just like …" I couldn't believe it, I forgot her name.

She stood up with a frustrated look, "You are one weird kid. What is your name anyway?" I couldn't remember anything, not even my name. "What's wrong?" she asked.

I looked around looking for a clue to what my name was. The sword that was floating in the air in my previous dream rested at my side.

"My sword!" I said, hugging it tightly. I unsheathed it alarming the girl. She unhooked from her back an even bigger sword, pointing it at me. "Hey! What are you doing?"

"Drop your weapon!" I immediately dropped it and raised my hands high. "You dare attack me?"

"No! I was just looking at my sword. See look," I said looking down at my sword. "My name is carved on the blade. My name is Ryushin." I looked at it funny. "My name is Ryushin?"

"Seems Gundita was right about this place," she said, placing her sword away. "We must get out of her quickly, it's not safe here."

"Why is that?" I asked.

Demons emerged from the ground.

The Adventures of Ryushin

"That is why," she said striking her sword out.

I grabbed my sword and faced the demons.

"It's so dark, I can barely see them," I said.

The demons jumped into the air, ready to attack all at once. I evaded to the side and challenged two of them; the girl took on four on the other side.

The first one attacked head on. I jumped to the side, striking it three times. The second one faded, reappearing right under. The demon swung its arms underneath my feet, launching me into the air. Blocking the first demon's attack, I retaliated with a quick strike downward. Back onto my feet, hanging into the fight, I struck the second one away.

I ran over to the girl to aid her but three more demons rose from the ground. They formed together an even bigger demon. It pointed its open claw before me, launching a dark bolt of lightning. I blocked with my sword, taking a bit of damage from the force. I sprinted toward the greater demon, delivering quick strikes. This time my attacks were invulnerable.

"Hey!" I called over to the girl. "How do I kill this thing if I can't hurt it?"

The greater demon struck with its claw, marking my arm with a light cut. I flinched backward, still waiting for a response from the girl.

"Use your mana or energy, whatever you use!" she yelled.

I looked at her confused.

"What the hell...?"

I gripped my sword tightly, gathering energy from within. An image of fire appeared in my mind so I focused on fire.

"You have to command it," she said, continuing to hack away at the demons.

"Command it... right," I said.

I called forth fire. My blade lit up with a fiery glow around it. I dashed again, slashing the demon with a fire attack. The demons all vanished, leaving the both of us victorious.

She was rather calm, but I couldn't help but jump into laughter.

"Wow! I never knew I could do that!" I said astonished. "That's kind of stuff I could only watch on T.V.!"

"Let's go, we don't want them to come again," she said.

"Oh, yes. We don't want that." I said.

She looked like someone I could trust. Her sword kind of doubted my mind, but I didn't really have a choice in the matter. I placed my sword back into its sheath and tied the blade to my waist.

We left the dark forest and out into the open, where I could see a lot better. The sky was a nice, shiny blue, mixed with the white of the clouds and the rays of the sun. Seems like forever since I saw an atmosphere this beautiful. Not too far in the distance, a large stone wall stretched a pretty good distance along the land.

"What's your name by the way?" I asked.

"My name? I haven't told you?"

"Nope, we were interrupted by those thingies."

"My name is Aida. A pleasure to meet you, Ryushin."

"Wow, that's a beautiful name," I said.

She smiled briefly.

"So what are you? Are you some kind of terminator or something?" I asked.

Aida was confused, "No, I'm a paladin, though not a holy one. You're name is Ryushin, right?"

I nodded, yet had no idea what a paladin is. "Yup," I answered on her question.

"I see. Your name is well known around these lands."

"Oh really? Why is that?"

"You will learn more soon enough."

We continued to walk down the dirt road in the dark toward the large wall. The lands around here were a lot different. Everything was so open; there weren't any buildings or anything in sight.

"Um, Aida?"

The Adventures of Ryushin

"Yes?"

"Where are we?" I asked.

She answered, "We are in the lands of Raigen."

"Raigen..."

"Yes, Raigen, Kingdom of the Land."

Now, Raigen wasn't familiar to me at all. I've never heard of Raigen, the Kingdom of the Land, before. This was all too new; I had to find out more.

I stayed silent the rest of the way, following her like a baby puppy. The long path only made me think about this new place I am in now. Where was home? Have I forgotten everything? What will I do now?

We approached the stone wall with a steel gate planted in it. Two guards saluted Aida with honor and opened the gate. I walked on in with her and to my surprise, the great Kingdom of Raigen lay rested before me in a giant ditch. The walls around it rose pretty high, not including the giant stone wall already atop of it.

"Why is the castle in a ditch?" I asked, "Isn't that dangerous?"

"It's actually quite a long story," she said.

We both continued our path down a long pathway, leading to a small lift with another guard on it. The guard pushed a button on one of the machines. With great speed, the lift jolted us right down to the city.

"Before we head into the castle, I want you to meet a friend of mine," Aida said.

We walked into a mechanical part of the city, filled with machinery and electronic devices.

I tripped over something heavy, falling flat on my face. I sat up, dusted my clothes off and looked to what I tripped over; it was a small little fox.

"Whoa, what the hell is that?" I asked.

"Excuse me?" it said.

"The fox can speak!" I gasped, "Wow..."

The Adventures of Ryushin

Tiny rays of light surrounded us on all sides, picking away at our skin. And in an instant, we transported up to Penyae's room.

"Whoa! What was that?" I asked.

Penyae chuckled with his arms up on hips, "I am glad you like it! It is my latest technology yet. Beats taking the elevator."

Penyae was taller than the other Kitsune, standing at about half my height. He must be a pretty old one, considering the white spots on his orange coat and the way he slouched forward like an old man.

"Aida, what can I do for you?" Penyae asked.

"First, I want you to meet a friend of mine. This is Ryushin."

Penyae became overwhelmed with the presenting of my name, opening his eyes wide and dropping his mouth open. He looked at me in shock for about a good moment before responding to Aida.

"You don't say?"

"I do say, I couldn't believe it myself."

"You guys aren't going to kill me are you?" I said frightened.

Penyae crept over to me with his arms behind his back. He took a good look, front and back side. He always did the humming noise, like all professors would do.

"What do you think Penyae?" Aida asked.

He turned the other way and gave a big long sigh. "I do remember him being a lot beefier in books."

I staggered to the floor in disbelief.

"What can you make of it?" Aida asked.

"The Legend as people would call it," Penyae said, walking around in laps, "was a Legend that was never really fulfilled back way before the War of the Exiled."

"What is this Legend?" I asked, running up to Penyae. "Please explain."

Penyae walked over to his computer station and sat down. He punched in my name in the search column and an article appeared.

"The world's leader says a quote in fine print disappeared shortly after the defeat of the warlock. His disappearance was unknown and shortly after, the banishing of Draconia took place."

"That means gibberish to me," I said.

"Ryushin was the royal leader of Draconia, also known as the Kingdom of the Dracolytes. A stunning race, half human and half dragon, conquered almost all the lands and put them into a state of serenity," Penyae continued to explain. "But everything has its price. The kingdom was also home of a deadly power source, a dark one. It is called Destati."

"What are you trying to say old man?" I asked.

"There had to be some involvement with the power source, a good reason why Ryushin had disappeared after that long war," Penyae said, "It is a mystery left unsolved to the world and your reappearance back into the world could possibly effect the world, the good and the bad."

Penyae walked over to a bed rest and patted it down.

"Come, Master Ryushin. We are going run a research file on you."

I walked over to the bed and lay down on it. A big panel hovered above me and sprayed on intense rays of light. Penyae walked over to his computer and pushed some buttons.

"Strange..." Penyae hummed.

"What is it Penyae?" Aida asked, walking next to my side.

"Very little information on him," he answered. His computer beeped multiple times. "This is all I could pull up for you."

Penyae:

Name: Unknown
Age: 20

Birthplace: Unknown
Class: Crusader
Weapon of Choice: 1 Handed Sword
Specialization: Energy Based Attacks

Aida was lost. "A Crusader? As in, a Crusader way before the war even started?"

"Possibly. Ryushin was part of the Crusader Brigade, a powerful elite squad that worked under the Kingdom of Reina," Penyae said.

I couldn't help but slide off of the bed and look at the screen myself. It was my picture, it was me alright. My clothes were a lot fancier though.

"What's this here?" I asked.

"That is a summary on the War of the Exiled," Penyae answered. "The whole point of the war was to banish Draconia's dark power away from any evil heart that wanted its power. The Kingdoms of the world did their best to keep demons from preventing the banishment, but Ryushin was able to lock it away for good."

"I should take him over to Gundita right away," Aida said.

"Yes I would too. Gundita actually knows more about Ryushin than my computer believe it or not. But, he can't go the way he is dressed," Penyae said.

"What's wrong with my clothes?" I asked.

"You look like you just came right out of a pile of trashed clothing," Aida laughed.

I grunted, "Well what the hell are you wearing eh?"

Penyae stepped forward and cleared his throat. "You are looking at one of the finest Paladins of Raigen. Let me introduce to you, Aida, formally equipped with the plated golden armor, quite flexible too."

Her armor was made of hard rock plate, tinted with shining gold and white, lined with a bright orange. A tabard tailored with orange red and yellow colors overlapped her armor, tied at the waist and dropped thinly to her knees. "She has one of the finest sets of gear. She is a defender the people and the world. And she's beautiful with her black silky hair and blonde streaks too."

"Okay, I get the picture," I said.

"Thank you Penyae, but you didn't have to do that for me," Aida smiled.

"So what do I wear to the kingdom?" I asked. Penyae scrambled behind the counters, pulling out a rusty old box. He pulled some clothes out and handed them over "What is this?"

"Just put it on. I am sure you will like it."

I came out of the other room in the uniform he gave me. I was dressed in black slops to go with my shoes, and a cut-sleeved red shirt. It provided a belt with a hook to attach my sword, black open finger gloves for my hands, and a black torn leather shoulder pad to cover my right shoulder.

"Not bad," Penyae said with his hand on his chin. "What do you think Aida?"

Aida and I smiled at each other.

"Now, before you take off, I want to give you something that will help you along your adventure. You have a lot to learn boy." He whipped out a black bracer and tightened it all across my right arm. "This will help you channel your energy when you decide to use your mana. But watch your mana consumption because if you overuse it, you will drain yourself of your life."

"How do I know if I'm over using it?" I asked.

"You'll know," Aida said, "You will feel tired."

Penyae was filled with laughter, "You look stunning in your attire boy, and it goes well with your hair. And Aida, try not to fall so fast for this boy as well."

Aida and I both blushed.

"Thank you Penyae, I owe you one," Aida said.

We walked out of the Mech Block and made our way down the long stair way. This long stairway was known to them as the Raigen Bridge, the only way into the castle and the

The Adventures of Ryushin

only way out of the city. The city was the shell of the castle. On both sides of the bridge were two blocks; to the west of the bridge were the Port and Trade blocks. On the east side was the Mech Block, home of machinery and technology, and the Air Station which supports aerial transportation. Then there was the castle, planted in the center of the city.

We approached the castle's front gate, where we were greeted by a tall man in about his late twenties. He wore iron shoulder blades with daggers attached to them, colored with a fine tint of gold. His body armor and leggings were strong and bold, almost defining a perfect resemblance to a statue. On his back, he carried a great hammer with spikes at the end of the stone. I couldn't really see his face though because it was well guarded by a helmet. The helmet ran into spiky ends with a sharp red fade to it.

Aida saluted, "Nomak."

"So you've return with him?" he asked.

"Yes. I am here to bring him to Gundita," Aida answered.

Nomak crossed his arms for a moment and inspecting me. "So this is him, huh?" Aida and I looked puzzled.

"The name's Ryushin," I addressed.

"I know who you are Scrub," Nomak snorted.

"What's your problem?" I said, getting in his face.

He raised his back hand, ready to strike. He laughed and said, "You dare stand against my rank Scrub? You best be kneeling before me."

"Now why would I go and do that for an ass like you?"

He grabbed his great hammer and slammed it on the ground, "What did you call me, Scrub?"

I drew my sword and said, "You heard me."

Aida jumped in our path, disconnecting us from each other. "We're not even into the castle and you two are already starting a riot."

Nomak spit on the ground and put his hammer back on his back. "Scrubs, both of you. I'd hand you your faces if you weren't trolls." He entered the castle and walked out of sight.

I put my sword away and asked angrily, "Who the hell does he think he is?"

Aida covered my mouth, making sure that Nomak was away from us.

"He is well-honored around here. It's just who he is. Whatever he says or does, don't take it personally but he has let people get the best of him before, he seems intent to never do that again."

"Yeah, well, he doesn't have to be a jerk to me," I said.

We walked into the castle, looking all around. There were two floors, the top and the bottom. On the first floor was the Grand Court, this is where the special events take place. They can either take place in the courtyard, the gardens, the royal room or the master's court. The top floor consists of five areas the training grounds, the armory, the infirmary, the cathedral and the magician's quarters. We were standing in the courtyard.

"Aida."

"Chrisa," Aida saluted. Chrisa looked just like Nomak, except Chrisa is a female. She carried a sturdy lance spear hooked onto her backside, unlike hammer or sword that Aida and Nomak wielded.

"Gundita is waiting for you," she said, "Please follow."

We headed into the Master's Court, just straight ahead. A young blonde haired girl stood next to a seat of the throne. She wore dark faded leather clothing. She had a black long sleeved shirt with leather guards on her shins, up to her knees. She had short black shorts that cut at the middle of her thigh with straps connected to her leggings. Her long blonde hair was tied in the center with a bandana, making it into a tail.

"Now, show your best manners. I know she looks young. She's actually eighteen but don't let her looks intimidate you. She is a well and high classed person," Aida explained.

"Aida, please report," she commanded.

Aida said stepping forward. "It's just as you said. A young man would be wandering the dark forest. He presents himself as Ryushin and his current status is unavailable, according to Penyae's database."

"That damn Kitsune's machineries couldn't save us if it was his last resort," Gundita said walking toward us. "So this is He, the Prince Ryushin… interesting. He's actually kind of cute." I staggered to the floor blushing rosy cheeks. "How old are you?"

"…I'm twenty…" I said, still blushing red cheeks.

She laughed, "Very interesting."

"What's so funny, Commander?" Aida asked.

She laughed even more, "He's cute. He's young enough for me to date." Aida balled her eyes away as I staggered to the floor again. She turned her back walking back up to the throne. "Let me introduce myself. I am Commander Gundita, leader of the Kingdom of Raigen. We are a nation of the lands around us. We stand together with great pride."

"You guys don't like, rule the world, do you?" I asked.

Gundita shook her head. "We work under as a missionary kingdom, allied with three other nations around the world. They are Imperia, Olida and Evangelista. We watch the world every day and every night, we balance the world with power."

"Okay, I really don't have any idea what you're talking about," I said. "I haven't the slightest idea what I'm doing here either, so bare with me."

"He doesn't remember anything, Gundita," Aida said.

Gundita was troubled now. She paced herself back and forth, with her chin resting between her fingers, thinking continuously.

"You don't remember anything at all?" she asked.

I shook my head.

"Well, the best we could do is take you in as one of our students," Gundita said.

"Wait what? I have to go to school?" I asked.

"Not just school, but more of a training program. With the right set of mind, you should be able to finish the program in less than a year. You will practice in combat skills, sword handling and cardio exercise. The world these days is filled with danger, knowing how to survive is the first thing you must learn."

"It's going to take that long?" I asked.

Gundita nodded. "I will do the best I can throughout the year to help you recover your memory. Just bear with us, okay? One year is all I need from you."

I nodded.

For the first three months, I underwent some training that helped me enhance my mind and my intellect. I trained under Chrisa, who helped me improve my mana pool. I able to harness my energy and conserve it, making me last longer in fights. Familiar words came to mind during the long training sessions. For example, two outward explosions that consume a lot of energy, I call Kagayaku Hikari and Seinaru Yoru. These are also known as energy blasts.

The next two months I trained in the art of sword specialization under Gundita. The whole plated armor wasn't my gig, so I remained in the outfit Penyae sported to me. Gripping and handling the sword were my toughest links. In the time to pass, I finally learned how to hurl the blade accurately. My trusty sword, that's been with me since the start, has never left my side.

And still, there were no signs of anything.

The next month I learned how to move with agility, becoming more evasive in combat and becoming more accurate on my attacks. Strangely, my vision would enhance at random times, giving me the upper hand during Gundita. Things would slow down for a bit, making the fight really easy to read.

When I wasn't training, I'd find myself walking around the city and castle grounds, minding my own business and getting to know the place better. Throughout the days in the weeks that passed in months, my loneliness began to pick up. There wasn't any one really to talk to, being a stranger and all, but I would have the biggest smile on my face, every time Aida would stop by and talk to me. She had this thing in her that really made me happy, and I would stay that way for the remainder of the day.

It had been six months and still there were no leads or any sign that related to me. So I did what no one else could, and that was trying to remember my own past. Nothing seemed to spark. The more the snow fell during the time I was here, the more I started to forget everything of my past. Is this what the boy meant when he asked me if I knew who I am? The only thing I know about myself now is my name is Ryushin.

Gundita and I clashed in the center of the room. I jerked onto my back from her forceful attack. She stood above me with an open hand.

"Take a break," Gundita said. "You've been at it for such a long time, maybe you should go out to town and take a rest."

"What's going on in town?"

"Nothing really, just enjoy the crowd and relax."

So I did what Gundita said and took a walk around the city. I ended up going to the trade district since there was no other place to go. The trade district was filled with a lot of people. There was always a trade or auction going on. People needed this, people needed that, there were auctions for food, armor, some valuable rings, even pets. There were alchemist shops, blacksmiths, weapon crafters, chefs; they had a lot of things here.

"Excuse me," someone said, bumping right through. She was carrying a whole bunch of vials filled with liquids inside. "Excuse me. I need to get through so I can put these on auctions."

She bumped into a bigger stronger guy, shattering her vials against the floor.

"Watch it you little runt!" the bigger man screamed. She stumbled to the floor to pick up the shattered vials before anyone could step on them.

"Did you need some help?" I asked crouching next to her.

She looked at me as if no one has ever helped her before. She had long brown hair down to her hips tied in a twist all the way down. She wore a purple robe with silver linen and very little shades of blue splashed into the cloth. On her back was a long silver staff with a red crystal implanted on the tip of it.

She shyly said, "Thanks... No one has ever helped me before."

I began to pick up the shattered pieces.

"Don't worry about it. What is this stuff anyway?"

She looked at them and then back at me, "There... there um, potions?"

I chuckled a bit and said, "You don't seem too sure about what they are."

"I think they're potions... I've been trying to learn alchemy so that I can combine it with my frost magic," she said, standing up. "I think they will be able to save us one of these days."

"What exactly do they do really?"

"Um... well... they can do a lot of things. They can make you stronger, immune to certain effects... restore health or mana... or do bad things to bad people... you know?" she somewhat explained.

I raised my eyebrow, lost forming confused at her response.

"Uh huh... what's your name?"

She saluted, dropping her shattered vials onto the floor again. She picked them back up and said, "I am Onry."

I looked all around at the staring people.

"Hey, put your hand down. No need for formal introductions. Your name is Onry. My name is Ryushin, nice to meet you."

She smiled, "Nice to meet you too Ryushin. You don't look like you're from around here."

"That's because I'm not."

"I usually stay at the castle. I'm under consistent training there," she sighed, continuing with, "its not easy being a mage."

"Oh, you're a mage?"

"Actually, I'm a frost mage... watch," she said, raising her hand.

At the flick of her wrist, a blue light wrapped around my body. A frost cloud emerged all around my body, that freezing anything that touched it. It froze my legs over, pinning me tightly to the floor. "Oh my! I am so sorry!"

I started to shiver all around, "Can you please remove it? I am freezing down there." She flicked her wrist again and the ice shattered off. "I can see why you're under consistent training." She felt discouraged. "Aww don't be sad. I'm sorry. I'm under consistent training too."

"You are?"

"Yup, it's been six months, too."

"I've been at it for two years," she said. She almost looked like she was ready to break down in tears. "I've been trying so hard to pass the tests for the missions but it seems like I'm never going to get there."

"Missions?"

"Uh huh..." she sniffled, "I want to be a part of Gundita's missionary groups, doing raids and investigations."

"Don't worry, you'll make it and you know what?"

"What?"

"I hope we both make the same missions," I said with a smile. "It'll be fun and you will be nothing less than perfect and we will own everything." She smiled back, still head down. "I gotta run now. I have a lot more training to do."

"Okay, take care! I hope to see you again!" she shouted.

The next two months I continued into deep sword training with Gundita. She was a mean teacher and a force not to take lightly. She was a master of deception making it very difficult for enemies to detect her movements. I had to concentrate my energy to seek her out, forcing energy waves in her direction. Even if I could reveal her position, she would be too fast to counterattack.

Still living the lonesome days here in Raigen, I found myself a comfy spot in the garden courtyard. I would lie there on the bench for hours, just listening to whatever sounds came by.

Then it happened that day.

Across the garden, I could see Aida dressed rather casually then geared. She was picking white roses off of the roses bushes, collecting them into a bouquet. Her voice was humming at first. She caught me watching her in the corner of her eye. She smiled and began picking the roses again. A beautiful song rose from her voice and it melted away my heart. She sang the words-

**Saigo no kisu wa ka ba tabako no flavor ga shita
Nigakute setsunai kaori**

**Ashita no imagoro ni wa
Anata wa doko ni irun darou
Dare wo omotterun darou**

**You are always gonna be my love
Itsuka darekato mata koi ni ochitemo
I'll remember to love you taught me how
You are always gonna be the one
Ima wa mada kanashii love love songu
Atarashii uta utaeru made**

Her voice was so beautiful, I couldn't stop listening. My heart was melting at the same time, it's like she was doing it on purpose.

I walked up to her interrupting the song. I pleaded, "Please, don't stop singing. You're voice is so beautiful, I just wanted to have a closer listen."

The Adventures of Ryushin

She smiled, holding her the bouquet of roses in front of her.

"Are you spying on me, Ryushin?"

"No... I... was just... you see..."

I just couldn't find the right words to say to her at that moment, she had already taken my breath away. With twinkle in her eye and a soft wink, she made me grow weak at the knees. She smiled, watching me crumble to the floor.

"Stay with me for a bit," Aida said.

Being alone for a long time, I stayed with her all night listening to her beautiful voice sing. Sometimes, my eyes would trick me. Aida would turn into someone else, that looked just like her.

I resumed my training the next day.

The next three months ended in physical training with Nomak. He was a prick when it came to training and he gave me the hardest time no slack, no rest. But I wasn't about to let him get the best of me. Nomak saw my progression rising giving him ideas to try and make things more challenging.

"You give up yet Scrub?" Nomak would always say when he knocked me down. But every time and all the times I stood back up, he would walk away somewhat impressed.

The last month, I pretty much rested, spending a lot more time with Aida in the garden at nights or helping Onry train for the mission exams. Even with the year going by so quick, there were still no leads from Gundita.

I cleaned off one of my blades with a towel, slowly wasting time away in the garden. Onry crept around the corner slowly, thought for a moment in her place, then finally sat down beside me.

"Hello Ryushin," she smiled, "How are you? I haven't talked to you in a while."

I smiled, putting my sword away. "What's going on?"

"What's going?"

I raised my eyebrow then said, "Nevermind, how are you?"

"I am doing quite well," she said nervously.

"Are you okay? You're acting weird."

She stood up clasping her hands together thrilled about some news, "Oh I am so nervous! Today I'm supposed to receive my score for my missionary exams." She jumped around in circles excited. "If I pass, then I can finally go on missions!"

I fell off the side of the bench surprised, "Calm down! You're gonna break my ear drums with all that yelling. All you gotta do is just wait it out and everything will be just fine."

She sat down again in silence drifting her mind out into space. "Now what the hell are you doing?"

"I am patiently waiting like you said I should," she said. She was faced straight forward, blinking not even once.

"You don't have to be weird you know, just relax," I said, relaxing her tense shoulders. "You're going to scare people if you keep doing that."

"Ryushin."

I turned around, finding Aida standing there with a big smile on her face.

"Aida!" I smiled. I was overwhelmed with happiness the moment I saw her. "Always a pretty face to see."

I could see her blushing.

"Anyway, to make things simple, I was inspecting a hidden area out by the canyon," she answered. "It might be a possibility that this is our first lead."

"Really?"

Aida handed Onry and me a report. "We must file an investigation, exploring the area and report back to Gundita as soon as the mission is complete. Onry, you are a part of this mission, so I suggest you prepare yourself with food and water."

"Yes ma'am," she saluted, taking off.

"She's a little whack," I said. "Anyway, who else is attending this mission?"

"Onry and I will assist you," Aida answered, reading down on the paper work, "and we are to meet two more, who are waiting patiently for our arrival at Returner's Hill. From there we will group up and carry out our mission. This area is known as the Canyon's Pass. The hidden area is actually hidden deep under the ground. While you have been in training this past year, Penyae's machines have been hard at work with the ground creating a tunnel deep enough for us to move through."

"Sounds interesting."

"Very. Up until now, the hidden area never existed."

I stood up with a smile and asked, "That's why it's a hidden area, yeah?"

Entering the Master's Court, Gundita bowed as Aida and I approached her. She looked up smiling and said, "See, I told you I'd do the best I could to help you."

I bowed in return to hers replying, "That you did. Thank you Gundita."

"Now listen up, if Aida did not inform you already. The two of you will be assisted along with Onry on this mission. You will head to a small base camp north from here and rest there overnight. The following morning, you will be accompanied by two explorers, entering the tunnel they have been digging for the past year. You will report to me when the mission has been completed."

"Now before you go," Penyae's voice echoed. A large screen slowly moved down in front of Gundita. "I have personally taken the time to make you a custom built RT for you, Ryushin."

"What's that?" I asked.

"It is called a Raid Tracker. It allows you to communicate with other RTs within range of yours. Aida and Onry should already be on your RT, thanks to Gundita. However, the RT can only keep track of member's status if they are within a fifty yard radius," Penyae explained.

"Oh, and don't think we won't be surveying your exploration down there," Gundita said. "We took the liberty of inputting a link-stone into your RT, which allows us to communicate back and forth between the both of us."

I took the RT from Gundita and placed it on my left arm, acting like a bracer. "What are you going to be up to while we're doing all the dirty work?" I asked.

"We will be monitoring the lands around us," Gundita said, "Ever since you appeared that day a year ago, the activity of all races have been picking up. When you return with your finding, I will explain more on them. Now get going."

Aida and I walked off leaving the castle.

There stood Onry, waiting for us by the platform with a large sack sitting at her side. We stepped onto the platform and were quickly taken to the gates, just beyond the city.

"From here, we will head north into the open fields then proceed toward Returner's Hill," Aida explained. "I hope you two are both ready for this." Onry lifted the sack onto her right shoulder and we entered the grassy plains.

Chapter Three
The Other Girl

That had to be the longest walk I have ever been on. I was way too tired and cramped up for the rest of the trip. We still couldn't see the lights from Returner's Hill. The night had fallen upon us, with all of us growing weary. I stumbled to my hands and knees trying to rest a bit.

"The camp is just up ahead," Aida said, carrying her legs over the hill.

Whining and moaning from the pain, I cried to Aida, "But I'm so tired!" Onry caught up to Aida leaving me behind. "Bah, you two are so nice you know that?"

I picked myself up and staggered my way toward them. A light at the bottom of the hill began to flash. It was Returner's Hill.

As we entered the base ground, troops in blue chain armor approached us. They saluted Aida, bowing in a graceful manner. The two troops ordered us to follow them back to their tent.

A map lay on the table as we entered the tent.

"Let's see… where shall we begin…" He took out his pen from his side pocket and marked an area on the map. "This here is the hidden area that we have uncovered in the last few months. From this point on, into the tunnel, we have not been able to advance any further," the troop informed.

"Why, can't you dig anymore?" Aida questioned.

"We have been wondering that since the minute we hit the stone. This stone we've dinged seems to be a special stone- a stone so strong that even the rain cannot dissolve its surface," one of the troops said.

Aida gave them a hysterical look and said, "So then, why did you bring us out here?"

The second troop replied with, "Well... since it is a special stone, it had special markings on it that maybe you can decipher."

"Special markings? What kind of markings?" Aida asked.

The troop pulled out a photo and rested it on the table. The writing on the stone was too blurry for me to see. Aida thought briefly then looked puzzled at me.

"Anything?" the first troop asked.

"We'll have to take a look at it ourselves."

"We will assist you to the stone and your party will continue investigating the rest of the area. The RT will record everything, so we should be able to collect any data needed during your investigation," said the first troop.

I stretched out my arms wide, "So when do we leave?"

"First thing in the morning," the first troop answered.

That night, Onry and I sat around a campfire as Aida's mouth went on a verbal rampage with those troops. I stared into the fire, watching the flames flicker in the same pattern. The same questions continued to cycle in my head- who am I? Why am I here? What is going on?

Aida finally shut her mouth, joining us around the fire. The troops, all talked out, went for their tents to rest.

I looked over at Aida as she glared into the small flames.

"So, what's your story?" I asked. She broke concentration. "Yes, I'm talking to you."

"Do you really want to know my story?" she asked.

"Of course, you seem like a pretty interesting person," I answered.

Onry didn't mind listening to what Aida had to tell. I zoned in, focusing more on her eyes, watching her breathe in long and then exhaling.

"I actually grew up as an orphan when I was about the age of thirteen. I really don't recall anything else before that but anyway... moving on," she said, introducing her story.

Aida was a girl without a past to remember, just like me. Completely different from my story, she doesn't seem to think much of it, telling by the way she spoke. She grew up learning the way of a paladin, alongside Nomak and Chrisa, elders in the paladin branch. Her reason of being a paladin was to repent everything in her past that she remembered that truly made her ill.

She would speak horribly of some guy she used to be in love with. She said she was treated badly like an animal and she regretted being in love with him. As long as she could remember, she hasn't been in love with anyone since. Being more concentrated on her work, Aida didn't pay too much attention to her love life, making it less stressful.

"I really hope someday, I can be in love and actually be loved in return," she said.

"And you will," I said, enlightening her. "Don't worry about this guy ya know? I'm the only guy ya need around anyway!" She smiled. "Well, in like a bodyguard kind of way..."

Onry passed out fairly quick, probably bored with Aida's story. I rested my back up against a rock, giving a wide yawn into the night. Before I could shut up my eyes, Aida sat down very close next to me.

"Aida..."

She smiled, pulling her legs together up against her chest. "Ryushin..."

"Is everything alright?" I asked, blushing rosy cheeks. She tucked herself under my arm, wrapping herself in my body. She rested her head softly on my chest, closing her eyes.

"Goodnight, Ryushin"

The next morning, we stood outside the grounds in the bright shining sun. "Ryushin, stand up straight. You're looking rather lanky this morning." I gave Aida a nasty look, barely listening to her. "Alright, Ryushin and Onry, set your RT to sync with mine, that way we can keep track of our locations and speak to each other if we are to get separated." We synced our RTs and their names became listed under mine. "Alright troops, move out."

We took off early, heading north to the mountains.

"Just up ahead, it's not too far," the second troop said.

We came to the base of the mountain where the pathways split into multiple directions. We followed the troops into the mountain and toward the area where the tunnel was being worked on. "Okay, from here on out, you will be on your own. We will be recording your investigation, so try and get as much as you can."

"Go ahead Ryu," Aida said.

I stepped backward after looking deep into the tunnel and asked, "Wait, why do I have to go in first?" Aida shoved me into the tunnel and off we went. We walked slowly down a dark tunnel that almost seemed so endless. "What if there are spiders in here? I can hardly see!"

"Oh hush," Aida said.

"Why don't you go in front of me then?" I continued making my way down the tunnel with my arms extended out in front. At that moment, the ground below us started to rumble a bit. "What the hell was that? That is so not cool."

My RT popped open and Gundita showed up on the screen.

"Listen carefully. We have been picking up a strange aura within your radius. It seems to grow stronger the farther you advance into the tunnel."

"Great, you mean there's a monster down there?" I asked.

"We aren't sure of its identification but continue to proceed down the tunnel. We will contact you if anything else grabs our attention," Gundita said.

I pressed up against a hard wall.

"I think this must be the stone they were talking about. Quick, give me some light." Onry flashed the torch in front of me, holding the light to the stone. Engraved in the stone was a very strange text. "Aida, move up front and see if you can read it."

The Adventures of Ryushin

Aida took a glance, wondering what the meaning was. She stayed quiet for a bit, reading it back and forth. "Very interesting..."

"What does it say Aida?" Onry asked.

"I have never seen this text before in my life, but somehow I can read it," Aida said. "Ryu, come and see if you can read it."

I stepped up to the wall, examining the text thoroughly. It seemed so familiar to me as well. It was as if I have seen it before but I just don't know where.

"A Link Between Two Hearts," I read out loud. "How confusing is that?"

"That's what I would like to know," Aida said, just as confused as I was.

"There must be a secret meaning behind it, a deep one in fact," Onry answered.

"Obviously," I said, crossing my arms. "My question is... how do we advance further into the tunnel when this stone is in our way?" I pressed up against the stone pushing as hard as I could... still no budge. "We can't do much damn it. We'll have to turn back."

Aida looked back up the long tunnel.

"If we're going to leave we'll have to move fast." Onry started climbing back up first, followed by Aida. I stayed a bit, examining the stone one more time. "Hurry up Ryushin," she called.

"A Link Between Two Hearts..." I whispered. On the stone a marking started to engrave itself. "What the...? Wait a minute, guys!" I called to them, "Something just appeared!" The engraving marked the word: Down.

The tunnel started to shake fiercely. The surface cracked below, engulfing me into a dark pit.

"Ryushin!" Aida shouted. I landed shoulder first into the ground with piles of rocks tumbling from above. I rolled out of the way, saving myself from being squashed. "Ryushin, are you alright?" Aida called from above.

I sat up and grabbed my tailbone.

"Freakin', what the hell was that? I think I just smashed my tailbone…" I cried. "I'm fine. Damn it, get me out of here. It's dark down here. There could be spiders or something."

"We'll find a way down to you," Aida said, "Check out the area and see what you can find."

"Onry!" I shouted, "Throw me down the torch!"

She gently dropped the torch so that the fire wouldn't blow out on the way down. I grabbed it and flashed the flame around the area. There were torches on the walls. I shared the fire, lighting up the room.

"Heads up Ryu," Aida called. The two girls came crashing down on a piece of ice. "We used Onry's ice magic to create a bed for us."

"Well, at least we found an alternative entrance," I said, inspecting the room. "Look, there's a tunnel up ahead. Maybe we'll be able to learn some more if we go take a look."

"Remember the way back. We are unsure of what can be ahead of us," Aida said.

We entered the dark hall.

The thick, dense air made it very hard for us to breathe. The walls were tiled with cracked rusted stone, moss hanging from the cracks and the fire burning very dim on the torches.

"Wait a second," Aida said, pressing her back up against the wall before entering the next room. "I sense a lot of evil in front of us. But I don't see anything."

"Maybe your head is broken," I insisted.

"What are those?" Onry pointed straight ahead.

In this next room there were round stones planted into the ground before us. They looked just like eggs. Oval shaped objects layered with a thick crusted, orange surface.

"Are these the things that are emitting the evil aura?" Aida asked.

I put my ear up against one of them to listen inside. I heard a heart beat inside the shell. Then an evil voice called out to me. *"We're…"*

I jumped back frightened.

"Aida … come here and listen. It's talking to us." Aida put her ear up to the surface of the egg.

Placing my ear one more time, the egg said, "*We're…coming for you…*" My heart started to pump faster.

"I don't want to be here anymore…" I said, frightened.

A gate opened up on the east side of this room. Aida and Onry ran to it while I trailed them from behind.

In the next room was a big space of nothing. In the middle of room was a tiny altar hoisting a shining orb. Aida ran up to it and examined the area. Onry and I ran up to the altar and looked around. Aida placed her hand on it but nothing happened. Onry gave it a shot, but still nothing. It was a white orb with no light or any aura around it.

I looked even closer at the orb. The closer I got the more the orb began to glow. "Do…do you see that…?" I asked.

"It took you a whole year to get here?"

The boy in the hood surprised me from behind.

"What is this place?" I asked.

"Beats me, but I believe it has something to do with you," he answered.

Aida and Onry were completely still. Time had stopped all around me. The boy in the hood walked over to the orb, examining it very carefully.

"Can't you at least tell me who I am? Or how bout you? Who are you?"

He turned his back and walked slowly away. "You are still fresh at the tip of the iceberg. Though you may have grown just a bit, it is still not enough. Check the orb one more time before you leave." He faded into the darkness with his voice trailing behind him with an echo. "And leave with haste."

The room went back to normal. Aida and Onry looked at me with a hysterical look on their face. "Are you there? Hello?" Onry said, knocking on my forehead.

"I'm here, damn it," I said. "Look, we can't stay here any longer, we must leave and fast."

"Why? We haven't learned anything yet," Aida said.

"Just trust me on this one."

Aida and Onry headed for the opened gate. I looked one more time into the orb, and there I was. I was sucked into a flash back. Everything was on a gray scale except me. I was still in color.

This must have been a clue to what the boy was talking about. I stood on the grassy hills at what seemed to be a school. There were a lot of teenagers around and I could see myself in the far back, standing alone.

"Hey!"

"Yo Ralph," I answered, "What's up man?"

He and I chatted for a bit. I turned to the side and there in the corner of my eye, she sat elegantly. "Hey, who's that girl over there?"

"I don't know," Ralph answered.

Someone from afar called out to me and Ralph. It was our friend Donna. She walked up with a big smile and said, "Whatcha guys doin?"

"This young fella here's been scoping out that chick over there," Ralph said.

"Oh!" Donna said excitedly. "Want me to go talk to her for you?"

"No! It's okay," I said, blushing red. Donna ran up regardless. I turned away acting like I had no idea what is going on.

Donna came back and said, "I told her you said she was cute. She has a cute name."

I jumped straight into another flash back. This time I was in a library studying with some friends.

"Are you okay man?" one of my friends asked. His name was Jude. A plump man for his figure but a very suave character at heart.

"This is stupid, how can she be so dumb to pick someone else over me when we were talking almost all the time?" I complained.

"Aww its okay," Jude's girlfriend said. Her name was Alyssa. She was a thin girl with a very big smile.

"I don't even know what I should do," I complained some more.

"Why don't you just go to her?" Jude suggested.

"You think I should?" I asked.

"It wouldn't hurt. It seems like you're hurting yourself more by not doing anything about it," Alyssa said.

I had another flashback right after the other. It seemed as a part of my past was flashing in different times. This time I was in a bedroom on the phone.

"So, what date should we actually make it official?" I asked.

She said, "I don't know, what you think it should be?"

I thought for a moment and then answered, "How about today? June 18, 2003?"

I could hear here giggling, "It's perfect."

"Ryushin!" Aida called. "What are you doing? You tell us to leave and you just stand there? Come on, let's go!" I came back to a conscious state. I grabbed the orb and sprinted for the gate. The gate closed and locked us in.

"Oh no…" Onry gasped.

A loud growl came from deep within the shadows. I turned around and looked, trying to see what it was. I put the orb into my pocket and stood my ground with my sword in hand. Aida joined my side, grasping her sword.

A dark scaled dragon flew out from the shadows, gliding over us in circles. The belly of the dragon was scaled with gray rough skin, while its hard skin was painted with a dark aura. The wings were ripped and torn in the web but was still able to fly. It had three spiked horns, two on the sides and one out the middle of its forehead. The dragon's eyes marked intimidating yellow that struck fear into its prey. Its talon claws were as sharp as daggers.

"Damn it all," I cursed at the dragon.

Gundita popped open on the RT. "The source of the strong aura is actually from that dragon. Be careful, it is an ancient dragon from the past known as Tiamat. Its shadow powers are hard to escape and can engulf you in one attack. Work as a team and you shouldn't have too much of a problem taking out the dragon. Best of luck," she briefed us and then signed out.

"Well, you heard the boss," I said.

I hurled my spinning blade up at Tiamat. It blocked it with its wing and came to a stop in the air. It roared fiercely throughout the room, shaking the area around us. I ran and picked up my sword, standing my ground. Tiamat took one deep breath and shot down a ray of fire. The fire turned to a dark wave of flames ready to burn us all. Onry blocked herself off with a barrier of ice. Aida jump over it quickly, drilling her sword into the wall using it as leverage.

I jumped up toward Tiamat, ready to strike. Tiamat spread its wing, smacking me away. I recovered off the wall, bouncing right back into an attack again. The dark fire below cleared and Onry discarded the ice barrier. She cupped her hands upward at Tiamat and launched a couple of ice shards. Aida planted two feet on the wall and pulled out her sword. She pushed off, aiming straight for Tiamat.

Tiamat flew up higher, pulling out of reach. The dragon quickly countered Onry's frost bolts with a shadow ball. Onry tumbled to the side as the shadow ball exploded on contact with the ground.

I hurled my sword again at Tiamat but the attack failed. Onry recovered to her feet, ready to attack. Aida jumped over toward Tiamat, looking to strike. Tiamat flew even higher. The three of us met together and stood our ground. Tiamat came down and stood on the floor waiting for us to attack.

"No wonder this room is so big," I said.

Aida was getting angry. She growled and asked, "Everything we do Tiamat just counterattacks."

I thought for a moment. "Well, we're just going to have to try harder," I said.

"What do you suggest we do?" Onry asked.

"We'll just have to counterattack Tiamat after he counterattacks our attacks," I suggested.

Aida responded, "Sounds like a plan."

"Just follow my lead."

I channeled my mana into my legs, increasing my speed. I hurled my sword one more time at Tiamat. It countered by bouncing the sword right back, then starting to take flight again. I left my place and aimed for a wall.

"Aida grab my sword and throw it above Tiamat!"

Aida grabbed my deflected sword, launching it over Tiamat's head. I bounced off the wall and into the air above the unsuspecting dragon. I grabbed my sword, striking it in the back. It cried an eerie cry. Tiamat was angry. It began to swing left and right quickly with its talon claws. Luckily my mana was still channeled into my legs. I was able to dodge the attacks in the air.

Onry encased herself in a block of ice. She cracked it from the inside and launched shards in every direction around her. The sharp shards bounced off the wall, scratching and cutting the rough surface of Tiamat's skin. Tiamat flapped its wing inward, striking me back down to the floor. I landed onto my back, knocking the wind out of my stomach.

Tiamat roared fiercely again and took a deep breath.

"It's weakened. I should be able to finish this," Aida said.

She gripped her sword in one hand and focused her mana into her sword. Her sword transformed into a golden hammer. Tiamat launched its ray of fire down toward us. The dark fire began to grow quickly toward us. Aida launched the golden hammer striking it from a distance. Tiamat roared in pain.

"It didn't finish it off," I said pulling myself back up to my feet.

I grabbed my sword and jump up toward the soaring Tiamat. I jabbed the point of my sword into Tiamat's body on the way up, pulling the blade through its body from waist to head. I landed onto my two feet as Tiamat came crashing down.

A small shard came from its ashes and into my hands. Could this be... a piece to the puzzle?

That night, we returned to Raigen reporting our investigation to Gundita.

"I must say," Gundita clapped, "I am very impressed with the way you three handle that." She crossed her arms behind her back and paced herself back and forth. "Tell me Ryushin, what is that you hope to find out of all of this?"

"I... uh... well, I want to find out who I am really." I answered.

"Funny," she said sarcastically. "That seems to run around in your head a lot. To me, I think you do know who you are. You just don't really know what you want." I was confused for a moment to what she had said. She wasn't making any sense to me at all, or at least I thought she wasn't. "I saw everything that you had seen in there. We all did. Aida and Onry are the only ones who didn't."

"Oh? How is that so?" Aida asked.

Gundita continued to pace herself again. She brought up a screen and displayed the recent events that took place. There he was, the boy in the hood talking. Then it went to my flash backs, they were able to record everything through the RT. "This boy seems awfully familiar. Something tells me, I've seen him somewhere before."

"Did you hear what he was saying?" I asked.

Gundita looked down on me and asked, "Who is this girl?"

"Girl?"

"You know, the girl in your past. There is the girl and the significant date you both were talking about, June 18, 2003." Gundita focused in on the girl, examining her closely. "It seems like you can't remember who she is. If I am correct, she

The Adventures of Ryushin

is somewhat involved in some way." She pointed at the girl one more time. "Doesn't she remind you of someone?"

I thought about it for a moment.

Aida and the girl looked rather similar to one another.

"She looks like Aida," I answered.

"She does almost look like her," Gundita agreed. "But, this flashback must have occurred some time when she was younger because Aida looks a lot older than her."

I looked over at Aida as she stared into the ground, deep into her thoughts.

"You three are to stay at ease until further notice. We will report back to you until we have come up with a conclusion to this."

Gundita saluted and walked off.

A few days have passed and everything stayed quiet around Raigen. I, at least, got my own bedroom. The only disturbing part of our rest period was the flash backs I've been having over and over again. I was haunted by her spirit in my dreams. The closer I stepped toward her, the more she began to move away. What was I suppose to do now?

"Wake up."

Aida smashed a pillow in my face. "Gundita needs us ASAP."

I growled tiredly and forced myself out of bed. I took a quick shower, dressed myself before heading out.

Onry and Aida were standing before Gundita, whom was pacing herself once again back and forth, as always. I joined their sides and paid close attention.

"I'm sorry Ryushin but we still haven't been able to gather any words about your past," Gundita apologized.

"Wait, so why am I here?" I asked.

A large screen popped up from behind her with a picture of a young man on it. "I am here to ask you for your help Ryushin. Since we have rallied most of our guards toward another part of the world, we need your assistance investigating an unusual movement."

"Okay, what is it that you want me to do?"

"Now let me do a brief of what is going on." She pointed at the man and a brief window of his data base opened up. "This man here goes by the name of Atlmaz. He is a young trained Warlock, who is able to enslave demons and dark spirits. It seems that he may be connected to the strange activity the beasts have been displaying."

"Do you want us to kick his ass or something?" I interrupted.

"Let me finish first Ryushin. He is also on a land where no aircrafts can pass. Seems he is using a strong aura to prevent the airships from staying in the air. So we suggested you three to travel from Imperia, the Masters of the Water, toward his dark kingdom by foot. Ahz-Bovan is a dark kingdom of the dark ages during the War of the Exiled. Maybe if you travel there, you will be able to learn something about your past," Gundita briefed.

"So, when do we leave?" I asked.

Gundita's screen displayed a map of this world. She pointed to a continent in the north and said,

"Commander Lecia will direct you about the whereabouts of where this dark kingdom rests. Please prepare yourself. You can be out there for days or maybe even weeks."

And so our adventure continued down the path toward Imperia.

Chapter Four
Ahz-Bovan

I stood on the railings of the airship, looking deep into the moon as the chill winds came passing by. The image of the girl took shape within the clouds, smiling down at me. I smiled back.

"You can feel her, can't you?" Aida asked.

"What do you mean?"

She placed her hand on my heart. "She's in your heart, I can feel her love. Though, I don't understand why I can feel it."

"It's okay, I try not to think about it," I said.

"You're head must be spinning ever since that trip down in the Returner's Hill," she said. "I hope everything works out for you."

I chuckled at her words.

"Don't worry, I'm still me," I said, happily, giving her the biggest smile I could pull out.

"Do you still love her?"

"I don't know what you're talking about," I answered pretty straight forward.

"You don't remember her at all?"

"Nope, I've been trying to remember but it just doesn't seem to want to come out."

"Keep smiling, okay?" she said. I gave her a confused look. "Just please, keep smiling, for me…"

"Okay," I answered, giving her a smile.

"We will arrive in Imperia shortly, just be on your best manners. We are entering the world's capital and home of the world's princess, Kirikah." Aida patted me on the back before walking away.

After a long night's flight, we arrived in the Kingdom of Imperia. The structure of the kingdom was far different as Raigen was built. Raigen was built into a ditch, surrounded by towering mountains as its border. Imperia's castle was surrounded by lakes of water which was created by a giant water fall that stretched for about miles. It looked like only Airships could enter the kingdom from what I saw, but it's possible there could be other ways.

We landed in the Airstation and were immediately escorted out and into the Master's Court. Imperia's Commander was dressed in a brown tunic with green lining stitched in finely. She wore a green short skirt that cut off at her thighs to go with brown boots that reached all the way to her knee. She had light brown hair that dangled straight down to her shoulders with a green beret on her head that had a feather sticking out of it. She looked like she was about in her mid twenties.

She sighed and said, "I expected a lot better than this from Gundita."

"Hey!" I started out angrily, "What's that suppose to mean!"

She bowed. "Sorry, I guess you three will have to do. Gundita did say she was short on people at the moment."

Aida bowed in exchange, "We are very sorry Commander Lecia. Raigen is still under a lot of work with our pupils."

"Very well, just call me Lecia. I, myself, am not used to the formality yet," she said. "I am currently waiting on some of my students to report in and assist you guys on your investigation in Ahz-Bovan. For now, I want the three of you to channel your RTs to sync with mine. You will be under my command for the time being."

"Lecia, what is going on?" Aida asked.

"Since my pupils have already briefed, I guess it wouldn't hurt to tell you three also," she said. "There has been strange activity coming from Ahz-Bovan, a once controlled kingdom of the dark knights. We believe a warlock by the name of Atlmaz has something to do with this strange activity and is at work to building an army. His strange behavior only recently occurred one year ago when an ancient temple appeared out of nowhere in the ocean, just outside of our kingdom."

"An ancient temple..." I said to myself. "Have you investigated the temple yet?"

"Apparently we couldn't advance any further into the temple because of a strange stone with an unknown text inscribed on it," Lecia informed.

"If it is okay with you, I would like to go and check it out for myself," I requested.

"I really don't care what you do with that temple, just so long you investigate Ahz-Bovan first," Lecia replied.

The door behind us barged open and five unique characters came bursting through.

One with a big mouth started boasting, "Alright! Who asked for the great Mordakai's help?" He had that kind of twinkle in his eye that could catch any girl's attention. He wore a red open vest that exposed his chest and stomach. His forearms were covered with silver plated gauntlets and had silver lined baggy shorts. Red chained boots locked around his calves and feet. His hair was blonde, long bangs dangled just a bit on the side and the rest slicked backwards. On his forehead was a red headband and on each of his side of his belt carried a hand-axe.

"Do you ever get over yourself?" the next character asked.

She was a short girl with blonde hair dyed, with purple tips that flowed down her left side and to her shoulder. She wore a purple tunic with her left sleeve stretched to her wrist while the right sleeve was torn off at the shoulder. Now her pants were unique. She had black pants on where her left leg was exposed while the right was covered. On her back rested a long thin blade, similar to Aida's great sword.

"You're one to talk Rheaa," someone said from behind.

This next guy was a little taller than most of us. He was well dressed in white and blue plated armor, covered from chest to toe. We couldn't see his face because of a white helmet in the shape of a dragon that covered it. On his chest plate read the name, Aeric.

"Shut up Aeric, no one asked you," Rheaa said.

Two more people entered the room both dressed in black leather. Strange looking but was cool in a way. They had black masks that covered the bottom half of their faces but displayed their eyes. One was a male and the other was a female.

Lecia sighed.

"Great students... Valen, do you have to wear your mask here? And Kirikah you need to start acting like a princess, not a ninja."

They both pulled off their masks, tucking them away in their sashes. Valen had blue spiky hair and Kirikah had very long brown hair wrapped with pigtails by bandanas.

"Now that you all are finally here, for crying out loud, we can get this mission underway," Lecia said, crossing her arms. "Here is how this mission will be taking place:"

"There will be two groups-

Group 1- Mordakai, Ryushin, Aeric, and Valen
Group 2- Rheaa, Aida, Onry, and Kirikah

You will---"

"Did you just say Ryushin?" Mordakai asked, cutting off Lecia's briefing.

Lecia began to shake with steam, "Yes I did! Now pay attention!" Mordakai flinched and stood quiet.

"As I was saying, you will enter the Imperia water canals and enter Ahz-Bovan from two different points." A screen popped up behind her similar to Gundita's screen. "Squad one, you will enter from the dining room and proceed to move on to the higher parts of the castle. Squad two, you will enter

The Adventures of Ryushin

from the courtyard, surveying the lower part of the kingdom. From both points, you will rejoin into one squad when you meet. Once finished, you will report back here. Any questions?"

Mordakai raised his hand.

"Yes Mordakai?" Lecia asked.

He looked at me and asked, "Are you really Ryushin?"

"Mordakai! You can talk about that when you guys are underway but please stay focused on the briefing!" Lecia shouted. Lecia sighed again and said, "Aeric, you are in lead of this mission. You are all dismissed."

Mordakai jogged over to me and stared emphatically. I stepped back a bit uncomfortably.

"So this is what a Ryushin looks like huh?" He shook my hand and said, "The name is Mordakai, I've heard lots about ya." He thought for a moment with a distraught look on his face, "Well, actually only in stories but I've always wanted to meet ya."

Rheaa walked over to me saying, "Don't mind him at all, he never shuts up." Mordakai snapped an angry grin at Rheaa. Aeric, Valen and Kirikah joined in on the conversation with Aida and Onry left on the side.

I chuckled just bit before moving over to Aida. Actually, I started to hide behind her.

"What are you doing?" Aida asked.

"I am afraid, very afraid," I said.

"They're just fans of yours, get used to it. Not everyone lives to see a Ryushin," she said, bursting out in laughter.

I lightly shoved her and crossed my arms, "Some help you are." Onry started laughing along with her.

Mordakai walked over with the rest of the group. "We have agreed to terms with these lackey girls we're teamed up with."

"What terms?" I asked.

"We noticed Lecia put us in groups of guys and girls, so we decided it was going to be a challenge," Aeric said. "First one there and back wins!" Valen, Mordakai and Aeric started taking off toward the door.

"Hey! That's not fair!" Rheaa yelled. "Kirikah, girls let's go!"

Rheaa and Kirikah started taking off.

Aida crossed her arms, thinking for a brief moment. "With the way they're acting, I wonder if it's possible to get this mission done." I started running toward the gate with Onry behind the rest of them. "Hey! Wait for me!"

I started to fill with laughter, "Now this is my kind of group!"

Aida, Onry and I arrived at the beginning of the Imperia Canals where the rest of them stood around in a huddle.

"What's up?" I asked.

Mordakai started laughing. "They thought it wouldn't be fair if we got the jump on them, so we decided to start the challenge when we come across a fork in the road. The split paths lead to one side of Ahz-Bovan."

"Is this how you enter Imperia by ground? You enter through the water canals?" I asked.

"Of course, they don't call us Masters of the Sea for nothing," Valen said. We continued to walk down the road with a little chit-chatter.

"I think it's kind of neat to have the princess joining us on this mission," Aeric said. Everyone started breaking out in laughter. Aeric stopped and asked, "What? What? What's so funny?"

Rheaa said, "Don't act like we don't know. We all know you have the biggest crush on Kirikah, just admit it."

Kirikah's cheeks started to turn bright red.

Aeric denied Rheaa and shoved her a bit. The two started to clash into a dust ball of thrown fists and kicks.

Aida and I walked behind the group, minding our own business. I looked at her and smiled. "Can I help you Ryushin?"

"Nope, just smiling," I said, continuing to smile. She smiled back.

Mordakai started walking next to Onry examining her. He asked, "How come every time I get near you, I'm freakin' cold?" Onry smirked and flicked her wrist, trapping his legs in ice just like she did to me back at Raigen. He started to panic, "That is so not cool!"

Valen put on his black mask and started sprinting all around us. "What the hell are you doing Valen?" Rheaa asked.

"Being super cool, that's what I'm doing," he said, still sprinting around us. Rheaa stuck her leg out and tripped him. He went sliding across the ground.

I started laughing. I looked at Aida and said, "I think we're all going to get along just fine."

"Are you really him?" Kirikah asked, walking next to me.

"Huh?"

"Are you really THE Ryushin?"

I became uncomfortable again, "I guess? I'm still in the process of trying to figure out who I am."

"Wait, you don't know who you are?" Aeric asked. Valen, Rheaa and Mordakai joined in on the huddle.

"Oh come on, do you guys have to do this to me?" I asked.

Mordakai patted me on the shoulder, "He's the Ryushin alright, I know for a fact."

Rheaa started laughing, "And what fact may that be?"

"Because he's a noob."

Rheaa bonked Mordakai on the back of the head. "You're an idiot."

"Here is the fork in the road," Aida said. "So we split up from here?"

"Yes, the boys will come with me and Rheaa will lead the girls," Aeric said.

So, Aida and I parted for the first time. I was kind of sad on the inside but I know I will see her soon.

Mordakai, Valen, Aeric and I climbed the hill and reached the left side of the castle. Valen jumped from the top of the hill to a side window and picked the lock. Aeric and Mordakai followed with trouble due to their heavy gear. I followed right behind and we entered the dining room.

We surveyed the room but nothing out of the ordinary caught our attention.

"You would think they would at least leave some food out. I'm starving," Mordakai said, holding onto his growling stomach.

"Hey, we can't go anywhere. This door is locked," Valen said, struggling with the doorknob.

"This place is so old and beat, we may have to find another way around," Aeric noted.

Mordakai grunted, "Yea right. Let's just break the door down." He sprinted into the door throwing his whole body at it. The door was sealed shut, bashing him back onto the ground. "That... is one... hard door."

"Take a look around, there has to be something," Aeric said.

I walked over to a fire place where burnt wood piled in the center. Above the fireplace was portrait. It was a picture of a girl, dressed in a black dress with a black pointed hat, that sort of dangled down at the tip. In her eyes she had this evil look and dark grin, quaking fear into my heart. Down at the bottom was a name, Jyn, Lord of the Darkness.

"Jyn..." I said to myself.

The door that Mordakai tried to break down opened on my command.

"Whoa! I got it to open!" Mordakai jumped with joy. "All I did was play with the candle holders. It was like they were a switch or something."

"Good job Mordakai," Aeric said walking into the next room. I started to laugh a bit on in the inside following right behind them.

As soon as all of us entered the next room, the door behind us closed shut again. We entered a room with a lot of tall statues with heavy gear on them. This must be an armory.

Aeric stepped forward to see further up ahead but the room was too dark to see that far.

"How much do you want to bet one of these statues is going to come alive and kill us all?" Valen asked.

"I bet you all of them will come alive," Mordakai agreed.

"Quiet," Aeric said, listening closely. "Do you hear that?"

In the distance was a faint sound. It sounded like a growl from a beast.

"I don't like the sound of that," Mordakai said.

It was a disturbing growl similar to that of a beast.

"There's something definitely down there," Aeric said.

I slowly moved toward the end of the room. "We'll never know unless we find out." The rest of the group followed behind me. Straight ahead was the door to the next room.

"Pfft, there's nothing in here," Mordakai boasted.

"I wouldn't quite say that," Valen said, looking at his RT. "There's definitely something here."

Aeric looked up and became tensed. I looked up as well to find a pair of yellow evil eyes glowing in the dark. Aeric and I quickly drew our swords.

"Look out from above!" Aeric exclaimed. The disfigured monster dropped from the ceiling and onto its front and hind legs.

"Whew, that has got to be the ugliest thing I have ever seen," Mordakai shrugged.

It resembled a decaying hound with its fur and skin peeling off, its flesh rotting all over its head and body.

Mordakai grabbed his hand axes as the hound started charging toward us. He jumped up into the air, ready to launch one of his axes. A dark glow wrapped around the hound and it disappeared.

"Look out behind you Mordakai!" I yelled.

The hound appeared behind the unaware Mordakai. Out from underneath, Valen surprised the hound an aerial kick.

Valen's kick had unexpectedly gone right through the hound. Another hound came from above pouncing on both of them.

I gripped my sword tightly and hurled it quickly at one of the hounds. My sword flew right through the transparent hound, causing a third one to pop out. Mordakai and Valen pushed off the hounds and recovered close to me and Aeric.

"Eh, we shouldn't do that anymore," I said. "Seems like our physical attacks just make the hounds multiply.

Aeric drilled his sword into the ground and palmed both of his hands toward the oncoming hounds.

"Chokusha!" Aeric casted.

Rays of light zapped from his palms banishing the hounds on contact. Suddenly, an even greater hound came from above, swiping Aeric aside with its giant claw.

"Oh great, an even uglier hound," Mordakai said.

I quickly sprinted around the giant hound, retrieving my sword. The hound chomped at Mordakai. He evaded to the side, countering quick with a couple of strikes to its snout. The hound roared upward. Valen pulled out a short sword from the side of his belt attachment as he leaped toward the beast's wide open chest. The hound struck down quickly with its claw. Valen countered with great agility, then slashed at its chest.

I focused my mana into my legs, moving quickly toward the hound. I jumped high onto the hound's back, jabbing the tip of my sword into its back. The hound jerked around, launching me into the air. It opened its mouth firing a fireball in my direction. I took the hit slamming into the wall off in the distance.

Aeric pulled his sword out from the ground and focused his mana into his sword. As soon as the blade of his sword started to glow with a blinding light, he slashed away at the hound from a distance emitting out waves of light energy. The hound took a couple of hits and sent back the last attack with a whip of its tail. Aeric took the counter attack in the stomach jumping backward a couple of feet.

"You damn pooch," Mordakai grunted, "If we let those blasted girls beat us, I'm gonna be very pissed."

Mordakai roared with vigor, filling the room with an echo of a lion's roar. I can feel an intense amount of energy exerting from his body. Strange markings that looked like whiskers appeared on his cheeks.

"What's he doing?" I asked.

"He's using the best of his ability of course," Aeric said. "They call this the Shishiku. Mordakai's class is a unique one. He is the only one I know that has been able to master The Berserker class. He can increase his strength and speed drastically but his defenses dropped poorly in exchange. It's a risk to enrage like that but I'm sure he knows what he's doing."

Mordakai chucked his left axe quickly into the chest of the rotting hound leaving no chance for the beast to dodge it. He then dashed so fast behind the axe, hardly able to keep up with his movements. He lunged up high into the air, hovering over its crying head. Mordakai thrusted his right arm with axe in hand, striking quickly yet fiercely at its face. For the final blow, he slammed his axe into its skull, crushing it into pieces.

His energy level suppressed as he jerked his axe out of the dead hound's skull. He chuckled, "That was pretty fun."

Point of View: Aida

We entered the courtyard, just as Lecia instructed. The area was still and was a big room to move across. Inside the courtyard were dead blue-leafed bushes and a dead water fountain in the center. Our group was very quiet and much focused at the moment. Our RTs didn't pick up any energy levels... only the one in the next room.

Kirikah stood close to me on her guard.

"What are you doing? There's nothing in here," I asked.

She somewhat stuttered a bit, "I've never been on a mission before… this is actually my first one."

"Just stay close as a team and don't get ahead of yourself. If we time things right, things will go smooth from here on out," I said, trying to encourage her.

"Come on, what is taking you two so long," Rheaa pouted, "Let's go, the boys are going to beat us." She crept on her tip toes over to the next door.

Onry, Kirikah and I followed close behind Rheaa, who opened the door to the room, sneaking her way into the dark.

This room was filled with shadows, not a pinch of light was in here. I channeled my mana, creating an aura of light from within, so that who or whatever was in my radius could be seen.

"You guys stay out of sight but don't go too far," I commanded. A high energy level started showing up on my RT. There was definitely something in this room.

Onry quickly fired an ice shard out from the dark, hitting something. I moved closely to it. It seemed to be a black bird of some sort, with evil eyes and decayed parts in its body.

"Think you can find a light switch Aida?" Rheaa asked.

I hugged the wall tightly, looking for a light switch to light. I heard more wings flap in the dark but Onry quickly shot them down with ice shards. I found a switch and turned it on. The door we entered from shut tightly and part of the floor began to collapse. I ran to the center to avoid falling in the pit.

"Aida! Get away from there!" Kirikah called.

I looked at what was behind me and to my surprise; it was a giant decaying raven. Pillars came falling out of the ceiling, turning this room into a giant birdcage with the door to the next room way out of reach. I channeled my mana quickly and created spikes of light around my body. A flock of tiny ravens flew out from under the wings of the greater raven, launching an all out assault at us. Onry quickly moved in front of me, countering with many ice shards. More ravens came out from under its wings, picking sharply at Onry. I unhooked my sword from my back and struck them away. Rheaa sprinted quickly toward the giant bird, pulling out that long thin blade of hers.

"Kyoufuu!" she said, performing a three strike attack at the bird. The air around us cut into sharp blades, circling its way toward the raven. The giant raven flapped once, then twice, performing the same attack as Rheaa.

The raven began to fly.

"Onry, fire a giant icicle at the stupid bird," I said.

Onry created an icicle and fired. I jumped onto the icicle riding it up. I hopped off the icicle, landing on top of the raven. I rose up looking to strike. The raven countered spun in a circle, tossing me off its back.

Smaller ravens came from below the pit and into the cage.

"Kirikah, don't just stand there you have to get moving," Rheaa said. There must have been thousands of them in here.

"I don't know what to do..." Kirikah cried.

"Damn it," I cursed.

I picked myself up and started attacking the smaller ones as the bigger raven took its time recovering up in the air. The greater raven came to a halt in the air and looked down upon us.

"I don't like that look of this," Rheaa said.

The greater raven screeched an eerie sound downward in our direction. It was a very disturbing sound, bringing us to our knees. The bigger raven opened its wings wide and flapped down fiercely. The wind attack it created started cutting against our armor.

Kirikah moved in front of us and lifted her hands into the air, palms up, as she took the hits to her body. She channeled her mana and created a shield around all of us, protecting us from the wind attack.

"I don't know how long I can hold this for..." she shrugged.

"We have to act quickly," I said standing back on my feet. "Rheaa, you think you can do that Kyoufuu of yours again?" She gripped her sword and nodded. "Onry, create a blizzard of your ice shards to combine with Rheaa's Kyoufuu. That way, the both of your attacks can push against the raven's attacks. I will finish it off from that point on."

"Release the shield Kirikah!" Rheaa called ready. Kirikah dropped the shield as we got caught in the wind attack again. "Kyoufuu!" Rheaa performed once more. Onry concentrated her mana, creating multiple sharp ice shards. She released them into Rheaa's attack, spiking through a lot of the smaller ravens. The ice shards and wind blades sliced through the air and into the body of the bigger raven.

I gripped my sword and transformed it into a Taigotettei, a hammer of light, with my mana. I aimed and launched the glowing hammer, striking it in the heart. The greater raven released another screeching roar, just before falling through the cage and into the dark pit below us. The wind attacks stopped and we were able to catch our breath.

The door to the next room opened up along with a pathway. We escaped that fight with little but many scratches.

Point of View: Ryushin

We entered the following room, leading to a throne. The seat was cracked into pieces and the banners behind it were torn all around.

"This place is a piece of crap," Mordakai said, "There's nothing even here. Lecia will hear it from me when we get back."

"Oh please. We just got here," Aeric said. "Start looking around."

I started searching the area for ways to move on but this time, I don't think there is a way to move on from here. On the wall was another painting of the same girl, I saw before in the other room, The Lord of Darkness, Jyn. This time it was a picture of her standing on an altar with three glowing circles above her. One orb was blue, the other green and the last one brown. On the bottom of the painting it said- Shiva, Titan, and Garuda.

I pulled the painting off revealing a hole in the wall. I peaked through and I could see a couple of men out on an open field. There were thousands of winged demons marching side by side.

There were three suspicious characters. They looked like elvens but taller than an average human with darker colored skin. One was dark blue and the other was dark purple. The dark-blue skinned elven wore red and black leather gear, exposing his ripped muscular arms. On his face, he covered his right eye with a black eye patch and his bottom half of his face covered with a mask. His green hair ran straight down to the end of his spine by his hip.

The dark purple looked just the same but with gray and black leather gear. His left eye was covered but had no mask on the bottom of his face. His white hair spiked in a wave backward. They both had pointy long ears and long eyebrows that trailed off their face like whiskers. They were broad in size and looked very powerful.

"You guys are still here?" the third shady character asked.

He wore all dark plated armor. On his back was a giant sword, bigger than Aida's great sword. His helmet was a round bowl shaped figure, covering the top and back side of his head but left the nose and mouth exposed.

The two elvens stayed quiet.

"Bah, you two were never really known for talking much eh? At least, that's what Lord Atlmaz told me. And you two best are lucky he picked you rejects out from the Elven Roots. Otherwise you two woulda been goners. What's your names anyway?"

"I am Deadsong and this is my brother Fearsong," Deadsong said. He was the one in red and black gear.

"Interesting, I like it. It has a tone in it that says kill or be killed," he chuckled. "The name is Corfits and proud right man to Lord Atlmaz. Why, I'd take an arrow for him if need it be."

"Corfits talks too much," Fearsong said.

"Corfits talks way too much, indeed," Deadsong agreed.

"Come on now, a little talkin' never killed anyone right fellas?" Corfits chuckled.

I pressed up against the wall a little more because their conversation was becoming faint. I pressed too hard that the wall collapsed, falling right through to the ground.

"Ey! What was that, you two go check that out, yea?" Corfits commanded.

I picked myself up and confronted the three characters with their army of demons right behind them. I looked quickly at Mordakai signaling for him to stay up there.

"I smell the blood of a Dracolyte," Fearsong said, pointing at me.

Corfits walked up to me, examining thoroughly. "Not much to look at really. Who the bloody hell are you?"

"My name is Ryushin," I answered.

The army behind Deadsong and Fearsong cowardly stepped backward.

"You mean to tell me a scrawny little puke like you is the Legendary Ryushin from five thousand years ago?" Corfits asked.

I shrugged my shoulders and looked at him. He took one swing and struck me very hard in the stomach bringing me to my knees. I grabbed my stomach and held it trying to ease the pain.

"Like I said, not much to look at."

"The blood of a Dracolyte flows within him, I can smell his blood," Deadsong said.

"Well, why don't we open him up, spill all his blood and find out, shall we?" Corfits said unsheathing his great sword.

I slashed my sword out knocking his sword away from him. I stood back up against the wall ready to fight. The rest of them drew their weapons, challenging me to attack.

"So the little chap has a little fight in him," Corfits chuckled grabbing his sword from the ground, "Well, he's got little time left to live."

Mordakai, Aeric and Valen jumped from the room above, just in time. Aida and the girls came from behind, killing most of the army by surprise.

"No Corfits, looks like you're the one that has little time left to live," I said.

"What is this? Is this a raid? Set up by whom?" Corfits asked.

"Where's Atlmaz?" Aida asked.

Corfits began to laugh at Aida. "You want to know where the great Lord Atlmaz is, do ya? Well shit out of luck honey, you won't escape from here alive."

Deadsong and Fearsong threw down a couple of smoke bombs and the three of them escaped.

Aida walked over to me as I continued to hold my stomach. She placed her hand over mine and asked, "Are you okay?"

I smiled and replied, "I am now."

"I really don't think its safe here anymore. We should really head back to Imperia and report to Lecia," Aeric suggested.

As we walked down the open field looking for a way out, a strange energy level started appearing on my screen. It was a huge one that overlapped this whole field. Beneath us, the ground started shaking.

"What the hell is going on?" Mordakai shrugged, falling off balance to the quake.

Out from the ground, eight spiky legs arose around us. We became separated, formed into two groups again. Onry, Aeric, Kirikah, and I were on the left side while Aida,

Mordakai, Valen, and Rheaa, were on the other side. A giant ugly, slimy head emerged from a hole with its gigantic body.

"Oh shit," Aeric gasped. "It's the Plague Spider. Be on guard and listen carefully to this fight. This spider has a timed attack that can devastate us all if we do not follow the right order. This attack can poison us all on contact and can quickly spread. First we've got to take out the legs in order for it to become immobilized. Shortly after that is finished, we must attack the body and prevent it from releasing any of its young."

"Onry and I will take care of the young spiders it adds," Rheaa said. "Just take down those legs."

"Go!" Aeric commanded.

I quickly moved to the side, running toward the front leg of the spider. Aeric followed behind me, striking the leg with his sword. I jumped high to where the joint was and jabbed my sword into it. The spider's leg stretched out swinging Aeric and I backward. Kirikah created a shield to break our fall.

Mordakai, Valen and Aida on the other side, tried the same thing, attacking the front leg. The spider growled, releasing its young out from behind its sack. There were thousands of them.

"I hope you're really cold Onry because we're gonna need all the mana you can dish out," I said.

Onry moved farther down at the end, launching multiple shots of ice shards at the oncoming spiders. Aeric and I continued hacking away at the front leg.

"Kyoufuu!" Rheaa performed, slicing the young spiders into pieces with her wind blades.

Mordakai growled fiercely and raised his energy level. He smashed the front leg with his Shishiku attack while Aida moved onto the next leg. Aeric channeled his mana into his sword creating a light aura around it. He sprinted up to the leg and sliced it into pieces.

"Kirikah, move over to Aida's side. They will need your shield soon," Aeric ordered.

Onry moved back toward me and Aeric, successfully clearing the first wave of young spiders. The spider growled and rotated its body, smacking all of us away and up against the wall.

"Quick, everyone bunch into groups, it's ready to attack," Aeric warned.

Onry moved in front of me and Aeric while Kirikah moved in front of Aida, Mordakai, Valen and Rheaa. Onry created a barrier of ice around us, as Kirikah created a shield around the rest of the others.

The Plague Spider launched a thousand needles toward us, shattering both shields into pieces but we managed to avoid any critical hits. Valen sprinted to the second leg, ripping it into shreds, then moving to our side. I hurled my blade at the second leg's joint, snapping the leg into pieces. The front body of the Plague Spider fell back into the hole it crawled out from.

"Good job everyone," Aeric said, "We're almost in the clear."

The second wave of young spiders came rushing at us. Onry and Rheaa tended to them with their Blizzard special abilities. Unexpectedly, the Plague Spider splashed out a huge net of webs, immobilizing us.

"Shit, I can't do anything," Mordakai said struggling to break free.

Aida channeled her mana and broke the web with her light that surrounded her. I channeled my mana, adding fire to the blade of my sword. I swung downward burning the webs. I quickly freed the others and continued attacking the third leg. Soon the room became a blazing firehouse. Aida struck down the third leg bringing it down one sided now. The Plague Spider slid into the hole.

"Where the hell did it go?" Valen asked, searching the area.

"Oh no... Everyone quick move together!" Aeric yelled with haste.

More webs sprung from the hole, immobilizing us once again. I swung my sword burning the webs that caught us. Kirikah and Onry moved over to the bunched up group. Another web caught Aida's leg, taking her to the ground.

"Aida!" I shouted.

I ran quickly to her and cut the web from her leg.

"No Ryushin! Get to them quick!" Aida yelled at me.

The Plague Spider launched thousands of needles out from the hole, ready to rain upon us.

I pushed Aida to Onry.

"Do it now!" I demanded of Onry. She didn't waste any time and created the barrier as Kirikah created the shield behind it. The thousand needles rained atop of me spiking into my body, arms and legs.

"Damn it!" Mordakai yelled.

Aida cried my name out, "Ryushin!"

The needle's poisons began to merge with the blood inside my body. The Plague Spider carried itself out from the hole.

I dropped my sword and faced the Plague Spider by myself.

"You stupid spider. Let's go," I said, faintly.

I positioned my hands to my right side, bending my knees. I formed my hands into a cup, focusing up at the Plague Spider, who released more young spiders. "It's over for you!" I snapped my arms forward, aiming at the Plague Spider and yelled, "Kagayaku Hikari!"

A giant beam of intense energy launched from the palms of my hand and into the face of the Plague Spider. The beam burned right through, bursting the spider into flames along with its young.

I fell to my knees weary and weak. Aida crushed the ice barrier and shield, running to my aid.

"Aida," Aeric called, "Grab him and let's go. We have to get out of here."

"You didn't have to do that," Aida said, holding me in her arms tightly.

I just smiled. She smiled, hugging me tight.

"I'll carry him," Mordakai said, lifting me into his arms. "Get going!"

The room started to burn up faster. I was cold though. I couldn't feel the heat. I closed my eyes and relaxed.

Point of View: Aida

All of us, except Ryushin, stood before the disappointed Lecia. Ryushin took the poison needles because of me. If I wasn't so careless, this wouldn't have happened.

"Don't worry about Ryushin," Lecia announced. "He will be fine. He has a strong will unlike anyone I have ever known."

"I..." Aeric said, before shortly getting interrupted.

"Overall the mission was failure," Lecia said. The rest of us became discouraged. "But in any case, I am proud of the teamwork you have displayed amongst yourselves. There is no I in team and you all saw that. You all ought to thank that young kid that risked his life for you. We will repay our debts by helping him in return when he is fully recovered. For now you are all relieved for the time being."

Chapter Five
The Great Divide

Point of View: Ryushin

"Are you okay?"

"I'm fine," I said, "I'll be up and running in no time."

"You don't sound okay."

I opened my eyes, looking up into the sky. It was partially cloudy and the fragrance of flowers motioned easily through the air. I was lying out in an open flower field with the fresh air running all over my body and the sun's rays of light soothing my wounds. Over to my right was Aida, sitting next to me. She smiled and faded away.

"Aida?"

I looked behind to find the girl from my flash backs standing underneath an apple tree. She wore a long white silky gown with thin straps wrapped over her shoulders. Her black hair with blonde streaks was tied upward by a white headband then fell into a ponytail. I walked over to her as she sighed and frowned downward at the grass.

"So you completely forget?" she asked. I didn't answer back. I thought for a moment and just watched her look down into the grass. "You have…"

"I didn't forget anything," I quickly cut her off. "I just can't remember. Trust me, if I wanted to remember than I would, but it's not that easy."

She placed her right hand over her heart. A very painful feeling overwhelmed me. It started in the center of my heart, breaking me down to my knees.

"It pains me right here… do you feel it?" She gripped her heart, creating more pain into mine. "It pains me to ever think you could forget about me."

"What is happening to me?" I said, drilling my fingers into the grass. The sky became dark and the clouds flashed with lightning. "What are you doing to me?"

"There was a time when you and I were one," she said, walking over to me. She knelt down in front of me and lifted my chin. The pain still continued to rupture my body. "I dream of the days we once had and hope that maybe they will come back. Someday, we will be as one again. I believe in you."

She began to fade away.

"Wait, don't go!"

"You will always be in my heart, my first love," she said. Her last words, first love, echoed all around me.

"Ryushin, wake up."

I opened my eyes to find myself in an infirmary, lying on a bed.

"You were having a nightmare."

"Aida... where am I?" I asked.

"Relax for a bit, you're safe," she said with a smile running her hand through my hair. "I'm just glad you came through. I thought I had lost you for good."

"What are you talking about? I feel just fine," I said sitting up.

"Take it easy," she said pushing me back down, "It's the first time you've moved in a couple of days."

"I've been out for that long?" I asked.

Aida pulled a needle from a tray on one of the counters. "We had to pull out nearly seventy of these. It wasn't fun but you looked almost dead."

I chuckled at her. "Thanks, but it'll take more than just some lousy spider to get me."

"Come on, everyone is waiting with Lecia," Aida said, pulling me out of bed.

I hopped out of bed, grabbing my gear. "Okay, let's get going," I said, slipping on my clothes and strapping my sword. I quickly rushed out the medic room and made my way to the

Master's Court with Aida. I entered and approached the awaiting Lecia.

"I see you're a lot better," Lecia said. "Thanks to you, we were able to alert the other kingdoms of Atlmaz's plans."

"I don't care about that right now," I said. "Where are the others? Are they okay?"

"We're just fine," Mordakai said entering from behind us. The others entered from behind him as well. "See! I told you he'd be fine. Valen, where's my money?"

"Put a sock in it," he answered.

"Hush you two," Lecia ordered. "I have a new mission for you all and it requires you to be away from the kingdom for a while. This is mandatory, so all of you will be a part of it..." I raised my hand interrupting Lecia. "Yes Ryushin?"

"I have a request before we actually take part on this mission," I answered.

"Very well, what can I do for you?" she asked.

"When I first arrived here, you mentioned of a stone with ancient text out in the ocean somewhere. I want to explore that place before hand and find out what's out there. I believe I have some sort of link there."

Lecia paused for a moment, poking at her forehead with her finger. "Fine, you can take one of our boats out at noon. Just be sure to be back by night fall so I can load you up for our dispatch."

So at noon, I took out one of Imperia's boats and sailed the deep blue ocean, also known as the Great Divide. The waves were calm, splashing salty sea water at my feet. Rheaa, Valen and Kirikah volunteered to accompany me on my voyage to the hidden temple. Aida, Mordakai and Aeric had to stay because their armor was too heavy to stay afloat. Onry, on the other hand, wouldn't be much help with her ice magic.

"Valen, are you sure these are the right directions Lecia gave you?" Rheaa asked.

"Damn it. How many times do I have to tell you yes?" Valen said, striking a grin.

"Don't you get fussy with me," Rheaa said.

Kirikah and I paid no attention to their quarrel.

"Sorry... they always fight like this..." Kirikah said.

"I don't mind," I said.

The two of us continued to scout the water, looking for anything unusual. There was still no sign.

"Are you and Aida...?" Kirikah began.

I looked at her strangely with one eyebrow raised.

"Are we what?"

"You know... do you love her?" I laughed. "What... what's so funny?"

"Aida and I are just friends. I think we both know that we're a little too busy with what's going on right now."

"But you two seem to work well together, I just thought..."

I continued to laugh, "You're so funny, Kirikah."

"Well, I think she likes you," Kirikah said. "And maybe you should like her too."

"She likes me?" I asked. I was a little shocked, yet still filled with happiness. Kirikah drew a big smile on my face; I tried my best to hide it away.

"She does. She was talking a lot about you while you were recovering."

I paused and then answered, "That doesn't mean anything."

"I don't know about that one..."

"Oh, really now?" I questioned.

Rheaa and Valen continued to wrestle off to the side, fighting for whoever was right, paying no attention to the ocean. Valen rolled out of the fight and dusted himself off.

"This can't be right anyway. We're moving too far from Imperia. Lecia said it was close by," he said.

I noticed the boat was slowing down. Suddenly, we came to a stop.

"Ryu...?" Rheaa called.

I quickly made my way to the back of the boat, looking over the edge. There was a large mass wrapped around the bottom of our boat. Rheaa rushed over and looked over the edge.

"This is exactly why I don't like coming out here," Valen panicked. "Sea creatures are going to eat us and we have no where to run!"

"Um, Ryu… I think you should come see this…" Kirikah said.

I ran over to her, witnessing the water slowly rising into the air. Soon, our boat was caught in a big cylinder of water, rising hundreds of feet.

"Great, just great. Now what the hell are we suppose to do?" Rheaa asked.

Up at the top off the wall of water I could barely see someone standing on top of it.

I pointed up at him, "Do you see him?"

The three of them squinted their eyes, looking closely.

"I don't see anyone," Rheaa said.

The person atop the water was the little boy in the hood. He smirked and pointed down at me. He lunged to the center, creating a bright light in his hands. With a light swing, he tossed it straight down toward our boat. The water began to cave in after the light.

"We are so screwed," Valen sighed.

I ran over to Kirikah and said, "You have to put a shield now or we'll be smashed."

"Are you kidding? I can't block something like that," she cried.

"If you don't, we're all going to die anyway so just do it. I know you can," I said.

Kirikah raised her hands and created a round shield around out boat. The water crushed up against the shield, flushing us deep into the ocean. The rest of us went flying up against the shield. Kirikah gave her best, keeping the shield strong and sturdy. We came to a halt as the boat lay upside down under the water.

Rheaa pointed at something in the water. Wrapped around our boat was the body of a very long giant serpent floating, there with us. It was motionless though.

"Is that thing sleeping?" Valen asked.

"We want to keep it that way," Rheaa answered.

Kirikah's power was growing weary.

"I don't know how long I can hold this up for."

I looked around for any ideas. In the distance, a bright light flashed atop the head of the giant serpent. It was the stone, the stone with the ancient text.

"Everyone, take a deep breath," I instructed. "Once Kirikah drops the shield, follow close behind." I nodded to her.

Kirikah released the shield once we took deep breaths. The water poured in, flushing bubbles of air back to the surface. I swam immediately toward the sleeping serpent, aiming for its head. The other three followed close behind. The serpent was very long and wide, covered with green scales that sparkled brightly in the water.

I raised my hand, telling the others to hold. The closer I swam to the stone, the more the belly of the beast would growl.

The text read- The Presence of Two Worlds.

Suddenly, I was able to breathe underwater. Valen eyes opened wide and pointed behind me. The eyes of the serpent were opened, glaring right at me. Stupid enough, I waved. The serpent opened its mouth and swallowed us whole.

"I don't want to die!" Valen cried.

"Shut up you baby," Rheaa said.

"We must be inside the serpent," I said.

"Strange. I don't see any flesh," Kirikah said.

The walls enclosed around us were made of hard stone, cover with moss between the cracks and a dense atmosphere.

The water below us was shallow, allowing us to walk. A dark tunnel was opened ahead of us.

"We'll have to move forward," I said, "It looks like we're not getting out the same way."

We walked down the stairway cautiously, not knowing what was below. The stairs suddenly shifted into an arc and changed directions.

"The serpent must be on the move," Rheaa assumed.

The torches on the wall lighted the stairway dimly.

We're coming for you Ryushin, echoed in my head.

I paused for a moment, listening to the walls. Those words repeated slowly, creepy and hoarse.

We finally came to an end of the stairway with a closed door. I placed my palm on it and the door started to shine. The door opened, revealing a large dark room. In the middle of it was a shining orb.

The four of us ran toward it.

The room began to fill with scenery the closer we approached the floating orb as soon as we reached it, we found ourselves in a whole new world.

"Where are we?" Valen asked.

There were people swarming this place, endless walking and talking, moving in every direction. There were machines moving at high speeds with people riding in them. I looked over at the sign that read, Knott's Scary Farm.

The girl from my dream walked out of a maze called the Abyss. She was holding onto someone's hand. It was my hand... a younger me.

"Hey, isn't that you, Ryu?" Valen asked. I looked a lot younger, thinner and had shorter hair. "Isn't that Aida too?"

Rheaa bonked him on the head. "Are you blind? That's not Aida. They look nothing alike."

"I think they look very similar in a way," Kirikah agreed with Valen.

"That's not Aida," I said. "That's someone else. I can't remember who she is."

The Adventures of Ryushin

The girl and I held each other's hands, looking deep into each others eyes. A ghoul came running through, sliding on his knees and frightened the girl. She jumped into my arms. He started laughing.

"Having fun yet?" I asked.

She smiled and replied with, "Yup, I'm glad that my mom let me come out here tonight with you." They both smiled at each other and gently kissed each other on the lips.

"Oh!" Valen giggled, "This is getting mushy."

Rheaa bonked him on the head again.

"It's sad."

The boy in the hood stood poised behind us.

Valen asked, "Who are you?"

He smirked and crossed his arms.

"Wait… why is it sad?" Kirikah asked.

The boy looked over at the girl. "First," he challenged, "I must test you, Ryushin. I must know if He is making a right decision, putting the world's destiny into your hands."

"What do you mean by test?"

"Enguarde, Ryushin."

I slashed my sword out of its sheath, watching the boy hover throughout the room. He landed on top of the coaster railings.

"You're going to have to do better than that."

I performed a high jump, landing onto the railings sluggishly. I attacked. He countered my attack with an energy ball. It bounced off my chest, bouncing me backward. My foot slipped against the railing, causing me to fall between. Grabbing on at the last second, I swung myself up and readied my attack.

The boy pointed behind me.

A roller coaster ride zoomed quickly toward me. The boy slammed me onto the ride with another energy attack. I growled ferociously at him. He smirked. Before I could attack, the momentum of the ride thrusted me downward. I held onto to the coaster, fighting the gushing wind against my face. The boy levitated before me.

"Seems like you need more time, Ryushin."

The ride began going upside downs in circles, looping in all directions, my head was about to spin off. I jerked to the side.

"Save me!" I cried out to the others.

He took to the sky, raising one hand up. A giant light of energy emerged from the ball of his hand, flashing endlessly with great power. He tossed it at the coaster railing, breaking it into two. I quickly released my hold on the ride, darting through the sky and down to the ground. Shifting my body weight, I was able to land onto my feet, grinding vigorously against the ground.

"Not bad," the boy clapped.

"Pretty good, huh?" I chuckled.

The boy crossed his arms again and vanished.

There had to be a glitch in his fast movement. I'll just have to guess his next attack.

I ran over to the girl and my younger self. The boy appeared behind me. I performed a somersault them and hurled my sword. "Gotta be quick," I said, dashing closely behind the spinning blade. With every ounce of energy I had, I jolted faster than the sword and behind the boy.

The boy was surprised.

I caught my sword and attacked. He evaded my rush, left and right.

The boy pushed off with an energy ball. I lunged backward, catching myself.

"Seinaru Yoru!" I yelled.

A bright energy blast exploded from my palm.

The boy slapped it away causing it to explode in the distance.

He smirked, "Is that what you call an energy blast?"

The boy palmed both of his hands. I shifted my hands into a cup, tucking them to my side. He launched a giant wave of energy from his palms.

"Kagayaku Hikari!" I yelled.

Bright blue energy emerged between my hands, burning powerfully into a large beam of light. The two beams exploded on contact. Both of our bodies wrenched backward from the force of the impact.

We both emerged from the smoke unharmed.

"Interesting, the Kagayaku Hikari attack. I don't recall Him using a technique by that name, but he had a similar attack just like it," he said.

"It's a special attack. It comes from my heart," I responded.

The others joined my side once again. The boy sat on a bench, resting from our little spar. We were still in the flash back, watching the people walk back and forth.

"So who are you?" Valen asked.

"I guess this would be the best time for this," he said. "My name is Astrae, a loyal sorcerer of Draconia, known as the Kingdom of the Dracolytes."

The three of them gasped, surprised at the boy's heritage.

"So the Dracolytes still exist in this time era?" Rheaa asked.

"We have never left this world in the first place. The kingdom is banished at the moment under a certain circumstances, preventing any evil disturbances from awakening the Destati. I am here not by choice but by force. My job is to make sure Ryushin grows strong before things start to occur, if they haven't already occurred."

"You mean, the building of the army of demons," Rheaa said.

"The young warlock, Atlmaz, is hard at work. He plans on retrieving the Destati and using it for his own evil deeds. The trick behind all of this is releasing Draconia from its hidden slumber."

"What does he have to do with me?" I asked.

"You are everything to do with this, Ryushin. You had performed some action long ago to banish the kingdom away from the dark. Unfortunately, I was far too young to even remember."

"You're pretty powerful for a runt, why can't you just beat Atlmaz?" Valen said.

"I've already fought with Atlmaz before. He is far more complicating than you would ever imagine. It's almost walking right into death's row."

"Astrae, do you know anything about this girl?" I asked, standing next to her.

"Not really. As much as I can tell you, she is connected to you," he answered. "You're the only one that really knows her."

"But why... why does she look so similar to Aida," I asked.

The boy didn't answer.

I pulled the first shard I collected from the first temple and showed it to him.

"These are the shards of your power. You will find them throughout the temples that you come across. There might be many, there might be little, you'll never know."

The area changed into a smaller room.

"Ayaka," I called.

"Wow, what a beautiful name," Valen said.

Ayaka and I were huddled around a bunch of friends in tuxedos and fancy dresses. Ayaka, beautiful as always, glimmered her way across the room in her light pink, diamond dress with her hair held up by a silver hairpin. I was dressed in a black tuxedo with a dark blue vest tucked underneath the overcoat.

"What school is this again?" a lady asked.

"Tesoro High School," Ayaka answered.

"Alright, everyone for Tesoro's Prom 2004, please come over to the counter," the photographer called.

Five couples, including us, gathered around the counter, waiting for our picture to be taken. Ayaka reached for my hands, pulling me inward against her. She looked into my eyes with a smile. I smiled in return.

"Aww, aren't they so cute?" Kirikah cried.

"Shut up, Kirikah," I said.

"Alright, you two, follow me," the photographer said, pointing at me and Ayaka.

The two of us followed her behind a red curtain. Kirikah, Valen, and Rheaa followed right in with them. I slowly passed the curtain, watching the two of us hold each other. Ayaka leaned up against a stand with her elbows, as I put my arms around her body, both heads tilting in sync together.

"I can't hold it!" I shrieked.

"Just hold it a little while," the photographer said, creating a frame with her fingers. "There, just perfect. Smile for the camera!"

We both smiled toward the lens. The photographer took the shot.

"You both look so cute together, almost perfect," she smiled.

"Did you hear that?" Kirikah asked, "She said you both look cute together."

"Ooooooh," Valen teased, "Aida is gonna be so jealous!"

"Aida? What does she have to do with this?" I asked.

The three of them along with Astrae started laughing at me.

I looked at Ayaka one more time before the room faded back to normal. Another shard appeared on the ground. I picked it up and I became fully re-energized.

"I will wait for you at the next temple that lies hidden in the skies," Astrae said.

He crossed his arms as glowing lights surrounded us all. In an instant, we appeared back in Imperia where Lecia was standing. Astrae was not with us however.

"Don't you guys ever knock?" Lecia asked. "At least now that you're back, were you able to find out anything while out there?"

"All that I needed to know," I answered.

Lecia smiled.

"Good, let's get this mission underway."

Chapter Six
The Elven and the Troll

That night, the eight of us gathered around Lecia.

Our mission was to form two groups, one heading west to Imperial Falls and one heading north east to the Elvara Jungle. The point of the mission was to find the whereabouts of Atlmaz's movements.

After the mission briefing, our group set out for the Elven Roots, home of the Elvens. To get to them we must pass through the Elvara Jungles, the defensive wall of the elven's homeland.

The jungle was painted with hot bright colors. Flowers were bright orange and pink, leaves showing a bit of neon green, even the bark of tress were high-toned brown. The trees were jagged at the center, blocking off most of the land in the distance. It was very easy to get lost out here.

Mordakai set out further ahead alone, scouting the area. Aida and Onry kept stayed close to my side, keeping watch for anything suspicious.

I took a good look at Aida.

For a second, she flashed into Ayaka and smiled. I smiled back.

"So what exactly did you find at the temple?" Aida asked.

I lied, "Nothing."

"I'm sure it was nothing," she said then bursted, "You big fat liar!"

"What makes you think I'm lying?"

"Damn it Ryushin, you haven't said a single word to me since you've returned to Imperia and now you're going to walk on like nothing happened?" she asked.

I chuckled as I continued walked, "Don't worry. I'm still me."

Now I began to think more about what she just said. Did the shards have an effect on my attitude toward things? In a way, I do feel different at heart. I feel stronger yet closed away from everyone else.

Mordakai came swinging down from a tree.

"Up ahead there's a camp in the middle of the road," he said.

"Awesome, that means we can take refuge there for a bit," I cheered. "My feet are killing me."

"Doesn't look like we can Ryu, the camp is run by trolls," Mordakai sighed.

"Trolls… I wonder what they're doing here…" Aida asked.

"Um… well… for quite some time now, the trolls have been trying to take the elven homeland for themselves," Onry explained. "They seek to expand their conquest and hope they can build a better kingdom for their kind."

"Sure," I said rushing ahead.

I leaped into one of the trees and squatted silently on one of its branches. I could see the whole camp from up here. The trolls were tall, skinny and lanky. They slouched forward just a bit and their giant hands hung over, touching the ground. Their noses were longer and their massive tusks spiked either down or up.

"Alright, you freaks best gather together now."

All the trolls huddled in the center. Onry and the others joined my side honing in on the camp. The man that came out was the fouled mouth Corfits, along with his two bodyguards, Deadsong and Fearsong.

"Hey, it's that loser, Corfits, that bastard," Mordakai growled.

"Quiet," Aida said.

"You morons still haven't located those poor excuses of life yet?" Corfits angrily asked, stomping his foot into the ground.

"The Elven move swift everyday," Deadsong said.

"Not in one place they will stay," Fearsong added.

Corfits lost his patience with the two elvens. "Thanks, I knew that already. Anyway, you damn trolls better find them before midnight or I will slice off your heads and feed them to the Rizaado!"

"Sir Corfits," a troll called.

"What is it, damn it all?" he yelled with fumes. "Can't you see I am talking here?"

"I beg for your forgiveness sir, but we were able to capture one of the Elven," the troll said.

Two more trolls entered the scene with an elven all tied up.

Corfits chuckled, "Make her tell us where the homeland is. Whip her until she gives in, that'll get the job done." The elven was a female. She's a little taller than the average human, but not as tall as Deadsong or Fearsong. She has blue eyes and a bright purple skin color. Her hair was blue as well, matching her eyes. She wore a green dress made from fine looking cloth, decorated with leaves of a darker green and some sparkling beads lined together with silver linen. "Do as you please troll, I take my leave."

Corfits vanished with a smoke bomb, taking Fearsong and Deadsong with him.

"We have to help her." I said, hopping down from the tree. Mordakai cracked the joints in his knuckles. "Think you can blind them with a thick mist Onry?"

"I think I should be able to," she nodded.

"We're going to have to be quick on this one," I said.

Onry concentrated her mana into a miniature cloud of mist and consumed the camp in her power. The trolls became aware of our presence, quickly drawing their weapons. The rest of us moved quickly, yet silently through the mist. I found my way to the elven and attempted to untie her. The elven squirmed fiercely, fighting desperately to break free. I paused for a second, losing attraction from the startled trolls nearby.

"Calm down," I warned her, "They're going to see us."

The elven still wouldn't stop squirming. I freed the elven from her ropes and she took off running into the woods. The trolls yelled and quickly chased after her. Mordakai and Aida stood, their just watching them run around.

"Don't just stand there, go after her," Aida said.

I quickly picked up the pace and caught up with the rushing crowd. I tugged on some of the trolls' arms, jerking them behind me. Momentum started picking up. Mordakai and Aida caught up with me. Out of nowhere, a pair of demons attacked from both sides. Aida and Mordakai defended them off.

"Just keep after her," Mordakai said.

The elven began to glow a strange color. She surprisingly changed into a cat. Her speed increased, building a gap between the two of us. I drew my sword, concentrating fire into the blade and hurled it toward the trees in front of the elven. The trees burned to the ground, blocking her path.

"Look, I just want to help you," I said.

The elven pounced on top of me. She raised her claw and took one swipe. I delivered a quick blow to her stomach with a double kick, knocking her off of me. The elven swiped her claw once more, knocking me back onto my back. She took off running into the jungle again. I quickly picked myself up and continued my pursuit.

Further ahead, the jungle became a little more complex then it was before. Great vines wrapped under and over each other making several different path ways. The vines must be the trick for the elvens to stay out of sight. I quickly saw the elven climb her way through the vines off in the distance.

"Ryushin," Aida called, "So where is she?"

I pointed her out in the distance, watching her jump out of sight.

"Great, how do we get through this tangle?" Mordakai whined.

"What happened to Onry?" I asked. Aida and Mordakai looked blankly at each other. "Don't tell me you forgot about Onry?"

"Bah, rock-paper-scissors, Aida," Mordakai said. They gamble their hands. Aida came up rock and Mordakai resulted in scissors. "Damn it, fine. I'll go find her."

"Let's go Aida," I said.

We both climb the vines upward, surveying the distance. It looked like the elven got away. The paths that we walked along were heavily surfaced great vines with old leaves and branches. Scratched into the vines were giant claw marks. The blue sky faded into a tropical orange and the night fell upon us.

"Maybe we should wait for Mordakai and Onry," Aida suggested. But I continued to move forward. "Ryu, are you even listening to me?"

"Don't worry, they'll find us."

"I don't know. Something isn't right here."

I stood still, sensing a presence around us. Aida was right. There was someone here with us. The female elven appeared and started running.

"There she is Ryu," Aida pointed.

Aida unhooked her sword and struck one of the vines below, snapping it into two. The vine dangled downward, knocking the elven off balance. I leaped downward onto a sturdy vine close by and grabbed the elven by the hand.

"Don't be afraid," I said, pulling her up. "We're not here to hurt you."

The elven sat down, a little frightened.

Aida leaped down next to us.

"We should get out of the opening. The trolls will see her from here."

We stood beneath a giant tree with lots of vines dangling upon us, blocking us out of sight. The elven stood there with her arms crossed.

"I knew it was you," the elven said.

"Say what? You can talk?" I asked.

"They're not stupid, Ryu," Aida laughed.

I felt embarrassed I began to blush.

"Ryu," the elven pronounced, "as in Ryushin." I nodded. "The Legendary Ryushin has returned, just as the elder prophesized," she said. "I am Rhyona, the guardian of the elvens. At birth, I was marked with gift to blend with nature."

"So that's how you changed into a cat," I said.

"A prowler is a better term, a cat is too puny," Rhyona corrected. "I must take you to our elder."

"We have to find our friends first," Aida said. "The trolls might find them."

She changed into a cat again and began to head off.

"We find your friends than you will see our elder. Follow me; it will be easy to find them."

We went back into the jungle to look for Mordakai and Onry. It was going to be a long night, and my legs were already cramping. We stumbled upon the same troll camp we ran into earlier. Still no sign of Mordakai and Onry…

The trolls were lively at work. I wonder what they could be doing.

"Rhyona," Aida whispered.

"Yes?" she answered.

"What are the trolls doing here?"

She grinned at the thought of it, "They're here to rid us of our land. For decades they have been coming in and out of the jungle finding ways to strip the vines away. That dark man is paying them off to do the dirty work."

"Damn that Corfits," I cursed.

"That bad man," Rhyona tearfully said, "He killed my brother, Rhyne, a few years ago. When Rhyne was around, the trolls dared not to come into the jungle. Without him, the elven have lost all hope."

"I'm sorry to hear that Rhyona," Aida said.

"They are up to something," I said. "Look at that."

The Adventures of Ryushin

The trolls were coming together, piling scraps of metal, bars and sharp swords. It looked like some huge contraption of sort, made for grinding things into pieces.

"The trolls plan on chopping down the jungle," Aida said.

"We have to stop them," I replied.

"Don't be a fool. These trolls aren't as dumb as they look," Rhyona said. "They're smart, just like the Kitsunes. They will trap you and ambush you at any given time and there are far too many of them for us to handle."

I responded, "Well, if we don't do anything, your jungle is gonna be nothing, literally."

"What of the people of your village, Rhyona?" Aida asked. "Can they help?"

Rhyona gave a long drawn out sigh.

"Most of the villagers aren't old enough to fight yet and the ones that are training are far inexperienced in battle."

I chuckled, jabbing my right fist into my left hand.

"If that's the truth than I will step up and help rid the trolls of this jungle."

"You would go out of your way to help us?" Rhyona asked.

I clinched my fist tight. "You know it." Rhyona started making her way away from the trolls. "Where are you going?"

"We cannot do anything right now," she said. "We must retreat back to the village and refuge there until morning."

"What about Mordakai and Onry?" I asked, looking over at Aida.

She shrugged her shoulders.

"They will be fine," she answered, "as long as they stay clear of the trolls."

After a long walk through the jungle, we arrived at a dead end where the vines all connected. Rhyona placed her palm in the center where all vines crossed and untangled them with her power. Aida and I followed Rhyona down a new path.

"I see," Aida said.

"What?" I asked.

"In order for the elvens to stay in hiding, they live under the great vines rather above them," Aida answered.

"Partially true," Rhyona nodded. "We are forced to live down here for our safety. We will move back up to the jungle when it is safe."

Rhyona opened another path and entered the village of the elvens.

Off in the distance were tree-houses with ladders leading out down to the surface. The surface was very narrow, filled with ponds of water covering most of the land. Some elvens tended the waters and plants for food, some younger elvens were hard at work cutting up wood. The area we entered was a colorful flower garden with butterflies flying all over.

"Butterflies down here?" Aida questioned.

Rhyona smiled.

"They are trying to survive just as much as we are."

We walked the path to the center of the village. As we walked through, the elvens of the village stared and gossiped amongst each other. They seemed frightened.

Beyond the city was a thick wood with a curtain covered door. An elven walked over to Rhyona and nodded to her, then entered the thick wood alone. Aida and I stood silently, waiting for something to happen.

"He will see you now," the elven guard announced, returning from the thick wood. "But you go in alone." I looked over at Aida, who shrugged her shoulders again.

Rhyona nodded.

I entered the thick wood alone, where the light was very dim and the air was very heavy with wood dust crawling all over.

A very aged elven sat on his chair rather lazily. He wore a tiara on his forehead with his old gray hair slicked back. He was dressed in very thick clothing with golden lining to keep him warm. His pale skin was wrinkled from head to toe.

"The world has been waiting for you, Prince Ryushin," the elder said hoarsely.

The Adventures of Ryushin

I could sense his energy level was very low and that he would soon pass on.

"Young prince?" I asked.

"You are once called Prince of the Dracolytes, during the days of the great war..." he coughed fiercely. "...Though it seems that your heart is slightly off beat." He pointed behind me, lighting up a torch on the wall.

There were some hieroglyphics of a story, painted amongst the walls with stick figures with wings and the lands around it.

"Long ago, during the War of the Exiled, there was a young prince who held the powers of both sides, the Dracolytes and the Humans. It was said- he would rise up and deliver the world an age of peace and prosperity."

Another wall lit up with a story.

"Shortly after the war, he had disappeared from this world along with the banishment of the Dracolyte Kingdom. In his absence, the darkness has emerged once again to this very day, seeking ways to conquer the world." He rested his hand and the walls went dark. "Only you can tell us what happened of the past and dark age from coming."

"How can I tell what's happened in the past? I have no idea what is going on," I replied.

"Close your eyes and feel what is hiding in your heart." And so, I closed my eyes and relaxed for a bit. I could see nothing but a black space. "Feel the past that is hiding."

I began to see images in my mind.

There was a black figure standing the dark with great wings expanding from its back. It hosted a wing of an angel and a wing of a dragon. It turned around slowly and looked at me with its pure red eyes.

I opened my eyes breathing heavily. "What was that?"

"I could see everything you felt," he said, coughing fiercely. "I understand."

"You understand what? Tell me, what happened?"

He closed his eyes and relaxed.

Soon, my heart became heavy. The dark figure appeared behind me with its claw raised. With one strike, I could feel its sharp nails digging deep into my heart. Flashbacks occurred left and right, showing motions of happiness and darkness. Ayaka filled in the void, smiling as she moved closer. I gasped for air, like I was choking and finally came to.

The elder opened his eyes… I was breathing heavily.

"What is most important to you, Prince Ryushin? What is it that you fear?" he asked.

"I don't know," I gasped.

"Did you not see what I saw? Our visions were similar to each other. What you saw was a glimpse of a possible future. It is what you fear; it is what is important to you. There will be a time when you will face a doubt in your heart. Whatever the outcome is, you must rise above it."

He rested quietly.

As I walked toward the door, I could hear him whispering in my head. But he was sound asleep.

Rhyona and Aida stood there waiting for me. I approached them with a little confused, but smiled to keep them on their toes.

"So?" Aida questioned.

I nodded to Rhyona and said, "First, we rid the trolls in the jungle and then we head for the Kingdom of Reina."

Point of View: Rheaa

Lecia had assigned me to lead this group to the west, hoping to accomplish the mission quickly. She wanted us to regroup with Ryushin's party as soon as possible.

To the west rested the beautiful waterfalls of Imperia. The waterfalls stretched hundred of miles westbound and dropped more than thousands of feet. It was beautiful at night. The water would sparkle so bright, it made the stars look tiny. There wasn't much dry land for us to walk on, so we dunked our feet into the water and made our way across the shallow depths.

Aeric and Kirikah stood quite a distance from Valen and me, spending quality time with each other. I was jealous in a way because Kirikah always attracted a lot of attention. They would always complain about my attitude and how mean I was. Still, I paid more attention to my work rather than someone else's life.

"You're always thinking," Valen said. "What could possibly go on in that brain of yours?"

"Shut up," I growled.

"Same old Rheaa," he said, amusingly.

"What's that suppose to mean?"

"Nothing, come on let's keep moving."

Aeric entered the conversation from behind. "Listen up. Lecia informed us of trolls running around in the area. Their reasons here are unknown and it can become a threat to the kingdom. We are to find the trolls and investigate."

I flicked my hand at Aeric.

"Blah, we know that already. Must you repeat everything?"

"Of course I do, especially with someone as ignorant as you Rheaa," Aeric answered.

We walked for hours across the waters. It was very heavy for us to pick up our feet in a continuous motion. I felt like falling into the water and drift away.

Everyone ducked into the water suddenly, stirring no movement. I ducked down too and followed their lead.

"What's going on?" Kirikah asked.

Aeric and Valen remained silent listening up ahead for any sudden movements. Aeric signaled for Valen to move in. Valen quickly hopped out of the water and moved swiftly up ahead into the trees.

"There is someone straight ahead," Aeric said. "I can feel it."

"Is it a troll?" I asked.

"Not sure, it could be anything," he whispered.

I swam steadily through the shallow waters, toward some trees. Valen was squatting next to a tree, spying on someone. In the middle of the water was a troll standing alone.

"That guy is just standing there," Valen whispered.

The troll stood with great posture. His right shoulder was shielded by a cracked plated shoulder pad while is left shoulder was exposed. Strapped on his chest was a vest on that opened down the middle revealing his rough body marked with scars and cuts. His pants were at the ankles. Rugged brown shoes covered his feet and Orange spiked hair shot in an upward diagonal.

"What should we do?" I asked.

"Just hold your position. There's gotta be more around here somewhere."

"You lied."

Entering the scene was Corfits whom we saw back at Ahz-Bovan.

"I did not deceive you," the troll said.

"Now Zandaris, I thought we had an agreement made?"

He turned and faced the dark man.

"I will not let you corrupt my people with your dark schemes. If we want to defeat the elvens, we will defeat them in our own way without help from a warlock like Atlmaz."

Corfits laughed ferociously. "Sorry troll, but you have no other choice." A couple of trolls bigger than Zandaris showed up behind Corfits. "You see, these trolls now belong to us and they will do our command. If you don't think that's fair, then die along with your rebellion."

The two trolls attacked Zandaris fiercely, whacking their sharp claws. Zandaris easily countered both of them, knocking them face first into the water. More trolls appeared. Zandaris fought hard to keep them off but there were just too many coming.

"Should we help him?" I asked.

"Are you crazy? Why would we help a damn troll?" Valen said, moving away.

"Not bad," Corfits applauded. "Can't expect anything less from the leader of the trolls, can you?" He drew his sword, slashing heavily at Zandaris. Zandaris rolled through the thick water, gathering some in his hand. He splashed Corfits in the eyes, blinding him for the moment and delivered a kick to his stomach. Corfits laughed punching his plated armor. "You're gonna have to hit harder than that."

The trolls began to surround him on all sides. Aeric and the rest showed up.

"What the hell? Why are the trolls fighting each other?" Aeric asked.

"They're corrupted by Atlmaz's darkness and Corfits is the one commanding them," I answered. "We have to help."

"What are you crazy?" Aeric asked.

"That's what I said," Valen agreed.

I grunted at both of them and drew my long blade out. Jumping into the mosh pit with slashes and cuts, Zandaris was able to break free. He looked at me as I looked at him, then I faced Corfits, holding my ground.

"Who the hell are you?" Corfits asked. "Wait a minute, I recognize you. You were with that Ryushin fella back at Ahz-Bovan."

"Shut up," I said.

A troll grabbed my arm, locking it tight. It was Zandaris. He pushed me into the trolls and took off running. Angrily, I started chasing him. Trolls jumped in my way, blocking Zandaris from my view.

"Kyoufuu!" I yelled, cutting right through them with my wind attack. Back to chasing Zandaris.

I turned around watching Aeric and the others confront Corfits. Catching up easily, I sliced my sword upward through the water, sending a shock wave toward Zandaris. It knocked him off balance, shoving his face into the water. I sprang out of the water, attempting to strike with a death blow.

Countering quickly, he raised his legs, planting them flatly against mine. He pushed off, catapulting me into the air. I landed onto the trolls from behind.

Recovering quickly to my feet, I tried another shockwave attack. Zandaris rolled to the side, evading the wave. Instead of rising into the air, I rushed with my blade down. His plated bracer on his arm blocked my attack. He rolled backward onto his hands and into a hand stand. He rotated on his palms, making it hard for me to predict his movements. He threw a swift kick toward my chest. I raised the flat of my sword, blocking his kick. His force was too strong, launching me onto my back.

Trolls began to attack from behind. Some rushed passed me, attacking Zandaris at the same time. I evaded their attacks and slashed them away. Zandaris pummeled his way through.

A tree log came out of nowhere. We both climbed the log and faced each other, pedaling our feet to keep ourselves balanced. The log was drifting too close to the edge.

"What the hell is your problem?" I said, "I was only trying to help."

"How do I know you don't work for that bastard, Corfits?"

"I just saved you back there and then you just throw me into those trolls?"

I attacked with my sword, barely nicking his chest. He threw a punch. This time, his force wasn't as strong. We both began losing our balance.

"Here come some more trolls," Zandaris said.

Zandaris hopped onto his arms into a handstand, attacking with his legs. He cycled strong kicks against my sword, throwing me off balance. I pushed away from Zandaris as the trolls jumped in between us.

"We're gonna go over the waterfall!" I yelled.

"Rheaa!" Valen came running.

My friends were close on our trail, running alongside the trolls. I drilled my long sword deep into the water and through the surface, delaying our fall as much as I could. Zandaris grabbed onto my leg, dragging more weight for me to carry.

"Let go of me you ass," I shrugged, losing grip on my blade.

"Care for a little dip?" he asked.

He yanked fiercely, breaking my sword free from the cliff.

Zandaris was falling right under me. He pulled on my leg again, bringing him up to my level. I dodged one of his punches. I pushed off his chest with a kick, creating space between us. I gripped my sword with two hands and started swinging. He was able to block all my attacks with his bracers.

He clasped his hands together, and then snapped them out wide open. Perfect clones emerged from his body.

A clone jerked me forward from behind with a straight kick. Another clone delivered a punch to my stomach. The third clone pushed off the fourth clone into a somersault. I forced my body to spin on its backside, blocking the somersault kick to my chest. I flushed downward, passing Zandaris and the clones.

I slashed my sword downward with a wind slash, pushing myself back up to Zandaris. I looped my sword around my body, striking the clones away.

"I got a good one for you," I said. Striking downward, I chipped his bracer and yelled, "Takuetsufuu!" A whirlwind glided out from the sharp of my blade and engulfed Zandaris in its spin.

The whirlwind pulled him closer.

I struck violently with a kick to his gut and continued with a spin kick to his face. I pulled my sword downward, launching him like a lightning bolt alongside the waterfall's momentum. The water from above crashed up on me, bringing me down to its base.

I opened my eyes slowly, floating along the still water. My body ached all over.

"You hit the water pretty hard shortly after I did," Zandaris said kneeling on the shore. "We were lucky to have landed in a deep part of the lake. Lucky for us I know where we are."

"Shut up," I said, gripping my sword. "Like I'd follow you anywhere." He nodded, then started walking the other direction. "Where are you going?"

"To Tru-Atgun, where my people need me."

"Tru-Atgun? What is that?"

"It is the land of my fortress," he said.

"Why don't I just kill you now?" I asked, lunging at him with my sword held high over my head. He blocked my attack with his bracer.

"There are far more important things going on right now than just our little quarrel," he said, flicking away my blade.

I didn't have much choice but to follow him. Plus, my RT wasn't functioning right. It'll take hours to find the others alone.

"What is the relationship between you and Corfits?" I asked.

"There is no relationship. He plagued my kingdom with his deceiving thoughts and took control of my own people. His source of power comes from the north... a dark area that none of my people dare to walk."

"Are you retarded? How could you let someone like Corfits enter your fortress like that?"

He growled, "I was forced to let him enter. If I didn't, he would have killed her. He entered the kingdom by force and there wasn't much I could do."

"Then why are we going to Tru-Atgun? Isn't that where Corfits is?"

"I am going to save my people, to save Her."

"But you would just walk into a slaughter. There has to be another way."

"You stupid fool. I wouldn't just barge in like that, throwing punches and kicks all around. You humans are all the same, no strategic plan whatsoever."

"That's not true."

"Then tell me exactly what you had in mind, jumping into my battle earlier against Corfits." I remained silent. "Be grateful human that I am joining with you for now... otherwise you would've been dead in your sleep."

Point of View: Ryushin

I jumped up top one of the higher vines, surveying the distance of the jungle. There they were. The trolls were up early in the morning, hard at work with that contraption of theirs. I signaled down toward Aida and Rhyona to move out.

I made my way to one side of the great vines, watching the trolls march with their machine. Rhyona and Aida opposite of me, waiting patiently behind some vines.

I nodded over to Rhyona.

She morphed into her cat form, jumping out in front of them. She provoke the trolls to follow her, leading them away from their machine. Aida and I jumped out and examined the piece of junk.

"How do you stop it?" Aida said.

On the top of the machine was a latch. Maybe that's where the switch was. I hopped up and tugged fiercely. Inside was a troll, maneuvering it. The troll jumped out of his seat and pulled out his javelin.

"Whoops," I smirked, "They left a buddy behind."

"Ryushin..."

Behind us were a horde of trolls staring us down. I waved.

"Aida, find a way to stop this thing. I'll lead them away from here." I picked up a rock and chucked it over at one of the trolls, crushing him right in the forehead. The troll fumed. I took off running into the jungle and hopped onto the great vines.

Rhyona was running around in circles just up ahead along the vines with a herd of trolls chasing her. I aimed there way and crossed paths with the other trolls confusing the two herds.

"Ryushin, over here!" Rhyona called.

She palmed her hand onto one of the vines, changing its pathway downward. I slid onto my side, riding the vine downward while Rhyona climbed upward.

"Whew," I said, jogging away from the hustling trolls. "This is a good workout."

"Stop playing around," Rhyona said, "We have to help Aida stop that thing."

Aida was helpless, beating the machine with senseless stares.

"What are you waiting for, Aida?" I called. "Just slice the damn thing with your sword."

"Do you see these cutter blades?" Aida pointed. "My sword would get crunched if I swung at it head on."

The trolls stopped, leaving me way up in front. I stopped running.

"Hey Rhyona, I think these guys are tired."

Rhyona stood still, staring at the frozen trolls.

"Something is coming," Rhyona alerted, "Get out of there, Ryu."

The only thing I heard was the machine chopping away at the vines. The trolls started to jump off the great vines, regardless how high it was.

Up in the distance, I can see a black coat moving fast toward us. It was suspenseful, watching the black coat shift its way toward us. As it came closer, I started to see yellow dots among them. They were demons, a mass army of them.

"Ryushin, get moving," Aida said, leaving the machine behind.

"Oh shit," I gasped.

I ran up the lower vine, making my way up and out of their way. Before I knew it, I was completely surrounded by hundreds of them.

The demons started flinging their sharp claws at me. Another demon grabbed arm pinning against the great vine. I flexed fiercely, trying to break free but the demon's strength was too great. More demons collapsed on top.

"Gaikou," Aida's voiced echoed from above.

A rain of light showered down on the demons, banishing them away.

"Look out!" I yelled, pushing her out of the way. A demon tackled me straight through the vine with power. I recovered from the attack, slamming my knee fiercely into its face. I grabbed a smaller vine to break my fall, climbing to the top.

Rhyona found her way to me.

"There is far too many of them. I didn't expect this."

I wiped the sweat off my forehead, smiling at her. "Sometimes, you just gotta expect the unexpected." I leaped downward toward Aida, knocking away some demons off the vine.

I gripped my sword tightly as Aida crunched some demons with her great sword. "Don't throw your sword," she said, "I know you're going to throw it." Jumping into the air, I slashed away at some oncoming demons.

"I like throwing it, Aida," I said.

"If you throw it, use your mana to control your sword. That way you don't have to go running after it."

A demon attacked from behind with its sharp claws. I grabbed its arm and flipped onto its shoulders, smashing it onto its knees. Launching high into the air., I gripped my sword tightly, wound my arm backward and let the sword fly. I palmed my hand at my sword, concentrating on its direction. The blade moved in a circle, swiping away the surrounding demons. I called back to my sword.

I laughed filled with excitement, "That was awesome!"

Someone attacked from above. I crossed my arms over my chest, blocking the direct attack. The force sent me flying downward and into the vines below. I slid across the dirt.

"You die here, Dracolyte," Deadsong said, equipping a claw to his right arm. Aida and Rhyona were too busy with matters above.

Deadsong charged with quickness. He shifted his weight right, vanishing, then reappeared on the left for the moment before disappearing one more time. Deadsong delivered a surprising kick from behind, cracking heel at the center of my spine. I lunged forward, rotating in the air. I caught myself on my palm, bouncing back onto my feet. I massaged my back, easing up the pain. Deadsong suddenly appeared on my right and smashed his knuckles into my face. I slid against the ground roughly.

Deadsong attacked from above. I rolled to my side, barely avoiding his fierce drill kick. I kicked into a leg sweep, knocking him off his feet. Pushing off my arms, I launched into the air and hung their for a while. He copied my same move, finding his way up to me. He pulled on one of arms and delivered a strong knee to my stomach. Clinching his hands together, he delivered a double punch to my upper back..

I gasped for air.

He stood their looking down on me. I launched my sword toward him, concentrating its direction. I pulled my arm, forcing the sword to race upward, catching his attention.

"Tricked ya," I laughed.

I slammed a jump kick into his stomach, and then slammed a fierce punch to his cheek. He went flew into a great vine. I palmed my hands in his direction waiting, for him to come out. He appeared behind me so fast, I couldn't see his movement. I grabbed his fist, tossing him over my shoulder. He caught himself easily and began sprinting toward me.

"Shadow punch!" he yelled, throwing a straight punch through the air. A wave of dark fists appeared in all directions. One at a time the fists would attack. I evaded and blocked all of them, rolling and jumping out of the way. Deadsong lunged forward and cracked his knuckles against my chest. I jerked backward, slamming against a great vine. I picked myself up slowly.

"Seinaru Yoru!" I casted, watching an energy ball fly out of my hand.

Deadsong rolled to the side, dodging the attack. I palmed my hand at my sword, directing it downward onto the unaware elven. He threw a straight jab but I countered his attack. I ducked under, rose up and crushed his jaw with a strong uppercut. My sword came down piercing through his left shoulder. I jumped high above him, launching another energy blast. The energy ball exploded on contact, creating a big wave of smoke.

The smoke cleared. My sword stood alone in the ground and Deadsong had escaped before the energy blast.

Demons attacked from above.

Large ice shards toppled on top of them, tearing them to pieces.

"Onry," I said happily.

Onry and Mordakai showed up on the scene just in time.

"Psh, worry about the girl why don't you."

"We should talk later," Onry said.

"That's fine with me," I said putting my sword away. "Let's get Aida and Rhyona and get the hell out of here. It's not safe here anymore."

Point of View: Rheaa

We stood underneath a cliff, looking upward at the edge of it. The wind chilled through our clothes and swirled its way the steep side. Zandaris stared blankly up at the edge, thinking endlessly.

"Go home," Zandaris blurted out.

I looked at him confused.

"Go home?"

"Yes, go home, this isn't your fight."

He walked up a fairly inclined slope alone.

"I'm not going anywhere," I said, running after him.

As he paced himself easily without a word to say, and he knew better than I did that he could not fight Corfits alone.

"Are you deaf? I said go home."

"I'm going with you whether you like it or not."

He stopped and stared deep into my eyes. "What business do you have here? You are just wasting your time."

I replied with a light shove, "Corfits is one of Atlmaz's goons. If we defeat him together, then maybe we can get him to tell us where Atlmaz is hiding."

He continued walking.

"Atlmaz does not hide."

"Then help me find him," I pleaded.

I stood in front of him, stopping him in his tracks. He shoved me out of the way and continued walking.

"No," he clearly stated.

I stomped my foot angrily into the ground. What was I suppose to do? I was separated from the others, I don't know my way back, and Corfits is just on top of this cliff.

"Zandaris!" I called out. "Please, you're the only one that can help me right now."

He finally stopped. I ran up to him, sneaking the puppy dog eyes on him. No one can resist these beautiful eyes of mine.

"Do you ever shut up?" he asked. My puppy dog eyes went from beautiful to sad. "First, we save Her... then I will help you."

I agreed, opening my hand for a shake-on-it kind of deal. He shook my hand and we walked together up the path.

After a long climb up the steep side, we found ourselves stuck outside the fortress walls. Zandaris walked over to the east side of the fortress walls and hugging it closely. He placed his ear onto the wall, listening as he shuffled further ahead. He stood back and punched his fist into one of the tiles. The tile slowly inserted itself opening a door to the side.

"Let's go," he said.

"How did you know about that?"

"You think I don't know my own fortress?" he chuckled.

He followed me in closing the gate behind him.

His fortress wasn't any typical ugly troll fortress. It seemed richer than the walls Imperia had.

We crept along the hallow wall quietly, keeping any sudden noises from alerting the trolls around us. As we got further down the hall, the walls became transparent for us. I could see the movement and activity that as going on outside the walls.

"Don't worry," Zandaris said, "They can't see us."

We turned the corner, leading to a staircase. Zandaris pulled on a torch light and opened another secret door. From there, we entered an unlocked cell room.

"Why would you put your secret passage in a cell room?" I asked.

He opened the cell door and scouted the area. There was no one in sight.

"Just in case I become locked in my own dungeon, I can escape easily."

"Smart…"

The fortress wasn't as big as Imperia, consisting of four different small rooms- the fort, the dungeon, the barracks and the courtyard.

Zandaris and I made our way to the upper tower on the east wall, which overlooked the courtyard. There were hundreds of them moping around, gambling or wasting time. Female and male trolls were equipped with fine metal armor and curved blades, dangling from their belts or sharp claws locked to their arms.

In the doorway of the fort, that lies north of the courtyard, was Fearsong, watching all of the trolls. Corfits was nowhere to be found.

"She must be inside the fort," Zandaris said, sniffing the air.

"How can you tell?"

"She has a different scent from the trolls."

"So how do we get to her with Fearsong standing middle of the doorway?"

Zandaris looked around for any ideas.

A long chain from the east tower to the west tower was our best chance. Another chain from the fort tower dangled from a hook, connecting the two chains.

"I will create a diversion. Reach the center of the courtyard by hanging onto the chains. Unhook the second chain and swing passed the elven." He hopped up onto the ledge. "Don't worry about me. Whatever you do, get her out of the fortress."

"Where do I find you?"

"I will find you. Now get going."

Zandaris slammed his claw into the wall and climbed down slowly. I quickly ran over to the east tower, hopping onto the ledge. The chain wasn't very sturdy. I drew my sword, balancing myself along the chain. Slowly, I grabbed hold of the second chain.

Fearsong spotted Zandaris.

He sprinted quickly over to him, alerting every troll he ran by. Zandaris pushed his back up onto the wall as he landed onto the ground.

I grabbed the middle chain, tried to unhook it but it was being stubborn. I had to unhook it without drawing any attention to myself.

Zandaris started clashing with Fearsong and the trolls.

Now would be the best time for me to get in there. I cut the chain with my sword, swinging down to the fort. Fearsong spotted me and started sprinting in my direction. Zandaris dove at his ankle, taking him down. The trolls piled on top of him, freeing Fearsong from Zandaris' grasp.

I ran inside the fort turning right into a mob of trolls.

Trolls defended a spiraling ramp. I took them out quickly with my sword and ran up the ramp.

Fearsong was right behind me. He bounced off a wall and threw a jump kick. I blocked the attack, nearly falling off the ramp. Zandaris, flying out of nowhere, kicked him strongly in the rib. Fearsong flew across the ramp, smashing into the wall and sliding down to the ground.

"Keep going."

I continued running up the stairway while Zandaris fended off the horde of trolls. At the top of the fort were two trolls operating on the other. I gripped my sword, catching their attention with the sparkle of my blade. The troll on the bed was a female. That had to be who Zandaris was talking about. They moved out of harms ways, letting me take the troll. I placed her onto one of my shoulders and took off running back down the ramp.

Fearsong headed me off.

"You go nowhere girl," he said.

Again, Zandaris flying out of nowhere, delivered a hard kick to Fearsong.

"You better not drop her," Zandaris warned.

I ran down the ramp, slicing my way through the trolls. Fearsong pushed off Zandaris, and then dropped the top. He tackled me from the staircase, knocking all three of us to the ground.

Fearsong raised his fist.

Zandaris was able to knock him off of me yet again.

"You dropped her."

"Sorry! It was his fault," I said. I placed the female troll back onto my shoulder.

I ran out into the courtyard, running into another group of trolls. Slashing my sword, I performed my Kyoufuu wind attack, blowing the trolls up against the walls of the fortress.

I made for the gate.

"Girl, I said you go nowhere," Fearsong called from behind. I turned around quickly performing Kyoufuu one more time. He timed the attack and jumped over it.

Zandaris tackled Fearsong.

I ran out of the gate, nearly running of the edge of the cliff. I spotted some trees to the north, so I made my way there.

In the area covered with little amounts of trees, I rested the female troll up against a tree and waited for Zandaris to show up.

"Where am I...?" The unconscious troll pulled through.

"It's okay, you're safe now."

She grabbed her head and said, "I feel like someone just dropped me on my head..."

Zandaris hopped down from one of the trees, landing next to me.

"Oh, Zandaris!" she said, leaping into his arms.

"I thought I'd never see you again..." Zandaris said.

This was too mushy for me. I left the two alone walking into the woods.

My RT came up with Aeric on it.

"Where the hell are you, damn it?" Aeric asked.

"You shut up. I'm in some kind of woods far west from Imperia Falls."

"Oh, you're not that far from us then. Listen, we got Corfits to spill some beans for us. Try and make it far north of your position. Something about the Kingdom of Reina... sounds kind of fishy to me but it's our best lead."

"I'll meet up with you guys soon."

I wonder if the team would let Zandaris join along. I walked back to him only to hear some harsh words mumble silently. I pressed up against a tree and honed my ears in, listening to what she said.

"You're so pitiful, Zandaris," she said. "Why do you refuse to join forces with Corfits?"

"I don't understand... I was too late to save you..."

I heard the sound of a sharp blade pierce into flesh.

"You are weak because you lack power. If you would just submit to his power, we would have done away with the elvens by now."

The Adventures of Ryushin

Zandaris dropped to one knee.

"What's happened to you?"

"When Atlmaz gains the power of Destati, the age of Dark Rule will arrive, leaving you all on your knees, begging for mercy."

"Destati…"

"Or I should just kill you now!"

I drew my sword quickly, slashing her across the spine.

"No!" Zandaris cried.

She looked down at him with blood dripping from her mouth, and said, "It's too late for you two fools…" then died.

"Why did you do that?" he asked.

"She was gonna kill you."

"I would have gladly died for her!"

"But why?"

"Because we do anything for the ones we love! Stupid human! Do you not understand anything?"

I grunted at him, putting my blade away.

"There is more than just her that you have to save. Maybe you can redeem yourself by killing the one that did this to her."

"I will. I will slay that dark man, Corfits."

I could see the anger in his eyes. He was enraged and I didn't know how to help.

I helped him up by the arm.

"Don't touch me!" he said, standing to his feet. He looked down on me with an angry look planted on his face. Then it slowly settled in. "I'm sorry… please forgive me."

"Just forget about it."

"I will do as I promised. We must head north into the woods. It's a long ways from here so don't expect any stops around here."

"I'm Rheaa, by the way."

I held my hand out for him to shake. He happily shook it, and we were on our way.

Chapter Seven
The Fallen Kingdom

Point of View: Ryushin

I think we were lost. But I didn't want to tell Aida that. She would be like, *'you don't know what you're doing'* or *'I knew I should have led the way'*. That was just her way of leadership.

"We're lost, aren't we Ryushin?" Aida asked.

I staggered to the floor.

"We're not lost, it's just a big world out there, ya know?"

"Yup, we are. I knew I should have led the way," Aida said, flicking open her RT.

Rhyona looked all around us, examining the place. "Actually, we're not too far off from the place you named."

I clapped my hands excitedly and said, "See! I told ya we're not lost."

"So where exactly are we?" Aida asked.

"If I remember correctly," Rhyona thought, "We should go west from here. What was the name of this place the elder spoke of again?"

"The Kingdom of Reina," I answered.

Mordakai jumped, "Are you serious?"

We all looked at him, confused about his reaction. He had this scared look on his face like he's been there before.

"What's up with you?" I asked.

Mordakai started biting his finger nails, "Any place but there! I swear you don't want to go there."

"Why not?" Aida asked.

"Don't you learn anything in your class? The Kingdom of Reina is a kingdom in ruins since 5000 years ago! There will be ghosts and everything in there, haunted I tell ya, haunted!"

Onry bonked him on the head. "Better?"

"A lot better," Mordakai said, "But still, I want out."

"Don't be a baby," I said, "We'll leave you here in the jungle with those demons."

"I don't care! I'd rather fight demons, millions of them in fact," he happily agreed. Onry bonked him on the head once more, and started dragging him by his arm.

We continued walking through the jungle to the west and just the thought of this place deeply caught my interest. It seemed oddly familiar to me.

"What else do you know about The Kingdom of Reina, Mordakai?" I asked.

He gulped and answered, "Well, if I'm right, the Kingdom of Reina was a dominant kingdom of the humans, hosting the princess of long ago. Its conquest was so great, the lands nearly stretched from one side of the continent to the other."

"A kingdom that conquered that much land?" Aida asked.

"Yes! So, we could be trapped down there forever and we wouldn't know it," Mordakai said, "Also, the kingdom had a major role in banishing Draconia."

"Draconia..." I whispered.

"You all need to pay attention in class, ya know?" Mordakai asked.

After about an hour of walking, we found ourselves at an open field of grass. There was no kingdom in sight, just a plain empty field. The five of us walked into the open, looking for some sort of clue or hint, but still, there was nothing.

"Now, if I'm correct, the kingdom actually sank back during the war and was buried. Maybe, the kingdom is right under our feet," Mordakai explained.

"Yea but that still doesn't help us get into the Kingdom of Reina," Aida said.

Out in the distance, I spotted a demon jumping into the ground. I ran over to the hole in the ground, just before it closed. This had to be place the Elder spoke of. I drew my sword, cutting through the grass, revealing a hollow interior.

"Over here," I called.

I jumped in first to make sure there was no one around. The rest of them followed after.

The place we entered was a hallway, with the lights dim on the torches, just enough for us to see further ahead. Mordakai jumped onto my back with shrivels running up and down his spine.

The next room we entered a giant room of dark space. There was somewhat little light, allowing us see just a bit. On the ceiling hung a chandelier, half-crooked and broken down. At the end of the room was a girl standing between two stairways, both leading upward.

I ran over to her. The closer I got, the room began to fill with life.

"About time you show up," she smiled.

I looked at my reflection against the shining tiles on the floor. I wore a red and black pointy hat with a feather sticking out from the side. A red dress suit with a white silk shirt replaced my other armor, and to finish the bottom, black tights and red boots switched out my slops and shoes.

"What's going on?" I asked her.

"You're silly, have you forgotten? We're celebrating our victory over Jyn," she answered.

"Who are you?"

She put her arms on her hips, "Are you mad? You must be sick or something."

"Yeah, I'm very sick," I joked.

"It's me, Reina," she smiled, flashing her white, sparkling dress.

I chuckled, "I knew that, I was just fooling you."

She smiled continuously, grabbing my hand, "You're always joking. Come on, let's dance." I had no idea what was going on, but I danced with her anyway.

She was beautiful. Her blonde silky hair lit up the night and the way she moved in her dress left the crowd stunned. And there I was, making her look bad in my tights.

The Adventures of Ryushin

Later that night, Reina and I sat around, eating and drinking.

"You seem a little tense, Ryushin," she said.

I choked on my water for a second, and then recovered. "What makes you say that?"

"You just don't seem like yourself…"

"I'm just really tired, that's all."

She grabbed my hand and held it tightly. "I'm worried about you, Ryushin. Even with Jyn gone, it seems like you get no rest."

"Jyn…"

She looked like she was about to burst in tears. "I shouldn't have said anything."

"Don't be sad, I don't mind at all."

She took my hand. We walked out of the giant room and into a room similar to a Master's Court. At the top of a small staircase was an altar with three baby dragons resting in a nest of soft straw.

She picked one up and cuddled with it.

"They finally hatched," she said, "This one we named Shiva." The baby dragon was wrapped with frost all over its blue scaled body. "Titan and Garuda are still very weak from the hatching, but someday I believe they will grow to be great guardians."

"These are baby dragons?"

"The dragons are to grow into guardians, each guarding the stones you created. With Draconia banished away from the world, they should be able to contain Destati from the hands of any darkness that seeks it."

"So that's why it was called the War of the Exiled."

"Yes. Exiling Draconia from this world prevented the humans from getting to Destati, which you had locked away in an altar atop your sword, the Trueblade."

"The Trueblade?"

She nodded, placing the baby dragon back into its nest.

"The Trueblade is the Holy sword of the Dracolytes. With one swing, you can easily sustain Destati's power."

"Where are the stones now?"

"They are in the crystal room. Once they have grown, the dragons will become secluded throughout the world, hiding the stones away."

We left the room, entering a courtyard. She would walk faster, and then looked back at me with a smile. She danced around in circles like music was playing all around us. She stopped, grabbed by my hands, and gazed into my eyes. I looked up at the moon, avoiding eye contact.

"It's so beautiful," she said.

"What's so beautiful... the moon?"

She pulled me into her arms, "This feeling. The beauty of serenity and peace, I can't recall the last time the world has ever been so calm." I chuckled. "What's so funny?"

"Nothing." We closed our eyes pressing our lips up against each others.

Point of View: Rheaa

Zandaris and I walked out of the woods and into an open field. Aeric and the others were jumping around like little kids. I ran up to them confused.

"What are you guys doing?" I asked.

"Aeric thinks there's a hollow space around here, so if we jumped, then maybe we can find it," Valen answered.

"Don't you ever pay attention in class?" Aeric asked, "The Kingdom of Reina was destroyed 5000 years ago, left buried underground." He looked over at Zandaris, who kept his distance. "I see you brought along a friend. Why don't you bring him here?"

I waved to Zandaris. He took his time on getting here.

"Don't be afraid, we're not going to hurt you," Kirikah cheerfully said.

The Adventures of Ryushin

"I recall your name being Zandaris, am I right?" Aeric asked. He nodded. "My name is Aeric, and this is Valen and Kirikah. Glad you could join the ride."

"Now, only if we just knew how to get in..." Valen said, continuing to hop around.

I spotted a demon up ahead climbing into a hole. I ran over there just before it closed. I drilled it into the ground with my sword, opening up an entrance.

"Hey, I found a way in," I called over.

Hopping in, the area looked pretty empty to me. The others followed right behind me one at a time. The area we entered seemed to be somewhat of a range, with a long dirt road paving the way to a shattered building.

"That must be it," Aeric said.

"Careful, I sense a foul smell in the air," Zandaris cautioned.

"Corfits could be inside that castle, possibly Atlmaz as well," Aeric agreed.

"Hey, look at that," I said, pointing at some man in a red suit. "Is that Ryushin?"

"That sure does look like him," Valen replied.

We ran up to the wandering man. It was Ryushin, but dressed in a different outfit. He surveyed the side of the castle, as if he was trying to get inside. Surprisingly, he walked through the walls. I cut open a locked window to the side, enabling us to follow.

It was very dark, hardly any light for us to see. This time, we were in a room with bunk beds piled against the walls. The room filled with life the further we advanced. The beds filled with injured people wrapped in bandages, blood nearly pouring through the cloth.

"Prince Ryushin," an injured soldier called. Ryushin walked over to him.

"Everything will be okay..." he said.

"Lord Jyn... she still lives... I saw her with my eyes."

"Though she is alive, she cannot grasp the power of Destati," he smiled, "It is safely locked away with Draconia."

"Prince Ryushin, I fear for our kingdom, she comes for you, she comes for you..." the ill soldier said, falling asleep.

Ryushin walked off through another wall. The five of us followed right behind him. This time, we stood there with Ryushin, looking down at three baby dragons. The names Shiva, Titan and Garuda, were labeled underneath their nests. A girl in a short pink skirt and white shirt walked in from the door on the other side of the room.

"Reina, you're still awake," Ryushin said.

She walked over to him and grabbed his hands.

"It's hard to sleep when my love can't sleep at all."

"I'm sorry, it's just that... the kingdom isn't safe anymore. Jyn is still alive."

"I understand. I will not leave your side."

Ryushin faded in his place, leaving the baby dragons behind. Reina walked over to the door she came in from and entered the next room. We followed her to the next room. The next room was a Master's Court. On the floor were injured soldiers, bleeding and dying from cuts and burns. Reina was on the floor, nearly half dead.

"Your majesty."

A group of soldiers barged in to her aid.

"Jyn, she's in the crystal room... you must help Ryushin..."

The soldiers ran into the hidden room behind a curtain just behind the altar. We followed them in. A girl with her back turned to us, stood before a large stone.

She wore a dark pointy hat with her black wardrobe all torn and ripped on every side. A scythe hooked onto her back. She looked backward at the soldiers with an evil grin. Her eyes lit up with a black light and she crushed them with her dark power.

Ryushin stood between the five of us, with his sword drawn.

"Finally, the stones are mine. Draconia will appear again and the Destati will be at my grasp!" She grabbed three smaller stones engraved in the tablet.

"Jyn, you must stop this."

"Shut up. Because of you, my family's kingdom fallen. But I will avenge them, the Destati will bring you your death."

Jyn and Ryushin faded away, leaving the room empty.

"Interesting," Aeric said.

"What's going on? Did I just miss something?" Valen asked.

Aeric poked at his head. He finally replied with, "The whole reason the war took place back then was because of the Destati."

"Meaning, it was really the battle between Ryushin and Jyn," I added.

"My understanding is Ryushin actually locked away Draconia with this power, so that no one can retrieve it," Aeric explained.

"Thus, it being called the War of the Exiled," Kirikah said.

"A war... It seems like Jyn was trying to stop Ryushin from banishing Draconia, so that she could get her hands on Destati. But it looks like Ryushin had succeeded in locking away the power."

"Come on, let's keep moving," I said.

Back in the Master's Court, Ryushin held Reina in his arms. All of a sudden, this sad overwhelmed my heart, and I felt like crying. Ryushin was crying, looking down at the injured Reina.

"Why did you jump in front of the attack?" Ryushin cried.

She smiled weakly and answered, "Because I love you."

"Everything's going to be okay, just rest for now," Ryushin said.

Reina nodded, falling asleep against the altar.

A bright light lit up behind the door. We barged through it alongside the enraged Ryushin. We were in a courtyard, filled with the bright moon. Jyn floated in the sky with a dark silver light flaring in the palm of her hand, raised above her head. She tossed it downward. The energy attack formed into a ring, absorbing right through the ground.

"Say goodbye to your kingdom, Ryushin," she laughed.

Jyn snapped her fingers, crushing the ground beneath us. The ground quaked throughout the kingdom and it seemed like the whole place was about to collapse.

"Don't worry," Aeric said, perfectly calm, "It's just an illusion."

The area returned to normal, bringing us to ruins underground in reality.

"Funny, meeting you guys here,"

Mordakai approached us alongside Aida, Onry and an elven.

"So you're mission took you this far as well?" Aeric asked.

Mordakai nodded, "Though, I really would like to get out of here."

Zandaris and the elven stared at each other uncomfortably.

"We meet again, Zandaris," the elven said.

"Likewise, Rhyona," he replied.

Mordakai looked at them both back and forth. "You two know each other?"

The two of them looked away at each other, crossing their arms stubbornly.

"Oh come on, can't we all just get along?" Mordakai asked.

"Where is Ryushin?" I asked.

They pointed at him, staring straight into a wall up front.

"What the hell is he doing?" Valen asked.

"He's been staring at that wall since we got here," Aida answered. "It's like he's hypnotized."

"Look at that!" Kirikah shrieked. Ryushin walked through the wall. We ran up to the solid surface but there was no way for us to get through it.

The Adventures of Ryushin

"Great, now we have to go looking for him," Aeric said.

We all decided to group together, feeling more comfortable in the search for Ryushin. No illusions occurred this time. We made our way into a strange room filled with many stone statues, half shattered but still standing.

Up ahead was Ryushin, looking deep into a strange stone tablet.

Aida ran up to him, tugging on his shoulder, but he wouldn't budge. Someone chuckled from the shadows to the side of her. Aida flinched onto her butt.

"Welcome to the Kingdom of Reina." A man walked out from the shadows. "What might we have here?"

"You must be Atlmaz," Aeric said.

He bowed before us, and then placed his arms behind his back. He wore a black wardrobe with dark purple linen stitched into it. The robe was nice looking, well designed with darker colors. His blonde hair was styled in all directions and he had the face of an innocent young teenager.

"Tell me, who is this young boy that stands before you?"

"His name is Ryushin," Aida said.

"Strange… I expected someone beefier," Atlmaz said. "If he is truly Ryushin, then he knows where the stones are."

"You mean, the stones to unlocking Draconia," Mordakai said.

"But didn't Jyn take off with them that night she infiltrated the kingdom?" Aeric asked.

"True, though I can't remember just how Ryushin was able to defeat Jyn with Destati in her grasp. Most of the story is only known to Dracolytes." He walked over to Ryushin looking at the tablet with him. "Ryushin was able to relock Draconia shortly after, sending the stones in different directions around the world."

"What do you want the Destati for, Atlmaz?" I asked.

He smirked, "Pure power, my friend. It is practically every warlock's dream to obtain such a power. And with such, I can conquer the world with my power, throwing everyone down to their knees."

"You'll never be able to conquer the world," I said.

He ignored what I said, continuing to look at the tablet. He looked at Ryushin and whispered, "Tell me, what you see."

Point of View: Ryushin

I smiled down at the baby dragons- Shiva, surrounded by frost clouds, was the guardian of the ice. Titan, the dragon with the skin as soft as quicksand, was the guardian of the earth. Garuda, with a tornado shielding its body, was the guardian of the air. These were the guardians of the three stones. If we find the stones, then we find Draconia.

But that's what Atlmaz wants. He wants to find the stones, so that he could unlock Draconia and retrieve the Destati.

Shiva flew north, Garuda to the East, and Titan to the south. Shiva is secluded where the mountains are cold while Garuda rides the winds and Titan shifts the moving sand.

"Thank you, Ryushin."

I flipped backward away from a tablet, landing on my back. Aida, along with the rest of the gang, looked down on me. "That is exactly what I wanted to know."

"What's going on?" I asked confused.

"You dope, that's Atlmaz," Mordakai said, bonking me on the head.

"That's Atlmaz?" I asked. I drew my sword from its sheath.

"Good going, you just told him where the stones are hidden," Aeric said.

He smiled wickedly. "Thanks to you, I will be able to find the stones and unlock Draconia from its prison. Destati will be mine and so will the world."

"You bastard, you tricked me," I said, angrily.

"Now that I know how to find them, I must be going now."

"Hold it. Don't think you'll get off the hook that easily pal," I said.

"Do you remember what you saw before coming in here?" Atlmaz asked. It was a demon. He snapped his fingers, unleashing demons by his side. The room became packed with them, all blocking our way from the out.

"Uh, we're screwed," Valen said.

"Take them, I want that boy alive," Atlmaz said.

"Scramble!" Mordakai shrieked, ramming shoulder through to the door. The rest of us fought our way out, slashing demons in our path, leaving behind Atlmaz.

We left the room and into the courtyard, filled with more demons. They closed in on us, pushing us back to back.

"We have to make our way to the top," Aida said.

"Which way is up?" I said, swiping at oncoming demons. We had no idea where we were running to. Everything was just a big mess to us. We made our way into the giant room with the chandelier in it only to find more demons waiting.

"That son of a bitch was planning this the whole time," Mordakai said, hacking away with his axes.

"Ryushin…"

It was Reina on her knees attacked by demons. I hurled my sword at them. I called my sword back and ran to her side. She surprisingly lunged at my face, nearly stabbing me with her sharp nails. I flipped backward away from her.

"Reina…?"

"Oh Ryushin, please join me. Let's destroy this world together," she said, licking her lips. Her skin melted away, transforming her into a rotting demon.

"Eh, no thanks." I faced her firmly with Mordakai and Rhyona next to me.

"That is one ugly girlfriend of yours," Mordakai joked.

We both rushed her head on, swinging away. Her arms molded into whips made of flesh, smacking us away. Rhyona transformed into a cat and pounced on her, clawing at her chest. Rhyona was knocked off and into a herd of demons.

The three of us were losing sight of the others. Demons filed in one at a time, blocking us out of reach. Aida called out for us to hurry up but Reina continued her assault on us. I dodged her whip grabbing, it quickly. I pulled her in and slammed a kick into her a stomach. She flew backward like a cannonball and smashed against the demons.

Mordakai and Rhyona took off running for the hall. I shortly followed right behind them. Reina's arm wrapped around my ankle, pulling me to the ground. Mordakai and Rhyona stopped to help.

"Come to me, my love," Reina said, with an even more hideous look on her face.

Demons picked me up by the arms, throwing my back up against a wall. Mordakai chopped at the demons breaking me free. Rhyona palmed her hands into the ground, summoning vines from the ground. The vines constricted Reina. Demons surprised Rhyona and Mordakai, slamming them fiercely into the wall next to me.

I flicked my head, telling Aida to leave.

"Onry, block the entrance off with ice!" I yelled.

"We're not leaving without you!" Aida cried, desperately trying to fight her way through to me.

"Don't worry about us, we'll be fine," I said. "Now go!"

Aeric and Rheaa pulled back Aida just as Onry closed off the door with ice. Mordakai, Rhyona and I were pressed tightly up against the wall.

"You almost got away, Ryushin," Reina said. "Lord Atlmaz, will be very pleased. As for these two, I taste death in their future."

"You ugly bitch, I'm gonna smash your face in," Mordakai angrily insulted. She knocked him out with a fierce blow to the head.

"Do you have any words to say, elven?" she asked. Rhyona said nothing. Reina grinned wickedly then knocked her out as well.

"As for you, Ryushin," she smiled, licking my neck. "Sweet dreams."

Chapter Eight
Kyugen, the Great Escape

Nearly half dead, dripping blood from the side of my head, demons tossed me into a cellar by the legs. The hideous Reina looked down on me with a sinful smile and locked the door. I was alone in the cellar. Neither Mordakai nor Rhyona were around.

My sword was missing.

I pushed up against the door with bars, trying to break through. It was no use. I wasn't strong enough to bust through.

On the other side of the wall, Mordakai was ramping on with his mouth. The sound of a hand slapping across his face echoed through the walls. It was quiet. Reina continued to blabber her mouth away at Rhyona and Mordakai about how they're lucky Atlmaz wanted them alive as well.

I searched the room for any clues to escaping, but the room was filled with nothing but a haystack for a bed and a pile of bones, with some flesh decaying upon them, dressed in ragged cloth.

The ruckus next door stopped and I could hear the door locking on the other side. I called out to Mordakai and Rhyona… there was no response.

Looking back at the pile of bones, an arm fully connected at the joints caught my attention. Maybe, I can use the extra arm as help to unlocking the door. Shaking it loose from the other rotting bones, I rushed to the door and slightly slid the arm through one of the bars, angling it so that it could reach for a handle.

"If you needed an arm, you could have asked me you know."

I looked behind, there was no one there. Pulling the arm back in, I put it back in the pile of bones. "Thank you very much."

"You're alive?" I asked frightened.

The pile of bones formed into a walking skeleton, dressed in thin cloth. The cloth wrapped around its knees, thighs and ankles. A tunic overlapped its body and a pair of leather gauntlets covered its forearms. Its hands and fingers, shin bones and next were exposed. A little skin covered the top of his face, leaving a bright blue glow in its eyes. A leather bandana wrapped around its forehead, spiking its gray, black hair backward.

"Well, I'm not but I am. I hope that makes sense to you," it said.

I was too freaked out to move.

"I'm sorry, but this is way too much for me," I said.

"Don't worry, I get that a lot," it said. I can tell by the tone of his voice that this skeleton was once a human male. "So, what ya locked up for?"

Still a little frightened, I backed up against a wall, watching it move closely toward me. He held his hand out toward me.

"I must be dreaming," I said, pinching my skin.

He grunted, "Come on, not all undead are evil ya know."

"You're an undead?"

"I'm a walking, talking, pile of bones, what do you think?" He sat against a wall across from me. "The name is Xamnesces. What's your name?"

"... Ryushin..."

He chuckled, "The Legend is back huh?"

Not so afraid anymore, I stood up and nodded. "Even the undead know of my name?"

"You make the undead fearful. Back 5000 years ago, you crushed our kingdom with a mighty blow."

"Interesting enough... why are you in here?"

"I've been locked up in here for some time now. I've seen prisoners come and go, usually taken to be executed by the Kyugen Marshals."

"Kyugen Marshals...?"

"Yes sir, the leading officers of this city. Kyugen is actually the base city surrounding a dark castle atop a mountain close by. The castle itself is hosted by a warlock by the name of Atlmaz. Powerful human he is, someone would have to be stupid enough to oppose his order," Xamnesces explained.

"Where exactly is Kyugen, Xamnesces?"

"If I remember one of the prisoners words right, Kyugen is an isolated island away from the main lands."

Just when I thought things couldn't get any worse, it seemed impossible to get back home. Even if we could get off the island, we would have no sense of direction whatsoever. The first priority is getting out of this cellar.

I looked through the bars on the door, looking around for any ideas to get out. So typical, a demon would be sitting there nearly dead asleep with a ring of keys under its arm. Now if there was just some way to reach the ring, then we could use Xamnesces' arm to unlock the door.

"Is there anyway we can get out of here?" I asked.

"Nope," he said, "Just through that door. I've helped lots of people escape before… they just die on the attempts."

"What do you mean you've helped them before? How?"

"Alright then, follow my lead."

I did everything he told me, picking apart his body bone by bone, sliding it through the bars. His arms would do the rest, building him together in one piece. The head was the only part that couldn't fit through the bars, so I held it up against the bars for him to see.

"And they never killed you for doing this so many times?" I asked, watching his body creep toward the sleeping demon.

"I'm already dead," he answered. "I got it."

Xamnesces slowly walked the ring of keys over to the door, leaving the demon sound asleep. Unlocking the door, we both crept out the cellar and into an even smaller room linked to more cellars. I looked over to Mordakai and Rhyona's cell while Xamnesces attached his head back to his body.

Without making the slightest sound, I unlocked the cellar and entered it.

Mordakai hung there in chains, half beaten from the waist up. Rhyona, chained up next to him, dangled half awake drenched in her sweat.

"I have never been locked up in chains before," she said, grinning at me.

"Don't look at me like that, how was I suppose to know we were gonna get captured?" I asked, unlocking both of them with the key. "We'll get out of here, I promise."

"Do you even know how?"

"Not really. We have to find our weapons," I said, picking up the wounded Mordakai.

Mordakai came to his senses, pushing off of my shoulders. He was upset, maybe even fired up about something.

"Remind me to slam that ugly bitch's face into the ground and spit on it." Rhyona and I looked at him worried about his choice of words. "She'll regret ever slapping me in the face."

"Let's get our weapons first," I said, moving slowly out of the cellar. Xamnesces waited for us in the other room.

"What the hell is that?" Mordakai lightly shrieked in a whisper.

"He's a good guy, I'll explain more when we're in the clear, we have to keep moving," I said, making a break for the door down the hall.

In the next room, our weapons were placed in a rack near a group of chatting demons. Rhyona sprung into action with her cat form, swiping them away with her claws. Fully equipped, we were ready to head out.

Following passed the door and into the next area, heat began to rise from below us. Turns out the prison was built in the center of a volcano. The only way out was through the long bridge, connecting to the other inner side of the volcano. Up in the corner of the volcano was His fortress.

However, the bridge seemed rather quiet, too quiet in fact. Reina wasn't too far from us either, sensing her foul saliva all over my neck. We crossed the bridge urgently, escaping the prison easily.

We entered the noisy, busy working city of Kyugen, and it didn't seem like anyone was gonna let up their busy work. The city was foggy from all the machinery working around us. Shops, merchants, restaurants all managed by trolls, humans and Kitsunes, bandits masked at the face robbing one another, seems like we walked into trouble itself.

"Look at this mess," I said, further surveying the city, "No wonder no one guards the prison. All the trouble is here."

"Ryushin, we have to find a way out of here. For all we know, Atlmaz is probably on pursuit of the stones," Rhyona informed.

"All we need is a ship," I said, looking around for ideas. There had to be something around here for us to use. How else would these people get their stock for marketing?

"I'm not leaving until I slam Reina's face in," Mordakai said, still steaming out the ears.

"You forgot spitting on it," I added.

"Oh yeah, that too."

Just at that moment, a sudden clatter of things happened around the corner. And here came sprinting very quickly a young girl dressed in a green vest and green mushroom cap, with a dirty white tank top underneath and brown baggy shorts. Her heavy boots, loose at the ankle, didn't slow her down a bit, leaving her pursuers in her dust.

"Talk about being at the right place at the right time," I said, ironically.

One of the trolls looked at us asking, "Why did you just let her go like that?"

We all looked at each other wondering what the hell he was talking about.

"Listen fool, we don't know what the hell you are talking about," Mordakai said, getting in his face.

The troll grunted pushing back on him. "I see how it is. You're all cohorts with her aren't ya?"

"You are whack," Mordakai snapped back. "We don't even know the girl."

"Then why did you let her go?"

"Oh my... Will you get it through your thick head, we don't know who the hell she is damn it!" Mordakai yelled infuriated. He slammed took a wide swing to the troll's face, knocking him out.

"What the hell did you do that for?" I asked.

"He was pissing me off, damn it," Mordakai answered.

A crowd of people surrounded us, hovering over the dazed troll. They whispered among each other, creating this awful buzzing sound to our ears. Rhyona started backing up slowly alongside Xamnesces, afraid of the angry mobs glaring upon us. Mordakai and I broke out of there with haste leaving behind the crowd.

"Better not look back," Rhyona said, catching up to us in her cat form. Xamnesces staggered quite a bit not used to the quick movements, but he caught on fairly quick.

Up ahead, I spotted the girl in the green vest stashing away a large sack of items. She heard the rampage of the mad crowd behind us and took off running nearly leaving her bag behind. Catching up to her, I reach for the satchel. She turned the corner, leaping onto some crates and over a fence. I slashed through the fence with my sword. Mordakai and the others were able to escape the mass mob.

We were in a dock where ships could sail away or dock. For this particular thief on our hands, she piloted an airship. The airship she attended was a large bullet-like jet. The steering panel floated on a mini stand similar to a pirate's ship, two silver wings at both sides and four propellers on the back for high speed. A cabin rested in the center with a large mast poking out of it with the flag of a smiling cat.

I leaped onboard unnoticed grabbing hold of the unguarded satchel.

The others hopped onto the airship as well, drawing her attention to Mordakai's heavy gear. She looked over at her satchel with my hand well in it and came after me. Mordakai jumped in the way.

"Hey girl, what ya got in the bag?" he asked.

"Their explosives," I answered.

Mordakai thought for a moment and asked, "What are you going to do with them bombs eh?"

She raced around Mordakai, aiming toward the bag. I lifted it up pulling it out of her grasp. The bag was heavy and I didn't want to drop them. Rhyona took hold as I blocked the girl's oncoming attacks. I grabbed her punch, swinging her inward and locking her tightly in my arms. She broke free of my grasp by slamming her heel into my foot.

Xamnesces bonked her on the head, hoping to knock her out but it just pissed her off even more. I grabbed her before she knocked out Xamnesces and tied her up to a box.

"Stop it, we're not here to hurt you," I said.

"What do you want from me?" she asked. "Let me go right now."

"Calm down, I'll let you go in a minute. I just need to ask a favor of you," I insisted.

"Oh yeah, name your price," she demanded.

Mordakai furiously pointed his finger at her and said, "Why you little ingrate! You're lucky we just didn't take off with your airship and leave you behind with those crazed people."

"So, go ahead. Why don't you?"

"We don't know how to fly the ship," I answered.

"Then learn," she said, looking away upset.

"Bah you little punk, fly us out of the city right now! Or else…" Mordakai demanded with a threat.

"Threatening me? What are you going to do huh?"

"I can either learn how to fly this ship through practice and turn you in to Imperia's command, and I know you know what that is, you being a thief or you can make it easier on yourself and fly us the hell out of here," Mordakai rudely suggested.

She didn't respond to either of the choices.

"Mordakai, just relax," I said, pushing him away from the girl. "Look, we mean no harm. We just want to escape this island and return home to Imperia."

"What's there for you?"

"There world is about to jump into a major problem and we must report back there to follow up on our previous mission," I explained.

"Wait so- you, this chatterbox, an elven and a walkin' sack of bones- are heading to Imperia?" she asked. "I don't think they'll feel comfortable with an undead stepping foot into their royal kingdom."

"She's actually right, Ryushin," Rhyona agreed. "With… what's your name again?"

"Xamnesces…" he answered.

"Right, with Xamnesces tagging along with us. It'll be very hard for Imperia to trust him by his appearance," Rhyona followed up on her previous sentence.

I looked over at the innocent Xamnesces who had no idea what were talking about. "We'll just have to dress him up with full on clothing. If Imperia can see that I put my trust in him then they will put their trust in him," I answered.

"Wait, what's going on…?" Xamnesces asked confused.

I untied the girl from the crate. She stood their undecided, whether to help us or not.

"All I have to do is take you to Imperia?" she asked. I nodded to her. "Well then, the name is Ksama. Welcome aboard the Feline! Everyone names their damn ship after a bird. Well I get to represent as a kitty, one of my favorite animals."

Mordakai snorted, "That's 'cause cats don't fly," at her as she walked over to the cabin. She brought out some extra dark clothing to help cover up the remaining bones Xamnesces was still showing.

"Like I said earlier, I'm not leaving until we get that wench," Mordakai repeated.

"We don't have time for that. We'd only be delaying our mission," I said.

"I don't care. Dude, she freakin' slapped us like dogs. I'm not gonna stand for that. Not me- no way."

"Then go ahead. Go slam her face into the ground like you said."

"…you're coming with me right…?"

I pointed at his fortress at the top of the volcano.

"His fortress is right there. Go knock and hope Reina answers it. Soon you'll find yourself being chased by millions of demons."

Mordakai face lit up like he came up with a great idea. But I didn't want to hear it. I walked away from him quickly and over to Ksama, who was wrapping Xamnesces up in the gear.

"Dude, that's his home! Let's go over there now and blow it up! We got enough fire power right here," he excitedly suggested, lifting up bombs in both hands.

"Hey, those are mine. You guys ain't said nothin' about using my stuff," Ksama said, pointing a finger at Mordakai.

"Come on. It's like the perfect chance. How much you wanna bet this will help us out in the near future?" Mordakai pleaded. "Dude, come on. You know you want to do it just as bad as I do. Do you know how sad he will be to find his home blown to pieces?"

"Do you know how angry he will be to find out it was us that did it, putting every kingdom in the world in jeopardy because of one stupid move?" I simply refused to his proposal.

"Don't worry about the kingdoms. Atlmaz can't do jack crap against the forces we have. If anything were to happen, it would slow him down in his pursuit of the stones, forcing him to put a hold on his task."

"He's got a point, Ryushin," Rhyona agreed.

"Not you too. Don't look at me, this is not my airship. If anyone is going to fly us up there, it would be Ksama's decision," I said.

Mordakai held both of her hands, pleading with her to agree. I couldn't listen to his whining. Sooner or later, Ksama would have to give in to Mordakai's annoying cry. And soon she did.

She flew us up toward the ring of the volcano, landing just a distance away from the dark fortress. The closer we flew in, the more its structure began to appeal. The surfaces of the walls were jagged, spiking upward at different spots of the wall. Yellow eyes marked all over the wall acted as a lookout, and the pure black color faded out the outline of the castle itself.

"I'll be damned if they didn't see us coming in from here," Ksama said.

"What do you mean?" I asked.

"You see those eyes on the walls? Those eyes aren't just there for decoration. They're a security watch to see whoever approaches the castle," she explained.

"So how exactly do we get in?" Mordakai asked.

"Two of us will have to zoom passed the eyes fast enough for them not to see us. I'll be one of them so that I can pick the locked doors. Who's comin' with?" she asked. Everyone automatically pointed at me. I snapped a grin at Mordakai who smiled innocently back.

"What? You move just as fast as we do," he chuckled.

"Once we get in, we will shut down the power source to the eyes, allowing the rest to come in," she said, stretching her calves.

"You sure do know a lot about this place," I said.

She smiled and asked, "Where do you think I got this airship?"

"Okay then, Mordakai. As soon as you see any sign of the eyes giving way, take the bag of explosives and come in. We'll meet you back at the door and work our way from there," I explained.

Ksama settled her feet into position and I channeled mana into my legs. With haste, we bolted onto the ring of the volcano, passed the eyes and up against the door. We entered the fortress soon as Ksama picked the lock.

It wasn't that bad at all. The room we entered was well decorated with bright lights, a large water fountain with a statue of an archer planted in the center, and a nice stairway leading upward to the second level. On the base floor, there were four doors- two on our left and two on our right. On the top floor, there were three doors. Judging the way the castle looked on the exterior, the three doors connected to higher floors of the fortress.

There were paintings of warlocks on his walls all around us with their names engraved on a tiny label below. The one closest to me, read Jyn.

Ksama was already on the move, picking the farthest locked door on our right. We entered the room leaving the door unlocked behind us. This room led to a long narrow hallway curved in the shape of a crescent moon.

"I'm surprised this place isn't swarming with demons," I said.

"Don't be, Atlmaz doesn't like company that much," she replied. We made it to another door, picked it and then entered the next room.

This room we entered was nearly pitched black. The most of light that gave way were rings of light purple energy, floating in the room before us. What are they, I couldn't help but wonder. Every ten seconds, a star field would appear in the center of the rings, bringing forth a demon. The demons, still asleep, were then transported through the ground by some sort of mechanical platform.

"This must be how Atlmaz has been building his army of demons," I whispered.

"Come again?" Ksama asked.

"It makes perfect sense. These rings are portals to the demon world and Atlmaz is summoning them in order for him to create his world army." Beyond the dark portals was a double sided door with bright lights shining though it. "That must be were the power source for the castle is."

We crossed the room swiftly without waking any of the demons. Ksama silently picked the lock, entering nice and quietly. In this room were thousands of screens, each locked to a set of eyes outside of the castle.

"Do you know how to work one of these things?" Ksama asked, fiddling with the control panel.

I took a good look at it but it looked just as confusing as Penyae's machines. Ksama, already frustrated as is, took my sword and smashed the facing of the control panel with it. The screens switched off and she tossed me sword back to me.

"Go get them. Putting the explosives in the room before with the portals will be our best shot," I said.

Ksama and I crept back into the portal room. I hid in a dark corner while Ksama crossed the room and into the long hallway. She returned back quickly with Mordakai, carrying the satchel of explosives. We placed one onto every platform that hosted a demon portal, and then left the room.

We still had a couple more left. Mordakai raced up to the second floor once we entered the main room. Ksama followed up as well, unlocking a door for the anxious Mordakai. The door they opened led to a room with a pretty big bed.

Mordakai laughed wickedly.

"This must be his room."

He planted a bomb underneath the bed. We made our way to the next door nearest on the left. Upon this room was a staircase leading up to the third floor. We found ourselves listening in on a conversation between two others.

"Atlmaz is in pursuit of the stones as we speak. You best better contain that fool in his prison."

A young girl nearly half dressed in plate armor spoke with a hoarse tone. She wore a visor across her face, shielding her eyes. Her straight brown hair mixed with a little bit of blonde dangled downward against her back. In her left hand, she held a long pole with a sharp blade attached at the point.

"Sithia," Reina nodded.

"There's that son of a bitch!" Mordakai yelled faintly.

Sithia turned her back to Reina, looking up at a giant screen with the world map on it. Two dots flashed continuously in the same positions, one in the north, and one in the east. Atlmaz has already located the whereabouts of two of the dragons.

"When Destati becomes ours, the world will soon bow to our order. We won't have to live in this dump we call home anymore. The lands will flourish with our dark aura. Everyone will live in fear, and no one will be able to oppose our rule," Sithia said. "If I must suffer this kind of life, so shall this world and everyone in it."

"Lord Atlmaz has gone after Shiva," Reina said, "Why don't we go after Garuda? Garuda's mark shows us she's very close by."

"You're right. But getting past Olida's air defenses will be a problem."

"...Yes, it'll be very hard indeed."

"Olida is known for their great forces in the air. They are the kingdom of the lands that sit on the clouds."

"A floating continent?"

"They can see everything around them, watching over Imperia and Raigen," Sithia said.

"I shall go check on our guest down at the prison cellar," Reina said.

A big 'uh-oh' hit my mind.

Just before Reina reached for the slightly open door, Mordakai shoved it open, slamming the door in her face. The rest of us ducked out of sight as Sithia turned around. Mordakai chuckled unhooking his two hand axes from his side.

"Who are you?" Sithia asked.

"I'm your daddy!" he shouted, rushing out of control toward both of them. I moved into the large room hiding behind a pillar unnoticed. Mordakai hacked at Reina, cutting against her rough skin. She cocked her backward and hawked a big wad of green spit at Mordakai's face. He shifted his head to the side, clutching her unguarded head with his hand. He pulled fiercely, shoving her face into the ground. Her head cracked the ground on contact.

"What up now, you ugly bitch?" he asked, standing on top of her with one foot. He spit on her face. She pushed off and retreated back to Sithia.

"That has got to be the most absurd thing I have ever seen," Sithia said, disgusted by Mordakai's actions.

I pulled out of hiding and confronted Sithia and Reina.

"Ryushin…!" Reina shrieked.

"You fail, Reina," Sithia said.

"I… I…"

With one move, Sithia pierced her blade through Reina's back and out the front. "You have no use anymore." Sithia pulled her blade out, jerking Reina's body to the floor. Rhyona, Ksama and Xamnesces entered the room following Reina's death.

"I'll be… Prince Ryushin, here before me," Sithia gasped.

"What's with the smile?" I asked, "We're not here to play around."

"Neither am I, Dracolyte. I am just surprised you're wasting your time here rather than finding the stones."

I drew my sword.

"Fool, you cannot defeat me," she said, snapping her fingers. Demons emerged from ground and to her side.

Rhyona took an explosive and moved to the side of the room with Xamnesces and Ksama. Mordakai and I stood side by side ready to take on the mob of demons.

I slashed away at the slow demons. Sithia leaped in between us circling her spear above her head. Mordakai and I stepped back opposite of each other.

"Rhyona, plant a bomb on the screen," I said. Sithia, aware of our actions, sprang for the defenseless Rhyona. Mordakai hooked her armor with his axe, holding her back. The two clashed away from the group.

Ksama vanished and reappeared behind Mordakai, surprising Sithia from under Mordakai's hand. Ksama, quick on her feet, moved behind Sithia and punched her in the spine. Provoked from her attacks, Sithia faced Ksama and barely struck her with her spear. Mordakai was on the attack. Blocking his attack with the pole of her spear, she pushed off of him with a kick to the stomach, and then smacked Ksama away with the flat of her blade.

"Okay, the bomb is planted," Rhyona said.

"Let's get out of here now," Xamnesces said. "I have a bad feeling about this."

Sithia and Mordakai continued to exchange blows while we made our way for the door. Pushing off her spear, Mordakai retreated and followed us in.

Back in the main room, the floors were heavily filled with demons, waiting all around the fountain. I formed my hands into a cup gathering energy on the move. Leaping over the railing, I fired an energy beam destroying them in one shot. The others ran down the stairs meeting with me next to the fountain.

Sithia lunged from the second floor, ready to swipe Mordakai. I pulled him out of the way, delivering a spinning roundhouse kick to her stomach. She landed fiercely against the statue.

"Get to the ship quickly," I said, confronting the warn-out Sithia. "Start it up, I'll be there fast." Ksama, without

The Adventures of Ryushin

hesitation, boosted her speed and sprinted for the ship. Rhyona, Mordakai and Xamnesces were right behind her.

Demons helped Sithia to her feet. I gathered more energy in the cup of my hands, filling the room with a bright light. The demons stepped in front of Sithia, blocking her from my view. Relentlessly firing an energy beam, the demons faded away and the point of my beam crushed Sithia against the wall.

I made a break for the airship.

Ksama got the ship started, lifting it off of the ground just a bit.

"Get moving Ryushin!" Mordakai yelled, sticking his arm out for me.

I rose up into the air grabbing onto Mordakai's hand, pulling myself up before the pursuing demons could grab hold of me.

With a narrow escape, we were home free.

Mordakai stepped forward with a remote control, denoting the bombs inside. One part of the fortress exploded, blasting black debris all over the sky. But then, the debris turned into demons. The fluttered quickly, heading toward our direction.

"Speed this thing up," I warned Ksama.

The swarm of demons glided their way over to us. Mordakai, Rhyona, Xamnesces and I fought the demons that landed on the ship while Ksama maneuvered the ship.

Sithia glided down on a giant crow with a smile on her face.

"You won't escape so easily, Dracolyte," Sithia said, hopping onboard.

Ksama turned hard left, jerking us off balance.

I grabbed hold of the railing, half of my body off the side of the ship. I flipped back on as soon as the ship was even. Sithia and Mordakai continued their fight from earlier while Rhyona and Xamnesces defended Ksama.

Sithia, deflecting Mordakai away from her, ran for Ksama. Rhyona tried pouncing on her but she countered with a strong backhand, sending her to the railings of the ship. Xamnesces couldn't do much, still getting used to his movement. Sithia took one swing slicing the undead's spine into two. Ksama's hard turn separated his two halves.

Xamnesces put himself together and rushed after Sithia.

She attempted to stab Ksama in the back. Ksama evaded to the side, dodging the pierce attack. Sithia's force carried her spear right into the steering wheel. With one pull, she snapped the wheel off, causing the ship to swerve out of control.

I jerked backward at the ship's toss, landing next to the propellers. There had to be a way to get them off our back. I formed my hands into a cup once more, powering up for one more energy blast.

"Ryushin, look out!" Mordakai called. Sithia was running my way. I didn't break focus, continuing to gather energy, more than I usually would.

"I got your back, brotha!" Mordakai yelled.

He gripped his left axe tightly hurling it at Sithia. Roaring with his Shishiku attack, he moved quickly behind his spinning axe. The axe pinged off of Sithia's spear and upward. Mordakai leaped into the air, thrusting his right arm with axe in hand and slammed downward upon Sithia's spear, crushing her through the ship and out the bottom.

She was quickly picked out of the air by her fellow demons.

"Kagayaku Hikari!" I yelled, firing a mass beam of energy. The bright beam of blue light lit up the dark skies around us, burning through the demons. The ship's velocity started to pick up as well. Mordakai and the others grabbed hold of anything sturdy, preventing them from falling off the ship.

With a one gasp for air, I released the energy beam, falling to my knees and hands. Sweat dripped from my drained face, my muscles tingling from my arms to my ankles. That was probably way too much energy for me to extract, but at least we escaped.

The Adventures of Ryushin

Everyone rushed to my side, helping me onto my feet. We moved over to the cabin resting onto a bed and sofa inside. I took my time, breathing heavily for air, letting my muscles relax from the tense moment that just occurred.

"That was probably the craziest thing that's ever happened to me!" Ksama excitedly said.

"Have you ever faced a giant spider?" Mordakai asked. She shook her head. "Then you haven't seen anything."

Still out of breath from the Hikari blast, I lied down listening to them chat away.

"I think I rotated the wheel just enough to head east," Ksama said.

"So you directed us toward Olida instead of Imperia," Rhyona said.

"We can't make it very far like this. It's too dangerous to be flying without a steering wheel. Who knows what kind of crazy stuff we'll bump into, ya know?" Ksama said. "I'll be right back. I'm gonna lower the ship into the water so that it can relax."

She left the room.

"Heading to Olida is probably a better idea anyway. With Aida on the other continent, we can actually cover more ground going after Garuda," I explained.

"Dude, I don't know about Olida," Mordakai insisted. "From what I heard from Lecia, Commander Craft can be a douche bag, a giant one in fact."

The ship landed softly into the water, floating east. Ksama walked in, sitting comfortably next to Rhyona.

"Even if Craft is like that, she'll have to help with the situation at hand," I said.

"What's going on? Who are you guys? What just happened back there? Who's Atlmaz? Ryushin's a prince? Are you rich?" Ksama asked, running her mouth endlessly.

"Shut up! We'll tell you everything we know so far in a damn minute, sheesh!" Mordakai snapped.

That night, I explained everything to Ksama- everything about Atlmaz, the Kingdom of Reina, Draconia, the Dracolytes, the stones, just about everything. I also mentioned my whole ordeal about my memory loss and my sudden appearance into this world. She seemed a little shocked about everything going on around us and the more shocking the stories got, the more she was interested in tagging along.

With an airship, we can move a lot faster throughout the world. Mordakai didn't seem so thrilled about her joining us, but I was happy to know that she was willing to assist us.

"So, we go after the stones before Atlmaz gets them, right?" Ksama asked.

"Ryushin…" Xamnesces interrupted, "What's going to happen to me? I don't really belong in this world."

"Don't worry. I won't let anyone hurt you," I said, patting him on the back.

"How exactly are we going to get to Olida? The damn kingdom is sitting in the sky above us," Mordakai said.

Ksama smiled, pulling out a map. "By the time it reaches day break, we should be here." She pointed at a small location on the map close to Olida. This part of the map was called, Ocean of Tornadoes.

Chapter Nine
More than just a Past

"Wake up... Wake up, you're so close." I could hear her voice calling out to me. It was faint but it was her voice. I remember.

"Wake up, damn it!" Mordakai yelled, shaking me back and forth.

Mordakai looked down on me. I noticed it wasn't him shaking me, the room itself was shaking. I suddenly hopped off the bed and ran out the door.

"About time," Ksama said, point out into the ocean.

Straight ahead were thousands of tornadoes, connecting from the cloud above us to the ocean surface. They were vicious cyclones, able to tear up a city in seconds. The base of the tornado circled roughly with water ripping along the winds. The dark clouds above seemed like it stretched for miles without an end, connecting to every tornado in the ocean.

"Why exactly are we here?" I asked shaking along with the ship.

"Simple," Ksama said, "We're going to ride the tornadoes up through the clouds and onto the continent."

"I think I'll wait here," Mordakai said.

"Oh come on, I've done it a million times. I have to leave the ship here, otherwise Olida will confiscate it," Ksama said, parking the airship on a little sand island. "Bigmouth, over here, crushed a hole in the ship so it wouldn't be safe to go into the tornadoes, without it breaking apart."

"Are you sure this is safe?" Rhyona asked one more time.

"Yes I'm sure," Ksama answered.

She dove into the water and started swimming toward the tornadoes.

"This girl is crazy," Mordakai said, jumping into the water after her.

Rhyona and Xamnesces followed in right after him.

"I like her," I said, diving in.

The closer we swam to the tornados, the more we got pulled in by the current. Ksama wasn't afraid and continued to swim toward the tornadoes. She would look back at us and urge us to hurry.

"Now, hold on tight," she smiled. The tornadoes forceful pull sucked us out of the water and into the cyclone. The five of us spun around a few times before getting tossed into the next tornado. The winds were gentle. They weren't as vigorous as I thought they would be. I opened my arms widely, letting the air underneath carry me.

"Aida would love this," I said.

The tornado carried us up a bit before separating us into our own tornadoes. Each tornado would throw us into another one further down the Ocean, as if they had a mind of its own.

"Whew, check this out!" Mordakai excitedly said, rotating around in his circles. Rhyona and Xamnesces were thrilled enough to be riding in the winds of a tornado.

Ksama found her way over to me and asked, "You okay there?"

"I'll be fine... it's been too long since I've been able to relax like this," I said.

She chuckled, pointing up ahead, "Better look up, we're about to run into traffic."

Other people were riding the tornadoes with us. They were travelers, with families and belongings at their sides holding onto each other.

"Where are they coming from?" I asked.

She answered, "They're coming from the lower cities around the world. These are people who want to live in the skies. Everything is so expensive up here. Craft did a major inflation on pricing ever since she's become the Commander of Olida."

"You'll see," she said, moving on ahead.

I flew into a cyclone connecting upward from one of the tornadoes into the cloud. People flew passed me with smiles or waving, or just join me for a few seconds before taking off.

Aida would appear lying there next to me, and then fade away. This sudden feeling I have for her is overwhelming and all I could think about was her. I wanted to be there by her side, forgetting all these missions- no Atlmaz, no troubles, and no problems. I just wanted it to be me and her.

The cyclone launched me into the mist of the cloud where I floated their slowly for a bit, then being snatched out of the cloud by another tornado field above. I surfed the winds as it picked up speed, tossing me from one tornado to the other.

A giant shriek trailed along the winds of the tornado. Over to the side, I saw a giant shadow with a pair of mean looking eyes, glaring down on me. At the moment I drew my sword, the shadow fled in the opposite direction. I put my sword away.

The tornado spun me upward through another set of clouds. I was able to gain my balance, landing on top of a cloud next to Rhyona.

"This is amazing," Rhyona said, surveying the field of clouds we were standing on. "Is it possible to be able to stand on the clouds like this?"

"The density of the clouds are just as solid as ground. Just don't stand in one place for so long, since we're breathing air up here too, the clouds oxygen slowly fades," Ksama explained.

Mordakai, nearly half sunk into the cloud, asked, "This is why?"

"No," Ksama answered, "You're just wearing plated gear." Mordakai dug himself out of the clouds and walked over to us.

The Kingdom of Olida wasn't too far, visible about a mile away. The city was built on different layers of clouds, showing some rocky mountains melded into the mist, some layers stacking on top of one another. The castle rested at the tip of a mountain, wrapped by a swirl of cotton clouds.

We entered the city of the kingdom, a nice peaceful area with the roads paved with thick clouds, market houses and homes made out of light wood. There was a fork in the road. A sign directed us straight ahead to a long stairway up to the castle. To the left upper layer was the dock, left lower layer was the trade district, right upper layer was the residential area and the right lower layer were the mech block. The people inhabiting the city were humans and Kitsunes, just like Raigen.

Ksama stopped for a moment.

"I'm going to get some supplies for the airship," she said. "You guys do what you need to do."

I began walking up the stairs until I looked back at Xamnesces, still afraid of what might happen.

"Come on, they won't hurt you," I said, pulling him by the arm.

At the top of the stairs, we were saluted by royal guards equipped with heavy armor, shining with a pearl white coating. At their sides were long polearms and a shield hooked to their other arms.

Mordakai saluted.

"The name is Mordakai, representative of the Kingdom of Imperia. We are here to see Commander Craft with urgency," he stated professionally.

"State your emergency," the royal guard requested.

"The actions of Atlmaz are at hand, we are running out of time."

"Please proceed. Commander Craft will be in the Master's Court," the royal guard stepped aside.

We entered a long hall with six doors, three on the left and three on the right. The doors on the left read: Armory, Courtyard, Classrooms. The doors on the right read: Weaponry, Ballroom, Master's Court. We approached the door marked with Master's Court and walked in.

"Who the blazes are you?"

She was in her mid twenties, still looked rather young with brown long hair, some strands clipped with diamond clips. A yellow tiara bearing a flame over her head wrapped around her forehead, matching her red flaming dress that was cut at the shoulders and ending at the thighs, mixed with an orange taint tied at the waist by a rope. White gloves guarded her forearms and hands, matching the long white boots.

"Private Mordakai," he saluted. "I am a representative of Imperia."

"Likely of Lecia to send me one of her own without letting me know," she said.

"Commander Craft, we need your help," I interrupted.

"Who might you be?" she asked.

I saluted just as Mordakai did following the same gesture. "I am Ryushin, representative of Raigen."

She crossed her hands, closing her eyes disappointed. "Gundita is also sending me her men too. Though you could only expect less from young nineteen year olds." She looked over at Rhyona. "What could an elven possibly be doing out of the jungle?"

"I am helping Ryushin throughout this journey of his," she answered.

She looked over at Xamnesces, squinting her eyes at him. Xamnesces tucked himself into the shadows, frightened by Craft's glare. She opened the palm of her hand, exposing an intensely heated fireball.

"What is an undead doing in my castle?" she asked.

I stepped in front of Xamnesces, defending him like I said I would. "He's with me. He helped me escape from Kyugen. There was no way I was going to leave him there."

She grunted, putting out the fireball. "Fine then, report."

"We recently stumbled upon a secret tablet hidden in the ruins of the Kingdom of Reina. The stone tablet explains the secret of Destati and the banishing of Draconia. We have confronted Atlmaz of this matter and he is hard at work in finding the three stones that unlock the world of the

Dracolytes. And one of the stones is near by," Mordakai explained.

"And how did you end up here?" she asked.

"We were captured. And we recently just escaped Kyugen's prison."

"Is there anything more to report?"

I stepped forward saying, "Atlmaz has been using multiple portals to open up gates to the demon world. He's been building an army of demons, preparing for an invasion of some sort. I believe he will be attempting to take Destati by force when he unlocks Draconia."

"Interesting... you know the whereabouts of the stones?" Craft asked.

"One is just south, close to this area," I answered.

Craft turned around, opening a large screen behind her. She opened a map pointing south of our location. "Just south of Olida you say?" I nodded. "There's nothing we can do right now."

"But why... if we don't hurry, Atlmaz will be sure to get it before us," I said.

"I know that you idiot. With the tornadoes to the south turning in their own direction, there's no way you can reach the Wingfields," she explained.

"How do we fix them?"

She thought for a moment. She turned around and said, "It's possible that stone floating in the sky is part of the problem. Our men cannot decipher the writing on the stone, so maybe you guys can do it. Ever since that stone has appeared, the winds have been very fierce."

"An ancient stone..." I whispered.

I remembered Astrae saying, *"I will wait for you at the next temple that lies hidden in the skies."* That had to be it.

"We'll take care of it," I said. "How do we get to it?"

"Take the road south. You will see a dysfunctional field of rough tornadoes. Ride the tornado up and you will see the stone," Craft explained. I nodded to her leaving with the others. Before I could reach the door, she called out to me. "The undead stays with me." I looked over at Xamnesces, who looked back at me.

I nodded to him.

"I will have Lecia contacted when you come back," she said.

With Ksama repairing the ship and Xamnesces in Craft's restrictions, it was just Rhyona and Mordakai left to accompany me.

We left the city in a hurry, heading south just as Craft instructed. The roads became clearer up ahead, the skies becoming darker and the winds much stronger. Before us was a black nimbus cloud, hovering tall and wide across the field. Along the field, dark gray tornadoes ripped apart the grounds, crushing anything around it.

"She wants us to go in there?" Mordakai asked. "No way, that thing will shred us up into pieces."

Without thinking about it, I walked a little closer to the field. I noticed even at our distance range, the winds were already trying to carry me in. A tiny sparkle of light appeared in the dark cloud.

"That must be it," I said, "We have to go now, just stay close behind me."

I ran further down the road picking up wind speed. A sudden wind curl snatched us from the ground, sucking us into one of the cyclones.

These tornadoes were rougher than the ones before. Surfing alongside Mordakai and Rhyona, I pushed my body with great force, just enough to jump into the next tornado.

"Wait here," I said.

I circled upward to the top of this tornado where the mouth opened wider. I channeled my mana into my leggings, boosting power for a long jump. Pushing off the dense air, trying my hardest to break free from the strong winds, I hopped into a rapid wind current, circling around the stone.

There was no way I can move around in these winds. I have to read from here. I squinted at the stone, trying to read the tiny text on it.

"Two Hearts, Two Worlds, One Destiny."

The winds became still. Everything that was floating around inside dropped to its hard surfaced texture, sliding all the way down to the bottom. I landed softly onto the surface of the winds. They were as hard rock, blades of winds sitting still motionless in the air around me.

Levitating above the ancient stone was a cloud with an orb resting on it. I hopped from each wind blade, using them as steps to make my way up. I grabbed it out of the air and entered a flash back.

"Is everything alright?" I asked.

She sat there ready to burst into tears. I faded out of my own body into a spirit watching them looking at each other. We were in a large room, filled with lots of frames on the wall behind her. The room connected to a backyard and a long kitchen.

"It's just..." she began tearing.

"Are you okay? What's wrong?" I asked, kneeling on the floor, trying my best to comfort her.

"...just that this college applications are killing me... and my mom is always getting mad at me and everything. I only have a month to do them..." Ayaka said.

"Don't worry, you'll pull through it. I'll even help you," I said.

She started crying. I didn't know what to do to stop the sadness. I had this feeling in my heart that I wanted to cry too. The tears ran down her red cheeks unending. She couldn't even look at me with a straight face.

"I can't do this..."

I stood up looking down at her and asked, "You can't do what? You just gotta be strong."

"I mean this. I think we should take a break..."

The Adventures of Ryushin

A sudden dreadful feeling overcame my heart, making my stomach really ill. I could sense it in my heart. She didn't want to be with me anymore. My eyes became watery, tears escaping out the side. I looked away trying to hold it in, but it was just too much to fight.

"Was it something I did wrong?"

"No... I just think we could use one. It'll give me the time I need to catch up on the things I need to get done," she answered.

"For how long?"

"I don't know. Maybe until I get everything done, I'll be ready..."

After a few nights, I felt really tired for some odd reason, so I passed out before midnight. I had dreams about what she said, I began fearing that I might lose her and I had no idea what I'd do if that ever happened.

I received a random phone call at about three in the morning. Ayaka's name popped up on the caller idea. I picked it up in a hurry answering it.

"Hello?"

"Hi... are you busy?"

"No... what's up? Is everything okay?"

There was a pause in her answer. She then replied, "We have to talk."

In my mind, I knew it was coming. It was over. I felt the blood rushing to my heart, pumping faster than it's pumped before.

"What... did you wanna talk about...?"

It just came straight out. "I think we should be friends." I couldn't help but cry... I saw every little moment that we had together crush away like a mirror glass, falling on the ground. Everything was shattered, making every part of my body numb.

"But why? What did I do wrong?"

"It's not that..."

"Then what is it?" I interrupted her, "Give me a chance to work things out. Everything will be fine, I promise…"

"I just don't feel the same way anymore…" she answered, pausing for a moment. "…Look, I gotta go. I'll see ya around or something…"

The dream state ended.

I sat there on the hard surface of the winds. The most I could do at the moment was think about what just happened. I felt angry and upset. I wanted to slam my fist into hard surface or yell as loud as I could, but I couldn't. It just hurt so much, watching what had just happened.

"Are you remembering everything?" Astrae said, sitting next to me. I was too ashamed of myself to look at him. "It's okay to feel the way you do. Not everyone is strong the way you are."

"I don't care," I grumbled, "She was a bitch anyway."

Astrae patted me gently on the shoulder. "Don't say that, you're just angry, that's all."

"I hope I don't ever see her again!" I stood up, yelling as loud as I could.

Astrae sat there absorbing the intense rise in my voice. He pulled me back down.

"You can't say that like it's a sure thing, Ryushin," he said.

"Of course I can, I'm not returning home anytime soon, and I don't want to! Not if she's still alive! I hate her!" I yelled, angrily.

"You keep that up and she won't ever come back to you," Astrae said.

"Shut up! Like I could give a damn if she'd ever come back!"

Astrae sighed, "Well, put that aside. Things are starting to fall into place and you probably won't see me for a good while. Just stay focused, Ryushin."

The winds motioned once again, engulfing me in its grasp. A cyclone picked me up into a hurry and carried me out to the still lands where Rhyona and Mordakai were waiting.

On the ground was a shard sparkling its shine into my eye. I picked it up feeling the rush of its power move all over my body.

"Are you okay? I heard you yelling up there," Mordakai asked.

I paid no attention to either of them. I was so upset, I nearly stomped my way back to Olida in a hurry leaving them behind.

I stormed into the Master's Court, standing there looking at Craft, who was with one raised eyebrow and a confused look. Mordakai and Rhyona stumbled in after me saluting her.

"So did you solve the problem?" she asked.

I said no answer. Mordakai and Rhyona looked at me with a confused look on their face. I crossed my arms and looked away.

"Ryushin, what are you doing? Tell her what happened up there," Rhyona said.

"Alright, someone explain right now," Craft demanded.

"Well, Ryushin told us to stay while we were in the tornadoes when he went up to the stone and then after that, Rhyona and I just ended up back on the ground," Mordakai explained his part.

"Ryushin, what do you have to report?" she asked.

"Nothing," I answered.

"Yo, Ryushin!" Valen yelled happily.

A large screen with Valen and Lecia appeared.

"Valen, get out of my seat!" Lecia said.

"You're such a meany. I just wanted to say Yo."

"That's not the Ryushin I remember back in Imperia," Lecia's voice said. Lecia looked disappointed. "What has gotten into you, Ryushin?"

"Look, I don't wanna do this anymore," I said. "I'm going home."

I barged out of the room not paying attention to them.

Chapter Ten
The Windfields of Garuda

Point of View: Mordakai

"Mordakai, what happened to Ryushin?" Lecia asked.

I shrugged my shoulders just as confused as she was. "I don't know. It probably had something to do with the stone earlier."

"What stone?"

"There was a strange stone with an ancient text preventing us from moving south. and ever since Ryushin went up there on his own, he's been a little cuckoo."

"Craft, is this your doing?"

"How dare you accuse me, you little wench!" Craft said.

"And your reasons for moving south, Mordakai?" Lecia asked.

"We were going after the Garuda," I answered.

"Continue your pursuit. I will inform Gundita of Ryushin's actions. Aida and the others are on their way to the north after Shiva's stone," Lecia instructed. "By the time you arrive back in Olida, an airship from Imperia will be waiting for you."

Lecia signed out.

"I don't think we can do this alone," I said.

"Stop rushing me," Craft said, "I've already assigned one of my own to assist you."

A young blonde girl walked into the room. She wore a red tunic with a hood attached to it, lined with a silver thread. The tunic was tied at the waste with a brown leather belt. The tunic also cut at the high part of the thigh into a short skirt. Her white leather gloves covered her arms and hands just like Craft, along with her long white boots. On her back was a staff with a black crystal ball attached at the tip.

"One of your apprentice mages," Rhyona said.

The Adventures of Ryushin

"Her name is Yoichi," Craft said, as Yoichi, bowed to her introduction. "She is a fire mage and her powers will be of great assistance to you."

"Nice to meet ya," I said, shaking her hand. Her shake was freakin' and she smiled like she was intentionally trying to burn me. I pulled away, smiling back a little frightened.

Xamnesces also joined.

"He will be joining your team as well," Craft insisted. "He had a barrier binding his power making him quite useless, so I disabled it. He is a warlock from the past, and his powers will be very useful."

"He's a warlock just like Atlmaz?" I asked.

"He is a warlock with a good heart, I have already looked into his inner feelings," Craft answered.

"Where is Ryushin?" Xamnesces asked.

"He's gone," I answered.

"Will he be back?"

"I don't know. I hope so."

We all saluted Craft, departing from the room and into the city. I kinda felt like a dope walking through the city without the slightest clue of where to go. Usually Aeric or Ryushin would be around to tell us what to do now they're gone. It was so unlikely of Ryushin to bail out on us like that, especially with someone like Atlmaz on the loose.

Ksama ran toward us, going from happy to lost.

"What's wrong? Where's Ryushin?" she asked.

"Gone," Rhyona answered.

"Say whaa!?" Ksama shouted. "What do you mean, gone? Just like that?"

"He just left without telling us why," I said.

"Where did he go? You can't just let him walk out like that," she said. "Where are you going now?"

"Supposedly, we're going to find Garuda and get the stone," Rhyona answered.

Ksama looked at the four of us. "Will you guys be fine?"

"Why, where are you taking off to?" I asked.

"I'm gonna get back to the airship, and try to find him," Ksama said, taking off in a hurry.

"Well, there goes another one," I said.

Rhyona crossed her arms, "Let's get moving. The sooner we find the stone the sooner we can look for Ryushin."

We left the city back to where the whole dramatic event started. The tornadoes looked a lot more calm this time, making it a lot easier for me to trust. The winds from the tornado picked us up, carrying us back into their spin. The four of us, riding the winds on our feet, jumped from tornado to tornado and reached the Wingfields on the other side.

The Wingfields stretched far out for miles, still a little misty from the clouds but visible through them. Small trees plucked out of the ground well spread apart. The clouds in the background rose up slowly, clapping loud sounds of thunder. Lightning bolts crawled all over the cloud like spiders.

"How could you expect a dragon to come flying out to this dump?" I asked.

"It's a dump. No one would look here," Rhyona answered.

Xamnesces stepped further out into the field, listening to a cry in the clouds. He would look up into the clouds for a moment than snap his eyes to another direction.

"Garuda is here," he said. "Garuda moves fast. It's very hard to keep up with her movements."

A bright green dragon darted out of the clouds off in the far distance. That had to be Garuda telling by the way it was shaped. The layer of its skin, coated with tiny cyclones, looked very soft and smooth. Its wings flapped outward very wide shaped thin and sharp for faster air movement. It was thin at the waist, packed with muscle everywhere else, its neck somewhat long and sticking out, its lower legs powerful and sturdy as well, able to tear an airship into pieces in a sec. Its long tail spiraled just like a tornado, helping it maintain perfect balance when in flight.

"Great, do you think it'll be fun getting a stone from that thing?" I asked, pointing at Garuda. She snapped a keen look this way, turning in flight toward our direction.

Xamnesces gathered dark energy into a ball in the palm of his hands. Before he could launch it, Garuda picked up speed, zooming in faster.

"You're not going to blast it out of the sky are you?" I asked.

Another cry came from behind Garuda. Through the clouds, a gigantic skeleton demon busted out, locking its sight on the green dragon. The skeleton demon was dressed in chains, its hair dried up and frizzy from the lightning. It had no eyes, scratched out by cut marks. A pale golden crown sat atop its head, hoisting Sithia above it.

"Just as I thought, a banshee," Xamnesces said. He launched the shadow ball at the banshee, damaging it just a bit. Garuda zoomed like a cyclone into the clouds and disappeared.

"You're not serious are you?" I asked. "Do you see that thing? That thing will eat us, its freakin' huge!"

Yoichi pulled me down to the ground, evading the banshee's giant arm.

She popped back up, gathering fire in both hands. "Hinotama!" she casted. She brought her hands together and blasted a large flamethrower, burning part of the banshee's arm.

The banshee swung her arm wide into the air, nearly swiping Garuda out of hiding. Garuda quickly picked up her balance, flying off into the clouds again. Xamnesces and Yoichi continued their long ranged magic attacks.

"If only I can get up to Sithia…" I said to Rhyona.

"Why do you need to get up there? It's the big thing we need to worry about," Rhyona said.

I ran out into the open field looking for Garuda. She was the only one that could help me get up top. I called out to her but no response. The banshee faced me, ready to swing a backhand. Grabbing onto one of the finger nails, the banshee pulled me up unknowingly.

Slowly making my way from the finger to the wrist, Garuda appeared once again, flying under and over the banshee's arms. The banshee's head was spinning all over while Garuda circled around it. A fireball came out of nowhere, knocking me off balance.

"Hey! That's not funny!" I yelled down to Yoichi.

The banshee finally noticed I was on its wrist, and it started wiggling its wrist around. I took one of my axes and rammed it deep within the bone, using it as a hook. One axe at a time, I would make my way upward from the wrist to the forearm and then to the shoulder. The banshee raised its other hand, getting ready to squash me.

Xamnesces launched a giant shadow ball at the hand, blowing it up into pieces. I continued to climb up, finding my way to its collar bone.

The banshee quickly picked me up with its fingers and held me out in front.

"Will you guys keep the damn thing off me, damn it?" I yelled down to the others.

Rhyona ran to a tree. She clasped her hands together, gathering energy. With one pump, she slammed her hands into the ground summoning a giant root vine. The vines grew fast, whipping their way around the banshee's free hand.

Yoichi's fireball blasted the fingers into flames, breaking me free from its grasp. I plummeted downward. Garuda swooped around the flaming bones and caught me onto her back.

Rhyona commanded the vines to constrict the banshee's arms.

"Garuda, take me up to the crown," I requested.

Garuda swooped under the roots, gliding into a diagonal upward along the banshee's backside. She turned the corner flying in front of its face. The banshee shrieked loudly, blowing a very disgusting smell our direction. Flying up to the

The Adventures of Ryushin

top, I leaped off Garuda's back and onto the crown where Sithia stood waiting.

"I'm surprised you're up here, pest," Sithia said.

"You need to shut up fast," I said, gripping my axes.

"Let's make this quick," she said, spinning her spear into her hands, "It doesn't look like my banshee will last any longer."

Sithia pushed off her feet, charging quickly. I crossed my axes, blocking her downward swing. I rushed her with a right swing, left swing downward, clanging the blade of my axe up against her pole. Sithia countered with a straight kick to my stomach. I ducked out of the way, evading one of Yoichi's oncoming fireballs. Another incoming nailed Sithia from the side, throwing her off balance. I rolled forward, pressing my lowered shoulder into Sithia's stomach and launched her into the air.

Sithia grabbed onto one of the banshee's hairs and pulled back onto the crown. We continued to attack one swing at a time. Sithia lunged fiercely with her spear tucked at her side. I staggered away from her pierce attack, falling off the crown. I grabbed a hair strand, dangling front of the banshee's face.

It broke free of the roots hold, swinging its burning hand toward its face. I let go of the hair strand and laughed as the banshee smacked itself in the face. Yoichi and Xamnesces continued to launch their magic attacks at the banshee's face.

"Get Garuda you fool!" Sithia demanded. The banshee searched around for Garuda but she was nowhere to be found. Garuda broke my fall once again, gliding under the banshee's arm.

"Look out!" I yelled, pushing off Garuda. The banshee grabbed Garuda, squeezing her in its hand. The dragon let out a giant cry of pain.

I landed on my back next to Yoichi. "What are you waiting for? Shoot one of your fireballs at it!" I yelled.

"I'm not gonna blast the dragon you idiot." Yoichi held her attack.

"Yes banshee! Squeeze the life out of the dragon. Bring me the stone," Sithia said excitedly. Garuda with a great cry spit out the stone from her mouth. Xamnesces leaped for the falling stone. "Get the stone!"

"I'm sick of this dumb crap," I said, pulling my hand axes down to my side. I concentrated my energy into my axes for one final attack. I growled ready my Shishiku, increasing my strength and power. "Taka no Hane!" I hurled both of my axes upward at the unaware banshee. The axes turned into discs of energy. The two discs pulled closer to one another, creating one giant cutter. The cutter pierced through the body of the banshee, splitting the banshee into two.

Yoichi and Xamnesces launched a final fireball and shadow ball at the banshee's hand breaking Garuda out of its grasp. My axes returned back to my hands.

Sithia called for her giant crow and flew away. Garuda roared victoriously in the sky, flying away into the clouds.

The four of us grouped together again, looking down at green stone.

"Let's hurry and return to Craft," Yoichi said.

Point of View: Ryushin

After the whole stunt I pulled up in Olida, I felt ashamed of myself. They didn't deserve that at all, especially Rhyona and Mordakai. I didn't care so much of the situation anyway. All I wanted to do was lie here, drifting away in the ocean and look up at the bright sun.

"You're not going to float there all day are you?" Ksama said, floating there next to me.

"How did you find me?" I asked.

She relaxed her arms behind her head, looking up at the sun with me. "I don't fly an airship for nothing."

"The airship is fixed?"

She nodded with a smile.

"What the hell is the matter with you?"

"She was everything to me, Ksama..."

"Who was?"

"Her name is Ayaka... she was the love of my life. I loved her so much," I said, closing my eyes. I remembered her clearly. A young girl with smooth silky skin, smiled a picture perfect image, and had this complexion no other guy could resist.

"You're such a little baby," Ksama splashing water in my face. I was ashamed. I floated alongside Ksama but looked away from her eyes. "Are you crazy or something?"

"What if I am? I am crazy about her, Ksama," I said, shaking her by the shoulders.

She shrugged her shoulders and slapped me in the face.

"That's for being an idiot!"

"I'm not being an idiot! It's true damn it!" I yelled.

"The only thing I see that's true is that she's not coming back for you and she never will! Get over it," Ksama said.

Ksama's harsh words felt like a dagger stabbing my heart. looked down at my reflection in the water, picturing myself in glasses and normal clothes that I used to wear. That was me. I was a lost boy without a sense of direction because I had lost something so dear to me. I knew who I was... I'm not a legend at all.

"I'm sorry, Ryushin," she apologized. "It's just that, when I first met you guys back in Kyugen, you guys showed me something I thought I would never find..."

I looked up at her distraught face.

"What did you see in us, Ksama?" I asked.

"The ties of friendship," she answered. "The way you lead them... a human, an elven and an undead... If I didn't want to help, I would have sat there tied to that crate. But your warmth, your character lightened my heart. And I'm guessing that you have that same effect on everyone around you."

I smiled at Ksama. I felt happy again.

"So don't let some girl get in your way," she pleaded. "Somewhere out there, there's someone waiting for you, and you wouldn't even know it."

When she said those words just now, Aida started smiling in my head. I could hear her singing again, that same song that she sang in the garden echoed all around me, entering my ears, running down my body and into my heart, melting it away.

I looked up into the sky and said, "I hope I have a place in your heart too."

I grabbed Ksama and hugged her tightly. I whispered into her ears, "Thank you." Looking down at my reflection behind her, I could see myself change into someone different, someone strong. My reflection smiled and waved. That is how I should be.

"Don't get all mushy on me now," Ksama said. "Let's head back to the ship. I'll take the time to listen about this Ayaka girl you're whining about."

And so we did.

I met Ayaka when I was about the age of seventeen back in high school. I never would have thought a girl like her and a guy like me would ever be together. Until one day, we just suddenly started talking. I was little shy at first but still curious about her background. As the days rolled on, problems and such getting in the way, we managed to stay close and find happiness from one another. Everyday that I would see her, I would have this smile on my face, just happy to see her. She would show the same kind of happiness by smiling back toward me.

Then we reached for one another and became one for almost three years.

Even though I am not in her heart anymore, she is still in mine and she always will be. I guess I was just too foolish to admit she had left and Ksama was right, she was never going to come back. But I'm fine with that because as long as she's happy, I will be happy too.

"So are you ready to get moving?" Ksama asked. I nodded a yes to her. "Where shall we go, boss?"

"Don't call me that," I said.

She giggled a bit waiting for a destination.

"Since Mordakai and the others are well after Garuda and Lecia sent Aida after Shiva... We should move south and see if we can find Titan," I suggested.

"Alright, what kind of region do we need in order for us to find Titan?"

"Somewhere where there is a lot of sand..."

"I know just the place. There are the Southsands a little southwest of Raigen. We can begin looking there."

"Alright, then we're off to the Southsands," I said, pointing outward into the sea. The airship lifted off the water taking off further ahead. Looking up into the sky, I could see Astrae smiling down on me. I smiled back, waving to him.

Chapter Eleven
The Dragon and the Snake

Point of View: Rheaa

Lecia proposed a mission for some of us shortly after our return to Imperia. We successfully cleared our tasks in the previous mission but at the expense of losing three of our own. To further cut the casualties within the party, Lecia selected just a few us to carry out this next mission, while the rest remained back at Imperia waiting for our return.

I walked ruggedly through the thick heavy snow, wrapped in a heavy brown fur coat and black sweat pants to keep me warm. Aida came along for the mission, wearing thicker plated gear covering all of her skin. Onry didn't seem to have any problems with the cold weather, being immune with her ice magic and Zandaris tagged along, fighting the cold in his normal clothes, not wanting to stay back at Imperia.

One of Imperia's airships dropped us off south of the icy mountains, known as the Glacial Front. Ryushin's clues to the dragons and the visions we saw of them were our only help to finding the stone. Shiva was wrapped in a mist cloud and the only place in this world covered with frozen solid ice would be here.

We walked along narrow pathways leading into the mountains. The narrow passes would become thinner and the icy winds would pick up the more we advanced deeper in. The walls were jagged surfaces of pure blue, dripping down from the top. Our images reflected back toward us. It was like walking through a fun house full of mirrors.

Coming to a fork in the road, Onry stood unsure of which direction to we should go. Aida looked down the left pass only spotting more narrow cliffs. Zandaris looked up the right pass seeing an opening to a cavern.

The Adventures of Ryushin

"If we head right, we can rest in the cavern," Zandaris supposed.

"It would be for the best," I suggested. "With this kind of weather, we might not make it all the way."

Aida, without contesting our decision, walked up the right path toward the opening and entered the cavern.

We rested on the snow that was piled up in the center of the cavern. The ceiling was uneven with sharp icicles dangling above us. Onry iced the opening with her magic, sealing off the door.

"This could take days," Zandaris said.

"Fire anyone?" asked Onry.

No one did.

I continuously looked over at Aida, who hasn't said a word since we arrived at Imperia. She crossed her arms over her chest trying to warm up. She was so cold, looked colder than the rest of us. Aida didn't have to hide the fact that she is sad about Ryushin. She never wanted to leave his side at all but we had no choice.

Zandaris took some rocks and branches buried from underneath the snow and desperately worked at trying to get a fire started.

"Aida, it's okay," I blurted out to her. "I'm sure they're just fine."

She became more distraught.

Onry nodded her head. "Cheer up Aida. We'll see him again soon. I just know it."

"So he has returned after all," Zandaris interrupted.

"What do you mean?" I asked.

"He is Prince Ryushin, am I correct?" I nodded. "You best all prepare yourself. With that name going around the world, I can sense something horrible about to start."

"Something horrible?" Onry asked.

"Ryushin is a warlord back 5000 years ago. But there is something about him I could barely understand as I watched the visions that took place at the Kingdom of Reina," Zandaris said.

"Visions… I didn't see any visions…" Onry said.

I couldn't help but wonder why our group saw the visions of the past while theirs didn't. We saw them very clear.

"His heart did not match his heart beat," Zandaris said.

"But that doesn't make sense," I said. "How does his heart not match his heart beat?"

Zandaris took a branch and engraved a heart into the snow. He drew another one linking to the first heart.

"If I am not mistaken," Zandaris said, "this is what his heart looks like." Aida's attention was deep during the explanation. "He may just be the Ryushin we all think he is. But I can see someone else right there with him."

"Now you're just being weird," I said.

"He is different, kind of like he is two different people in one," Zandaris assumed.

"It somewhat makes sense," Onry agreed. "Ryushin from 5000 years ago alive during this time, how can it be any different?"

"He probably found a way to lock himself up for thousands of years and just magically pop back alive," I suggested.

"If this is true… then he is the most powerful human walking this universe," Zandaris said. "Once he learns how to combine his power into a perfect heartbeat, there is no stopping him. He would make the Destati look like a joke."

"But he's on our side right?" I asked.

Aida looked a little upset.

"Even if he's two different people, that doesn't change who he really is," she said.

Ignoring her attitude, I asked, "So how do we get his heart to beat in sync of the other?"

"Don't know. He'd really have to find a way to tap into his power but…" Zandaris said.

The Adventures of Ryushin

"...but if he were to break away completely from the second heart..." Onry added.

"Then we could be dealing with an all powerful Gisuru," Zandaris said.

"I don't understand..."

"He's talking about a mimic," Aida said. "When you lose sight of who you truly are, you become a mimic. Those are kinds of people identical to your true self but in a darker state of mind, where everything is plunged into sorrow, despair and darkness."

"In other words, they are called the Gisuru," Zandaris said.

"How do you know about that?" Onry asked.

Aida looked away with no reply.

"Usually, that only occurs when one loses something dear to them. It can happen to anyone," Zandaris said. "It happened to..."

"Your wife..." I finished off the sentence for him. "She was a Gisuru. But your wife was plagued with a dark controlling power different from what a Gisuru. What is that called again, Kenboushou?"

"Kenboushou... amnesia," Zandaris answered.

"Tsuikai would be the cure to such power," she answered. "During my studies as a paladin, there are ways you can purify someone of the mind, and the best way would be recalling experiences of the past."

"Reminiscence, understandable," Onry said. "And if they can't remember anything?"

No answer.

"Ryushin would never submit to such a dark state, if that's what you're getting at," Aida said.

I sighed, "Let's go."

We left the cavern after our little talk about the Gisuru, heading down the other path. The icy winds were just as cold as before and the snow storm picked up fiercely as the pass became narrower.

After all that talk about the Gisuru, that made me question Ryushin's origins more. With Zandaris' eyes, he can understand better than any of us what Ryushin is going through. If there are really two hearts within Ryushin, beating off sync of each other, is it possible he could turn his back against us?

After a long walk down to the base of the mountains, we found ourselves staring out into a pale blue, almost faded white, sea of ice. It was a long stretch ahead of us, leading to a smaller island of glaciers.

"I bet you Shiva is on that island," I gambled.

Aida, in a hurry, stepped onto the icy ocean. Zandaris pulled her back urgently away from the ice block. The ice cracked rapidly, shattering into water. The water dried up slowly, attaching back into the ice block.

Onry knelt on the ground, running her hand back and forth over the water.

"This ice is synthetic," she said. "Must be Shiva's power."

"So now what do we do?" I asked.

Onry stood back up. She raised her hand forming an orb of mist with her mana. Pushing the orb out into the ocean, her power absorbed the blanket of fake ice in a small radius around it. "We have to stay close to the orb or we will freeze instantly on the ice."

The four of us paced ourselves, timing our footsteps with the movement of the orb. The air froze into icicles every once in a while, hanging motionless in the air, then would return to normal and continue to flow gently through the icy land. Underneath the thick ice, I could see frozen serpents.

The closer we approached the smaller island, the more the temperature would drop. Our footsteps would fill quickly with ice, locking us to the ground. Onry would have to stop and intake the ice with her powers, freeing us from the snares.

We finally reached the base of the smaller island, ragged along the coast with small sharp edged hills. The brown dirt underneath the snow began revealing itself. There wasn't anything unusual here, just the sounds of the icicles pinging their sharp tips throughout the hillside. Onry, with haste, stomped her way through the snow and released the orb.

"Someone is here," Zandaris said. "It is the scent of a human."

"I wonder who it could be." I thought.

"It's probably Corfits," Onry suggested.

"No. It's a female," Zandaris said. "She works her way around the small island without wasting time. She's a blonde girl with long hair, equipped in thin, light but powerful armor." He continued to read the movements in the air. "A long blade... similar to Rheaa's weapon of choice."

I smirked, "She must be an elemental."

"Sparks of lightning wrap her blade," Zandaris responded. "We must be careful."

Onry entered a narrow pass between two hills. As the pass thinned further down the distance, the hills on both sides began rising into mountains and suppressed the cold dry air around us. Beyond the pass we came to a basin created by long pathways spiraling downward to a smaller lake.

"Shiva is here," Onry said, "I can feel the mist trail she leaves behind when she flies." She pointed at a trail of mist twirling all over the air, in and out, over the mountains that create this basin. "Something isn't right here. She is on the run from something."

"Maybe she's running from that girl Zandaris can sense?" I suggested.

Zandaris shook his head no.

"That person is definitely here, along with something bigger," Onry said, feeling the mist with her hand.

"What could possibly be that big?" I asked.

Onry leaped from the edge, falling toward the small lake, bypassing the long spiral walk. She created a ramp of ice down to the water. The three of us slid down to Onry, who was feeling the water with her bare hand.

"The water is warm," she said. A moment of silence broke in around us. Onry couldn't help but think.

Out of nowhere, a blue thin dragon swooped from the sky. Shiva was beautiful. Her dark blue skin covered her body with swirls of clouds that looked like cotton. The frost clouds were coated with diamond looking ice particles. Shiva's wings were long and flat so that it could gain height advantage among its enemies.

But Shiva was not afraid of us.

Shiva pointed her head upward.

"I think that means we should leave," Zandaris supposed. "Like, right now."

Shiva flapped her wings fiercely toward the ground, pushing herself back up into the air.

"Peons, Atlmaz was sure to find you guys out here."

The girl Zandaris described stood across the small lake holding a long blade on her shoulders. Little tails of lightning crawled all over her sword and body armor.

"You work for Atlmaz?" I asked.

She smiled wickedly. "You're just lucky he isn't around finish you all of. He sent me to find this stupid dragon and kill it. But I just find a bunch of nubs playing with water."

Shiva fired a frost beam from its mouth toward the girl. The girl easily punted the beam away with a spinning uppercut with her sword. "Hekireki!" she yelled. With another swing, she launched multiple jolts of lightning toward Shiva.

Onry created a disc of ice from the water. She tossed it in front of the jolts, absorbing the energy attack. Shiva retreated higher into the air.

The girl looked over at Onry.

"A frost mage are ya? It's been a while since I last killed one of you. The name is Linwe, learn it well, and fear it well. Denkouissen!" She slammed her long blade into the water, conducting the lightning on her blade to jolt. The water and the lightning combined into a sharp harpoon, flashing endlessly toward us. Regardless of Onry's ice wall defense, the lightning of the attack pierced right through it, shocking her hand that she had in the water earlier.

I jumped in Onry's way and slashed out my sword. Onry palmed her slightly burnt hand over the water, transforming it into a solid surface. Zandaris and Aida joined my side, sprinting along the ice toward Linwe. A mass group of demons appeared behind her. In spite of their numbers, I continued my relentless assault.

"Kyoufuu!" I called, creating a fierce wind with the swing of my sword. The wind attack froze just a bit, converting the wind cutters to ice.

Aida and Zandaris fought their own horde of demons off to their side. I lunged at Linwe with my sword tucked down at my side. I landed on the ground and swung upward with an uppercut. She swung downward countering my attack. We began to clash with our blades, each impact creating a spark of lightning or a force of wind.

I slashed sideways. She blocked with her sword, delivering a kick to my body. I slid on the ice. I drilled my sword into the ice, cutting out a chunk of it. I flung it out in front and slashed them into smaller chunks.

Onry moved behind the small chunks and fired them like bullets. Linwe responded to Onry's attack, batting them away. With a spinning attack from her blade, she flashed another harpoon of lightning and water our way, crushing the ice surface as it crawled its way toward us.

"Hyoushin!" Onry chanted. She clapped both of her hands quickly and laid them upon the ice surface. The area around us quaked heavily, breaking the surface into pieces. The harpoon split into different directions, destroying some of the demons that were attacking Aida and Zandaris. Onry raised her palms upward, launching the bigger chunks of ice toward Linwe.

I jumped onto the large pieces, on the move toward her.

Linwe smirked. "Rurukai!" she yelled, raising the point of her blade up into the sky. Thunderbolts came crashing down from the sky. I leaped swiftly from piece to piece avoiding the bolts of lightning.

I gripped my sword with both hands. "Takuetsufuu!" I said, creating a mini tornado of strong winds. The tornado wrapped around Linwe, locking her in place. Linwe slashed her sword right through, sending it back toward me, this time with lightning crawling around inside. I was locked in my own attack. The lightning trails shocked me endlessly throughout my body.

Zandaris pushed off one of the demons and grabbed my arm. He pulled me out quickly and we both landed in the water. Zandaris and I saw a mean pair of giant eyes looking up at us from down below. Frightened, we both climbed out of the water quickly.

"Did you see that?" I asked.

"We're in deep trouble," Zandaris said, catching his breath. "We need to leave now or we're all going to die."

Onry and Linwe continued to tango with their powers while Aida fought her way toward us.

"What's going on?" she asked.

"There's something in the water," I said. "It isn't pretty either."

"Well, let's get Onry and get out while we can," Aida said.

Onry creating two walls of ice both on Linwe's sides. She clasped her hands together smashing her between them. Aida grabbed her by the shoulder and the both started to make their way toward us.

Zandaris and I ran away from the herd of demons with Aida and Onry following close behind. Shiva flew by gallantly. With one breath, she froze the herd of demons chasing us.

A blade of lightning sliced through the path, cutting us off from the rest of the trail. Linwe stood there with her sword in both hands.

"You nubs, you will all die here!" She pierced her sword into the ground and raised both of her hands high into the air. "Leviathan, kill that dragon for me and get me that stone!"

Sparks of lightning crawled its way from her blade and into the water, causing the area to quake violently. Out of the water, a giant serpent's head emerged. Shiva took to the sky, on the run from the serpent. The serpent was similar to the one in the water back near Imperia, not made of stone but its rough neon green skin was just as tough. It slithered away out of the water.

It's body grinded up against the interior of the basin, causing it to break apart. Zandaris and I leaped from one cliff to the other. Onry followed close behind, but Aida was nowhere around us.

"Where's Aida?" I asked Onry.

She looked back, just now noticing she was missing.

"I swear she was right behind me."

"I'm going to go back for her!" I yelled, barely able to hear with all the rumbling going on. Leviathan's body rammed fiercely against our side, breaking the cliff into pieces. I grabbed Onry's hand, holding onto Zandaris' hand, nearly falling off of the cliff. Onry looked downward as she hung there, still no sign of Aida.

With all his strength, Zandaris was able to pull us up.

"It's too dangerous. We have to get out of here."

"But we can't just leave Aida here," I said.

"Are you blind? This place is falling apart," Zandaris said. "We'll all die. Aida wouldn't want this."

I looked over to Onry. She nodded, "He's right. We have to get out."

"Aida..." I cried. Zandaris pulled me away from Leviathan's body, dodging a falling chunk of ice. "How do we get out?"

Shiva swooped in around Leviathan's body toward us. She turned around, signaling for us to hop onto her back. Zandaris quickly hopped on without any question, Onry followed and I as well. Shiva lifted off, slowly flying close to Leviathan's body.

We were out.

Leviathan, the giant beast of the sea, twisted and turned endlessly from the basin. He screeched loudly as we flew passed him, cracking the solid field of ice below us.

"Lecia, are you there?" I asked, punching buttons on my RT.

Lecia appeared onto my screen. "What's going on?" I raised my RT so that she could see the enormous serpent behind us. "Oh wow… I'll send in an airship now."

Zandaris grabbed my arm and yelled, "You better make that quick!"

Leviathan slithered its way along the ice very swiftly toward us. Shiva aimed upward into the clouds. I looked back. Leviathan, with his mouth wide open, trailed very close behind.

The giant serpent chomped at us. Shiva evaded to the side, firing an ice beam. There wasn't much of an effect. She continued to flee from the persistent serpent. We turned sideways, upside down, doing roundabouts, and I felt like throwing up.

Onry created a sharp icicle in her hand. She darted it downward on the way to Leviathan, pricking the skin underneath his eye. The serpent roared fiercely in pain.

"If only you could do that continuously," Zandaris said, "You would be able to tear away at it's from skin."

"I can't make that many in a short amount of time," Onry explained. "I need to concentrate my mana long enough."

"Shiva, look out!" I warned, nearly evading Leviathan's swipe. We were almost over the ice field, managing to pull Leviathan's full body out of hiding. The gigantic serpent look like it was able to crush a kingdom in swipe of its body.

Leviathan whipped its tail at us, hitting Shiva strongly. The three of us along with Shiva shot downward toward the ice field. Onry with a quick reaction, created an orb to prevent us from freezing. Our bodies slammed up against the surface.

I rushed over to aid Shiva. The tail whip from Leviathan caused way too much damage, bruising almost her entire body.

With a gasp of breath, Shiva released the stone from her mouth. She slid it over to my feet with her nose.

"Onry, think you can take that thing down?" I asked.

She brought together her hands, palms flat, almost up against each other. She bent her knees concentrating as much as she can to create as many icicles.

"Here it comes," Zandaris said anxiously. He slammed his fist into the ground, cracking the icy surface below us. Onry triggered her arms outward to her side, lifting the chunks of ice from the cracked surface out of the ground.

Leviathan slithered too fast for Onry to respond. Desperately, she launched the icicles and chunks toward Leviathan. The pieces broke upon its skin, scratching just a bit.

"Okay, we're screwed," I said, mocking Valen's responses to tight situations.

Ironically, Leviathan stopped in its own path. It raised its body higher into the sky, ready to attack. The area around us began to quake viciously, knocking all of us off balance. The waters behind Leviathan, from under the ice and before us, began to spout powerfully into the air like geysers. The waters all gathered into a sphere above the serpent, blocking out the sun.

We tried so hard to get to our feet, but the quakes were too powerful.

"If only He were here," I cried. "Ryushin would never have let this happen!"

The sphere of water slammed back into the sea creating a gigantic ripple in the water. The ripple crushed downward. The power of the ripple created tidal wave, slowly growing higher to the clouds, swarming its way in our direction.

"Ryushin..." Onry whispered.

Even with the quakes around us, Onry managed to stagger up to her feet. She unhooked the staff from her back, pierced it into the ice, and used it as a support to help her stand.

"Onry, what are you doing?" I yelled.

The tidal wave was growing higher as it moved closer toward us. Onry palmed both of her hands at the distant tidal wave. I could feel her mana increase quickly around her. Her robe lifted upward with ice wrapping around her body. She closed her eyes shut, pushing with every ounce of mana she had. The wave overlapped us with Leviathan underneath it as well.

Onry was completely frosted in ice. Her eyes were pure blue, her hair frozen into spikes, her robe breaking off little pieces at a time and a cloud of mist wrapped around her body in a swirl.

"Get ready!" Zandaris said, shielding himself from the oncoming tidal wave. The water came booming down on us.

With an instant cast, Onry pumped her arms inward then outward, freezing the entire tidal wave in an instant. She gasped for air, nearly frozen to death. Grinning toward Leviathan, Onry closed her fists cracking the tidal wave into millions of spikes.

The sounds of chimes tingled throughout each spike. Onry opened her closed fists, darting every spike of ice above us back toward the giant serpent. Fiercely, piercingly and quickly, the spikes tore at the serpent's skin, continuously grinding right through.

Onry casted away her shell of ice that covered her completely with one push. The shell converted into a keen lance and zoomed its way toward Leviathan. Onry clasped her hands together and yelled, "Hyoushou!" The ice lance pierced through the serpent. Leviathan's torn up body, crashed to the water, and froze completely.

The quakes stopped and the area became calm again.

Shiva weakly flew away into the air, leaving us behind. I crawled my way to Onry, who was unconscious on the ice. Zandaris picked her up and we escaped into the mountains from where we first began.

"We must find a place to rest her," Zandaris said.

Slowly, we took Onry into the cavern, resting her onto a bed of snow.

"Damn it, where are those guys?" I asked, keeping lookout for the airship.

"She's rock solid," Zandaris said, holding onto her arm. She must have completely transformed herself into ice. If she used her full potential in her magic, she could have iced her entire interior, completely putting out her body heat.

"Onry will be okay though, right?"

"We need to get her out of the cold."

I continued to look back outward, hoping that Aida would appear, but there was still no sign of her.

"Please be okay…" I whispered to myself.

Chapter Twelve
Bandits of the Southsands

Point of View: Ryushin

I woke up slowly in the cabin of Ksama's airship. It was the weirdest dream I've had this entire adventure, was as if it were real. A yellow light converted to a darker shade of purple along a black empty space, similar to the colors Atlmaz wore.

Something was wrong.

"Ksama," I called. I opened the door to find her quietly piloting the airship. She looked back at me, eyes wide open. "Where are we?"

"Take a look," she said, pointing outward into the distance.

Breezes of light sand swirled by, making it somewhat difficult to see. This must be the Southsands. It was still dark out. Just barely enough to see the gray sand below sift silently under the moon's light.

"This is the Southsands?" I asked.

She nodded.

There wasn't much out here, not even dunes or wastelands of bones. The sands seemed like a pretty mellow place and no signs of a dragon around.

"Is everything alright?"

I paused. She can sense something wasn't right either.

"Well, I had a pretty irrational dream just now."

"The light was it?"

"How did you know?"

"That was no dream, Ryushin. That light was so strong. You can see it while your eyes are closed. I'm sure a blind man can see it too."

"What does it mean?"

"The light turned into a darker shade. That must be Kenboushou," she explained. "Usually the light never is that

The Adventures of Ryushin

strong, but this must have happened to someone that harnessed it pretty well."

"What is Kenboushou?"

"Someone has been plagued with darkness," she said. "In shorter terms, it's a curse. You become seduced to one's power, a puppet more likely. I have to lower the ship. We've been flying for almost fifteen hours straight," Ksama said, sailing right. "There should be an oasis around here somewhere."

She descended toward the sands, quite a distance away from a small lake. From our landing, we walked toward the bright lights.

"Oh, be careful what you say around these people," Ksama warned. "These people are dangerous. Trust me."

The two of us entered through a small gate which wrapped around the lake with tall wooden logs. The desert palm trees were decorated lights in the shape of a flame, the huts all around the lake were closed off with guards, and a huge statue of a reptile stood tall in the water.

"Halt, what brings you here to the Oasis?" asked the Kitsune guard.

I looked over at Ksama.

"Just passing by," she responded. The Kitsune searched the both of us thoroughly. He tugged on my sword and looked back up at Ksama.

"What's with the sword?"

"Sorry," I apologized, unclipping it from his paws. "I need this."

Still uncertain about my character, he dropped his guard allowing the two of us pass.

"I'll be watching you," he said.

Ksama paced herself along the edge of the waters, carefully scouting the area for anything suspicious. Without turning to face me, she whispered, "They're watching you very closely. You might want to keep your guard up."

"Are you going to tell me what's going on?" I asked, trying hard not to move my lips.

"They're thieves, Ryushin. They'll do anything to pilfer anything that you possess."

A middle aged man with a black eye patch, torn clothes, brown long bushy hair and a rune machete blade on his back, approached the two of us with the most peculiar smirk on his face. He raised his arm preventing us from passing.

"Ksama, long time no see," he said.

She looked up at the man. "Sorry, have we met?"

"Numerous times, my lady, it's quite shameful that you don't remember me at all." He lifted his shirt up revealing a long gash of a scar that started from his lower right hip and wrapped all the way around to his left shoulder.

"I did that? Wow, that's gotta suck."

He grabbed his sword angrily, striking downward at her. She evaded to the left. I delivered a straight kick to his face, jerking him onto his back. He rolled backward flipping onto his feet.

Enraged, he pointed the tip of his sword at me. "Who could you be?"

"That's right, he's my bodyguard," Ksama said, dusting off the dirt on her clothes. I bonked her on the head. "Okay, okay, you tell him who you are."

"Ryushin," I said, unsheathing my sword. "You'll end up face first into the ground before you even know it."

He chuckled, "The Prince Ryushin. The name is Demarcus, I'm sure you have heard of me as well."

"Nope," I replied.

A ghostly pale covered his face, shocked that I did not know his name. He grabbed his hair with his hands, falling to his knees. Ksama and I looked at each other confused.

"My name goes a long way, Ryushin. I am the great sand bandit of the desert. There isn't a battle I haven't fled, or a treasure I've never taken. My great speed cannot be matched

The Adventures of Ryushin

and my strength can only be compared to a God!" he cried proudly flexing, his muscles.

"You're nuts," Ksama said walking away.

I joined her side as well, putting my sword away.

"Wait!" he called. "Give me a chance to prove it!"

Ksama and I ignored him, as he cried loudly behind us. With sudden swiftness, Demarcus snatched something from my pocket and took off running.

"After him!" Ksama shrieked.

"But I don't even know what he took," I said, searching myself. I had my sword and shards and I know for sure I didn't have any money. Disregarding my words, Ksama took off sprinting after him.

We raced out of the oasis in pursuit of Demarcus, who led us out into the open desert. Demarcus ran up and down hillsides, into raging sand storms. Ksama vanished in her place leaving me behind. I dashed toward Demarcus, easily catching up. Ksama appeared in front of him, slamming her hard knuckles into his nose. He wrenched passed Ksama and onto his back.

He got up to his feet ready to fight. Demons and strange deformed lizards emerged from the ground.

"Demons..." I said.

Ksama screamed in horror, pointing at the lizards. "It's the Rizaado!"

Demarcus laughed while wiping the sand off his face. "Since my run in with the dark knight, I've been given the power to control demons and the lizard race, Rizaado."

"A dark knight... that must mean Corfits is here," I said.

"So you know the dark man," Demarcus said, amusingly. "I will do him the favor of killing you both. Attack!"

Alongside the demons and Rizaado, Demarcus launched a full on attack.

"I'll get the tiny satchel," Ksama said, squaring up with Demarcus. The demons and the Rizaado blocked me off from the other two.

I slashed my sword out slicing through one of the demons. One of the Rizaado attacked from behind. Rotating onto my knees, I cut my blade into the thick skin of the lizard. Another demon slashed downward with its claw. Pushing off the lizard with a kick, I grabbed my sword with two hands and sliced off the head of the attacking demon. More of them appeared.

I formed my free hand into a claw, building up energy. I fired energy blasts right, left, the slashed away with my sword right, spinning in the air and kicking a Rizaado in the face. Quickly, I hurled my sword like a boomerang at an oncoming demon. I forced my sword left, up, into the sand, back out from underneath, behind, in a circle around me, wiping them out in large numbers. A second wave of energy trailed behind the circle of my blade, destroying the next wave of mobs emerging from the sand.

"Ryushin, catch!" Ksama called, tossing a small satchel. I caught the tiny bag and stashed it away into my pocket. She moved quickly behind Demarcus grabbing him by his shirt. She jumped over him, overlapping his shirt around his head and blocking out his sight.

"You little rat!" he yelled angrily. She grabbed him by the head with both hands and slammed her knee into his face. Demarcus wiggled down to the sand.

I finished the last of the demons and Rizaado off and joined alongside Ksama, who had Demarcus tied up by his own shirt. He looked up at me with a dazzled look.

"What's with you?" I asked, pulling out the satchel from my pocket.

"You still amaze me, Ryushin. You're technique is so flawless," answered Demarcus. "Corfits warned me of your coming. So you seek this dragon by the name of Titan, is this true?"

"What do you know about that?" I asked.

"Since I like you that much, I will tell," he said. "If you head north from here, you will reach the North Dunes. It's a dangerous place filled with carcasses of the Rizaado, whirlpools of quicksand traps and raging sand storms strong enough to grind the skin off a human's body but with a person like you, I'm sure that place is nothing more than a playground."

"Corfits is up north?"

"He is at work trying to capture the rock stone dragon with intentions of reviving an ancient Rizaado," he explained. "That big statue in the center of the lake at the oasis is Kroasha, the Lizard King. He is about one hundred times larger than that stone statue."

Dawn came with the yolk of the sun rising beyond the sands.

"We'll go to the North Dunes," I said nodding to Ksama. "And you're coming with us."

There we were, standing on the border between the Southsands and the North Dunes. You can see the difference in the color of the sand, the south in a smoother tan shade and the north in a rough orange shade, scarred with bones of Rizaado and humans that dared to walk it. As if the place weren't ironic already, the raging storms ripped up the skies but never crossed the border to the Southsands.

"So Demarcus, how did Corfits move around the North Dunes?" I asked.

Demarcus shrugged his shoulders. "Corfits is a very strong man. I'm not sure how he moved diligently through the sands."

"Have any ideas, Ksama?" I asked.

"If I'm correct, the North Dunes was once a hideout for many of the Rizaado thieves. If only you can find the correct whirlpool, you could probably enter their underground refuge," she supposed.

I pushed Demarcus across the border. The raging sand storm ripped up his shirt in a flash. He crawled back over the border breathing deeply.

"Whew, that bad huh?" I asked.

"What did you go and do that for!" he shouted.

I laugh at him.

"Just wanted to see how bad the storm is. Not even the airship can fly through this huh?"

"Nope, no fleets have ever been able to fly over the dunes, making it easy for the Rizaado to escape. And since they have very rough skin, they were able to move in the storm with ease."

Now we were completely stuck between a rock and a hard place. There was no solution to passing the storm. How did Corfits get through it? How did he manage to walk through the storm so easily?

I placed my hand across the border. The raging storm ate through my leather glove slowly. I'd have to move fast in the storm, but there was no where to move too.

"Ryushin, look over there," Ksama said.

A large dragon with soft looking skin was gliding closely over the sands of the North Dunes. That must be Titan. His wings looked heavy but powerful, making it difficult for him to fly higher. Titan would spring into the air for about a second, then come diving back down to the sand.

I called out to him. No response. The storm must have been too loud for him to hear us. Titan sprung one more time into the air and dove straight down into the middle of a whirlpool, disappearing from the surface. That must be an entrance to the Rizaado hideout.

Forming my hands into a cup at my side, I used my Kagayaku Hikari energy beam to create a temporary hole in the sandstorm. I grabbed Ksama's hand and dashed for the whirlpool leaving behind Demarcus. The sandstorm closed in behind us, inches away from touching us. I dove for the whirlpool, holding Ksama tightly in my arms. The quicksand gobbled us up, spitting us deep into a dark cavern.

The sand from above slid slowly down the ceiling, crawling along the walls or dripping like water. Inside the cavern was very dim light coming from holes along the ceiling,

The Adventures of Ryushin

showing bits and pieces of crushed building, hiding underneath the sand. Sharp bones from ribcages emerged from the ground along with skulls of lizards and humans. The sound of sand sifting through the cavern echoed in the distance.

"Wow, this place is pretty crappy," Ksama said, dusting off the dirt on her clothes.

I continued deep into the cavern, curious of what lies ahead. The cry of a dragon shrieked along the cavern walls, creating a shockwave behind it. This continued throughout the tunnel.

Beyond the cavern was a deep abyss. Small pillars rose from the bottom creating an odd pathway of steps to the other side. One pillar at a time, Ksama and I hopped on one foot to another across the small pillars and over to the next tunnel. The cry of the dragon continued to shake the walls.

"We're close," I said. "I can feel Titan's power."

The next room was filled with a giant statue, one hundred times bigger than the statue in the oasis Demarcus. Well, it was half of a statue. The bottom half of the statue was alive and moving well. The tail of the Rizaado heavily swayed back and forth, causing light tremors when it hit the walls. Underneath the statue was Corfits, with his hands thrown up in the air.

I slashed my sword out drawing his attention.

"Ryushin, what a surprise," Corfits said facing us.

"Is it really?"

"You know, you're right," Corfits chuckled, "I was wrong about you the first time and I'm sure as hell won't be wrong about you the second. You see, I underestimated you Ryushin. Atlmaz was indeed correct on his presumptions about your power. You are truly growing too fast for us to even comprehend."

"What exactly are you trying to say?"

"Tell me Ryushin, what is the secret to your power?" Corfits asked. "You've come a long way and it seems there is no ending to your growth. He fears you, and now he seeks the power of Destati to destroy you."

"Is that all this is about, Power?" I brought the blade of my sword to my throat. "Why don't I just kill myself now and end all of this?"

Corfits laughed wickedly.

"I wish it were that simple but I'm sure you're well aware of the fact that you killing yourself would only quicken the death of many people in this world. You are the sworn protector, the prince, the most powerful warlord, and you think killing yourself will do the world a favor?"

"Where is Atlmaz?"

"Lord Atlmaz is very tied up at the moment," he said.

"Building up that army of demons right? Sorry to break it to you but I destroyed the dark portals inside his fortress."

"Hmph, destroying the portals means nothing to us. Atlmaz can create portals to the demon world in a short matter of time; just he doesn't need to anymore. The army of demons is already complete. And soon they will be unleashed when Draconia is open."

Corfits laughed wickedly. "Even if I fail here, you will lose no matter what."

Titan flew in from one of the holes in the ceiling, landing between the two of us. He faced Corfits with anger. Corfits drew his great sword, calling forth a group of demons and Rizaado to his aid.

"Ksama," I called. I tossed her my sword so that she may defend herself. I'll have to use my mana to defeat the mobs. Corfits turned his back toward us, clapping his hands together at Kroasha.

I rolled to the side evading a couple of Rizaado attempting to tackle me. Ksama moved from behind, sneaking in some attacks from behind. I performed a leg sweep, knocking a Rizaado off its feet. Kicking it in the stomach, it flew backward into a couple of demons. A demon attacked from behind. I grabbed its claw countering with a toss over my shoulder and into the ground. I flipped backward, slamming my feet into a Rizaado's face. I pushed off into the air and threw a punch into a demon's face.

Ksama slashed away at the demons, evading left and right.

"Ryushin!" she called, tossing my sword toward my direction.

I moved it all around with my mana, destroying demons on the attack. Moving it back to Ksama, she grabbed the sword and slashed at their stomachs. Ksama drilled the sword into the ground, held onto it tightly, holding herself upside down in the air. She kicked backward onto a Rizaado, rotated on her palm spin kicking another two away with both legs.

I tucked myself under an oncoming demon, slamming the point of my elbow into its stomach. Quickly, I rose up and delivered a fierce uppercut to its jaw. I rotated on my heel continuing with a roundhouse kick to its stomach.

"We have to stop Corfits from reviving that Rizaado," I said, pummeling my way through. I leaped into the air firing an energy ball toward his direction. A Rizaado moved in the way, taking the hit for him. I launched a couple more, demons dived in front of it.

Corfits laughed, "You won't stop me Ryushin!"

Titan flapped its wings onto the ground creating a shockwave, knocking everyone off balance.

"Ksama," I called.

She hurled my sword passed me destroying the staggered mobs ahead. Running along the flying sword, I snatched my blade out of the air continuing to rush the emerging mobs. I aimed straight for Corfits. He pulled onto his sword, swinging fiercely at me. I rolled under his attack and poked the tip of my sword toward his chest. He dodged out of the way, raising his sword high and striking downward. I blocked with my sword and we clashed into a cyclone of swinging swords.

"Ryushin," Ksama called. She vanished in her place, reappearing behind Corfits. He deflected me backwards, dodging Ksama's punches from behind. With a hard back kick to her stomach, Ksama jerked backward into the foot of the statue. The statue raised its foot. She jumped out of the way just before Kroasha slammed downward.

Corfits was angry. He ran underneath Kroasha and raised his hands. "Come forth Rizaado King, and do me my bidding. Get me that stone!"

The statue began to shake violently, withering away the solid stone case around its body. Kroasha was revived. His skin was green scaled covered in pale red, heavy leather armor. His yellow eyes blazed open, muscles in its body flexed and one very big sword similar to Demarcus' blade hung from its hand.

"We can't fight that thing in a very small place like this," Ksama said, "We should move to higher ground."

Titan nodded his head toward us.

"I think Titan wants us to hop onto its back," I assumed. Ksama grabbed my hand and we both jumped on his back. In a flash, Titan sprung up into the air and into a whirlpool hole, bringing us back to the surface. Kroasha's hand emerged from the quicksand, pulling him out to the surface.

We flew low to the ground but at a very quick speed, leaving the North Dunes and into the Southsands where the sand storm sub-sided.

"Here he comes!" Ksama shouted. Kroasha was on the move, taking giant steps through the sands. Titan glided hard left heading back the other way. Kroasha swung downward with its sword. Sand raised a couple of feet creating a sand wave from impact. Titan sprung upward in time to jump over Kroasha's quick swing behind us. We flew lower to the surface again.

Titan flew into the sand storm of the North Dunes again. He took a deep breath and lunged into the air, spiking back downward into a whirlpool. We were inside the cavern again. Kroasha slammed its fierce claw into the ground attempting to grab us. Titan sprung out of the cavern and back onto the surface, barely escaping his grasp.

The Adventures of Ryushin

"Bah, we can't just run the whole time. Titan, move toward Kroasha," I commanded. Titan turned wide heading straight for the giant lizard. Kroasha raised his foot high into the air. "Seinaru Yoru!" I yelled. I fired an energy blast into his foot. The explosion knocked him back onto his back.

Titan landed onto its feet spreading his wings out. With one push, he flapped them into the ground, causing the sand to wrap around Kroasha. The sand attack crushed its body downward and back into the cavern. Kroasha pulled himself back up quickly. Suddenly, we were ambushed on both sides by smaller Rizaado and demons. Titan pushed off, flying away from the mobs. Out from the ground, Kroasha's tail sprang upward, knocking all of us high into the air. With one swipe, Kroasha grabbed Titan from the air and began squeezing him tightly in his grasp. Ksama and I hit the ground.

I launched an energy ball upward towards Kroasha's hands. The explosion didn't break him free. Kroasha opened its mouth and hurled a ball of green spit downward. Ksama and I rolled opposite directions. The green goop burned away in the sand, creating a hole into the cavern.

Titan cried in pain. With one breath, a tiny stone flew from its mouth.

"Ksama, get the stone," I said. Ksama, quick on her feet, rushed over to the stone's position.

I cupped my hands for a Kagayaku Hikari beam. Kroasha swung downward with his sword. I flinched back, breaking concentration. He swung multiple times.

"Ryushin, I got the stone," Ksama yelled.

"Nice, now it's time to take this big thing down."

Countering his next attack, I quickly jumped onto his hand and ran swiftly up the side of his arm. I fired a couple of energy balls at his face. The explosions blinded his eyes. He raised his arm and covered his eyes. I ran along his collar bone firing continuously from under its chin.

Rizaado appeared around his neck.

I ran away from the Rizaado and back to his shoulder. There was no other choice but up his bicep and onto his forearm. I made it to his wrist. Recovering from the blindness, Kroasha wiggled his arm back and forth. I grabbed onto one of the links on his arm, holding on tightly.

Still in his grasp, Titan continued to cry painfully. He created an energy ball in his mouth, firing it upward to Kroasha's face. The energy ball exploded, dealing heavy damage to the lizard's face. He raised his arm again, making it stable enough for me to continue running. I cupped my hands while running and powered up. With one long leap, I somersaulted from the tip of his hand and positioned myself in front of his face.

He opened its mouth as soon as he dropped his hand and fired his acid spit. I flexed my arms tightly and launched the energy beam against the spit. My energy beam burned right through the spit and into Kroasha's opened mouth. I forced more energy into his mouth. "Kagayaku Hikari!" I shouted. The beam burned through the back of its head. A giant explosion erupted within his mouth, destroying the Rizaado's head into pieces.

Titan snagged me out of the air and we both watched the dead Rizaado tumbled into the ground, burying underneath into the cavern. We flew down to the sand, picking up Ksama.

The rocky dragon dropped us off back at the oasis, where Demarcus was waiting. I lowered my shoulders irritated by his presence. Titan nodded and flew away.

"Ryushin," he called, staggering hastily over to us. "You are all right, I see. I could see Kroasha from all the way over here. You killed him didn't you? I knew it!"

I raised my hand, stopping his endless talking.

"Please, could you at least give me a moment to breathe?"

He stopped for a moment, giving me the chance to rest, and then he began again saying, "So did you get what you were looking for? Where will you go now? May I go along with you?"

The Adventures of Ryushin

"NO!!!!" I yelled, angrily. "Demarcus, you are not coming with us. I'm sorry but we've got to go." I nudged Ksama in the side. "Go start the ship quick..." Ksama took off running. I followed right behind her, leaving behind Demarcus.

"Please! Give me a chance to prove myself!" he cried in the distance.

Ksama and I stood around the steering wheel, just drifting to wherever on the airship. I held the tiny bag in my hand, but I had this feeling I shouldn't open it. Deep down in my heart, that feeling Ayaka left in my heart a long time ago was there. Sad to say, but I can't stop thinking about the past anymore. There was so much left unsaid and so much left to learn, it makes me want to stop in time and not do anything at all. I came here with a reason and I'm going to finish what I've started.

"Where to now Boss?" Ksama asked.

I bonked her on the head. "I told you not to call me that. That light, it still bothers me. We should refuge close to a kingdom."

"Great, the Kingdom of Raigen just lies north east of here."

"Then to the Raigen we go."

The gates of Raigen opened and gave us a place to land. We docked the ship and exited the Air Station. Raigen guards approached us in haste.

"Ryushin," they saluted. "Gundita has been waiting for your arrival. Please come with us."

I was escorted alongside Ksama by the guards and into the Master's Court. Gundita had this awful look on her face, as if something terrible has gone wrong. Ksama and I saluted Gundita, but she was so troubled she flicked her hand, minding the salutations.

"Gundita... what's wrong?" I asked.

"Lecia has informed me that Aida has gone missing," she said.

I suddenly shook at the knees. It was nerve wrecking to know that Aida has disappeared.

"When was this?"

"She disappeared on a mission with Onry. Nomak and Chrisa are searching for her right now, trying everything in their power to find her light aura. But so far, there has been no trace of it."

"Ryushin…" Ksama called. "The light that turned to dark… could that be Aida?"

I stomped my foot into the ground, clinching my fist as tight as I could. "Shut up Ksama! There's no way."

Gundita thought about what Ksama said. "I don't know how strong Aida's will is, but her fragmented past has left a big hole in her heart. It's possible for darkness to corrupt her soul in an instant."

"But she's a paladin! Paladins are holy! That doesn't make any sense to why as Aida would do such a thing!" I was so angry I wanted to slam my fist into the wall.

"Aida is the fighting type of Paladin, Ryushin. To become truly holy, she must first cast aside her dark side," Gundita explained. "I do recall her telling me about some guy she fell in love with a long time ago. She was treated horribly, like a dog, someone that took advantage of her and would play with her heart and step on it just to make himself feel better. I'm sure that was very painful for her to go through."

"She's a Gisuru," Ksama said.

"What the hell is a Gisuru?" I asked outraged.

"The darker presence of one's soul… only if you've lost something so dear to you."

I let out my bitterness.

"Bah, that's a bunch of load. I've lost someone dear to me and I'm still perfectly fine!"

"Even so, you are an easy target for Kenboushou, just as Aida is," Ksama responded.

"I'm sorry Ryushin," Gundita apologized. "There is not much we can do with the current situation at hand."

The Adventures of Ryushin

Penyae walked into the room unexpectedly.

"Master Ryushin, what a pleasant surprise," he greeted.

"Penyae...?"

"I am glad you are doing well. You look a lot bolder than the last time I've seen you," Penyae said. He handed Gundita a stack of papers. "Since you are here, you might as well listen in on my report."

"Report? What report?"

"The secret of Ifrit's Ring," he answered.

"The secret of who, what?"

"While you and your comrades have been out on your journey, a surprising item has come up," Gundita explained. "To the south east of the world map, the Kingdom of Evangelista has reported a very odd disturbance west of their kingdom."

"The Kingdom of Evangelista..."

"Yes, The Kingdom of Evangelista is known as the Masters of Fire, led by Commander Cildiari. She's a very sweet girl, still quite too young to lead a nation perhaps," Penyae said.

"Cut to the chase damn it. I don't have time to ramble on about this. I must find Aida, she needs me more than ever," I said.

"Patience Ryushin. We need you to investigate this so-called secret," Gundita said.

"Bah, why? Aida is more important right now!"

"Ryushin, please, Nomak and Chrisa are already on the case. Have faith in them," she said. "The reason I need you to investigate this mission is because it has something to do with the current state of affairs that's happening."

"How does this have something to do with me?"

"Ifrit is one of your dragons."

"What?" I exclaimed. "There's a fourth dragon?"

Penyae brought up a screen with the world map on it. "Ifrit is guarding something very vital to you. My research indicates that it is a ring that connects the three stones of Garuda, Shiva and Titan."

"But my visions in the Kingdom of Reina showed nothing about a dragon named Ifrit," I said.

"Ifrit is there, and he is alive causing multiple volcanoes to erupt," Gundita said.

"Fine, I accept the mission. How do we get there?"

"You will take an airship to the Kingdom of Evangelista. Some friends of yours are waiting there for you. Dock your airship and move by foot into the volcano. Inside the volcano, there should be a temple alongside bridges connecting the inner walls together," Penyae said.

"Ryushin, please don't worry about Aida," Gundita pleaded.

"I promised I'd be there for her."

I didn't waste any time. Ksama and I took off on her airship heading Far East from Raigen. My only concern right now was Aida and finding her, making sure that she is alright. Now I was caught between two different people, her and Ayaka.

Chapter Thirteen
The Secret of Ifrit's Ring

It was a long flight. Both Ksama and I had fallen asleep for seventeen hours, resting from our previous battle in the Southsands. And after that long rest period, we had arrived to the Kingdom of Evangelista, a work in progress.

The main castle sat in the center of the city. A ring of grass, filled with roses and small trees, looped around the castle separating it from the city. The ring of the city was split into arcs, the Air Arc in the top left, Tech Arc in the bottom left, Trade Arc in the bottom right and Residential Arc in the top right.

Ksama docked the airship in the Air Arc station. Kitsunes rushed to our ship, connecting it with pipes and wiping the dirt off of it.

"Their hospitality is great isn't it?"

I looked over the ledge, finding a girl with a dark bluish tabard sort of like a short skirt with a baby blue tie tucked underneath her dress shirt. Black tights strapped on tightly to her thighs, a pair of dark blue boots with a black front cover locked around her calves and her feet.

"I'm not paying for this," Ksama said hastily. "I didn't ask them to do it."

"It's alright," she responded, "Most people that fly in I give them the works for free."

Ksama lowered the bridge.

"You must be Cildiari," I presumed, walking down the bridge toward her.

She bowed gracefully. "That is correct, Ryushin."

I nodded. "And this is Ksama."

"Nice to meet you Ksama," she bowed.

"You're not like the other Commanders," I said.

She chuckled. "That's because I'm the youngest out of the four of us. Hard to believe but I never would have imagined leading a completely new nation."

"So you're even younger than Gundita."

"Yup, I'm only seventeen. They are far stricter than I am because they say I'm still a child at heart. Someday I know I will prove to them that the leadership inside of me is there."

I smiled. "I'm sure that you will."

"Now, it would be for the best if we spoke in the Master's Court. Some friends of yours are there waiting for me," she said, walking off.

The three of us entered a transportation carrier, riding along a tram that ran in twisted angles all around the city. Since it was a new kingdom, Cildiari is trying her best to promote the city.

After the short ride, we entered a castle smaller than the other kingdoms. The first room we entered was the Grand Hall, pretty spacey but quite empty. There are three doors, one in the front and two on each side opposite of one another. The left door was labeled Armory, School Grounds on the right and Master's Court in the front.

We entered the Master's Court.

"Yo Ryushin, what's up?" Valen asked excitedly. Kirikah and Aeric were standing there with him.

I laughed happily, just as excited as Valen.

"It's good to see you again," Aeric saluted.

Kirikah agreed. "We thought we were never going to see you guys again?"

"And of Mordakai, where is he?"

"Wait, just a minute. You're all talking too fast," I said. Cildiari smiled along with us. I pulled Ksama by the hand and introduced her. "This is Ksama."

She blushed, "Nice to meet you."

Cildiari raised her hand. "I'm sorry to break your re-gathering but we must work quickly, Gundita's request."

All of us stood in a line shoulder to shoulder.

"You all are here for a reason. There is a disturbance in the volcanoes to the west of Evangelista, also known as Ifrit's Cauldron. A sighting of two unfamiliar characters has been reported by one of our guards that was patrolling the area. When he approached the two characters, the characters fled into the greater volcano. These characters were elven males dressed in leather clothing," she explained.

"That's probably Deadsong and Fearsong," I informed.

"We believe that those two are attempting to summon the sleeping beast, the Phoenix. Reasons are the volcanoes high activity in eruptions. This is not an optional mission, for this is also for the safety of our kingdom."

"We'll get this done, no problem," Valen said. "We got Ryushin with us."

"Shut up," I smirked.

"It'll be hard to fly with an airship since the lava blocked off all landing spots. It'd be best to travel by land. I'm sure you will find an easier way in, as did the two elvens," she said. "Best of luck to you all."

We saluted.

Before I walked off with the others, Cildiari pulled me to the side.

"Yes?" I asked.

"Gundita and Lecia have well informed me of a certain stone with ancient text inscribed on it. They say that you have an attachment to them. The guard also seemed to see a stone just as they described, emitting a strange glow. It might be possible the strange eruptions are coming from the stone and not the Phoenix. If you have the time to investigate it, please be my guest."

"Thank you," I nodded.

The five of us moved quickly out of the city and onto the grassy plains. Far beyond the plains, I could see the greater volcano surrounded by smaller one, similar to the size of hills. Smoke rose from the plains in the distance and the lava was moving fairly quickly toward Evangelista.

I jumped from open spots toward open spots that lava couldn't overlap, moving far left to where the side of one volcano was safe. The others were following close behind.

"Ryushin, there's a trail," Ksama said.

The pathway was between two smaller volcanoes. We moved inward to a long staircase leading to the top. The railings were built high so that the lava could not cover the stairs.

As I climbed the stairs, a strange headache randomly started to occur. It was a sharp pain nearly enough to black out my sight, sometimes making me weak all around my body. I sat down for a moment catching my breath. The air was very thick. It seemed like everyone else was doing fine but I had the hardest time inhaling. My head started spinning, eyes opening wide, body becoming numb... what is going on?

"Ryushin..." Kirikah said, confused. "You don't look so good."

"I'm fine," I replied. In a split second, I stumbled over the staircase, unable to move. "What the hell? I can't move at all."

Point of View: Ksama

Ryushin closed his eyes. I shook him fiercely but he didn't budge. He was unconscious. I looked over to the others whom shrugged their shoulders.

"Anyone know what's wrong with him?" I asked.

Aeric knelt beside him checking his status. "He's burning up. I think the heat might be getting to him."

"Oh come on, you gotta be kidding, right? We're doing fine aren't we?" Valen asked.

"Look at him," Aeric said, pointing at his face. Drops of sweat poured down his face to his neck, enough to make a full bucket of water.

A loud cry zoomed through the air all around us. Out of the blue, a bright red dragon swooped down and picked

Ryushin from his place, flying back up into the air. It flew upward against the volcano's side and into the crater.

"Good job," Aeric said. "You just watched the dragon take him."

"Like you did anything, you jerk," I snapped.

Valen and Kirikah took off running up the staircase. Aeric and I grunted at each other, then following closely behind. At the top of volcano was a stone with strange text inscribed on it. Around the stone was a whirlwind of fire blocking off the entrance into the volcano.

Kirikah said, "It's just like the stone before."

"What are you talking about?" Aeric asked.

"That day we arrived back from Ahz-Bovan, Ryushin took Rheaa, Valen and I with him to find a stone. It looks like the one we found back in the ocean," Kirikah explained.

"So, what do we do now?" Aeric asked.

"I guess ya gotta read it, ya know?" Valen answered. "Anyone know this mumbo-jumbo?"

I took a good look at it.

It was a similar text I remember seeing on some of the treasure I used to find all around the world. The words seemed perfectly clear to me.

"Loss of One, Gain of Much, Gain of One, Loss of Much," I read out loud. The whirlwind of fire vanished, opening a spiraling path into the volcano.

"What was that you said?" Aeric asked.

"It's an analogy," I repeated.

"It must apply to Ryushin," Kirikah said. "Remember, that girl Ayaka was in that last place we had gone."

"Ayaka? I don't remember any Ayaka," Aeric said.

"She is the first love of Ryushin," Kirikah replied. "I think..."

"Forget that, we gotta find Ryushin. That dragon is gonna eat him," Valen said.

The inside of the greater volcano was filled with bridges, all connecting from the inside of the walls to a center floating island, similar to a spider's web. On that island was an old rundown temple.

We walked onto one of the shaky bridges, slowly crossing from one side of the volcano to the other. The bridges bounced every step we took, making it nearly difficult for us to pass. The lava beneath us wasn't making it any easier either. It was a long drop down.

"Ryushin has to be in that temple," Aeric supposed.

"That's way over there man," Valen said. "How do we get from here to there?"

I continued to pace myself very slowly down the bridge. Suddenly, a dagger darted upward cutting one of the bridge lines. The bridge tilted onto its side. I grabbed hold, my legs as stiff as tree logs, maintaining my balance.

"Ksama!" everyone gasped.

My weight was causing the bridge to tilt more. The loose side of the bridge snapped. I hopped at the last minute, landing on the thin side of the bridge. The others slowly made their way to me. As the bridge would wobble, they would retreat back to a safer bridge.

"Valen, down there!" Kirikah pointed.

There was an elven standing their in a dark unique outfit, smiling wickedly toward me.

"Hold on, we'll try and find a way to you," Valen said.

The elven leaped high, cutting the last line as he zoomed by. He landed on the closest bridge from above. I plunged downward with the bridge in a long angle. My body thudded against the wall of the volcano and caused me to lose grip on the bridge line. I dropped down just a little bit, able to hang onto the last thread.

"Just take your damn time!" I yelled toward the others. The others were trying to get to me as fast as they can, hopping from one bridge to another.

Another elven came into view. He raised his hand with daggers between his fingers and tossed them at me. I pushed off the wall just in time to escape the sharp knives. Without any choice, I began climbing the thin bridge line. The elven continued to dart daggers at me.

Valen confronted the elven.

He looked at him in a funny way and asked, "Which one is you again? I forgot."

"My name is Fearsong, remember it," he answered.

The two of them clashed. I desperately continued to climb up the bridge line. Grabbing hold of an open ledge, I pulled myself up watching them fight.

Fearsong threw a jab at Valen. He countered, grabbing his arm and tossing him over his shoulder. Fearsong used his free hand to grab hold of the bridge, swinging upward and bashing his heels straight through the bridge. Hanging in the air, he launched a spinning kick. A transparent bubble wrapped around Valen, deflecting the attack.

Kirikah bravely dropped from a higher bridge and pounced onto Fearsong. The elven caught her by the legs with both of her hands. Valen flipped forward into a somersault, slamming his heels into Fearsong's shoulders. The force for both Kirikah and Valen smashed him right through the bridge and down to a lower one.

The elven from earlier, who snapped my bridge line, split Kirikah and Valen apart with a double kick to their chests. Aeric retaliated with a surprise attack from above to the back of the elven's head with his shield. The elven flinched, nearly stumbling over the bridge line.

"You must be Deadsong than," Aeric said. "Either way, both of your names don't mean anything to me." He unsheathed his sword, swinging and slashing away at the evasive elven. Aeric palmed his hand quickly, "Motatsuku!" Deadsong's speed started to decrease. Valen kicked Deadsong easily in the spine, flinging him forward. Aeric slammed his plated covered left fist into his stomach and smashed him through the bridge with the bottom of his sword.

Fearsong grabbed onto Deadsong's hand, swinging him back onto the bridge. The two jumped opposite angles onto higher bridges. Aeric put his sword back into his sheath, spread his arms wide open, each hand pointing at one of the elvens.

"Kinbaku!" Aeric casted. A small wire of energy wrapped around the elvens, constricting them tightly. Valen bounced from bridge to bridge toward one elven while Kirikah was on her way to the other. Raising up, Kirikah and Valen delivered a flying kick to both of their faces. The elvens flipped over the bridge heading straight down toward the lava.

An eerie screech boomed from below. The screech was so loud, the force of the sound swayed the bridges back and forth.

Out from the lava came soaring a gigantic bird drenched in liquid magma, great flames burning off it's wings, its eyes pure red and its beak long and pointy.

Deadsong and Fearsong grabbed hold of the giant bird as it flew upward. The bird snapped the bridges in half with its wings or burning them to ashes with its flames.

"We're screwed," Valen cried.

The three of them ran toward the walls of the volcano, looking for a safe place to hide. I tucked myself into my ledge and out of sight.

"Now what the hell are we suppose to do?" Aeric asked, who was on a ledge close to me. Valen and Kirikah were on the opposite side.

"Can't you use your mana spells?" I asked.

"Yeah right, his magic sucks," Valen yelled over. "He's more of an assist fighter than he is offensive."

"We could really use Ryushin right now," Kirikah said.

"Let me give it a shot," Aeric said determined. He popped out of hiding with a raise hand at the flying bird. "Chokusha!"

A ray of sunlight beamed downward from the sky and into the volcano, burning the bird. Aeric's attack just caused the giant bird to burn even more.

"Good job you idiot!" Valen yelled from the other side.

The giant bird raised its beak and blasted a wave of fire along the walls, almost catching us on fire. At most, all I did was hope for Ryushin to come back.

Point of View: Ryushin

I opened my eyes, still unable to move. The dragon stood there with its wings closed, glaring deeply into my eyes. The room we were in was filled with a golden yellow light emitting from torches on the walls. Behind the dragon was a stand with an orb floating above it.

"Ifrit, I know it's you. Let me go," I demanded.

The red dragon didn't budge.

"Are you serious? What the hell are you doing? You're supposed to be on my side." I noticed a strange collar around his neck. A tag hung from a small chain with the word Jyn written on it. I squirmed. "Damn it Ifrit, don't let Jyn control you."

The orb in the back began to shine brightly. An image of the past began to zoom in closer the more I stared into it. The room faded black and to another scene. I remembered the place well. I was at my formal high school, Tesoro. I continued to watch, struggling to free myself at the same time.

"I don't know if you should do it," Ralph said.

"Don't worry, I don't see any harm in it," I said.

Ralph and I were standing quite a distance away from someone. Over ahead was a group of three girls, one of them being Ayaka. The girls were talking and eating lunch on the cemented floor, leaning up against a pillar.

I walked toward them a few feet, and then turned back to Ralph. He grabbed hold of my shoulders and spun me back toward Ayaka. I took a deep breath.

Ayaka spotted me in the corner of my eye, a little curious of my actions yet a little confused at the same time. Since she saw me already, I had no other choice but to continue walking toward her.

Her friends looked at me blankly, continuing to chomp into their sandwiches.

"Excuse me, can I talk to Ayaka for a second?" I asked, politely.

"Go ahead," they answered. They sat there not budging at all.

"I meant alone?"

Ayaka balled her eyes and walked passed me. "What is it?"

She was already annoyed, I could tell by the way she stood there, slouched and arms crossed, one knee bent while the other perfectly straight. I was so nervous at the moment, my eyes would wander off trying to find words to say. She raised her eyebrow waiting for an answer.

Ifrit continued to glare into my eyes without blinking. The memory continued to carry on. I didn't want to see this, I didn't care at all. All I could think about was breaking free from Ifrit's hold and finding Aida.

"Well, if you're not going to say anything, can you please leave me alone?" she asked angrily.

"Wait, I'm sorry," I apologized. I had no choice but to start off with the gift. Out from the back pocket of my shorts, I pulled a long thin jewelry box. She was surprised. I opened the box handing it to her.

Her jaw dropped slightly and I couldn't tell whether she was happy or upset. Ayaka continued to look at the gift. It was a golden heart shaped locket with two pictures of her and her friends inside.

"Look, this isn't about me or about us, this is about you. And I just want you to know that I feel like an idiot not accepting your proposal as best friends and I should have. Now I'm stuck without you. Just, I hope you have a happy eighteenth birthday and always remember where you're from," I stated. I recklessly turned around and tried to take off running.

Her words stopped me in my tracks. "Was it expensive?"

The Adventures of Ryushin

"No," I lied. "I gotta go Ayaka, happy birthday."

The room returned to normal with Ifrit still glaring in my eyes. I squirmed around in my place bouncing like a fish fresh out of the water.

"Let me go, damn it!" I yelled. Another image zoomed in from the orb. "I see how it is, just trying to piss me off, aren't you?"

There I was, standing outside of her house, looking up at her window with my phone ringing.

"What do you want? I'm sleeping," her tired voice said.

"Ayaka, come outside," I requested.

"What's outside?" she asked.

After a few seconds, she raised her blinds and shot a hysterical look down toward me. "Are you crazy? It's passed midnight. How did you get in here anyway?"

"Just come outside and I'll tell you."

She took her time, keeping me out in the cold for about ten minutes. She finally came out, wrapped in a big blanket.

"Well, what is it? You have to be quick, otherwise, if my parents find out you're here, we'll both be in big trouble."

"Come walk with me," I said, walking down the pavement. I paced myself quite slowly, attempting to make this last as long as it can. She walked by my side, faced straight forward, wrapping the blanket tight.

"Are you going to tell me?" she finally asked, breaking her patience.

The image forwarded further into the night.

"Ayaka... get out of here," I grudged. I stood up once more, facing the four demons. She couldn't move. She was too afraid. "Ayaka, they're not after you, get going now!"

I could feel the blood drip from my mouth caused by the blows to my stomach. I could barely feel my body. I've never endured this much pain before.

"Ayaka... you gotta get out of here..."

"I'm not leaving you," she said, tears falling from her eyes. I looked up at the night sky as the demons were coming toward us.

Anger started to build in my heart. I felt infuriated, upset and raged. I shook violently on the floor trying frantically to break free of the Ifrit's hold. A white flame began wrapping around me. This had to be my energy building up from inside.

"Ifrit, let me go!" I roared. The flame sparked, causing Ifrit to flinch. I broke free with just enough time to attack. Time slowed down, every step, every breath was vital in this moment. I drew my sword from its sheath quickly before Ifrit recovered his glare and sliced off the collar around his neck.

The dark aura of the collar faded away, allowing Ifrit to regain consciousness. I put my sword away and slowly pet the confused dragon. His breathing was soft and silent.

"It's okay, everything will be alright," I said to Ifrit.

My memory continued to play on, skipping a few scenes. Ayaka and I were sitting in a room up against a couch. She dropped something into my hands and I stashed it away into my pocket.

"Okay, sheesh," I said.

"Don't forget it! Don't forget me, promise?"

I chuckled, "What makes you think I'd forget about you?"

"Just don't or I'll be very mad." She frowned at me. "Stay strong, right here…" She rested her hand upon my chest where my heart was. "If you're strong here, then you will never forget."

The room returned to normal once again. A sudden heat began to boil all over the room, steam rising from the floors, off the walls, through the ceiling. The room exploded from the top, jerking me onto my back. The smoke cleared, showing a giant flaming bird hovering above us.

"Ryushin!" Ksama called from the side of a wall.

I was in a volcano, with a big bird on fire, a confused dragon and friends stuck along the inside of the walls.

"Ksama, what's going on?" I asked.

The Adventures of Ryushin

She pointed to the flaming bird. On the shoulders of the bird were Deadsong and Fearsong, smirking down on me.

"I don't have time for this," I growled. "We have to find Aida."

The giant bird flapped its wings ferociously, sending blazing winds toward me. Ifrit grabbed me by the shirt with his mouth tossed me onto his back and took off flying.

"Ryushin... Aeric and I will assist you from here," Kirikah said. Ifrit swooped downward evading a flamethrower from the bird, and picked up Ksama and Valen.

"Alright, let's teach this damn bird a lesson," I said slashing my sword out. Valen drew his short sword from his side.

Ifrit made a hard turn aiming straight for Phoenix. The bird fired a long flamethrower from its mouth. Ifrit flew over it, using his feet to run on it. Our speed increased.

"Mekurumeku!" Aeric casted from the side. A flash of light blinded the Phoenix's eyes. I fiercely hurled my sword at the bird, cutting right through its shoulder. My sword returned and Ifrit made a sharp turn away from the Phoenix.

"You two are gonna have to take care of Deadsong and Fearsong up there," I said to Ksama and Valen.

Valen nodded. "Get us up there and we'll do our part."

Ifrit flew upward along the inner walls of the volcano. He turned sharply toward the Phoenix still blinded by Aeric's magic attack. Phoenix recovered with a quick fire blast from its mouth. Kirikah's shield bubbled Ifrit, protecting us from the fire attack. I hurled my blade at the same shoulder, piercing right through again. Ifrit glided straight up and over the damaged bird.

Phoenix raised its mouth toward us, building up heat from within.

"Aeric, do it now!" I called.

"Mekurumeku!" he responded. The flash of light blinded the bird again preventing it from attacking. "Motatsuku!"

Ksama and Valen leaped from Ifrit's back and onto the Phoenix, kicking and punching the slowed elvens. I lunged forward toward the face of the blinded bird with my sword raised. My blade slashed a couple of times between the birds eyes.

The bird countered with a headbutt, knocking me away. It opened its mouth ready to attack with another fire attack. It launched a flamethrower from its mouth and a blazing wind from both of its flapping wings. Kirikah's shield protected me. Ifrit plucked me out of the air and onto his back again.

"Seinaru Yoru!" I yelled, launching an energy ball. It exploded between its eyes, blinding its sight. Ifrit paced around the blinded bird slowly while I watched Ksama and Valen rumble with the elvens.

Deadsong and Fearsong kicked Ksama and Valen back to back, then lunged at them with another continuous attack. Ksama vanished and Valen blocked both of their attacks. She reappeared behind Deadsong, grabbing his shirt from behind. She jumped over him, bouncing off Fearsong while Valen delivered a straight kick to Deadsong's stomach.

"Otoroeru!" Aeric casted. A blue light wrapped around the elvens but they still continued their relentless rush. Ksama and Valen attempted to block. Deadsong threw a punch into Ksama's stomach, but his attack didn't do anything. Ksama, surprised, threw a fierce punch into Deadsong's face, jerking him on his back. Valen laughed at Fearsong's weak punches. He spun on his left heel in a circle delivering a spinning roundhouse kick to Fearsong's face. The elven spun in the air multiple times before landing on his stomach.

The Phoenix recovered.

Ifrit swooped downward, away from the angry bird. The Phoenix shot multiple flamethrowers at us but Ifrit was too fast. I turned, confronting the bird with my sword gripped tightly in my hands.

"I got a new one for you, Phoenix," I said. "Shiden'issen!" My sword flashed in my hand, creating four

The Adventures of Ryushin

perfect replicas of energy. Hurling my sword, the energy copies flashed as fast as light through the bird. The real sword split right down the center of its body creating an opening in the wounded bird.

Ifrit flew above the Phoenix, picking up Ksama and Valen. We glided downward helping Kirikah and Aeric from their spots.

"Ryushin, the Phoenix is still alive," Aeric cautioned.

I cupped my hands, tucking it down at my side for the final blow. The Phoenix raised its head for a last attempt to shoot us down. Energy gathered in my hands, emitting a bright light within the volcano, turning the lava light blue, the walls to brighten. The giant bird launched a huge flamethrower.

"Kagayaku Hikari!" I yelled. I snapped my arms forward and blasted a beam of energy at the Phoenix. The powerful beam of light energy singed right through the flamethrower and into the bird's mouth. The bird's head bursted up with its body, plunging into the lava.

A shard dropped from the smoke.

"Ifrit, over there," I demanded. I snatched the stone out of the air, grasping it tightly in my hands. I could feel my energy restoring from inside, my power growing stronger. I put the shard away alongside the other three as we flew out of the volcano.

After a short quick flight, Ifrit dropped us back in front of the gates of Evangelista. With one breath, Ifrit created a large ring with its fire. The ring cooled down quickly.

"Thank you," I said. The red dragon flew off back toward the volcanoes.

"Think this is it Ryushin, what Gundita was talking about?" Ksama asked. The ring had three points on the inside of it. I pulled out the stone I got from Titan and placed it within the center of the ring. Titan's stone instantly attached itself one of the points.

"Yeah, this is it," I answered. "Let's go see Cildiari."

In the Master's Court, Cildiari waited for us. We lined up and saluted her at the same time. She bowed in return.

"Report anyone?" she asked.

"We were able to retrieve Ifrit's Ring and take down the Phoenix," I stated. "The elvens are taken care of and the volcanoes have stopped erupting."

"Perfect, a mission well accomplished," she applauded. "Unfortunately, your stay here is going to be limited. Gundita needs you all to return to Raigen, especially you Ryushin."

"Does it have anything to do with Aida?" I asked anxiously.

"I believe so," she answered. "Though I must say, Gundita seemed so poignant. I fear the worst four your friend."

"Let's go Ksama," I said. The five us made it to the door. I looked back at Cildiari with a smile. "I'm sure we'll meet again very soon."

She nodded in return.

Chapter Fourteen
First Love

We all boarded Ksama's ship, blasting off into the air in a hurry. I couldn't sleep the whole flight, worried that something might have happened to Aida. All I could think about was her, if she was okay or hurt or anything. I just wanted to see her. As soon as the ship docked in Raigen, after a seventeen hour flight, I raced to the Master's Court ahead of everyone else.

"Gundita, what's up?" I asked, completely out of breathe, hands on my knees.

She looked down in dismay. "While you, Nomak and Chrisa were away, I had received an anonymous letter. I couldn't tell who it was, but the letter demanded that you be somewhere at a certain time, alone."

"Alone, but why?" I asked.

Gundita shrugged her shoulders.

"Ryushin," Mordakai called from the side. Alongside Mordakai was Rhyona, Xamnesces and another girl I've never met before. "Good to see you bro."

"Mordakai..." I sighed. "I'm sorry about what..."

"Bah, forget about that. I know you were going through a hard time," he smiled. "By the way, this is Yoichi."

We both shook hands.

"I know you have to go alone, but I still don't trust the letter," Rhyona said.

"It's too risky to be out there by your self, especially with the madness going on around here," Xamnesces agreed.

"Ryushin, we're here by your side," Rheaa said, coming from the other corner. Zandaris took a good glimpse at me then turned around. I noticed Onry wasn't around.

"Where is Onry?" I asked.

"Don't worry about her, she is recovering in Imperia with Lecia," Rheaa answered.

"Look, bro, we all managed to get a stone," Mordakai said, pulling out his stone. Rheaa handed me her stone. I pulled out Ifrit's Ring with Titan's stone attached to it. The two other stones attached themselves to the ring, creating a Triune.

Everyone was amazed at the light of the Triune, slowly flashing back and forth. I looked closely at the stones. Between the caps edges of the stones, I could see something connecting. They looked just like bridges.

"No way…" I gasped.

"What is it Ryushin?" Ksama asked.

"Draconia is in our hands…" I answered, looking closer toward the Triune. "There, each stone has a certain piece of the kingdom. The ring must be the barrier that's keeping it sealed."

"So Draconia is still closed off right?" Aeric asked. "That's what we want. We don't want Atlmaz to open it, right?"

The door slammed open and Penyae stepping through it.

"Just as I predicted," he said. "I now understand the stones and the ring well enough."

"What are you talking about Penyae?" I asked.

"The ring and the stones you see before you aren't just hard rocks made as keys, but they are shrunken pieces of Draconia. It's nearly impossible to banish a whole kingdom in an instant, so what Ryushin did was divide them up into three parts,"

Penyae explained, "Ifrit's ring acts as a barrier, some sort of key to prevent the kingdom from expanding. The Triune you see before you is Draconia, but it cannot expand until it is returned back to its original location."

"And Atlmaz would know where this would be?" I asked.

"I believe he's a step ahead of us in every level. All we can really do is prepare for the next series of events," he said.

"Ryushin, we're running out of time," Gundita said. "The letter demands you bring the stones. I really don't consider you going, but I have a gut feeling that this has to do with Aida."

"What if he's demanding a trade, ya know?" Valen asked. "Aida for the Triune, am I right? That has to be it."

"There's no way I'd ever trade Aida for some stupid stones," I said angrily. "I don't care, he can have the stones. He just better make sure that Aida is alright. I promised I'd be there for her, and I'm not going back on that."

Rheaa patted me on the back. "Besides, even if he opens Draconia, we'll stop him either way."

"Ryushin, you have my grace," Kirikah said.

I smiled. "Thanks Kirikah. Gundita, where is this place?"

"It's just a little south of here," she answered, opening a map on her screen. "To the world, this is known as the Arcs of Heroes, a very dry place where thousands of rocky arcs raise high into the sky from the grounds, overlapping or arcing under one another."

"Similar to the great vines in Elvara Jungle," Rhyona added.

"They raise too high, Ryushin. Death awaits you at the bottom of the arcs," Gundita said.

I clinched my fist tightly. "I'll be fine."

"I'll go with you, Ryushin," Ksama said. "You need an airship to get there."

I nodded to her. "Everyone, wait for me. I'll bring her back safe."

And there we were, faster than one could ever imagine, flying over the Arcs of Heroes, just as Gundita described. They were giant arcs, even bigger than the greater vines in Elvara Jungle, over lapping one another, rising as high as the clouds, the texture of the arcs as hard and rough as metal.

"Ryushin, I still don't think you should do this," Ksama warned.

"Wouldn't you do this for someone you love?" I asked. "Regardless of how dangerous this might be, I will not break my promise to Aida."

"Okay then, but I will be here waiting for you close by. If anything gets out of hand, I'm gonna jump in and fight no matter what you say."

Ksama lowered the airship slowly onto one of the arcs. The wide spans of the arcs were hundreds of yards long, just about perfect for a battleground. The arcs curved all the way down to the solid ground in length.

Black clouds hovered overhead, clapping thunder loudly as it passed by. Thick rain began to pour in slow spurts, pounding fiercely against the arcs. Strong winds, blowing through my clothes and wet spiky hair, rushed in whirlwinds under and over, curving the strong rain sideways.

I jumped off the airship in a hurry, scouting the area around us. No one was in sight. Ksama lowered the ship's bridge and walked cautiously out.

"There's someone here," I said, hearing quick movement all around me.

"It might just be the rain," Ksama suggested.

"No, there is definitely someone here. This doesn't feel right, Ksama."

"And you just notice that now? We've been telling you that since back at Raigen."

I pointed at the black clouds. "The setting is too dark, too gloomy. It would be for the best if you left, like right now."

It was a trap. I had this sharp feeling in my heart, the kind of feeling that makes you weak all around the body and makes you just wanna leave. There was definitely someone here, I could feel it.

A shadow in the distance jumped from one arc to another. I began my pursuit, leaving Ksama behind. I leaped, lunged, jumped from low arc to high arc, in between arcs and under arcs, chasing the speedy figure. Where did it go? It disappeared. I stood still under one of the higher arcs, listening carefully for any sudden moments between the raindrops.

The sound of blades came rushing from below. I rolled to the side just barely dodging a thin energy attack. The energy cut through the solid arc as a knife would through bread. A couple of more attacks came zooming upward. I slipped onto my stomach as the cutters sliced a square chunk free from the rest of the arc.

Picking myself up back to my feet, I jumped to a higher arc in time as the piece plunged all the way down to the bottom, slamming into lower on its way. More blades of energy came shooting from below. I flipped backwards, evading a couple, and then flipped to my side, dodging more. I bent my legs and sprung upward like a frog, back to the top of the highest arc.

"Not bad."

I turned and faced the shadowy figure. Standing there was Atlmaz, with an evil smirk on his face. A large scythe was hoisted onto his shoulder, with a hooking blade that looked sharp enough to slice the world into halves.

The rain continued to pour heavily against our clothes, water dripping from our faces, down our arms, through our clothes, making it difficult to see. Thunder would crash downward, nearly striking us.

"Ryushin," Ksama called, rushing over.

Atlmaz chuckled, "I expected nothing less from Prince Ryushin. It has been quite some while since we last encountered one another and your performance back at the Kingdom of Reina was, what's that word… quite lackey."

"Shut up, where's Aida?" I growled. "If you…"

"Hah, how do you know about this girl?"

"She's my friend and I know you have her captive, you son of a bitch."

"The girl is just fine, so don't worry." He lowered his scythe to the surface of the arc, relaxing for the time being. "So you got my note? I figured you would be dumb enough to come out here."

"You want to trade for the stones, don't you?" I assumed. "I'll do it, I'll trade for Aida."

"So hasty, so sad, that you would consider your friend a materialistic item that you can just gamble with. I haven't yet even mentioned the stones once to you and all you can think about are giving them up. Is this girl really that important to you?"

"Yes," I answered.

"That important to you huh?" he smirked. "You will see her soon enough. But please, let me tell you something, I have nothing to hide from you anymore. Every time I try to do something, you and your comrades manage to screw it all up. But it matters no more."

"You won't succeed either way."

"Determined enough? I will unlock Draconia and harness the power of Destati. The world will kneel at my power or die rebelling. Can you see it? Can you see the world of darkness? That is my world, a warlock's dream, to enslave the world with demonic power, creating fear in everyone's mind. This time, I win Ryushin, I win. The path to power will open and you know it. Destati will be mine."

I motioned my hands into a cup, tucking them to my side and gathered energy into my hands. He raised his free hand toward me with a sick smile on his face.

"Not a chance!" I yelled, launching an energy blast.

Aida swirled in front of Atlmaz, shielding him from my attack. I pulled up the energy beam, watching it rocket into the sky and back down, exploding brightly in the background.

"I told you already, this time I win," he laughed out loudly.

Aida swaggered helplessly with her arms tied behind her back. She was weak, her eyes closed and legs too tired to keep her standing.

"You bastard, what have you done to her?" I growled.

"Who me? You should be thanking me. I found this girl trapped beneath the ice over at Shiva's Basin, so consider her lucky enough to be alive. You have no idea about how many

The Adventures of Ryushin

ways I tried to make her useful to me. Trade was a perfect idea."

"Ryushin…" she called weakly.

"Aida, don't worry. I'll be there soon," I said.

"Now, I'm quite the generous person," Atlmaz rudely interrupted. "I'll make you a fair deal, one that you simply cannot refuse."

"Is that joke? Are you screwing around with me?" I raged.

He chuckled, "Give me the stones and I will give you the girl." I stood motionless, trying to bypass the trade and find a way to keep the Triune, saving Aida at the same time. "Come on, there is nothing you can do if you truly want to save this girl."

"Ryushin," Ksama whispered, "What are you waiting for? Give him the Triune."

I looked back at the waiting warlock. "You first," I demanded.

Atlmaz shook his head. "Nah uh, do you take me for a fool, Ryushin?"

"How can I trust you?"

"Easily, it's either you do or you don't. I'll let you make that decision."

I grunted. There was no way I could win against Atlmaz in this hostile situation. I was afraid that he may take the Triune and Aida, killing two birds with one stone, or possibly kill me at the same time. What was I going to do? I've never been a situation like this before.

She looked so lifeless. I felt so guilty about leaving her side, making me want to trade positions with her, my life for hers.

"Ryushin, make the trade now so that we can take her back to the kingdom. She looks too ill to be out here in the rain," Ksama said.

Thousands of thoughts circled around my brain, confusing me even more. I couldn't take this anymore. I pulled the Triune out from my pocket and looked closely at it. Draconia was shining brightly against the dark grey sky.

"Draconia..." Atlmaz gasped. "How long I've waited to see it..."

"We trade at the center at the same time, no funny tricks," I said.

"As goes for you Ryushin," he agreed.

I slowly walked toward Atlmaz and Aida with the Triune in my hands. Everything became silent, the thunder, the crashing rain, the fierce winds, and the footsteps. All I could hear was my heart beating nervously. Atlmaz walked slowly toward the center with Aida in one hand and the point of the scythe underneath her neck.

We met at the center of the arc.

He reached for the Triune with his arm wrapped around Aida's waist, cautious whether I would take the wanted item back. I gave in, releasing my grip from the Triune. I grabbed Aida by the arm and pulled her into my arms, retreating backward to Ksama. The sound began to boom in my ears again.

"Aida... I'm so sorry for leaving your side," I apologized, running my hand down her frail face.

"It's okay, I'm fine now," she said. She fought hard to stand on her own two feet. "You must stop him..."

Atlmaz began walking off with the Triune in both of his hands, his eyes bedazzled at its glow. I ran halfway toward him. He turned around and grinned. "We made a deal, now keep it."

I slashed my sword out of its sheath. "There is no deal, I'm gonna take the Triune back right now."

"Is that so? You have other things to worry about right now and I as well," he laughed.

"Ryushin, look out!" Ksama yelled.

I turned around to find Aida high in the sky with her hand raised above her head. Her sword slowly formed in her hand, but a darker shade. A dark lining outlined her eyes and her pupils turned yellow. I raised my sword above my head just in time to stop her attack. Her force was so strong, the surface below me cracked.

She had no emotion in her face, just the dark eyes.

"Aida... but why?"

"It's no use. She's subjected to my will. She can no longer hear you," Atlmaz laughed.

I pushed her upward, rolling under her body and over to Ksama.

"What did you do to her damn it?"

"Kenboushou..." Ksama said.

"Ken what? What is that?" I asked.

Atlmaz chuckled with Aida defending him. "So you know of Kenboushou, the dark spell to control one's mind. I knew you would try to pull a fast one, Ryushin, but I knew better. She's my puppet now and she works for me."

"You bastard, just you wait 'til I get my hands on you!" I yelled. The instant I took a step forward, Aida went on the offensive. I blocked her attacks, barely able to keep up with her fast movement with the rain getting in the way. Each strike between our swords caused thunder to boom. "But she was a paladin, how could she give into such an evil power like that?"

"Regardless if she harnessed the light, the light could always black out. It was quite sad really, I almost felt sorry for the girl."

"What are you talking about?" I asked, deflecting Aida's relentless attacks.

"Her heart was not whole, as if she had no heart beat," he said. "So I filled the void with the power of darkness, making it way too easy for me to enslave her mind. She cannot hear your voice, Ryushin. I've already consumed her for too long. She will kill you and then she will die along with you."

"Aida, no... I won't let that happen."

"I take my leave Ryushin. Until we meet again, that's if we meet again."

He created a portal and walked right through it, vanishing into thin air.

I pushed Aida backward, halting her with my hand.

"Aida, please listen. It's me, Ryushin," I pleaded. "We don't have to do this. Look, I'm disarming myself." I sheathed my sword again. "Aida, you gotta come through."

She was still numb in the face, the rain not even causing her to blink. Her great sword flashed a dark light, creating a dark aura around it.

"Ryushin, bring your sword back out, are you crazy?" Ksama yelled.

As the thunder clapped, Aida's eyes would turn pure black leaving only the yellow pupils visible.

"The pain…" she said.

"Aida, please."

"It hurts right here, Ryushin," she cried, grabbing the area of her heart tightly. "Why did you hurt me? Why? I gave you everything?"

I was confused. "What are you talking about? I did nothing."

"You left my side, leaving me alone to myself. I was so frightened… afraid I was going to be alone forever."

"Aida, I have no idea what you're talking about!"

Her blade glowed even brighter with dark energy. "I will share my pain with you. Kurai Shuuha!" She swung her sword in a diagonal, launching a dark wave of energy. I grabbed Ksama's arm and leaped off the arc down toward another.

"Ksama, you have to get out of here," I said.

"I can't just leave you here, you have no way out," she cried.

"That doesn't matter. I don't want you to get in the way. There has to be something we can do to break her of this spell."

"You have to bring her memory together, Tsuikai, reminiscence of the past," she explained.

"Reminding her of the past? But we don't have a past."

The Adventures of Ryushin

"You gotta try, it's the only way."

Aida leaped downward toward us. I pushed Ksama out of the way, dodging Aida's deathblow from above. She quickly retaliated with a spinning kick to my stomach. I used my hand to flip myself back up. Aida appeared way too fast in front of my eyes with her sword raised to her side. I evaded a couple of her swings and jumped upward to the high arc again. Aida surprised me before I could land with a punch back down to the lower arc.

I landed onto my back, taking in the pain slowly.

"Ryushin!" Ksama called.

I flicked my hand at her, signaling her to leave.

"Yami no Hikari!" Aida yelled from above.

A shower of thin dark energy beams came toppling downward on the arc. I shifted quickly from side to side, evading the attacks. I stumbled to my feet and took a hit to my back. Aida was in front of me again with her hand raised across her chest. She triggered her arm, delivering a fierce backhand to my face. I flipped to the side and onto my stomach.

The blood from my lip began to drip out of the cut slowly with the rain keeping it from drying up. The sharp pain from a cut above my eye began to bleed as well. Aida walked toward me with her sword down at her side. I got to my feet and leaped to the high arc again, this time I was on the run.

I flipped downward to the lower arcs, bouncing back and forth between high and low with Aida on my tail. I needed time to find a way to attack without hurting her physically.

"Aida, stop this now, please!" I cried. She caught up to my side, still emotionless in her face. She swung at my legs. I flipped forward over her attack, bouncing all over the arc, trying my best to avoid her endless attacks. "Don't you remember me? I'm Ryushin. We met in a forest just north of here, remember?"

"Share my pain, Ryushin," she said. She placed her flat hand onto my stomach and yelled, "Seinaru Yami!" a dark

253

energy ball carried me across to the side of a higher arc, exploding on contact. I closed my eyes and took the hit. I peeled off the side of the high arc slowly, tumbling to a lower arc on my stomach. I felt burned all around my body, my clothes torn from the explosion.

I stood up weakened at the knees and at the shoulders, it felt like a giant was stepping on my back. Aida grabbed my torn shirt, tossing me to the side. I slid on my arm taking more damage.

"Ryushin," Ksama yelled from above. She leaped from the higher arc. She drew my sword and said, "If you're not going to fight her, then I will."

"Ksama, I am fighting her," I said hoarsely. "I'm trying to make her remember. You have to wait it out just a bit. She will come through with it, I know it."

"Still though, that doesn't mean you should be taking a beating like this."

"It's okay, I don't mind," I chuckled.

"Are you crazy?" she asked. Aida charged. Ksama vanished quickly using her sneak attack technique. Aida was no fool though. She turned around and grabbed Ksama before she could reappear.

"Ksama!" I cried. She slammed her knee into her gut, knocking the wind out of her and then tossed her to the side. Aida turned her attention back to me.

She raised her foot over my stomach, looking deep within my eyes. "I want to hear you suffer, just as I did when you left me. This is how much it hurt." She bashed the heel of her plated boot into my stomach. All I could feel was the wind getting knocked out of my stomach. She did it continuously, listening to my cry of pain, enjoying it.

"Aida, no more, please…" I said, too weak to keep my eyes wide open. My sight was blurry, only able to see red mixing with the water, my own blood. There was no more pain from her attacks, just a numb feeling.

The Adventures of Ryushin

"Ryushin!" I heard Ksama cry out loud. I heard the sounds of swords clashing, a kick to someone's flesh and a body thudding against a puddle of water. "Ryushin, I'm here. Let's get out of here as soon as we can."

It was Ksama.

"I'm too weak to move…"

"Then I'll carry you if I have to," she grudged as she threw half of my body over her shoulder.

Aida appeared in front of us.

"He is not leaving here alive," she said.

"Aida…" I sighed.

She moved in between, separating the two of us in different directions. Aida grabbed my shirt and slammed me hard into Ksama, sending her off the arc and down to a lower one, and then jerked me backward free from her hold. She aimed her open hand at me collecting dark energy into one spot.

"Ankokuseiun," she said.

The dark energy bloomed wide open like a flower, splitting into multiple energy beams. The energy beams, one by one, hit me from all over the place. A darker energy ball came crashing down from above, exploding on top of me.

I jerked backward onto my back once again, unable to move.

"Aida…"

"Can you feel my pain Ryushin? This is nothing compared to the hollow cavern you have built inside my heart," she said.

"There's no way I'm going to let you beat me, not a chance," I growled, slowly pulling myself up to my knees. I pushed as hard as I could to stand straight but I was too weak, I slouched to my knees. Facing forward to the dark Aida, grabbing my right shoulder to ease the pain, the best I could do was staring her down.

"It hurts so much."

"Shut up already... You think you're the only one with a broken heart?" I asked. "You have no idea what kind of storm I was caught up in. I had my heart shattered, just like you. She was important to me and maybe she still is but you don't see me whining about it and hurting others, do you?"

The shards from the temples lifted out of my pocket, surrounding me on all sides. They glowed strangely. I've never seen them glow like this before. In the blink of an eye, the shards flashed a ray of light, creating a cylinder around me and Aida. The memories of the temples I visited began to replay themselves.

"Ryushin..."

I maintained focus on Aida while she watched everything. The memories rotated all around us, switch from the time I first met Ayaka to the night we had our first prom to the night we broke up and to the night we reconciled our friendship.

"I don't care if someone broke your heart," I said. "Everyone experiences that kind of pain. Despite how painful it may be, only the strong rise and learn from it. I did, I learned a lot coming to this world. You have no idea what I have been through to get here; you have no idea how painful it was to recall all those memories of mine and you have no idea how hard I worked to grow!"

Aida dropped her sword, closed her eyes and shook her head back and forth violently. The memories of my past were having a definite effect on her.

"You can be afraid to love again. I was just afraid as you are now, but not anymore Aida. Because you know what, ever since I met you, I have been able to do something I have never been able to do before, and that's look forward."

She fell to her knees, ready to pull her hair out. "Stop it!" she cried.

Everything became silent.

She grabbed her sword and rushed toward me. She raised it to her side, aiming at my heart. Unexpectedly, Demarcus' tiny bag began to glow, lifting into the air by itself. The bag opened and out came the golden, heart-shaped locket that Ayaka gave me the night before I left.

"*Aida, please remember,*" a familiar voice said. The locket unlocked itself, opening up to the two pictures that were inside. "Please remember where you're from." The locket flashed brightly and filled the area with a bright blinding light.

Aida raced through the light, passed the locket, with her sword still raised by her side. She skewered forward. With enough energy, I shifted my body to avoid contact with the point of the blade. Her force carried her into my arms. I wrapped my arms around her waist, closed my eyes and gently kissed her softly against lips.

In the empty blank space of my mind, I stood there with Ayaka in my arms. She was dressed in a pink flower designed Kimoto dress with her hair up with chopsticks. I remembered this feeling. It has been too long since I last had this feeling in my heart. Ayaka wrapped her arms around my neck pulling more against my lips.

She pulled back, still wrapped around my neck, looking deep into my eyes. She smiled and asked, "See? Didn't I tell you I'd be there for you whenever you're stuck in a bind?"

"That you did," I smiled back.

"No matter the distance, nothing can ever come between us."

I pulled her in more, resting my head against hers as she held on tightly. We stood there for a long while just holding onto each other, just like we used to way back then. There was no greater feeling in the world then this, to be held by someone that you love and to be loved back in return.

All of our memories from the past circled slowly around us, reflecting perfect images of different times we held each other tightly. I remembered her soft warm cheeks and her silky skin soothing my body by just a normal touch. We rested foreheads against each other, looking with a deep passion into one another's eyes.

"So, I have a place in your heart?" I asked.

She nodded, "And I hope I have a place in your heart too."

A piano began playing all around us. It was a harmonious tune, quite relaxing and soothing to the heart. Ayaka closed her lips and hummed along with the tune.

"You know this song?" I asked.

"Of course, it's the song that beats inside of your heart. Do you know how it goes?" I shook my head.

"Listen…"

<u>First Love – Jessa Zaragoza</u>

Once in a while
You are in my mind
I think about the days that we had
And I dream that these would all come back to me
If only you knew every moment in time
Nothing goes on in my heart
Just like your memories
How I want here to be with you
Once more

You will always gonna be the one
And you should know
How I wish I could have never let you go
Come into my life again
Oh, don't say no
You will always gonna be the one in my life
So true, I believe I can never find
Somebody like you
My first love

Once in awhile
Your are in my dreams
I can feel the warmth of your embrace

And I pray that it will all come back to me
If only you knew every moment in time
Nothing goes on in my heart
Just like your memories
And how I want here to be with you
Once more

You will always be inside my heart
And you should know
How I wish I could have never let you go
Come into my life again
Please don't say no
Now and forever you are still the one
In my heart
So true, I believe I could never find
Somebody like you
My first love

You will always gonna be the one
And you should know
How I wish I could have never let you go
Come into my life again
Oh, don't say no
You will always gonna be the one
So true, I believe I could never find
Now and forever

At the end of the song, I opened my eyes to find myself holding tightly onto Aida in the rain. Still too damaged from the battle, I leaned onto Aida unable to stand. She knelt onto the ground resting me onto her legs.

"Are you crying?" I asked, looking into her beautiful eyes.

Her face scrunched up, unable to hold back the tears. She rested her head onto my chest, weeping sadly. "I'm so sorry... what have I done?"

"Aida, it's okay," I chuckled with pain in my ribs. "I knew you would come through. I had faith in your heart." Still crying, she held me closer in her arms. I smiled, wiping her tears from her red cheeks. "I think I just had Deja Vu," I chuckled.

"You didn't have to do that."

"I wanted to. It's something you do when you love someone."

"Please forgive me…"

I shook my head. "No, please forgive me. I should have never left your side back at the Kingdom of Reina. Never again will I leave your side, I promise." I grabbed her hand and kissed it softly. She gently kissed my forehead.

Ksama slowly walked over to us with her arm holding her stomach. She knelt beside us, "Are you alright?" she asked.

I nodded. "Ksama, meet Aida."

"I'm sorry…" Aida apologized.

"It's okay, it wasn't your fault. But damn, you sure do pack a mean one."

An airship flew in from the sky, landing onto the higher arc above us. The rain came to a stop and the black clouds began to part, uncovering the sun from its curtain. The rays of sunshine warmed my body as it shined upon us. Nomak and Chrisa leaped from the higher arc down.

Nomak grunted. "Scrub, I knew you wouldn't have lasted five minutes."

"Oh please, stop it. He's wounded," Chrisa said. She carried Ksama over her shoulder, while Nomak carried Aida in her arms.

"Hey! What about me?" I asked, still lying helplessly.

"You see that?" Nomak said, pointing at my legs. "They look fine to me, so use them."

"Nomak, you jerk!" I yelled.

I pulled myself up slowly and followed right behind them. The locket glowed vividly on the ground. I picked it up finding the two pictures missing.

Then Ayaka's voice said, "Now it's your turn. The two hearts that are empty represent you. I'll let you decide what picture to put this time."

"Two Hearts…"

"Scrub, we're leaving you! Hurry your slow ass up!" Nomak yelled from a distance.

"I'm still waiting for you," she said her last words. I could feel her spirit disappear. I put the locket around my wrist, wrapping it tightly.

Ksama and Nomak docked the ships back in the Air Station of Raigen where everyone was waiting for us. Mordakai rushed to my aid, helping me onto his shoulder. It was such a quiet moment, everyone in shock to find me all beaten up. Rheaa, Kirikah and Yoichi stood there looking back and forth between me and Aida. Valen and Aeric stood tall but depressed alongside Gundita. Xamnesces and Rhyona, with their mouths tied up, watched helplessly as I was gimped my way into the castle. Zandaris leaned up against a wall with his arms crossed yet still caring about my condition with a stunned look upon his face.

Mordakai helped lie me down easily onto an empty bed in the medical room. I rested my arm across my heart and drifted my head to the side where the door was. The door opened and Aida, in her golden dress and out of her plated armor, came into the room along with Nomak and Chrisa. As she walked passed me, she smiled, then rested onto a bed beside me. The three others left the room, leaving the two of us alone.

Aida and I exchanged deep sighs, waiting for one of us to say something first. I was a little nervous, being the first time we've talked in such a long time. It was different this time, our feelings that is. She knows that I have strong feelings for her. I lied there opening my mouth, ready to say something, then closed it shut.

"You're just like me," I started.

She turned her head slowly to me. "What do you mean?"

"Whatever that thing is called, a Gisuru, right?"

"I don't understand, what do you mean by that?"

"I know it. That's why since the start of all this, I didn't want to mention anything about it to you." She was confused. "You are her. You knew that all along didn't you?"

She nodded. "I'm still not sure why though. Ever since that day we learned about your memories, I started to remember them too. I can't seem to remember all of it, kind of like I'm missing a whole other half. I only know what is going on now, not what happened in the past."

She looked at the ceiling thinking very hard. "Sometimes, I can feel her by my side and when she's not there, I feel sad. I have this awkward emptiness inside. Do you feel that way too?"

"As long as she's happy and you're happy, I will be happy."

"Do you still love her?"

"I don't know what I feel anymore. It's kind of a shocker to find out that you are the other half of Ayaka. That just means I fell right back in love with the same person."

There was a long pause.

"I want to meet her," she said. "When this is all said and done, I want to go back with you."

"Back where? Back to my world?" She nodded. "I don't know if you want to do that, Aida. It's boring over there. You don't get to fight evil monsters and stuff like you do over here. All you do is work, work, work, and you just work so much for what, nothing."

She smiled, "But here, you work too."

"Yeah, but look, we get to go on missions and ya know. It may not look like it, but I really do enjoy doing this. If I were to go back, it would be just to retire sort of."

"Like settle down you mean?" I nodded. "I wish to retire with you."

I was shocked, my eyes opening up and all. I couldn't help but laugh at Aida and say, "Aida, we are a long ways from retiring, especially if you go back to my world."

"Then we'll walk the long path together."

I smiled. "Okay, together it is."

Chapter Fifteen
Path of Memories

It had been three days since I was planted on that bed and I feel just about ready to get back on my feet. There hasn't been any serious situation since that day Aida and I reunited but that didn't stop anyone from drifting their attention away from the problem at hand.

All of my friends relaxed for a few days in the city of Raigen, preparing for whatever lied ahead. Of course, we have been doing most of the work days on end and we were practically worn out.

Onry was able to make it to Raigen fully restored. She told me about her unexpected power breach in Shiva's Basin and how she found the courage inside by thinking of me. I felt encouraged at the time and she hopes that she could show me someday.

Rhyona and Zandaris were able to put aside their differences, for now, just like they said back at the Kingdom of Reina. Hopefully, they won't have to quarrel among villages and races anymore.

The five from Imperia all hung out in the pubs in the city. Mordakai and Rheaa would talk about their journeys apart while Valen and Kirikah were bouncing around the city, looking for things to do. However, Aeric would sit in the garden in the kingdom, just as I would back then; thinking of what he can do to be supportive. I sat their sometimes with him just talking about just random stuff.

There were other times I would just walk around the city alone, looking down at the empty locket, thinking of what I could put inside of it. Yoichi would be in the kitchen helping the cooks with fire, getting free meals for her work. We sat down one day at a shop and just talked, getting to know each other a little bit. Mordakai would pop in and out to check on her, I could tell that he had a crush on her.

The Adventures of Ryushin

Xamnesces had a hard time fitting in around here; in the world of the living is what I mean. Aida and I took him out on a gear run and we pretty much changed everything he wore. But he didn't like it too much. He stopped caring about what people thought of him. He was a good person, even if he was undead.

And of course, Aida and I would sit together under the stars. We talked about the past, what I remembered and what she remembered. I kind of felt bad since I did most of the talking. She didn't mind, I don't think.

I don't know how I should have felt during those nights but I felt happy, it was almost like a dream come true. She would look just like Ayaka with the chopsticks and I felt as if we were back together. That, of course, had to be a dream.

One night, I sat around the Master's Court watching Gundita just stand there. She did nothing but stand there the whole night, so I got mad. She used some stupid excuse that it was her job and she couldn't do anything as long as there was trouble leaking around the corner. Even though she is eighteen, that didn't mean she had to be a statue all day all night.

After about a full week, we all found ourselves back in the Master's Court waiting on the word from Gundita.

"I hope you all had a good rest," she said.

"You bet your ass we did," Mordakai laughed. "Now I'm ready to kick some demon tail!"

"Good. From this point on, there is no turning back." She opened her large screen with the world map on it again. There was a new continent on the middle of the map between all four kingdoms. "Draconia has been unlocked during your resting period."

We all gasped.

"So he succeeded in finding the Kingdom of the Dracolytes," Aeric said.

"That he did. The Commanders of the Kingdoms were just waiting for it, that's all," she said. "Now we must prepare for either the worst or the best."

"Is that why you had us rest for a whole week?" I asked.

She nodded. "That rest was just to relax the tension in your body. You have all been working hard nonstop and that really won't help us in the long run. Just think, if we had you all looking for Atlmaz and Draconia, you would be too tired at a difficult situation."

"I see, good call," Aeric said. "So what is it that you want us to do now?"

"Your next mission is to head over to Draconia and secure the place as much as you can. Lecia, Craft and Cildiari are hard at work preparing young students and troops for a long battle. I will do my part here in Raigen and prepare everyone as well."

"If we're going to go, we have to move now," Rheaa said.

"Yea, Atlmaz may be after the Destati as we speak," Valen agreed.

"You all will depart on Ksama's airship early in the morning," Gundita said. "Try and keep a straight face while you're there. Things may be a lot harder than you think they will be."

"Don't worry," I said. "Together we can do it, all of us."

Aida nodded and so did Onry.

"I am sorry that I cannot get my own people to join us," Rhyona apologized. "They don't want any part of this."

Zandaris nodded.

"The undead are not ones to rely on for this fight. Subjected to evil will, it'll be hard for them to resist Atlmaz's dark power," Xamnesces said, his way of saying sorry.

"Don't be sorry. This is our fight and we don't mean to drag anyone into it," Gundita said. "All I can ask for is that you all give your best."

"And we will give it," I said. I held my hand outward. Mordakai placed his on top of mine, then Aida, then Onry,

The Adventures of Ryushin

then everyone else. Zandaris' big paw covered all of ours. I laughed and said, "Together."

Everyone agreed, "Together."

The following morning, all of us walked along the Air Station in a straight old-fashioned line, saluting Gundita who was standing there with her arms behind her back. She saluted for the final goodbye as Ksama lifted the airship into the air. With one boom, we blazed into the sky.

Even as far as we were, we could see Draconia emerging behind the horizon, slowly creeping up on the sun as the airship flew closer.

My heart was racing, jumping, just too excited to finally see it but yet a little nervous at the same time. We were at the end of our journey; the final destination is just ahead of us. All of us stood around the steering wheel, too nervous to say anything. I could see the focus on their faces: Mordakai, Rheaa, Valen, Aeric and Kirikah from Imperia, Yoichi from Olida, Onry and Aida from Raigen, and Xamnesces, Zandaris and Rhyona from their homes.

"Listen up," I said. Everyone but Ksama, who was flying the airship, turned their attention to me. "I know you're all nervous. I'm just as nervous as you are but don't let this shake your composure. If you do then Atlmaz will win. He gains power from our fear and we can't let him do that. I am here with you all. No matter the odds, we will come out of this with a win, I promise."

"We won't let you down," Mordakai said.

"Not just me you dope," I laughed, "We do this one together."

"Ryushin, look," Ksama said.

From above, the four dragons, Shiva, Ifrit, Titan and Garuda, glided down and flew close by.

"Wow, that's tight!" Valen said excitedly.

Laughter and joy overcame my heart for I was too thrilled to see them flying in sync together. Shiva and Ifrit moved in front of our airship, guiding the way.

Here came the sun, shining brightly above us with its warmth. I had this pumped upbeat feeling in my heart and it felt like a high tempo song was playing all around us. Then the wind came, gently brushing through our hair and clothes, smoothly massaging our skin.

"Hey, I can't control the ship anymore," Ksama said. "It's flying on its own."

The morning sky faded quickly into a night sky, filling with millions of stars and the sun still shining brightly above us. It looked as if were in space with shooting stars shooting right passed us.

Garuda and Titan zoomed incredibly fast along with Shiva and Ifrit, leaving a sparkling trail of their color. The ship sailed far right with the track. Amazingly, the trails started projecting images all around us, similar to the shards from the temples. My friends, Ralph, Justin, Jeice and Alex from the other world, were running alongside the ship in a green grassy hill. They all looked at me with a smile and waved.

On the other side, Ayaka, with her blue tank top, jeans and hair tied up with chopsticks, was standing with her arms behind her head, waving and smiling too. I looked over at Aida, but she was looking at the other side at another projection. I walked over and watched it with her.

Ayaka and I were running around chasing one another. Aida saw the laughter and happiness between us and it made her a little sad. She had this distraught look on her face, so I grabbed her hand, locking my fingers with hers and smiled.

"Do you think things will ever be the same?" she asked.

"Are you kidding? Why would you what things to go back to the way they were before?" I chuckled. "Things are just as great as they are already."

She smiled, tightening her hold on my hand.

Everyone was amazed at all the stars flying by. They were running around chasing the stars, or looking over the edge to see what was below.

The Adventures of Ryushin

Suddenly, the airship plunged downward in a sharp angle. Two roller coasters, one on each side, rode in next to us. All of my friends, Ralph, Jeice, Justin and Alex were had their arms thrown up in the air on one side, while Ayaka and I were on the other. The ship jerked back to a straight path. The projections faded and we were just about ready to land next to Draconia.

The night sky still remained the same.

Ksama regained control of the airship, slowly dropping the ship's speed. We landed on the shore of the new land, just a mile away from Draconia's gate. Ksama lowered the bridge of the ship and we all stepped on the soft, white, crystal sands.

Up ahead was an altar of some sort. I ran up to it, everyone else followed close behind. There was an inscribed text on it saying: The Kingdom of Two Worlds.

"Took you long enough."

Sitting there on a log was Astrae, still dressed in his mysterious hood, still arms crossed. "I hoped you enjoyed the show, He thought you would like it."

"He? He who?" I asked.

"Don't worry, you'll meet him soon," Astrae said.

I noticed that the kingdom was perfectly calm and Atlmaz was no where to be found or any of us goons.

"Where's Atlmaz?" I asked.

"Oh, about him. I'm pretty sure he's at home preparing," Astrae answered.

"Preparing for what?"

"Invasion. Unless you prefer hearing the word, war," he said.

"And you're calm about all of this?" Mordakai asked.

Everyone else was shocked.

"What's to be all jumped about? It's not like you haven't fought his demons before, am I right?" Astrae asked.

"I guess you're right," Valen said.

"It'll be better if you hear this from our Commander back in the kingdom," Astrae said, "So follow me."

Chapter Sixteen
Last Minute Tactics

He led the way into the Kingdom of the Dracolytes. There were four different blocks, known as the hexagons- the Hexagons of Shiva, Titan and Garuda. Shiva's Hexagon was the Airstation which lied in the North West, Titan's Hexagon was the Trade Hex with the entrance gate in the South, and Garuda's Hexagon was the Residential Area which was opposite of Shiva's Hexagon in the North East. It was just like the Triune, the green grass, the bridges and everything.

"What are these people?" I asked.

They looked like humans but didn't. Their skin was solid in color, each having a unique shade. Some had mouths, some didn't and their eyes looked sharp and mean, almost like a lizard's eye. Most of them were half human with some human features such as arms, legs, some had wings, smalls ones and big ones, or even both. There were male and female, males with either spiky or long hair or females with tied or curled hair, all with interesting colors mixed in.

"These are the Dracolyte Citizens," Astrae answered.

Mordakai poked Astrae in the cheek. "How come you don't look like them? You look like a little boy."

Astrae flicked his hand away and answered, "I was just born this way. Not all Dracolytes look like dragons. Most of them are hybrids, crosses between humans and other Dracolytes. It's the hidden power of turning into a full fledge dragon that they have forgotten."

Astrae took us inside the castle walls of Draconia where hundreds of Dracolytes stood in two straight lines, looking across from each other. Their armor was unlike any that I've ever seen using their wings to wrap around their bodies as breastplates and wore black slops similar to mine. Behind them were stairs, rising to another floor level with three doors on each side.

The Adventures of Ryushin

Two Dracolytes stood before us in front of a throne. The Dracolyte on the left was a male with a human face, covering his forehead and eyes with a visor but his spiky hair surfaced above the visor. His wings wrapped around his body just like the guards, arms equipped with shiny plated armor, black tights and silver long boots. The Dracolyte on the right was a female. She looked fully human dressed in a pure white silk long dress with diamonds embedded all over the body. Her wings were closed behind her back, with her blonde hair splitting the pair right down the middle.

"Commander Ragnorak, Commander Kaisera," Astrae saluted.

He bowed alongside the female Dracolyte. "Is this him, the one with the wings?"

Astrae brought me forward. I looked back at everyone else with a confused look on my face.

"This is him, just as Master Ryushin wanted," Astrae answered.

Ragnorak looked a little disappointed. "I expected someone a little beefier." I couldn't help but stagger to the floor. "But if that's what He chose, then he's putting a lot of trust in you."

"I don't understand, who is He?" I asked.

"I think it would be best if they met," Kaisera suggested.

Ragnorak nodded. "Ryushin, please follow me. Everyone will wait for your return here."

He pulled open a curtain from behind the seat of the throne, revealing a closed crystal door. He opened it.

"Take as much time as you need," Kaisera said, standing next to me.

I walked through into a room of shining crystals. The floor was tiled with crystals, the walls made out of crystal mirrors and the ceiling was decorated with thousands of them. In every crystal was my reflection, glistening with a small twinkle. Before me was a mirror with my confused reflection on it.

"I knew you would make it this far."

I jumped in place, frighten of the surprising voice. "Who's there?"

"Look in the mirror."

I slowly crept toward the mirror only to watch my reflection look back at me.

"Okay, now what?"

My reflection bowed to me. I was just about ready to make a break for the door. "Wait," it laughed, "Don't be afraid." My reflection walked through the glass mirror, becoming a solid figure of its own. When it walked out, it was dressed differently than me, bearing the similar clothing I had on back in the Kingdom of Reina- the red tights, suited armor and red hat with a feather in it.

"Wait, you're him, aren't you?" I asked.

He laughed, "Sort of, I'm also you. Well, now I am, at least."

"The Legendary Ryushin at last," I said, bowing to him.

"I'm sorry to drag you into all of this. I know how important you're home is to you. But you have to understand that you were the only one that I could rely on," he said.

"But why me? Why not some other beefier guy, as everyone would say?"

He raised his hand over his chest.

"For a long time now, I've been waiting patiently for that heart."

"That heart?"

"The Heart of Confidence, Love and Courage."

"And you saw that in me?"

He nodded. "I was right about you, the never ending growth to your power."

"Why didn't you just destroy Destati back in your time?" I asked.

"I couldn't. I can't really explain it, you and your friends will have to see it for yourselves. The Destati is well contained in the center of the castle. You will find it alongside the

Trueblade at the top of a tower that's built deep into the castle grounds."

"And what of that thing I saw in the visions of the Elder back at the Elven Roots? Was that a Gisuru?"

"I cannot say."

"Why not?"

"It is something you'll have to see for yourself."

"And Atlmaz?"

"I am counting on you to stop him from breaching the castle and obtaining the dark power. I will be at your side at all times. Seek the Trueblade and you will learn everything that you need to know."

He palmed his hand at me, creating trails of red glowing lights all over his body. His body transformed into a wave of light and raced right into my body, the red glowing lights now flowing all over my body. The lights flashed, covering every part of my body in a new uniform.

"What is this?" I asked.

"I was once called the Prince of the Dracolytes. It's about time you looked like one." The black sleeve on my right arm was now dark red, wrapping over my right shoulder where my black shoulder pad was, and over my left collar bone. Underneath the red shoulder pad was a black long sleeved tunic, extending to my thighs, tied at the waste by a red sash. On my forearm was a red bracer with my RT attached to it and both of my hands were strapped with black open finger gloves. I wore the same black baggy slops, along with black stitched moccasin looking shoes similar to the Dracolytes.

"Thanks for all of this," I said. I took my sword and drilled it into the crystal right before the mirror. "I will not fail." Before I left the room, I looked back at the mirror, examining my newly equipped gear. "Can you answer one more thing for me?"

"Go for it," he answered.

"How is it possible that Ayaka was split into two different people? And it led her other half to this world?"

"Ardon is a parallel world to Earth. When a Gisuru is born, the heart splits into two, leaving two different people, the dark and the light. Aida was born of dark, another reason why Kenboushou was easy to get to her, but she's been trying hard to cast away the darkness by following the path of a paladin."

"Interesting... what about me?"

"Only you can decide what you are," he said. "We may be two hearts, but you are still in control of your destiny."

I walked out of the crystal room, back to where everyone was waiting. They looked at me, surprised at my sudden change in gear, even Astrae. Ragnorak and Kaisera knelt before me, crossing their left arm across their chest. Astrae did the same as well.

"Prince Ryushin," Ragnorak said. "We have been waiting for you."

"It's okay, you don't have to bow," I said. Aida was stunned and amazed. I gave her a wink and smiled. She blushed.

"So He did choose you after all," Astrae supposed.

"Come Ryushin, we have much training to do," Ragnorak said.

"Training? We don't have time for that. What if Atlmaz strikes while you're training?" Mordakai asked.

"Atlmaz is a strategic person. He will not rush into a battle unless he was sure he would win. I give him three days at the most, two to prepare and one to fully restore his energy. He knows that against Dracolytes, he will need all the power he can get," Ragnorak explained.

"What is there to train anyway? I'm pretty sure Ryushin knows what he is doing," Aeric asked.

Ragnorak looked over to me, examining my character thoroughly. He looked over to Astrae and said, "His wings are still closed. He doesn't know he can fly, does he?"

Astrae's flinched, absentminded about something he forgot to tell me.

"I forgot…"

"Wait, I have wings?" I asked, looking over my shoulder. There was nothing there.

"Trust me, they're there. I can see them clearly with my eyes," Ragnorak said. His eyes were different than any others in the room, with a black liner outlining his eyes.

"Some Dracolytes are born with invisible wings, some choose not to reveal them, where as others use them as armor. The flap of the wing is thick and powerful, capable of doing many things," Kaisera explained. "Since you are half a human and half of a Dracolyte, you're wings are only visible to the eyes of the Dracolytes."

Mordakai and Rheaa poked my shoulder blades. "But if they're invisible, couldn't we at least feel them?" Rheaa asked.

"The wings of a Dracolyte are only felt when they are visible. In battle, the visibility of the wings can become crucial at a time of need. As far as Ryushin goes, I believe his wings are permanently invisible," Kaisera answered.

"He is the one with the special wings," Ragnorak said. "He bears the Dragon Wing and the Angel Wing. I can't really explain what that means."

"Other than my wings, what else must I go into training for?" I asked.

"You're eyes," Kaisera answered. "You have a pair of beautiful eyes, Ryushin. With Dragon Eyes, your visibility will increase in range and your awareness will heighten greatly. You will be able to detect fast attacks that you never could have detected before."

"And what about us? What do we get to do while he's in training?" Valen asked.

"You have two choices," Astrae said, "You train for the next two days and rest on the final day, or you relax for the next three days, waiting patiently."

"Yea right, if Ryushin is gonna train then I'm gonna train too," Mordakai said.

Everyone nodded and agreed along with him.

"Anything you need before we start, Ryushin?" Kaisera asked.

I nodded. "You must take me to the Destati."

Everyone gasped.

"But why? I don't know about you but the sound of that name just gives me the chills," Mordakai said, shaking all over.

"I must see for myself," I answered. "Only then will I understand the truth behind the past."

Ragnorak nodded.

He and Kaisera walked toward the left side staircase, moving passed the guards, and up to a door on the second level. I nodded to everyone else and followed him. The rest followed closely behind.

The halls were grand and rich, filled with a mass quantity of jewelry. There were diamonds everywhere, gold lining, shining armor, crystal tiled floors, and even the statues were dressed in rich gear. We walked through several doors and hallways before making our way outside to a center court. The court was somewhat of a ditch with a long narrow stairway leading down.

"You can see the Destati from here," Ragnorak said.

Rheaa pointed out to the light that was shining brightly at the top of a shrine. "You mean that light, right?"

"I want a closer look," I said.

Kaisera led us down into the ditch and up the long staircase. We entered the shrine. It was shaded with a pale, worn out looking gold color. The pillars that held the ceiling up were cracked and the tiled flooring was smashed into pieces in some parts. It was a fairly large open room, long and wide enough for a battle.

Destati levitated before us dead center of the shrine, emitting a strong silver light with a black purple-ish interior. I can hear it talking to me. It made a bee like buzzing noise. It was powerful, leaving a fearful mark inside everyone's heart, even mine. Everyone stood a great distance from the Destati, afraid to go anywhere near it.

"Why don't we just use it to blow up Atlmaz if it's so powerful?" Mordakai asked.

"Go touch it, you will see why," Astrae insisted.

Mordakai hid behind Yoichi and said, "No way. I don't trust it."

"And no one should. Its energy is made from darkness, pure evil intention. Only one subjected to evil can harness its power," Astrae explained. "If a good hearted person would take hold of it, it would fill its heart with greed, ambition, power, corrupting the person's heart."

The Trueblade slept on a stone underneath Destati, unsheathed, shining its keen edge. The handle was wrapped with fine black leather, lined with silver color. The blade was pure white with splashes of the rainbow's colors. I can feel its power as well. It was a calm feeling that rested everything around us- the trees, stars, clouds, lands.

"That must be yours, Ryushin," Aeric said.

Astrae nodded to me, so I slowly paced myself toward it. The force from Destati was pushing me back as if it were afraid, while the Trueblade insisted that I keep approaching. I held the shining sword by the handle, gripping it tightly, and hoisted it into the air, striking Destati in the center. The room in the shrine dimmed, bringing me to a flashback.

Jyn, in her warlock robe and scythe down to her side, came sprinting up the stairs in a hurry. I lost control of my body, forced to re-enact the past.

"Ryushin, how did you beat me here?" she asked.

"I'll never let you get your hands on Destati, Jyn."

"But I left you for dead with the Kingdom of Reina, I watched you die in that explosion!" she growled.

"It's too late. The Dracolytes will be here shortly," I informed. "You alone are no match for the Draconian Dragoons. You are no match for me either." I held the sword down to my side, knees bent, ready to fight.

Jyn dashed with her scythe gripped tightly with both hands. She swung with an uppercut. I stepped onto the rod of the scythe, hoisting myself above her and delivered a spin kick to her face. She flew into her shoulder, sliding across the floor. She got right back up and back on the offensive. I evaded her swings, stepping backwards, sideways, ducking, and also deflecting her attacks with my blade. She hooked the scythe around my neck. I countered, grabbing the rod of the scythe with my free hand, holding it firmly while she fought desperately to pull me in.

She raised her open free hand and yelled, "Fuereasei!" launching a giant, disoriented, red-orange energy ball. I sliced right through the attack with my sword and pulled myself inward. I landed a dropkick to her chin and she jerked backward onto her back. The sliced halves of energy exploded right behind me.

I lowered my shoulders. She was too tired, weak from her surprise attack back at the Kingdom of Reina. She slowly got to her feet, blood dripping from her mouth and scraped skin.

"Ryushin!"

A wounded Reina ran into the shrine.

"Reina, what are you doing here?" I asked.

Jyn smirked and wiped the blood off her lips. She took her scythe and swung a wave of dark energy toward her. I ran to Reina's aid, deflecting the attack away with my sword. Her attack knocked my sword out of my hands. The wave of dark energy sliced through one of the pillars and into the sky.

"Ryushin, I'm sorry!" she cried.

"Oh no, the Destati!" I gasped. I turned around, finding Jyn with her arms raised into the air. Her eyes were different, almost demon possessed. The Destati flashing above her arms, wrapped around her body like a snake, and increased her power.

"How do you want to die, Ryushin?" she said deeply. "Shall I make it quick and easy for you?" She blasted into the air and through the ceiling of the shrine, positioning herself in the center of the moon.

"Ryushin!" the Draconian Dragoons called, rushing up the staircase. They picked Reina up. The night sky faded a bright gray, slowly painting itself over the lands of Draconia. Everything was now gray.

The tower began to quake at its tremendous force. I slightly flew into the air and formed my hands into a cup, tucking them down to my side.

"With this power, I will destroy this world!" she laughed wickedly. She thrusted her arms tossing the small power downward. As it slowly fell from the sky, it grew into a colossal energy attack enough to wipe out the entire kingdom in an instant.

I whipped my arms forward, launching a heated red energy beam upward, clashing with the Destati. The two powers emitted intense flashing lights and the force of the collision knocked everyone off of their feet. I was pushed downward to the very bottom of the courtyard. The stairways on both sides started to deteriorate into the Destati.

Reina got to her feet and tried desperately to get to me, but the tower started to break apart. I continued to push as much energy as I could, resisting the attack. My legs crushed right through the ground, burying deeper with every passing second.

Reina fell from the tower and to the ground.

"Ryushin, the Trueblade!" she yelled.

The sword was just out of my reach. I released one of my hands from the energy beam, reaching desperately for it. The Destati pushed me further into the ground; I had no choice but to place my arm back into the attack.

Reina jumped from the floating tower, nearly tumbling to death on the ground. She crawled to the sword, grabbed it, and continued crawling toward me. I freed my hand once more, reaching out to Reina. I was almost there.

"How dare you!" Jyn yelled.

She took her scythe and swung downward with her dark wave attack. The wave nailed Reina right in the middle of the spine, slamming her body fiercely into the ground. She dropped the sword.

"Reina!" I yelled, pulling my arm back into the energy attack.

"I win this time Ryushin!" Jyn laughed.

The force of Destati knocked me out of the dream state. I rolled around on the grass while the event still carried on. All I could see was an energy beam shooting out of the ground in a massive gray light up against Destati. Reina lied there helpless, she was dead.

"Ryushin?" Astrae called.

Everything returned to normal again- the shrine, the stairs, the courtyard and the night sky. I found myself at the bottom of the tower at the same spot Reina died. There was no hole in the ground though. The memory finished before I could see how He defeated Jyn.

"Dude, you were like bouncing all over the place," Mordakai said, "It was like you were possessed, kinda creepy."

"That's strange," I responded, "It didn't let me finish."

"You saw all you needed to see," Ragnorak replied. "Jyn was defeated by Ryushin, but by a Ryushin we all don't want to remember."

"What the hell does that mean?" Valen asked.

"I understand. That's what He said to me back in the crystal room," I said. "He said, 'far worse' than a Gisuru."

"That night, he was standing their in a form we have never seen him breach," Kaisera said. "It was something I've never seen before. His power, it was too powerful, far greater than the Destati."

"The form of a Dracolyte, wasn't he?" Zandaris asked. "The second heart." Ragnorak and Kaisera felt displaced with Zandaris' response.

"It took us many days and nights to calm his spirit down. He was too enraged, we thought we would never get our prince back," Kaisera said. "When he was able to regain consciousness, he asked to be locked away."

"So I locked him in the mirror you saw in the crystal room," Ragnorak added.

"It all makes sense now," Rheaa said, amazed at the whole ordeal, "The only ones that knew of his disappearance were the ones in Draconia. After you locked him away in the crystal room, Draconia was banished as well."

Ragnorak nodded.

I walked away from the scene, uneasy and shaken up about the whole mess. I felt like sitting alone for awhile, recapping the events that took place during this journey. Everything was once so empty and now everything is whole. His story and my story are now both known to this world, but I just didn't know how to end it.

All of this talk about this 'far worse' characteristic just killed the rush inside my heart. I didn't want to fight anymore, afraid that I would turn into something dark, but I had no choice. If I fight then something bad will happen, if I don't fight, Atlmaz will destroy everything in his path, a lose-lose situation.

Later in the evening, I stood along a ledge staring deep into the night sky. It never turned day here, it was always night. Aida entered the scene from the open door behind me. I looked at her with dismay, then back into the stars.

"Is everything okay?" she asked.

I sighed, "Aida, I don't know if I can do this. I'm afraid that I'll end up hurting everyone. I'm not afraid of Atlmaz, I'm more afraid of myself at the moment."

She stood by my side, looking into the stars as well.

"Don't be afraid." I looked at her, confused. She smiled, grabbing hold of my hand. "If you're afraid then it'll be hard for you to fight it, but if you're strong than it cannot overtake you."

"Were you afraid?"

"Of course. Then again, I'm not as strong as you are," she answered. "When we were fighting at the Arc of Heroes, I was afraid. I was afraid that you would leave me again. Just the thought of it alone was painful enough. But you showed me the other side of me, the happy side of me. So I became strong."

I remembered, the night before I left, Ayaka said something dear to me. Aida said the same thing just now. "Stay strong, right here…" She rested her hand upon my chest where my heart was. "If you're strong here, then you will never forget."

"I understand," I said. "I haven't forgotten."

The next day, I spent most of my day training with Ragnorak and Kaisera in an isolated field away from everyone. For hours, they would stand on opposite sides of me, holding their arms out like they were draining my energy. I could feel two sharp pains emerging from my shoulder blades, but I still couldn't see anything. The two of them would step back at times, almost as if they were stretching my invisible wings out.

"Okay, you're wings are fully stretched," Ragnorak said. "Try giving it a go."

I was so lost.

"How the hell do I flap my wings? I can't even see them."

"It's almost the same thing as using your mana," Kaisera answered. "You do know how to use your mana right?"

"Of course I do, but only as energy based attacks."

"Try concentrating your mana toward your shoulder blades," Ragnorak suggested.

Still nothing budged, "This is hopeless. Are you sure I can fly?"

"I can see your wings perfectly fine," he said, swiping his hand in the air. "I'm even holding one of them right now. It takes a lot of mana concentration to start flying."

Kaisera agreed. "Only fly if you have to. Otherwise, I suggest using a flying mount, such as one of your guardians."

"My guardians?"

Ragnorak chuckled, "Astrae forgot to tell you another one."

The Adventures of Ryushin

"You can summon Shiva, Titan, Garuda or Ifrit, with a simple call. But if they are a distance away, you must use your Trueblade to summon them," Kaisera explained. "We'll explain more on that later."

"Keep trying, Ryushin," Ragnorak said. "You almost got it."

"Dude, I didn't even leave the ground yet, what are you talking about?" I grunted.

"Focus," he said.

I closed my eyes, thinking about pushing my mana to my back. If I could use my mana in my legs then I'm sure I could use them for my wings. My body was slowly lifting off the ground, pushing downward like the propulsion of a rocket. I opened my eyes to find myself just inches off the ground. The wings on my back outlined then faded away.

"Come on, use your mana," he urged. "You're not even trying."

"What the hell? I'm trying!" I shouted Ragnorak broke my focus and I ended up landing onto the ground.

Both Ragnorak and Kaisera gave a long sigh. "We'll move on to something else for now. Let's test your Dragon Eyes," Ragnorak insisted.

For next few hours, I was staring into the eyes of a statue of a dragon. Ragnorak and Kaisera had way too much patience for this; I was about ready to leave. They eyes of the dragon were rock solid, no texture in them at all, how would this enhance my eyes?

I slightly looked away.

"Ryushin," Ragnorak snapped.

"He's just as ignorant as your were," Kaisera chuckled.

"I wasn't this bad," he grunted. "At least I was able to do it faster."

I continued glaring at the statue. I began toying around with myself, playing that child's game to see how long you can stare without blinking. Swiftly, the eyes turned to flesh opening up. I wrenched backward onto my back. The eyes were stone again.

Ragnorak and Kaisera bursted out in laughter.

"What's so funny? Did you see that? That was crazy," I said, still jumpy.

"It's looking right at you," Kaisera said.

The eyes were still stone to me. "But they're rock solid."

"You're Dragon Eyes will enhance when you can see the true form of the dragon," Ragnorak explained. "Keep trying, the eyes were the hardest part."

So, I got back to my feet, staring right back into the statue's eyes, leaning toward it. The closer I zoned in on it, the eyes would slowly open. It stared right back at me. I slowly pulled back, examining the whole body of the statue. The stone began to turn to flesh.

"Commander Ragnorak."

I broke my concentration and the dragon returned to stone. It was one of the Draconian Dracolytes. I gave him the angriest look I could come up with, burning with fire behind me, smoking out of the ears.

"You, son of a bitch! I almost had it!" I pounced on him, strangling him by the neck.

"Prince Ryushin... please..."

Kaisera bonked me on the head. "Please report," she said.

"There are thousands of airships flying in from all directions," he said. "I think you should have a look."

"So much for your three days," I said, rubbing the back of my head.

The four of us walked out of the castle calmly looking into the night sky. Everyone was on the bridge looking up at the sky as well. The whole kingdom was enclosed by airships from all sides. Was it an invasion?

Ragnorak took the sky along with Kaisera. I tried to but I didn't get very far.

"Ryushin," Aeric called.

"Aeric, what's up?" I replied.

The Adventures of Ryushin

"I think that's the Commanders Fleet," he assumed. "They are here to fight with us."

Ragnorak glided back downward to the ground.

"They're your commanders all right," he said.

"So, why don't they land?" I asked.

"There's nowhere to park thousands of airships," he informed.

I staggered to the floor. "Have them park in the distance away from the kingdom," I said. "We can use the airships as an escape plan if all else fails."

"Smart thinking," Aeric agreed.

Ragnorak took to the sky. Four other ships landed in the Airstation of Shiva's Hexagon. Moments later, Lecia, Craft and Cildiari approached the kingdom, Gundita was right behind them. Ragnorak and Kaisera them.

"Gundita!" I said excitedly.

"Good to see you again, Ryushin," she bowed.

"Bah, we haven't much time left so it'd be best if we explained the situation at hand," Craft suggested.

"Right this way. We will talk in the Master's Court," Ragnorak said.

All of us, Imperia, Raigen, Evangelista and Olida, entered the throne room, with Ragnorak taking the floor. We all stood there quiet waiting for them to talk. Ragnorak coughed, "Ahem", looking at the four commanders.

"Oh, durh, I knew that," Gundita said, knocking herself in the head.

The four commanders took the stage next to Ragnorak and Kaisera, looking upon us with passion.

"As all of you know," Lecia started, "A big war is about to begin. Based on our reports from our scouts all around the kingdoms, a giant mass of black is heading this direction as we speak."

"That would be the millions of demons," Cildiari added.

"See we don't have quite of an estimate on how many will be attacking the kingdom, this fight may last all day and possibly all night," Lecia said. "We all encourage you to rest as much as you can until they arrive."

"We got less than seventeen hours before they arrive," Gundita informed.

"So much for resting," Mordakai sighed.

"Don't worry so much, we all have come up with a strategy to defend Draconia," Lecia said. "We have four kingdoms here on the defensive end. We will have enough to defeat Atlmaz's army."

"It's not so much as defending Draconia, but protecting Destati from being taken," I said. "There's no telling what kind of plan Atlmaz has up his sleeve."

"We will get to that soon enough," Gundita said.

"For now, we must talk about the groups and assignments we have for each and every one of you," Cildiari insisted.

All night, we honed in on the strategic plan the commanders had come up with. Atlmaz's army can breach the kingdom from three different points- Shiva's Hexagon through the air, Titan's Hexagon through the beach, and Garuda's Hexagon by ground. They saw Atlmaz's plan to create a triangle offense to keep us busy on all sides. Once all of us are completely occupied, then he will attempt to head straight into the kingdom.

They split us up into five different groups -

Team 1- Imperia [Shiva's Hexagon]
Valen, Kirikah, Aeric, Mordakai

Team 2- Raigen [Titan's Hexagon]
Rheaa, Aida, Onry, Ksama

Team 3- Olida [Garuda's Hexagon]
Yoichi, Xamnesces, Rhyona, Zandaris

Team 4- Draconia [Draconia's Castle]

The Adventures of Ryushin

Lecia, Gundita, Cildiari, Craft

Team 5- Support [All around]
Ryushin, Astrae, Ragnorak, Kaisera

Chapter Seventeen
Battle For Destati

There wasn't much time left. The massive black wall was growing in the sky by the second. Ragnorak and Kaisera urged me to finish my training as soon as possible, leaving me no time to recover. After all the training was said and done, I slept for a bit, waking a couple hours before the war starts.

"Ryushin," Kaisera called, as I was strapping the Trueblade to my side.

"Yes?"

"Before you step out onto that field, I want to teach you the art of summoning," she said, "So that if you ever need to escape, your guardians will come to your aid."

"Escape? Trust me; I don't plan on leaving any of you behind."

She smiled, "That's what He said long ago. Anyway, in order for you to perform a summoning, you must concentrate all your mana in your sword. The Trueblade will be your key to performing this hard technique. Concentrate the auras of your dragons- fire, ice, wind and earth, and release it into the air. They will come to your call."

I nodded, "I'll give it a shot."

"Prince Ryushin," Ragnorak called, "They wait for your speech."

A face lit up, "Are you serious? I have to give a damn speech?"

He nodded. "You are the Prince of the Dracolytes."

"Well doesn't that just beat all," I joked. He continued to wait for me. "Oh, fine."

I followed him through the door and up a stairway, all the way up to the highest tower and pulled open a curtain.

"Just say something encouraging," Ragnorak suggested.

I stepped out onto the balcony, meeting with the hundreds of thousands of people standing on the floor, the bridges, and on top of buildings. Aida, Onry, Ksama and Rheaa looked poised at the edge of Titan's Hexagon- Mordakai, Aeric, Valen and Kirikah saluting from Shiva's Hexagon- Yoichi, Xamnesces, Rhyona and Zandaris watching from Garuda's Hexagon- and the four commanders, Lecia, Gundita, Cildiari and Craft with their arms crossed down below on the bridge to the castle.

The sun continued to shine brightly in the night sky. The air was silent and the trees were quiet, only the crashes of the waves along the shores could be heard. The people, Humans and Dracolytes, were calm and focused.

"I don't what to say, Ragnorak," I whispered.

"Just speak what your heart feels," he replied, "You can do it."

I gave a deep breath with my head down, thinking of any encouraging thing to say. All of the events that took place began to come to my mind, especially how I have drastically changed in the short amount of time I've been here. A hand rested softly on my shoulder. I looked back finding my friends- Ralph, Justin, Alex and Jeice, standing there with me.

I smiled and said, "You know, it's been a while since I've been able to relax. Sometimes, all I can think about is home and when I'm going to see it." My voice echoed through the kingdom, using the stars to guide its way all around the people. "When I first came here, I was afraid. Not afraid because of this adventure, this journey that took place, but afraid because I was no one. Then I realized something... We are who we choose to be, not what someone makes of us in there own eyes. To be honest, I am Ryushin yet I am not but I choose to be that one person that everyone wants to see, and that is hope. So all I ask is that you be yourself when you're out there on the battle field, giving it your best."

The crowd started chanting along each other. I can hear them chant, "Ryushin" throughout the kingdom.

"I guess all I'm trying to say is..." They stopped their chant waiting for me to finish. "...let's kick their asses and own their face!" The thousands of people roared fiercely, raising their weapons into the air.

"Not what I had in mind, but it'll do," Ragnorak said.

"What? I'm no hero," I laughed, heading toward the door.

"Not yet you aren't."

As I walked down the stairs, everything became slower in movement, the flicker of the fire on the torches, the sounds of the footsteps offbeat, the loud chanting of the crowds outside echoing. My heart was pumping slowly, knowing that the demons were near.

In the Master's Court, Kaisera and Astrae were waiting for my command.

"I will assist Titan's Hexagon. Ragnorak you stay with the four commanders and do not let anyone pass. Astrae, find Mordakai and assist Shiva's Hexagon. Kaisera, you will assist Yoichi in Garuda's Hexagon," I detailed. "Let's give them a run for their money."

I ran out of the castle and onto the bridge, watching the black mass of demons fly toward us. Pumping my legs with mana, I sprinted into Titan's Hexagon toward the beach. Onry, Aida and Ksama followed closely behind while the troops all around us watched nervously.

We leaped out onto the beach, heading straight on toward the demons. In the distance, thousands of them splashed out of the water, quickly zooming toward us. Leaving the others behind, I channeled the mana in my wings and glided along the surface of the water. Thousands of icicles fell from the sky, pinning some of the demons into the water. I dodged and evaded right through them.

"Ryushin," Onry called.

She slammed her flat hands into the water turning it into a solid icy surface. I pushed off the ice and launched myself into a somersault like a catapult. I slashed my sword out, slashing at the flying demons.

The Adventures of Ryushin

Point of View: Aida

Thousands of flying demons raced passed us and into the cities. I drew my great sword alongside Onry and Ksama. Ryushin took to the sky, fighting in the air. A herd of demons were on the attack. I slammed my heavy blade upon one, crushing it into the ground, and then slashed another away. I gripped my sword with two hands, delivering an uppercut swing to another.

Onry fired bolts of ice in all directions like a gun, shooting down any demon that was coming our way. Ksama vanished in her place and reappeared behind me. She darted her dagger into the air, creating multiple ones as they shot by, tearing through the skin of the demons.

"Aida," Ryushin called.

He swooped downward and grabbed hold of my arm. We took to the sky and into a mob of flying demons. I held my sword out as Ryushin fiercely rotated in a circle. Concentrating my mana, my sword flashed with a holy light, generating a cyclone of energy, burning hundreds of demons to death.

Ryushin released me slowly back onto the beach.

"Everyone together," Onry said, encasing ourselves in a block of ice. With a single push, she blasted thousands of shards in every direction, piercing right through the demons.

"It's not safe to fight here," I said. The demons were outnumbering us all over the beach; we had to retreat back into Titan's Hexagon. I made a break for the city with Ksama and Onry following right behind. Ryushin flew into the city ahead of us.

Rheaa sprang from atop a building, striking demons out of the air. "Kyoufuu!" She fanned her sword upward, netting hundreds of demons in a fierce cutting wind.

"Gyoukou!" I casted, slamming my sword into the ground fiercely. A shockwave of holy light emerged in four different directions, banishing the demons. One of the trade buildings came crashing down in the distance. The demons were ripping this place up too easily; we have to up our defenses a bit.

"Aida, look out!" Onry yelled.

She launched an ice shard, picking the flying demon out of the air. Ksama was pulling sneak attacks off from behind our troops, stabbing demons unknowingly, vanishing and appearing all over the place.

Thousands of demons came storming through the front gate, blowing everything up in sight with energy blasts. Rheaa stood by my side ready to go on the offense. The two of us sprinted toward them, ducking and sidestepping their flying energy balls with our swords grinding against the ground.

Bolts of sharp ice darted from behind, taking out the first wall of demons. Rheaa and I swirled in, chopping any demon that dared to strike. Ksama joined in the attack from behind us with her sneak attack, bouncing from one place to another.

"You know," Rheaa panted, "We can't keep this up forever."

"Don't give up," I said, slashing at multiple of demons. Ksama appeared between us, all of us pressing up against one another's backs. "Let's show them what we can really do."

Rheaa and I hooked arms, holding tightly onto our swords with one hand. "Takuetsufuu!" Rheaa yelled. A cyclone emerged from the ground, spinning us fiercely in a sharp twister, pulling in any demon that was nearby.

Point of View: Mordakai

"That is a shitload of demons," I cried.

Aeric, Valen and Kirikah were hopping of buildings, away from the flock of demons that just pulled in. Astrae jumped onto my shoulders with his arms crossed.

"What are you doing just standing here?" he asked.

"Dude, we're getting owned," I said, watching the demons circling us.

"So, why don't you do something about it?"

The Adventures of Ryushin

"I can't beat all of these ugly things. There's way too many," I said, "And the others fled to the other side of the hexagon."

"Are you not paying attention? You're on the back side of the hexagon. The demons are flying in from the Airstation. They're heading there to fend them off."

"Oh, well, let's head to the Airstation then."

Astrae flashed a bright light, banishing the demons around us, and then took to the sky. I moved quickly behind him, hopping from building to building, smashing demon faces in with my hand axes.

I landed onto the ground, running into a thick wall of demons trying to get into the Airstation. I sharpened the blades of my axes up against one another, drawing their attention.

"Taka no Hane!"

I launched both axes right down the center, creating my cutter energy attack. The two discs pulled closer into each other creating one giant cutter, slicing through the wall of demons and opening a path for me to go through. I called my axes back, ready to fight the approaching group.

Three were on the attack. I dodged their consecutive claws, landing counter attacks with my axes. More jumped into the fight. Clinching my axes together in both hands, I batted a demon up against a pile of them, knocking them onto their backs. A bright light showered atop of them, killing them.

"You're taking too long," Astrae said.

Valen and Kirikah were flying out of the sky, riding on top of the backs of demons with thrilled looks on their faces. Aeric raised his hands into the air and yelled, "Kinbaku!" He yanked down several demons with his binding spell, slashing at them as they fell from the sky.

"Hey Mordakai, check this out," Valen said.

Aeric used his Motatsuku spell to slow down the movements of the demons. Kirikah lunged from her ride to Valen, grabbing hold of his arm. Valen rotated her around in the air, delivering strong kicks to the incoming demons. He then sharply tossed Kirikah downward toward a building. She pulled out her short blade, swinging at the demons that were flying upward.

"You show offs," I grunted.

"You guys, they're trying to destroy the airships," Aeric informed. "I wonder why though? We're not going anywhere."

"Who cares? Don't let them destroy the airships anyway," I said.

Valen and Kirikah joined up with us again. "Alright, that sounds like a bet to me."

"Betting at this time?" Aeric asked.

"I'm in, what's the wager?" I agreed.

"See how many demons we can round up," Valen said. He dodged a punch from a demon, sending it back with a back fist. "Aeric and Mordakai versus me and Kirikah, deal? After this is all said in done, I say losers pay for lunch."

"Deal," I responded.

"I don't know about this…" Aeric sighed.

"Go!" Valen said, heading for the airships with Kirikah.

I ran toward the airships behind the others punching Aeric in the shoulder, "Come on, it's free lunch!"

Point of View: Yoichi

Xamnesces and I tried our best to keep them out of the residential hexagon, firing and blasting fire and shadow attacks, but they grew by the number, turning the sky completely black. I couldn't see the stars anymore.

"They're rushing us," Xamnesces said.

"Hinotama!" I yelled, destroying a line of demons with a powerful fireball.

"Kogasu," Xamnesces said. The leftover fire from my fireball spread out along the demons, burning them out of the sky. Xamnesces waved his hand back and forth, burning as much as he can.

The Adventures of Ryushin

Demons flew overheard, ignoring our presence, ripping the rooftops off of the Dracolyte's homes. A large vine whipped them off of the houses. Rhyona was conducting the vines from underneath the soil with trees near by, while Zandaris was defending her with brute force.

An aurora wave of light wiped the sky of the demons, allowing the sun to shine through, but was quickly eclipsed once again by the numerous amounts of demons. Kaisera glided downward toward us while Xamnesces and I continued to attack.

"Kaisera, they're growing too fast," I cried. "We don't have as much force as they do."

"I noticed," she replied. "I think they're trying to zerg as much as possible."

"Then they will unleash the beast to take advantage," Xamnesces added. "That's what I predicted as well."

"If we keep this up, we'll be out of mana by the time Atlmaz strikes with stronger forces," I said.

"We must do our best to hold them out of the castle," Kaisera encouraged. "I will not leave your sides."

I gathered power from within my body and converted it to an outward explosion, blasting away demons around us with a crawling wave of fire. Xamnesces followed up with multiple shadow balls, destroying the second coming.

Point of View: Ryushin

I swooped out of the air and toward the bridge filled with demons, connecting to the castle door. Suddenly, the demons were banished away at the spark of a strong holy light. Nomak and Chrisa were dusting their armor off, emerging from the pile of demons.

"Nomak," I called, landing right next to him.

"What are you doing here, Scrub? You're supposed to be assisting the Titan Hexagon," he said.

"I just came to check on the bridge," I answered.

"We have this place covered, Ryushin," Chrisa informed. "Aida needs your help. I suggest you return to her side as soon as possible."

Hundreds of demons approached the bridge from the air. Nomak took his hammer and batted away at them. "All of them are scrubs. I can take on this whole army by myself if I wanted."

Knowing that they couldn't get passed Nomak and Chrisa, the demons slammed fist first into the water and through the ground.

"They're gonna enter from underground, Nomak," I said.

"Bah, who cares? They don't stand a chance against the Commanders anyhow," he laughed.

"Ryushin, go now," Chrisa snapped. I took to the sky, quickly growing weaker. I was too worn out to fly any longer. I returned to Titan's Hexagon on foot, slashing through demons in my path.

Into Titan's Hexagon I entered, finding Aida and the others surrounded by hundreds of mobs. Most of the troops were defeated already in this hexagon. It would be for the best for them to retreat to Nomak and Chrisa.

"Aida!" I called.

I hurled my blade toward their direction, rotating it in a circle with my mana. The blade sliced right through the demons surrounding them, giving them a chance to rest.

They were worn out, breathing heavily and their armor scratched and torn. I stepped forward in front of them, blasting an energy beam with one hand. The beam burned right down the center of the incoming mobs.

"Ryushin, there are way too many," Aida said.

"I know. I want you all to retreat back to the castle," I insisted. "I'll try and slow them down here."

"No," Onry said. She stepped forward, determined to fight with everything she had. "If we back down now, this whole attempt to defend this block would be meaningless. I'm not about ready to give up just yet."

Rheaa agreed, gripping her sword tightly with two hands.

"Onry…" I sighed. "Alright then, together we will take the Titan Hexagon."

For hours on end, we continued to fight against the relentless horde of demons, endless slicing, energy blasting, jumping, running, hurting. It was probably the longest fight I've ever put up and it seems like it wasn't going to end. The Titan's Hexagon was pretty much obliterated on all ends, taken in by the demons force.

Onry, Rheaa, Aida and Ksama were forced to retreat toward the bridge, where more demons were ganging up on Nomak and Chrisa. I stood strong alongside of them, continuing to defend as much as possible.

Demons would fly in, launching dark energy attacks into the buildings, bringing them down to the ground. The whole front side of the kingdom was up in flames for we failed to defend the entrance.

"We don't have much coverage," I said. "If there was only some way to take them out in mass numbers rather than a swing of a sword, then we would be able to turn this fight around."

"Rheaa and Onry are giving it their best shot, give some consideration," Ksama said.

"No, he's right," Rheaa said. "They're taking us out from the sky. It's almost impossible to separate them if they overlap us like this."

"I got an idea, but I need some time to gather power," I said.

Everyone looked at me surprised.

"You have a trick up your sleeve?" Rheaa asked.

"Of course. I need you guys to defend me. I need to concentrate on this as much as possible. This is actually the first time I'm attempting to pull this off, so pray that it works."

Everyone staggered to the floor.

"You better be right about this one," Ksama said.

All six of them moved arms apart, ready to protect me. I took my sword, held on tightly, and motioned it slowly down to my side. I can hear the vibe of the blade echo throughout my soul. I was getting too distracted by their fighting so I closed my eyes.

"Come on, concentrate," I whispered. Four different colors began to grow in the darkest of my mind- a snowflake of blue, a leaf of green, a stone of brown and a flame of red. I lifted the point of my sword to all of the colors, tapping them one at a time. My sword left a line mark in a certain formation, could it be the technique of summoning?

I opened my eyes, slashing my sword in a diagonal upward across my chest, slowly moving the blade over head back to the right, slashing quickly downward across my legs. I swung upward, grabbing the sword by the handle with both hands, positioning it horizontally aligned with my eyes, looking straight forward.

"Ryushin, hurry up!" Aida cried.

One of the demons knocked her flat onto her back, racing toward me with its sharp claw raised. I skewered the point of my sword forward into the heart of the demon and twisted it. A bright light exploded from within and wrapped all around the blade of the sword. I took the sword and hurled it high into the sky, opening a large hole in the demon wall.

The bright light caught everyone's' attention, watching the sword zoom into the stars. I raised my right arm into the air, holding onto my forearm with my left, concentrating my mana to the sword.

The sword flashed once, then twice before plummeting downward. I can hear the warcry of the dragons ripping through the air, growing closer and closer. Out from the flashing light came Shiva, nose diving toward Draconia. Garuda and Titan were to follow closely behind. Ifrit, lit up in flames, burning through the sky like a missile.

"A summoning?" Aida asked.

I nodded.

The Adventures of Ryushin

The four dragons blasted countless numbers of demons out of the sky with their elemental breaths, allowing the stars and sun to shine through. Shiva, Titan, Ifrit and Garuda then flew sharply down to us.

"Rheaa, Onry, let's go. The rest of you defend the bridge," I commanded. The three of us sprinted along the bridge, swatting demons off our trail. Titan lifted me up with his nose and onto his back. Shiva picked up Onry while Garuda took hold of Rheaa.

"Ryushin, look," Chrisa called.

In the sky, we could see the head of a giant beast far off in the distance. It was slowly creeping its way through the ocean and heading for the shores. The demon was humongous, with muscular arms and a strong looking upper body. It had tiny legs. It was wearing a golden neckpiece with big diamonds on it, a crown on its head with long horns sticking out of it, and a big loincloth to cover its midsection.

Rheaa, Onry and I took to the sky on the back of the dragons, only to be confronted by Linwe on her black crow.

"Ryushin, long time, no see," she smirked.

"So, one of Atlmaz's goons decides to show themselves," I replied, "Where is Atlmaz anyway, not here to fight his own battles?"

"Atlmaz is as deep within the castle, better than any of you nubs would know," she said. "Why, he might even be near Destati by now."

"That's a bluff. He could never make it passed the Commanders," I said.

"Better think again, Dracolyte," she laughed.

I grinned. She may be right, Atlmaz may be in the castle and we might not even know it. I had no choice but to fly back down to Aida.

"Aida, I need you and Ksama to head to the shrine and check on Destati," I said.

"But why?"

"No time for questions. We might just be in trouble."

She nodded. Ksama and Aida made a break for the closed door to the castle. Once open, the two went inside. Titan hoisted me back into the air to confront Linwe, but she was gone.

"Ryushin, we have to stop that giant from reaching Draconia," Onry said.

"I know, we'll have to come back later," I answered. "Ifrit, find Yoichi in Garuda's Hexagon and bring her here. This is gonna be a hard one."

Point of View: Mordakai

"Aeric!" I yelled.

"What is it now?" he grunted.

"You're not binding them up fast enough!"

Valen and Kirikah had a whole bunch of demons rounded up, enough to make a hill. I sighed sadly, knowing that I lost the bet. Astrae blasted the hill of demons away, bonking Valen on the head.

"Hey, what was that for?" Valen growled.

"This is no time for games," Astrae said. "We have to refuge at the bridge to Draconia, seems the Titan Hexagon was overtaken."

"What about Shiva's Hexagon?" Kirikah asked.

"We have to forget about it. Preventing them from breaching the castle walls is more important right now. I'll be waiting for you at the bridge."

Astrae took off into the sky.

"Alright, Mordakai," Valen said, dusting his hands together, "You owe us lunch."

I walked away. Just then, a giant sword slammed into the ground in front of me, Before me was a gigantic, armored giant. Its armor was blue and rough like the surface of a crab's shell. It had no eyes, just a black empty space in its helmet, but it did have the smallest, thinnest legs I've ever seen, smaller than mine. The giant swatted me into Aeric with the flat of its blade.

"What the hell, Mordakai?" Aeric shouted.

I dusted myself off. "It was that thing, right there."

The giant crept closer. It swung downward. Kirikah bubbled us with her shield, preventing the giant from damaging us. The bubble looked like it was about to pop. All of us scrammed in opposite directions away from the iron giant.

The demons left the Shiva's Hexagon, allowing the Iron Giant to do its work. Aeric and I hid behind an airship while Valen and Kirikah ran into a building.

"How the hell are we supposed to beat this thing?" I asked.

"Looks like we're going to have to break through its armor," Aeric answered.

"Are you crazy? Look at that thing. I'd be better off crushing my axes through brick walls."

"Okay then genius, you tell me what we're going to do."

"Nevermind."

I rushed around the corner of the ship, launching a full on attack from behind. Lunging into the air, I slammed the blade of one of my axes upon its back. The attack reflected off of its armor, vibrating all over my arm and my body. The giant turned around slowly. I dived to the side, evading the giant's attack.

I couldn't help but run back to Aeric in hiding.

"Way to go," Aeric chuckled. "You sure put a dent in that thing."

"Shut up! I'd like to see you attack that thing," I insisted. The giant's sword ripped through the airship between me and Aeric.

"Kinbaku!" Aeric casted.

His power wrapped around the giant's tiny legs, causing it to fall off balance. Valen and Kirikah jumped from the building window, darting smaller daggers at it.

"You idiots, that's not going to do anything!" I yelled, watching the daggers bounce right off the giant. The giant launched itself up into the air grabbing its sword with two hands. "Oh shit," I cried as it aimed for me.

"Otoroeru!" Aeric casted. I raised my axes in time to block the weakened attack. "Chokusha." Aeric palmed his free hand, blasting the giant away from me with a light energy attack.

"Dude, this sucks," I whined.

"There has to be a way to beat that thing," Aeric thought.

"It's coming back!" Kirikah shrieked.

"Run!" I screamed, racing passed the others and into hiding once again. The others split up in all different directions.

Point of View: Rhyona

Ifrit swooped down and took Yoichi onto his back, leaving me, Xamnesces and Zandaris to fight for Garuda's Hexagon. Kaisera was still here fighting with us. Suddenly, all of the demons fled away from the area. Zandaris let down his guard while I reverted back from my cat form.

Xamnesces approached us in a hurry. "You might want to get to higher ground," he said.

In the distance, we both heard a calamity of some sort, like a train was bulldozing everything in its tracks. As the sound got closer, so did the destruction. Homes were flying into pieces in the air, trees slamming outward and smoke trailing in the distance. Frightened, Zandaris and I jumped onto one of the rooftops of the houses. Xamnesces followed shortly.

"What the hell is that noise?" I asked.

"That would be the sound of a demon beast wrecking everything in its way," Xamnesces answered. "It doesn't care who's in its way, demon or human, it just wants to bash everything into pieces."

The Adventures of Ryushin

A giant purple beast with long curved horns raised half of its body into the air then slammed downward causing a tremendous force quake, rumbling some houses to the ground.

Zandaris thought for a moment. "That would be a behemoth."

"We have to stop it from going on a rampage," Kaisera said, gliding downward to us. "If it were to reach the castle, there's no telling how far its destruction will go."

Xamnesces launched a shadow ball toward the rampaging beast, exploding on contact. The smoke cleared, barely leaving a mark on its rough skin. Xamnesces attempted one more time.

The behemoth roared fiercely in our direction, causing tremendous pillars of fire to burst from underneath us. All of us retreated away from the rooftop of the house, avoiding the giant blazing fire.

Charging with full force, Behemoth caught Zandaris off guard. It catapulted him high into the air, using the side of one of its long sharp horns. I conducted a vine, latching it around Zandaris' ankle. Behemoth performed a tailwhip and dragged the vine with full force, wrenching us into a burning building.

Kaisera levitated between the fires, extinguishing them with her light power. Xamnesces continued to fire shadow balls, only further annoying it.

"Does this thing have a weakness?" I asked.

"It doesn't look like it," Kaisera said, shaking her head.

Just then, Zandaris caught a glimpse of something. The more I honed my eyes in on the giant beast, the more I can notice it as well. The lower waist of Behemoth was rather thin than any normal beast.

"Maybe we can snap the best in half," Zandaris suggested. "But we're gonna need it to hold still."

"How do you suggest we do that?" I asked.

"You're gonna have to use every root in this area to tie it down to the ground," he answered.

"But that blaze burned almost everything up."

"Well then, search deeper. There has to be some plant life down there."

I leaped downward to the ground, hoping that the behemoth did not see me. I gently rested the palm of my hands onto the ground, feeling the life underneath. It was faint, but it was there.

"I need time to gather them all together. They're way deep," I called. Kaisera and Zandaris nodded, heading out to help Xamnesces fight. I concentrated my mana as fast as I could, seeking out any available root or vine strong enough to tie the behemoth down.

Kaisera hovered over the behemoth, evading its snapping jaw and countering with light energy beams. Xamnesces continued to pick at the beast with every attack he could pull out of its arsenal. He tried shadow balls to dark waves of energy. It just didn't do enough to hold out. Zandaris was on the ground provoking it away from the other two with an awkward dance.

Zandaris started rushing over to my direction.

"Are you almost done yet?" he yelled from afar. He turned the corner sharply, heading straight for a house. I triggered the attack, raising a vast amount of vines from behind the behemoth. One vine latched onto one of its hind legs. A couple of more roped around the behemoth's upper legs, crawling to its waist.

"Zandaris, it's not working," I called. The behemoth was still too lively for the vines to hold it down. Enraged, the behemoth broke free of the vines' grasp, continuing to charge head on toward Zandaris. He rolled to the side, avoiding the sharp horns of the beast. Behemoth retaliated, catapulting him again with the side of its long horn.

I used the vines to break his fall. Xamnesces and Kaisera attacked with consecutive energy blasts. The behemoth, charging head on, rammed its way through the explosions with its head lowered. I tangled as many vines as I could around the neck of the beast, using its rampage to its disadvantage. The vines clutched downward, forcing the behemoth to nose dive.

"Do it now!" Zandaris yelled.

Kaisera and Xamnesces charged up power into their attacks. Behemoth roared fiercely, blasting pillars of fire out of the ground again. The two broke concentration, moving out of the way of the attack. The vines burned off around its neck, setting it free again.

I grunted, "Stupid dog. We have to try it again. We almost had it."

Point of View: Gundita

I sprinted smoothly across the side of the wall, escaping the Giant Eye's laser beam. Craft and Cildiari blasted the white of the eye with multiple fireballs and ice bolts. Nothing was working on this damn beast. I believe it was the lack of teamwork involved in the matter.

"Cildiari, stop cooling down the heat of my pyroblasts," Craft whined.

She responded, "Well, you stop burning up the frost from my ice attacks."

The two of them have been going at it the whole fight, it was ridiculous. Lecia and I were practically the only ones damaging the giant eye. Other than that, Ragnorak was nowhere to be found either.

I pushed off the wall, flipping onto the ground and rushing straight for the unguarded eye. I slashed out my two swords from my side ready to strike. Lecia popped out of hiding with her crossbow armed, locked and ready to go.

"Hamaya!" Lecia casted, triggering the crossbow. The arrowbolt spun keenly in a perfect straight line through the air, creating a wind tunnel around it. I stepped in from behind, cutting and slashing away at the white. The arrowbolt pierced right through the pupil, expanding it from the inside with the force of wind. The eye exploded, leaving an icky mess all over the room.

The four of us gathered around the minced eye, splattered all over the ground. The pieces began to melt into millions of smaller eyes with tentacles attached to their bottoms.

"Talk about seeing eye to eye," I joked.

The little eyes were no joke to be playing around with. As soon as one eye blasted a laser out of its pupil, so did the rest. We jumped apart from each other, dodging the obstacles of burning lasers all around the room.

Craft jumped into the air, hurling a flat bed of fire among the eyes, while Cildiari froze them over with a thick blanket of mist. The most Lecia and I could do was squash them to death under our boots.

The rest of the leftover eyes gathered together, fusing back into the giant eye. It launched an even greater laser than before. Lecia and I took cover behind a pillar on the second floor while Craft and Cildiari hid behind a pillar on the first floor.

"Hey!" Craft called out to us.

"What is it?" Lecia responded.

"Got any ideas?"

"There's always the old-fashioned bum-rush," I suggested.

The giant eye crawled through the room, searching for our whereabouts. It had no ears, making it impossible for it to hear out movements, but its vision was very sharp, catching any sudden movements in the corner of its eye.

"It's been too long since we've been working together," Lecia panted.

"Come on, we communicate all the time on the large screens," Cildiari said.

"Tell me about it," I agreed, "Our teamwork was unmatchable back then, remember?" Lecia nodded.

"Oh quiet. You act as if we've aged that much," Craft said.

"Let's give it the Four Corners technique, what do ya say?" I suggested.

"Think it'll work?" Lecia asked.

"We just have to get in position, and then it's time to own."

Point of View: Ryushin

I zoomed through the night sky on the back of Titan, gliding up against the water toward the demon king. The demon grew larger in size the closer I approached it. Each step that it took created a giant ripple to block our path. But that didn't stop me.

Rheaa, Onry and Yoichi shot forward ahead of me, drifting upward toward the head of the demon. I remained low to the water due to Titan's disability to fly higher.

The demon king attempted to knock them aside with its enormous forearm. The dragons swirled and twisted around the arm easily, too fast for it to keep up. Onry and Yoichi countered with ice shards and fireballs to the upper body.

"Incoming, get ready," I called.

Hundreds of demons attacked from behind. Rheaa dropped from Garuda's back, performing her Kyoufuu wind attack. The wind blades cut through several of them. I jumped toward Garuda, switching places with Rheaa. The demon king swung a backhand. Timing the attack, I jumped off Garuda and onto the demon king's arm.

Swarms of demons flew in. I charged sluggishly toward the demons while the king slowly raised its arm. A demon slashed downward with its claw. I countered with a cut straight through its body, gashing away another to the side. Another demon grabbed hold of my arm. I yanked it backward, countering with a backslash to its neck. Onry's ice shards and Yoichi's fireballs blasted the others away. The demon king raised its other open claw.

"Ryushin," Rheaa called.

Titan sprang into the air as high as he could. I dropped from the air in time to avoid the demon king's hand. Rheaa lunged onto the other arm of the demon king, switching places with me.

The four dragons did their best to keep the swarms of demons off our tails, using their elemental breaths. More swarms of demon began to pile in the air. The demon king grabbed a hand full and darted them toward us. Onry blocked all of them with a shield of ice and Yoichi with her fire wall. Titan glided quickly along the waters, avoiding the kamikaze demons.

Rheaa hacked away at the neck of the demon king. It tried to flick her away. Garuda swooped down in time, snatching her out of the attack.

The demon king held its arms out wide. With a quick spin, it created a cylinder of dark energy around it, blasting all of us out of the sky. I jolted through the water off of Titan's back. Rheaa and the others soon followed.

Demons plunged into the water after us. Countering their assault, I blew up each and every one of them with an energy blast. Rheaa slashed away at her oncoming demons with her long blade, while Onry and Yoichi swam to the top.

Rheaa and I were quickly picked up by Garuda. Shiva and Ifrit returned to Onry and Yoichi. A flock of demons were on Titan's tail. I grabbed hold of Rheaa's arm and chucked her downward toward him. Titan sprang up, leading them into Rheaa. She swiped her sword through all of them with her velocity. Titan glided back downward quickly, catching her on his back.

"This giant isn't gonna let us get anywhere near its body," I said.

Onry and Yoichi's power wasn't near enough to take down this overgrown demon. There had to be a way to destroy this thing in a single blow. I had no choice. I tucked my hands down to my side in a form of a cup, gathering energy from within. Spotting an opening, I launched my

The Adventures of Ryushin

Kagayaku Hikari beam upward. Just then, a giant wing wrapped around the body of the demon, blocking my attack. The giant wing expanded open, striking me off the back of Garuda.

"Ryushin," Rheaa called again.

She grabbed my arm and swung me back upward onto Garuda's back. The four of us were on the run from multiple swarms. The demons were growing smarter in their tactics, using energy blasts to try and knock us out of the air.

The four dragons came together, crossing paths one by one. We switched positions, attacking demons on the switch. Rheaa switched with Onry, and then I switched with Yoichi. The demon king continued to wave its giant arm around. Most of our concentration was on getting away from the swarms.

"Ifrit," I commanded. Ifrit blasted a flamethrower out of its mouth toward a pack of demons. I hurled my sword within the fire, conducting it with my mana and circled the sword all around us, cutting and burning the demons. I called for my sword. Ifrit shot upward toward the upper body of the demon king.

The demon king attempted to grab us out of the air. Ifrit dove downward toward the water with the giant claw on our tails.

"Ryushin," both Yoichi and Onry called. They blasted the hand with their elemental attacks.

Shiva and Rheaa combine their elemental attacks, creating a fierce blizzard all around them. The ice storm vacuumed up multiple swarms, tearing away at their bodies with sharp icicles.

"Let's try this one more time," I said to Ifrit. The red dragon summoned up a blaze around its tail, gaining momentum. The demon king launched an attack with its claw. I evaded in time, leaping onto its arm. "Cover me!" I yelled out to the others. I slowly ran up the rising arm while Onry and Yoichi blasted the demons away, giving me time to make it up to its shoulder.

I drilled the tip of my sword through the thick skin of the demon, ripping a cut open. The Trueblade released a light aura within the cut, causing the demon king to burn from the inside. It counterattacked. I darted toward the oncoming claw sharply, slashing right through. Ifrit caught my fall and flew downward. The sliced off claw fell to the water, knocking swarms of demons with it.

"Ryushin, we're running out of time," Rheaa said.

"Don't worry. We can do this," I replied.

Point of View: Aida

Ksama and I made a break for the crumbling door. The room behind us collapsed, continuing to rupture the walls of the hall we just entered.

"Why was this so much easier without the obstacles?" Ksama asked.

Both of us jumped from the falling staircase, grabbing hold of a ledge. We pulled ourselves up, taking a deep sigh of relief.

"I know what you mean. It seemed so easy walking through everything," I answered.

A pack of demons came flying in.

Ksama and I easily booted them out of the way. We then made a break for the next door. Suddenly, a dark energy blast exploded out in front, causing the ledge to crumble.

"Aida!" Ksama cried.

As we were falling, I drilled my sword into the wall to catch our fall. Ksama grabbed hold of my arm. I pulled her up to ledge, and then she helped me up. I took my sword out of the wall, continuing on down the ledge.

The castle walls started to shift erratically, creating an awkward path for us to step. We jumped from step to step toward the next door. Another energy blast exploded above us and the top of the castle tower came crumbling down upon us.

"Ksama, quick, we have to move downward."

We both climbed down in a hurry, racing against the falling chunk of stone. The erratic ledge gave us time to move cautiously.

"Here it comes!" Ksama cried, looking up.

"Don't look up!" I shouted. We both hit the bottom as far as we could. We dove to the ground and barely escaped the stone.

"Are you okay?" I asked.

The smoke cleared, revealing a new path for us to follow. The large stone blocked off the previous path, so we had no choice but to move forward. We rushed as fast as we could through the shaking room, avoiding falling debris from the ceiling.

Demons emerged from the ground but Ksama and I bulldozed right through and into the next room.

"There are demons from underground?" Ksama asked.

I nodded.

"Ryushin knew that Atlmaz had some sort of trick to bypassing the fight. We have to hurry to the shrine before he gets there."

I raised my sword, cutting a lock off a shut door and busted through. The land underneath us started to shift apart, some parts rising and some parts lowering. I slashed my sword upward with an energy attack, opening a hole for me to shoot through. Ksama climbed right after.

We were out in the night sky again. Demons flew in, swinging their claws as the passed by. Ksama and I didn't mind them and continued to run down the path.

"We're almost there," I panted, "We can do it."

Ksama and I reached the courtyard with the long stairway plunging downward. The courtyard was filled with Dracolytes and demons, clashing near the bottom of the tower.

"Oh no, we're too late!" Ksama wept.

I ran down the long stairway, Ksama followed shortly. Demons emerged from the steps, blocking our path. Before I could strike, the stairs broke apart in sections, separating me and Ksama. The demons climb to our steps.

"Hikari!" I casted, blasting the first wave of demons. More continued to pile onto my step. I thrusted my sword downward, delivering an uppercut through two demons. I rotated once more, rising into a flying uppercut, blasting a wave of energy out from my blade, slicing right down the middle.

Ksama bounced from step to step, avoiding the demons as much as possible. Their claw attacks would carry themselves into each other, making it easy for Ksama. She jumped high into the air, darting her dagger downward.

"Dokubari!" Ksama yelled.

The dagger split into multiple daggers, dropping upon the demons like rain.

I jumped off the step, bouncing on top of the demons heads. Ksama followed closely behind with the same tactic.

"Not far, we're almost there," I said, running through the crowd of clashing Dracolytes and demons. The battleground seemed so much larger than it did when it was empty. It seemed like I was running for miles toward the tower.

"There, Aida!" Ksama called.

A young man in a dark robe was walking through the crowd. That had to be Atlmaz. The Dracolytes tried to stop him, but he easily cut them down with his scythe.

"Atlmaz!" I called.

He turned around slowly. He had this sick evil look on his face.

"Look at his eyes," Ksama said.

His eyes were a dark shade of purple, emitting an evil presence from inside. He raised his hand slowly into the air, licking his lips. With great power, a dark light rose from beneath the ground, causing an explosion all around us. The ground cracked into pieces, shifting the area awkwardly. I shielded my eyes from the intense light.

The Adventures of Ryushin

Once the smoke cleared, the area was quiet. Everything was still. Atlmaz cleared the area of demons and Dracolytes with one attack. Ksama sat there frightened. He was gone.

"Let's go, Ksama," I said.

The two of us ran up the empty stairway to the top of the shrine. Inside, we found Atlmaz waiting for us. I clutched my sword tightly.

He grinned wickedly.

"Atlmaz, how did you get through everyone?" I asked.

"I'm too smart for those incompetent fools," he answered. "Though I would like to figure out how you were able to break free of my Kenboushou. My dark will is too powerful for a weakling like you to ever comprehend."

"Easily, I believed in the goodness of my heart," I answered, "the true path of a paladin."

He laughed.

"You honestly believe that you can defeat me?"

I remained poised. "I will do the best I can to stop you."

He opened his hand, emitting a dark familiar energy. I dropped my sword and grabbed my head with both hands. The pain was building deep from within.

"You heart is still hollow enough for me to consume it."

"Aida..." Ksama cried.

"Kenboushou!" Atlmaz casted.

The pain grew deeper inside. All of the dark memories I remember from before started to breathe life again. A dark purple flame encased around me, discharging a dark presence.

"Aida! Don't let him do this to you," Ksama said.

She took her dagger and sprinted toward him. He raised his arm and delivered a backhand to the side of her head. She grinded, shoulder first, into the ground.

"Ryushin..." I called.

Atlmaz grunted, "That guy again? This time he's not here to save you."

I closed my eyes, trying my hardest to resist. It was nearly impossible to bounce the dark aura back. My legs grew weaker, dropping me down to one knee.

I can feel Ksama trying to help me up. I tried to hold back but my body was out of control. I pulled my arm back and swatted her away.

"Aida..."

A familiar voice called out to me. In the darkness of my mind, Ayaka approached slowly toward me.

"Ayaka...?"

"Be strong," she said. "Be strong here."

She placed her hand gently over her heart, unleashing a white light from within. The light wrapped around my body, renewing my cuts and scratch marks all over my body. The blood that dripped from my lip cleared and the power within me grew stronger.

I opened my eyes, standing up to Atlmaz. The dark flame around me transformed to a white flame. Atlmaz was surprised. The flame grew bigger, sending out a shockwave in all directions.

Atlmaz laughed.

I picked up my sword, aiming the point of the blade to him. "Let's go." Ksama got to her feet, joining my side.

Atlmaz thought for a second. "I guess I have some time to play with you both." He twirled his scythe down to his side.

Ksama and I spread out.

Atlmaz glided swiftly along the ground with a shadow trailing behind him. Flashes of dark lightning jolted out of his body, protecting him from any physical attacks. Atlmaz attacked.

"I'll teach you," he said, swinging downward. The sharp blade of his scythe collided with my sword, sending sparks throughout the shrine.

"Aida," Ksama called. She vanished, appearing behind me. She struck Atlmaz twice in the arm with her dagger. He flinched back, and then continued to glide against the floor. "No blood?"

"That was a little too easy, don't you think?" I asked.

Atlmaz came again.

I swung heavily from the side. He glided around my attack, countering with a swing of his own. Pulling my sword back, our weapons collided again. This time, a trail of lightning crawled from his blade and shocked my arms. Ksama ducked under, delivering a kick to his stomach. Following through, I slammed my sword into the ground, sending a shockwave of light energy. Atlmaz glided out of the way.

"Nakkura," Atlmaz said. The shrine transformed into a black void.

Ksama and I moved on the offensive. I swayed my sword side to side, ready to strike. Atlmaz twirled his scythe from left to right, preventing us from attacking inside.. Ksama took the challenge. She evaded inside the spinning scythe and found an opening. She poked away at Atlmaz's stomach. I lunged into the air, delivering a hard blow to his shoulder with my sword. All he did was flinch back with a smile.

"What is going on?" I asked, watching him continue to glide along the black. Our attacks didn't seem to have an effect on him.

He hooked his scythe in a circle, pulling the black inward. As the black peeled off of the shrine, it began to explode all around us.

Ksama and I jerked onto the floor, taking the hit. We both struggled to our feet just as Atlmaz attack. He swung with his scythe. I blocked with my sword. He retaliated quickly, hooking his scythe around my waist and tossed me up against a pillar. Atlmaz glided swiftly over to me with his hand palmed.

"Suneku Kage," he casted. Dark energy formed in his hand.

Surprisingly, Ksama struck him from behind. Unguarded, I gripped my sword and fiercely bashed him away from us. Still our attacks weren't damaging him enough.

"We're never gonna win at this rate, Aida," Ksama said.

"I know, but I can't find a way to defeat him," I answered. "His skin is as hard as rock."

"We gotta think of something fast or its lights out for us."

Atlmaz glided in circles around us, laughing wickedly. Ksama and I poised ready, waiting for him to come. He lowered his shoulder and bolted toward us with intense speed.

Point of View: Mordakai

I stood low with my back up against a wall, hiding from the iron giant that was creeping around the corner. Aeric, Valen, Kirikah and I tried our best to slow the monster down, but our attacks and techniques weren't doing jack squat.

Coming out of hiding, I rushed the iron giant head on with my axes lowered at my sides. It chopped downward with its heavy sword. I sidestepped. Aeric wrapped around the corner and tied its tiny legs up with his binding spell. I rose up above the stumbling monster, crushing the sharp blade of my axe against its armor. The iron giant struck back, slamming the flat of his sword against my body like a ping pong.

"Mordakai," Kirikah called, wrapping her bubble shield around me.

I caught my fall and continued to rush relentlessly at the giant. I hurled my left axe, dinging off the armor of the giant's body high into the air.

Valen appeared in front of me.

"Alley-oop," Valen said, catapulting me into the air. I flashed down faster than lightning, hacking away with a couple of blows to the iron giant's face. My left axe fell back into my hand, emitting a red powerful light. I thrusted both of my axes forward and swiped the helmet of the monster off.

"Whoa, look at that," Aeric said. I retreated back to his position.

The iron giant had no head underneath its helmet. All of us stood around it, wondering what it was. It scrambled to its knees, swaying its hand back and forth, looking for its helmet.

"Don't let up," I panted. "If we're gonna beat this thing, we have to blitz it as much as possible."

I continued to attack.

Regardless of it being headless or not, the iron giant took hold of its sword, swirling it wide. I jumped backward, just in time to avoid the attack. The head on the ground could still see us.

"Hey, check this out," Valen chuckled. He punted the helmet into the sky. "Anyone want to play?" Kirikah somersaulted into the air, kicking it back downward. The helmet cracked on the ground, causing the giant's body to flop.

That gave me an idea.

"Valen, kick it over here," I called.

He booted the helmet in me. I rotated, holding tightly onto my axes clasped together, I batting the helmet fiercely into a wall.

"Hey!" Aeric cried.

The body of the giant was on hot pursuit after Aeric. He hopped from the ground onto the top of a building, escaping heavy blows from the giant's sword. Aeric casted his Otoroeru spell, preventing the sword from damaging him. He then fired his Chokusha attack into the midsection, blasting it feet away from him.

"I don't think there's any possible way to beat this thing," Kirikah said.

"No way," I said. "Just you watch, I'll put a crack in this monster's face."

"You better hurry, Astrae is probably waiting for us at the bridge," Valen said. "Sounds like a bet, wanna play?"

"What's the bet?" I asked.

"I'll give you a chance to redeem yourself. Take down the giant and you won't have to owe us lunch," Valen explained.

"You're on." I rushed recklessly toward the helmet, punting it into the air and batted it toward the body of the giant, knocking it away from Aeric.

"I owe you one," Aeric cried.

The giant screwed its helmet back on. I lowered both of my axes to my sides and gathered energy from within, pushing as much energy into my attack as I could. A red light surrounded both axes.

"I hope you're watching this one, Valen," I said.

The iron giant rushed with its sword raised into the air. Aeric casted his Motatsuku spell, slowing its movement down drastically. This time it was too slow to evade my attack.

It swung its sword downward, creating a tremor. I snapped my arms forward, launching the two axes. "Taka no Hane!" They formed together, creating its giant disc of energy.

"Kinbaku!" Aeric casted.

The giant stumbled forward with its legs caught in Aeric's binding spell. My attack slammed through the helmet, cracking it right down the center. It didn't stop there. The energy disc carried further into the giant's head, crashing straight down the center of the giant's body and splitting through the legs. The two halves slowly picked apart before exploding with incredible force.

The smoke cleared and we've become victorious. We all huddled together, applauding to our victory.

"Good job, but you still lost the bet," Valen said.

I shocked. "Why, how come?"

"Because, you didn't take it down by yourself. Aeric helped you," he answered.

I staggered to the floor. "Are you serious? I'm never betting with you again, you phony!"

"Don't be mad at me. You should be mad at Aeric," Valen chuckled.

"Guys, look," Kirikah said, point in the sky. Swarms of demons swirled their way toward the castle.

"Right, let's go," Aeric said.

Point of View: Rhyona

Behemoth continued its rampage through my vines and wasn't showing any signs of slowing down. Zandaris was still playing as bait out there, risking his life for us to win this battle.

I tried one more time. The roots from the ground wrapped around the body of Behemoth, fighting hard to hold it back. It urged forward, snapping the vines into pieces. Zandaris was again launched into the air.

"Rhyona, what are you doing?" he called, as he spun in the air.

I sighed. "I can't do it. The behemoth is too powerful."

Zandaris landed on top of a house hiding away. The behemoth went on a rampage, looking for him. Xamnesces and Kaisera popped into the scene, drawing its attention with their magic attacks.

"Kurai-Shuuha!" Xamnesces casted. He swung a dark wave from his hand, attempting to slice through the thin waist of the beast. Behemoth smacked it away with its tail.

It then rose up onto its hind legs. With great power, it smashed his front legs into the ground, causing the ground to shift levels. Behemoth roared fiercely into the night, bringing forth walls of great fire from the cracks in the ground.

I switched to cat form, bouncing away from the fire. Kaisera flew in from above, weakening the firewalls with her light magic. Zandaris jumped through the fire, throwing a punch at the behemoth's eye. It roared in pain, rubbing its eyes with its paw. Zandaris was swiped down to the ground.

"Zandaris," I called. The behemoth didn't know that Zandaris was right under him. He fled to a safe spot, hiding behind a broken building.

"That has to be an advantage," Xamnesces said, joining my side.

"You think?" I asked.

"That punch to its eye blinded it for the moment. If Zandaris can continue to do that, we might just be able to find an opening. When that time comes, you're gonna have to lock it down with every vine that you can conduct."

I nodded.

Xamnesces made his way over to Zandaris to inform him of the strategy.

"Alright, Rhyona, come on. You can do it," I encouraged. I gently rested my hands into the ground, concentrating my mana into every vine I could find.

Xamnesces clasped his hands together, summoning up as much dark energy between both hands. He roared into the night, casting a shadow flame around his body. I yelled along with him, raising every vine out of the ground, ready to go.

Kaisera picked up Zandaris by the arms, carrying him over to the behemoth. He dropped onto the snout of the beast, right between the eyes. Behemoth swayed his head back and forth, brushing its paw at its face. Zandaris held on tightly to one of its whiskers.

"Hold on, just a little longer," I yelled out. I conducted more vines to rise from the ground. I was not going to let everyone down on this one. This time, I was more focused.

"I'm ready," Xamnesces said, burning with power from deep within his flame.

Zandaris pulled on the whisker, springing forward toward one of the behemoth's eyes. He took a shot at its pupil. The behemoth raised into the air in pain, tossing Zandaris aside.

"Here it goes!" I cried.

I conducted every single vine around behemoth, locking him high into the air and exposed its thin waist to Xamnesces. The vines wrapped around its paws, body and hind legs, constricting it perfectly still. The behemoth struggled to break free.

"Shisou!" Xamnesces yelled.

He scooped his arms from below, causing a giant shadow flame to rise from the ground. The shadow flame crawled its way toward the behemoth like a train on its tracks and burned right through the thin waist, separating the behemoth into two halves. With a burst of light, the behemoth exploded, erupting all over the land of the Garuda Hexagon.

The smoke was difficult to see through. Zandaris' hand dug through the smoke, picking me up from off the ground.

"Good job, elven," he said.

I applauded him in return.

Xamnesces joined our side sluggishly, weary from his last attack. "We did a great job."

"I guess that changes things between our kinds," I said to Zandaris.

He dusted off his shoulder and said, "Not likely." He walked off toward the castle, then turned his shoulder and said, "But we'll see what happens from here. If anyone is to kill your kind, it's going to be me, no one else."

All I could do was smile. He was still stubborn about the past, but he knows deep down inside his heart, things have changed. I admit myself, I don't think too badly of the trolls. Hopefully, we can work together more often, setting aside the past and looking toward a new future.

"Thanks Ryushin," I whispered.

Xamnesces smiled, "He does make a difference doesn't he?" I nodded. "Come on, let's assist the others."

Point of View: Mordakai

The four of us left Shiva's Hexagon and toward the bridge. Countless numbers of demons were still picking at Nomak, Chrisa and Astrae. They would swoop down, slapping them, then take off into the air again.

Kirikah bubbled all three of them with her shield. Nomak and Chrisa were able to bat away oncoming demons.

"Kinbaku!" Aeric casted.

The swarms of demons flew slower in the air. Astrae flashed a powerful light from his body, banishing the slowed enemies. Valen and I raced along the bridge, hacking away at the unaware demons.

"Where have you guys been?" Astrae panted.

"Sorry, we had our hands full with an iron giant," Aeric apologized.

The three of them were worn out from battle. It looked like they haven't been able to find the time to rest.

"Here comes another wave of them," Kirikah said.

A shower of bright light burned through the oncoming demons from above. Kaisera glided downward like a heavenly angel, joining us by our side. Zandaris, Xamnesces and Rhyona came to our aid as well.

The swarms of demons circled around us by the number, looking to strike all at the same time. We all stood together strong, ready to take them out.

"This is pretty fun," I said.

Nomak grunted.

"Bet?" Valen suggested. "Let's take them down yea? Whoever strikes down the most is the winner."

"Prize?" Zandaris asked.

"Losers pay dinner to the winners for a week," he said.

"I'm in," Nomak agreed. I agreed as well too.

Valen nodded. "Let's kick some ass."

At that moment, all of us standing on that bridge did not let them pass. We displayed a great show in teamwork, working together to take out the swarms.

Nomak and Chrisa used their brute force to rip down countless numbers of demons. They would lock arms, performing a cyclone spin, bashing and hacking away at any demon that closed in on them. Astrae and Kaisera used their holy light magic to burn them in groups. Wave by wave, they single handedly took them out in the sky. Rhyona and Zandaris' bond grew stronger during this fight, being able to trust one another. She defended with the long roots from below while Zandaris smashed his knuckles and heels into the demons faces. Aeric used his binding technique, gathering as many demons as he could within his grasp. Xamnesces performed his shadow wave attack, cutting them into pieces. Kirikah shielded Valen and me with her magic while we moved onto the offensive. Valen and I would switch off positions, attacking from below and above one another.

Afraid to attack, the swarms of demons retreated for the moment.

Our group cheered on one another. For the first time since the battle had started, we've been able to sit down without worry.

"Must have water!" Valen choked. He dropped into the water under the bridge, desperately drinking from the moat.

"Do you hear that?" Aeric asked.

All of us sat silently around the bridge, honing our ears on anything peculiar. There was a buzzing noise flying all around. It was coming from inside the castle. I ran to the door, placing one ear on it.

"It's coming from inside," I said.

The door exploded outward, knocking me backward into Aeric.

"Damn it, Mordakai," he grunted, "That's twice now."

"Dude, it wasn't me. Look," I said, pointing at the smoking door.

A red laser beam shot through. All of us screamed and dove into the water. Out from the smoke crawled out a giant eye with tentacles underneath it.

I remained low underwater; afraid it was going to see me. It twitched around from side to side, looking for any sudden movements.

"Don't move," Chrisa informed.

"What is that thing?" I asked.

"It's an eye," she answered.

"Durh, I know that it's an eye," I said.

"Well, then why did you ask?"

"Look at it. It's freakin' huge," I answered.

An arrowbolt stung the eye from behind. Lecia and Gundita popped out from the smoke. A great fireball and ice shard darted out of the shadows behind Lecia and Gundita, exploding on contact with the eye.

The eye melted.

"Damn it, you guys," Lecia said. Craft and Cildiari emerged from the shadows. "See, now it's gonna be hard to kill that thing."

"Hey! I can't help it if I'm that powerful," Craft boasted.

Gundita smacked her forehead in disappointment. The melted parts of the eye transformed into smaller ones. They dropped off the bridge and into the water, looking at each and every one of us.

"Screw this," Valen cried. He spit out the water he drank earlier and swam for dry land.

We all made a break for dry land, avoiding the tiny lasers from the eyes. Rhyona, in cat form, scratched away at them with her claws. Everyone else squashed them underneath their feet.

"Die!" I shouted, stomping all over them.

The smaller eyes gathered together, fusing back into the giant eye. It whipped its tentacles, slapping all of us away.

Craft shot a giant fireball against the eye. "Hey, you're fight is with me," she said. Lecia, Gundita and Cildiari joined her side.

"Ready for the Four Corners technique?" Gundita asked.

"Eh? What's the Four Corners Technique?" I asked.

"Just watch," Chrisa said.

The four commanders vanished in their place, leaving nothing but a tiny cloud of dust behind. Even the eye could not keep up with their movements.

"Here it comes," Nomak said.

First, the eye was slashed with many cuts, stunning the eye completely. Second, the cuts filled with tiny arrowbolts, locking it down to the bridge. Third, a fire tornado rose from under the eye, tangling the eye in flames. And the final attack, a small blue waterfall, covered the fire, encasing it in a barrier of ice.

"Wow, the flames are frozen inside the ice," Kirikah said.

One by one, the commanders appeared in different corners, surrounding the eye like a box. Two lasers crossed into the eye. Lecia and Gundita were connecting, Cildiari and Craft connecting from the other. A strong white light burned its way from the ground to the sky, creating a pyramid.

"Zettaizetsumei!" all of the commanders yelled.

The pyramid deteriorated from the top to the bottom. Magically, the eye was gone. The commanders had completely banished the eye.

They all stood tall across from each other.

"It feels good," Cildiari said.

"Good team work, all of you," Gundita said. "I can't say best about the kingdom but I know you all fought your hardest."

"But there are still countless numbers of demons left," Aeric said.

"From here on, we fight as one. There's no way they can beat us anymore," Lecia said.

Everyone nodded in agreement.

"Look, that must be the source of the demons," Kirikah said.

In the distance, Ryushin and the others were trying their best to hold back the demon king. It was the supply of demon swarms. If they can just take that thing out, then Draconia will finally be safe.

"Here comes more," Chrisa said.

Another wave of demons emerged behind the demon king like a firework, filling the sky with black once more. We all stood together as one.

Point of View: Ryushin

The demon king powered its way through our attacks, continuing to walk toward Draconia. The smaller demons were the ones giving us a hard time. We were getting tired, especially Onry and Yoichi.

"You guys, we have to pull it back," I said. "If it reaches Draconia, there's no telling what it'll do."

Ifrit pulled backward, avoiding contact with the swarms of demons that were up ahead. With a mighty blow, Ifrit shot a flamethrower from his mouth, burning the swarm to ashes.

Rheaa flew underneath us on Titan.

"Did you find a way to stop this thing yet?" she asked.

I shook my head. "Do anything you can to either bring it down or provoke it away from the city."

Four demons were on the attack. I jumped over one, tossing my sword at the others behind it. Countering their assault, I commanded my sword left, then to the right, back to the center and behind me in a circle, striking the demons away. More demons were incoming from below. Ice shards and fireballs picked them out of the sky. Ifrit took the upper path, circling the demon from the backside to the front.

I formed my hands into a cup, gathering energy for another attempt with my Kagayaku Hikari energy beam. The demon king came to a stop, shielding itself with its wings.

"Ryushin, it's no use," Onry said on a flyby.

"You got any other ideas? The damn thing is too big to take down," I responded.

Yoichi glided down on Garuda's back. "Then, we'll just have to cut it down to size."

"Cut it down? Cut it down... hmmm," I began to think.

The Trueblade flashed brilliantly in my hands. This had to be some kind of clue to defeating this overgrown demon.

The demon king opened its wings fiercely and blew us away. It blasted a dark wave from its mouth, separating the three of us.

The Adventures of Ryushin

Rheaa flew in front of the demon king, provoking it with the raspberries. The demon king became infuriated, swinging its claws at Rheaa. Titan glided downward, wrapping around the side of the demon and to its back. The demon king turned around and chased them.

Ifrit and I took to the sky right behind them. Yoichi and Onry crossed paths simultaneously, causing the chasing swarms of demons to collide with one another. I performed smaller energy attacks on the demons that were on the attack.

Ifrit was gaining speed.

Then I saw it. There was a perfect opening for a one hit knock out. There was only one chance to get it and I'm gonna need everyone's help on this. I called to Onry and Yoichi.

Rheaa turned around, performing her windslash in front of the face of the demon. The demon king was blind. Rheaa and Titan swooped passed the head and huddled right next to us.

"You got a plan now?" Rheaa asked.

"Yea, I'm gonna need all of your help for this," I answered.

"Make it quick," Yoichi said, "We're running out of time on this one."

I pointed at the back of the demon king.

"That's our opening. Its wings cannot guard the back side, so if I can just get above it some how without it knowing, then I can strike from above."

"This will work?" Yoichi asked.

"Trust me," I answered. "All we need is a diversion. How big of a fireball can you create, Yoichi?"

She examined her hands quickly and answered, "Enough for one attack. Once I create this thing, I will be at the peak of my mana."

I nodded.

"All we need is one shot. Rheaa and Onry will keep the swarms off. Position yourself, so that you are point blank in front of the demon king's face. Power up as much as you can and give it something to be scared about."

The demon king recovered its sight.

"Ryushin, it's on the move again," Onry informed.

"Alright," I clapped, "Let's do this."

Suddenly, a flash of light struck my eye sight. I could see Aida fighting Atlmaz at the shrine. She and Ksama were in trouble.

"Ryushin, are you okay?" Rheaa asked.

"Aida, she's in trouble," I answered. "I have to save her."

"Go, we'll take care of this thing," Yoichi said.

"No, this first than Atlmaz," I responded.

The demon king blasted a dark wave. All of us broke apart, flying toward the giant demon. It launched another one. Ifrit and I shifted toward Rheaa and Titan.

"Switch," Rheaa said.

The two of us jumped from one dragon to the other, switching positions. I patted Titan on the back, signaling ready to attack.

"Let's go Titan," I commanded.

Rheaa and Yoichi crossed paths, switching on the fly by. Yoichi zoomed upward with Ifrit, while Rheaa and Garuda defended her with their wind attacks. Onry and Shiva flew close behind me and Titan.

"I'll cover you, Ryushin," Onry nodded.

The demon king spotted me below. It raised its claw high into the air, readying its attack. Onry shifted out far away while I stood firm waiting.

"Steady now, Titan," I said. The demon king swung downward. "Wait for it. Wait for it." The claw swiped. "Now!" Titan sprang high into the air from the water, avoiding the attack. I jumped off Titan and started running along the arm of the demon king once more.

Demons emerged from its skin but ice shards pierced right through them one at a time. Onry swooped downward, flying close by. Every demon that emerged, she picked apart easily.

The demon king raised its other arm, ready to attack.

"Yoichi, do it now!" I yelled.

"Moetatsu!" she cried out loud. She and Ifrit became encased in a great burning flame. She brought her hands together and gathered power. Ifrit charged, increasing the fire's power.

The demon king was frightened, the holding back its counter attack and shielding itself with its wings. It gave me time to make my way up to its shoulder.

"Only got one shot, Ryushin," I said to myself. I concentrated my energy into my legs, springing from its collar bone to the top of its head. With a final push, I launched off the top of its head and rose well above it.

The Trueblade started to glow emphatically.

"Ryushin!" Yoichi called. She hurled the encased flame around her and Ifrit toward my sword.

The sword was engulfed in their fire. In an instant, I flashed downward, slicing the sharp blade right down the middle. Titan bolted underneath, catching me with his back. The fire between the two halves exploded, smoldering the two halves to dust.

"You did it!" Onry cried with joy.

"Don't let up yet," Rheaa said, "There are still swarms of demons left over."

Another vision of Aida fighting Atlmaz occurred.

"I'm sorry you guys," I apologized, "Aida needs my help."

The rest nodded.

"We understand," Yoichi said.

"Go! Don't keep her waiting!" Onry said excitedly.

Titan and I raced for the distant kingdom, while the others remained to finish off the remaining demons.

Point of View: Aida

Ksama struck Atlmaz from behind with her dagger but he was still invulnerable to our physical attacks. She and I switched out. Atlmaz's scythe met with my sword, causing sparks of black and white. I countered, lowering his weapon to the ground, and then crushed my blade against his stomach. Atlmaz flung to the ground, able to take the fierce hit. Ksama continued the chain with a sliding kick to his face. I rose above the fallen warlock. With great force, I landed a deathblow with my sword to his chest, breaking him through the ground.

Atlmaz was smiling at me. My attack didn't work. I lunged backward, avoiding his shadow energy attack.

"What are we doing wrong here?" I asked.

Atlmaz dusted off his shoulders.

"It's like he's invincible," Ksama said.

He hasn't grown tired one bit and our attacks aren't damaging him at all. I just don't understand why this was happening.

"Are you done yet?" he asked. "'Cause if you are, then I will kill you both now."

Atlmaz disappeared.

Ksama and I put our guard up. He was either moving too fast or he disappeared from the shrine.

"I can't see him anywhere," Ksama said.

"He's still here, I know it," I responded.

Atlmaz chuckled from behind. He swirled his scythe in a circle, launching thin rings of energy toward us. One ring cut Ksama in the shoulder as she attempted to dodge it while another ricocheted off my armor, cracking it in the center.

He disappeared again.

This time, he launched a surprise attack from above. He disappeared on the way down. Catching me off guard, the warlock reappeared from the side, swinging upward with his scythe. I stepped to the side. He quickly hooked onto one of the straps of my armor. The blade sliced right through, cutting my inward shoulder.

Ksama attempted to surprise him from behind but he was no fool. He blasted her away with his shadow ball attack, and then fired one into my stomach, flinging me backward onto my back.

"Worthless girl," Atlmaz said, standing atop of my stomach with one foot. He applied more pressure, deepening the crack in my armor. I can feel the blood flowing through my mouth and drip down the side of my lip.

"Aida," Ksama cried, unable to move.

"All of your efforts to stop me were in vein," he chuckled, lowering his scythe to my neck. "How do you want to die, paladin? Shall I make it painful or quick?"

I gripped my sword tightly, attempting one more attack. He caught the sharp blade with his hand. He was too powerful for me.

Atlmaz threw my sword aside and raised his open hand into the air, creating his shadow ball. I closed my eyes, just before he pulled the trigger. In a few seconds, a tiny cut scratched my neck and an explosion erupted from the side.

"Are you okay?"

I opened my eyes. Ragnorak was kneeling next to me, tending to my wounds. Atlmaz was blown off of my body by a surprising energy attack by Ragnorak.

Over to the side was a half chewed out Atlmaz, missing one side of his body.

"Who are you?" Atlmaz asked.

"I'm your next opponent," Ragnorak replied. He lifted me up, carrying me over to the side. He carried Ksama over to me.

"Damn you, Dracolyte," Atlmaz cursed.

Ragnorak stepped toward him, ready to fight.

A wicked smile grew on Atlmaz's face. The destroyed side of his body grew back, completely restored. Ksama and I were shocked at this technique, where as Ragnorak was clearly unimpressed.

"I should have known you would have entered the castle disguised as one of your pathetic demons," Ragnorak said.

"Not as dumb as I look, do I?" Atlmaz laughed.

"It matters no more. Your fight is with me," Ragnorak said.

"This fight will be over in five minutes," Atlmaz guaranteed. The two vanished in their places, leaving nothing but a trail of dust behind.

"Where'd they go?" Ksama asked.

"I don't know," I answered, "They're moving too fast."

The two super powers clashed in the center of the shrine, vanishing and appearing from one spot to another.

Ragnorak appeared in the center of the shrine. Atlmaz emerged from the side, swinging his scythe into an uppercut. Ragnorak stepped to the side away from the attack. He turned around quickly, delivering a fierce punch to Atlmaz's face. The sound of his hard knuckles wrenched Atlmaz off balance. Ragnorak continued his rush with a series of punches and kicks.

Atlmaz countered with his shadow ball. Ragnorak flicked it away, launching an energy attack of his own. The attack burned right through Atlmaz, leaving a big hole in his stomach.

"No, this can't be," Atlmaz stuttered. He fell back onto his knees in disbelief.

Ragnorak stood before him, readying an energy blast for the final blow. Atlmaz's shocked expression on his face changed quickly to a wicked smile.

"Just kidding!" Atlmaz laughed, grabbing hold of Ragnorak's arm. He shoved his open hand in front of Ragnorak's face and released a powerful energy blast. The shrine filled with a blinding dark light, followed with a thick cloud of smoke.

"Can you see anything?" Ksama asked.

"Hold on," I answered, "I think I see someone."

The left side of the shrine cleared, revealing Atlmaz standing with his arm extended. The right side of the shrine cleared slowly. Ragnorak's hand emerged from the cloud, gripping onto Atlmaz's head tightly. The rest of Ragnorak's body appeared. His wings were raised above his face, shielding him from the previous attack.

"Damn you, Dracolyte," Atlmaz laughed.

Ragnorak exerted a powerful energy attack of his own, blowing Atlmaz up from within.

"He did it!" Ksama cheered. We slowly got to our feet and ran toward Ragnorak.

"I wouldn't be so happy if I were you."

Atlmaz was standing next to a pillar untouched.

"How...?" Ksama asked. "That attack was point blank. There's no way you could have survived that."

"That was a fine show all of you have displayed," he laughed.

I grinned. "What are you talking about?"

Ragnorak stood tall, dusting his wings with his hand.

"He was watching the whole time," he said.

"Now, wait just a damn minute," Atlmaz chuckled, "I was doing something."

Destati was missing in the shrine.

"Where is it, Atlmaz?" I asked.

He smirked and shrugged his shoulders. "I had snatched myself enough time to consume all of its power. The thing might have been small, but it was filled with intense power. What a rush it was."

"Oh no," Ksama cried, "He has the Destati."

"How did you do it, Atlmaz?" I asked.

"Easy. While you were fighting my silhouette replica, I was hiding behind the shrine, absorbing all of its power. With you pests in the way, I wouldn't have enough time to get it all," he explained. He let out a loud belch.

"Even if you have Destati, you need time to gather its power," Ragnorak informed.

"Trust me," Atlmaz smirked, "I already knew that."

Ragnorak looked uneasy, dropping sweat like rain down the side of his face. As Atlmaz paced himself toward us slowly, Ragnorak would retreat one step at a time.

"I'll never give you that chance," I said. I grabbed my sword from the ground.

"Must I?" Atlmaz posed.

He snapped his chest forward, triggering the dark energy inside his body to explode. A clear flame with a gray outline wrapped around Atlmaz, burning with great force. The room's color was changing from gold to pure white. Waves of smoke rushed against us, slowly pushing us back.

"Everyone, get down!" Ragnorak yelled. All three of us hit the deck.

"You all fail!" Atlmaz laughed. The flame around him expanded, rupturing the shrine into pieces. With a great boom, the shrine exploded, throwing us into the air.

I lunged backward onto the ground while Ksama hit the floor next to me. The shrine continued to spark with energy, nearly crushing the tower down to pieces.

"Ksama, let's move," I said, slowly climbing to my feet.

The ground below us started to crack. A strong quake came from the base of the tower, separating the courtyard into different pieces. Ksama and I were separated by the leveled land.

"Where's Ragnorak?" Ksama asked.

"I don't know," I answered.

The grounds shifted from side to side, colliding into one another.

"Up there!" Ksama pointed.

Ragnorak shot from the smoke and into the air. He gathered energy into his hand and blasted an energy attack downward, causing the smoke to divide from the explosion.

Atlmaz appeared behind the unaware Ragnorak. He raised his arm up and delivered a forceful back swing. Lightning sparked from the contact, flashing Ragnorak straight into the ground.

"Ragnorak!" I called.

I raced over to him, jumping from high grounds to low grounds.

Suddenly, Ragnorak zoomed from the ground and back to Atlmaz. With his fist clinched, he swung back and forth with both hands. Atlmaz was too fast, dodging and blocking his attacks all too easy.

Atlmaz snuck a strong knee into Ragnorak's stomach, knocking the wind out of him. He clinched both hands together and slammed fiercely upon his head, sending him right back down. Atlmaz raised both of his hands above his head, and then fired a barrage of shadow balls. The grounds exploded below with Ragnorak.

"How is Atlmaz able to fly like that?" I asked.

Atlmaz glided downward, filling one hand with intense energy. The land exploded when he collided with it, knocking Ksama and I back onto our backs.

"There's no way we can beat something like that, Aida," Ksama said.

"We can't give up now," I responded.

Another explosion occurred in the short distance and Ragnorak came grinding against the land, all worn and beaten. Atlmaz was on the attack. I got up quickly and sprinted toward the fallen Ragnorak.

I gripped my sword tightly, ready to attack. Ragnorak slowly found his way to his feet. Atlmaz bounced right over me, darting straight to Ragnorak. He dropped kicked Ragnorak into the air and followed with a beam of dark energy.

Atlmaz vanished before me. He reappeared above Ragnorak and delivered a very strong blow to his back.

Ragnorak snapped downward back into the ground. The force of the impact jerked me onto my back.

"Ragnorak..." I cried.

"Aida, you have to get out of here," he struggled to say. Ragnorak was a mess.. His armor was cracked and torn from grinding along the ground.

"Time to die!" Atlmaz laughed, charging up for another attack.

"We won't make it in time," I said.

Atlmaz launched a giant shadow ball upon us. A bubble wrapped around us, shielding us from the attack. The ground dissolved underneath us but the force still slammed us against the remaining walls of the courtyard.

"Aida!" Kirikah called.

The others ran down the stairway in a hurry. Kaisera and Astrae took to the sky, confronting Atlmaz. Mordakai and Aeric rushed to our aid, lifting the fallen Ragnorak.

"Aida, are you okay?" Mordakai asked.

"Thankfully we made it just in time," Aeric said.

Atlmaz laughed from above. "Just spoil my fun why don't you."

The four commanders aided Astrae and Kaisera. Craft, Cildiari and Xamnesces launched energy attacks at him. Atlmaz was able to avoid them all.

"He's too powerful," I said.

"It's okay, we're here now," Kirikah said.

"You all want to play?" Atlmaz asked. He raised his hands upward, unleashing countless numbers of demons upon us. We were covered by thousands of them in seconds then soon millions.

"Damn it," Valen cursed, "and here I thought I wouldn't see another demon for a good while."

"Later suckers!" Atlmaz laughed, blasting off into the distance. Demons grabbed hold of Astrae and Kaisera, buying Atlmaz enough time to gain distance.

"Aida!"

The Adventures of Ryushin

Ryushin jumped from the back of Titan. The dragon left to aid the others against the demons.

"Ryushin!" I called. We both caught each other in our arms and held on firmly.

"Sorry I'm late," he said.

Point of View: Ryushin

"Prince Ryushin," Ragnorak said, "You can't let him get away."

I looked all over the place, watching everyone fight off the demons.

"Where's Atlmaz?"

Ragnorak pointed the direction. "He's heading north."

"Let me see," I responded. I changed quickly to my Dragon Eyes, seeing passed all the demons. In the distance, Atlmaz was on the run by foot. "I see him. He's moving by ground."

I began to take off.

Aida pulled back on my arm and said, "You can't go alone."

"Why not?"

"He's too powerful for you to fight alone," she answered. "I felt how strong he is. Look at what he did to Ragnorak."

"Listen to her, Prince Ryushin," he said.

There was an opening just ahead of the demons. Everyone was too tied up to assist me in the chase. "Mordakai," I called.

"What's up?" he answered.

"Still got enough fight in you?" I asked.

He nodded. Valen and Aeric joined in as well. "We're with you all the way."

"Me too," Kirikah answered.

I looked over to the four commanders, fighting off the demons around them.

"Gundita," I called.

"Ryushin, just go! I'll catch with you guys later," she said.

"Alright, let's get moving!" I commanded.

Aida pulled on my arm again. "I'm going with you."

I shook my head, "No, you're too badly injured to fight. There's no telling what could happen out there."

"I don't care," she said. "You promised never to leave my side again. I'm going with you."

I sighed, "Okay Aida, let's go."

Ragnorak stood to his feet slowly, ready to fight the demons. "I wish you the best of luck."

"Don't worry," I said, "I can do this."

The six of us made a break for the opening in the wall. A group of demons flew in from straight ahead. Aeric, Valen and Mordakai took them down quick, giving us breathing room.

Chapter Eighteen
The Dragon's Den

Mordakai, Aida, Kirikah, Valen, Aeric and I- sprinted down the road in pursuit of Atlmaz, who was just a distance away from us. This was the final chapter of this long adventure. We have to do whatever it takes and stop him from using Destati on the world.

The blood in my heart continued to pump wildly, nervous yet excited about the battle up ahead. I was tired, a little numb in the legs, but I couldn't rest now. We have come too far to let him get away.

"Ryushin!" Kirikah called from behind.

Deadsong and Fearsong lunged from the bushes attacking with a surprise punch. Kirikah shielded me while Valen stepped in to counter their attacks.

"Go, you guys. Kirikah and I will hold them off," Valen said.

"Are you sure?" I asked. The two of them nodded and the rest of us continued our pursuit.

We ran along a small river bend, spotting Atlmaz speaking to someone in the distance. I launched an energy ball their direction. Atlmaz smacked it away and continued to run. The other person drew their lance.

It was Linwe.

"Ryushin, go around her. I will take her head to head," Aeric said.

Aida, Mordakai and I ignored Linwe, leaving Aeric behind.

"He's heading for the mountains," Aida informed.

"Atlmaz needs time to build up power for Destati. He needs a secluded area in order for him to concentrate enough time," Mordakai explained.

A shadow fell from the trees nearly swiping him. He rolled to the side and drew his axes.

Sithia stood poised with her spear in hand.

Mordakai nodded to me.

"Don't worry," he said, "I'll be there right behind ya."

Aida and I spotted Atlmaz flying up against the side of a steep mountain. An energy blast exploded in front of us, knocking Aida and me onto our backs.

"You're not going any further," Corfits snorted.

Aida drew her sword. I drew my swords as well.

"What are you doing?" Aida asked. "Get going, we can't let him escape."

I hesitated looking back and forth at Aida and Atlmaz.

"What about you? I can't just leave you guys," I said.

"Don't worry about us," she replied.

"But…"

"Go now, Ryushin!" Aida yelled loudly.

"Oh no you don't!" Corfits shouted, lowering his sword. He swung upward, sending a dark wave attack. Aida reflected the attack with her sword. The two of them clashed.

I ran for the base of the mountain quickly and jumped high.

"Atlmaz!" I called.

He pushed off the wall with his legs and fired a shadow energy ball downward, pushing him up faster. I flapped open my invisible wings and flew to the right. He fired another one into the mountain, breaking chunks of rock above me. I shifted back left.

"You're very persistent!" Atlmaz yelled.

"Seinaru Yoru!" I blasted.

He caught my energy attack and shot it right back down. It bounced off my chest, flinging back downward.

I looked up at him. He flipped over the top of the mountain hanging still upside down. He unhooked his scythe and sliced an incredibly large mass of the mountainside off, following with multiple shadow balls before going out of sight.

"Need a lift?"

The Adventures of Ryushin

To my left was Alex. He smiled as we both fell downward.

"Alex…? What are you doing here?" I asked.

Ralph, Jeice and my brother flew in from behind him.

"Whew, that's one big rock," Jeice said.

"Yea it is. Alright, what's the plan?" Ralph asked.

"Huh? What are you talkin about?" I asked.

"He's talking about getting over that thingy comin' your way?" Justin said. "Let's run that play we always ran in basketball," he pointed at me, "you're going to be the ball."

"Tight, let's do it," Ralph said. Justin, Jeice and Ralph spread out along the mountain side.

"Grab my hand," Alex said.

I grabbed his hand. He swung me downward, building momentum and then launched me into a somersault upward. I darted upward head first again, spreading my wings wide.

"Over here, I'm wide open!" Jeice said.

I pushed off the mountainside just before a shadow ball hit, spinning over to Jeice. He grabbed my arm and chucked me further upward.

Ralph flew in from underneath and catapulted me upward from underneath my feet and said, "Alley-oop!" I became encased in a clear white flame.

I pushed off the side of the mountain as I was going up, rotating into a somersault toward the giant boulder that was still in my way.

"You owe me one for this."

Right next to me was my brother.

"Justin…?"

"You know you can't do anything without me."

I smiled at him, pulling my clinched fist way behind me. His spirit jumped into my body, giving me more strength. I fiercely threw the punch forward, cracking the large mass into many pieces. I pushed off one of the pieces with my hands and flipped over the side of the mountain.

I landed onto a small island inside of a basin.

"I thought you would never make it," Atlmaz smirked. "But please tell me, who the hell are you?"

"Don't be stupid. You know who I am."

He laughed. "I know you are not Him. I can see it in your face."

I looked down into the water at my reflection. I saw myself, the person who I really am. But I could also see Him standing there next to me.

"My name is Derric," I said.

He chuckled, "So I was right. Where exactly did you come from and why are you here?"

"Like I'd tell you where I'm from. I might be Derric but I'm Him also, Prince Ryushin."

"Interesting..." Atlmaz said. "Who would have thought Ryushin would revive himself through another? He must be that desperate."

"Less talking, let's go," I said, slashing the Trueblade out to my side.

The two of us remained quiet, glaring directly into each other's eyes. My hand filled with sweat, holding tightly onto my sword while he levitated with his scythe in both hands.

He laughed, "Time to die." He opened his eyes wide revealing a dark red glow around his pupil. A strong force pushed me backward into the water. I pulled myself up back to the little island watching his power grow around him into a purple flame. The basin around us started to shake violently, cracking chunks of land off the wall. Atlmaz gathered dark energy into his hand, making it grow larger every second.

I placed my sword back into its sheath, bent my knees, and fought to resist the force of his attack. He fired it with great speed. I motioned my hands into a cup and gathered energy quick.

"Kagayaku Hikari!" I yelled.

Our energy attacks collided. His attacked overpowered my energy beam. The dark energy attack shattered through my counter and pushed up against my hands. The muscles in my body were cramping up tightly, so I lifted up and tossed the attack behind me.

The dark energy attack exploded into the walls of the basin, emitting a very bright, blinding light. Atlmaz and I both shielded our eyes.

When it cleared, he was gone. I can hear him though. He was moving too fast for my eyes to see, but he was still here.

I looked into the water, spotting Atlmaz's reflection above me with his scythe raised. I blocked his deathblow with my sword. The force from his attack flushed me deep into the water. I floated in the water just a little above the ground, looking for Atlmaz. He surprisingly tackled me from the side and placed his hand onto my stomach. I pushed his hand downward. His energy attack exploded on the ground, sending us both in opposite directions.

I flew out of the water and into the air. Atlmaz was moving fast along the basin once more. I turned around quickly to block his scythe with my sword. He rotated in the air and delivered a spin kick to my head. Black dots started wrapping around my body. Atlmaz struck from above with his scythe. I raised my sword in time to block his attack, but his force bashed me back into the water.

I pulled myself out and flew in front of him.

"What's the matter?" he asked.

Blood dripped from the side of my head and lip. How can I keep up with something like that?

"Feeling weak are we? Looks like my dots are working on you," he said.

All of his attacks are just now beginning to sink into my body, making it harder for me to fight back. I felt weaker, my muscles tense and tired.

Atlmaz disappeared again.

I can feel a fist slam from behind onto my back. Every attack he delivered caused black dots to absorb into my body. I flipped downward jaggedly but flapped my wings to stay above water. He appeared from behind and punched me in the back. I jerked forward. Atlmaz appeared out in front and began throwing punches and kicks. He flipped backward and slammed his foot up against my chin. He grabbed my ankle as I wrenched up and launched my body downward into the water.

I landed onto the ground underwater and just lied there. I couldn't move. The pains from his attacks were settling in. The effects of the black dots were weakening me.

"If you're not coming come out, I'm going to flush you out!"

An energy ball splashed into the water exploding right next to me. The force launched me out of the water. Atlmaz floated there next to me as I slowly lifted into the air.

He chuckled, "The Mighty Prince Ryushin."

Atlmaz clasped his hands together and bashed me in the stomach with a strong blow. He fired an energy ball, slamming me deep into the water. The explosion carried me afloat to the surface. I lied there all beaten and my clothes torn.

Suddenly, an energy beam exploded upon Atlmaz's back.

"Are you okay?"

It was Astrae, floating there next to me.

"Astrae, what are you doing here," I asked.

"I'm here to help," he answered.

"Watch out, I think he's using the Destati to increase his powers."

"I can't say that I can beat him, but I'll do what I can to slow him down."

An energy ball zoomed right passed us, exploding in the water.

"Are you two done squawking down there?" Atlmaz called.

Astrae pointed over a small island over at the side and said, "Take a seat."

I slowly floated my way over to the island and sat down, watching Astrae glide toward Atlmaz.

"Dracolyte," Atlmaz said pleasingly. Astrae had no words for him. He stood strong motioning his hands into a stance.

Atlmaz opened up the fight with an energy blast. Astrae vanished and reappeared behind Atlmaz. He planted his hand onto Atlmaz's back and fired. Atlmaz lunged forward. He flew up higher, gathering more energy between both hands. He launched it downward but missed Atlmaz. The energy attack exploded underwater.

Atlmaz created a barrage of energy missiles and fired them one by one.

"Look out!" I yelled.

Astrae created a shield around him. The energy missiles reflected off the shield and scattered all over the basin, exploding everywhere it landed. Astrae pumped his arm backward, triggered it like a gun, and fired multiple energy attacks.

I rolled to the side barely dodging a chunk of rock.

"Not bad, Dracolyte," Atlmaz said, continuing his relentless attacks of energy, "but you don't have enough mana to compete with me."

The area continued to explode with tremendous force.

Astrae was slowing down on his responses to Atlmaz's attacks. I can see it in his fight. I then remembered what he said before.

"You're pretty powerful for a runt, why can't you just beat Atlmaz?" Valen said.

"I've already fought with Atlmaz before. He is far more complicating than you would ever imagine. It's almost walking right into death's row."

He knew he couldn't win but still, he insisted in fighting for me.

Astrae was on the run, avoiding the energy blasts.

Why did he fight Atlmaz knowing that he couldn't win? One of Atlmaz's energy blasts knocked Astrae off balance.

"I got you now you little runt!" Atlmaz yelled, firing a giant dark energy beam. Astrae took the hit, exploding along the mountainside.

A blue circle wrapped around Atlmaz, locking around him tightly. Astrae sprung from the mountainside high into the sunlight, holding a bright light in the palm of his hands.

"No, I got you, Atlmaz!" Astrae yelled.

"You little punk," Atlmaz grunted, struggling to break loose.

"The more you try to budge, the more you're wasting your energy."

Atlmaz squirmed even more. Astrae blasted a massive ray of energy into the sky. It showered downward like hundreds of arrows, all crushing into Atlmaz. The light exploded brightly, emitting a blinding light.

I covered my eyes just barely able to watch Atlmaz take the attack.

The light cleared, leaving the basin covered in smoke. Astrae floated their breathing heavily. I can hear him though… Atlmaz was still alive.

"Astrae, get away from the sky!" I yelled.

Atlmaz, with a big surprise in his hands, bolted above Astrae. He launched the dark wave downward, crushing Astrae in the back and into the water. The water erupted high into the sky, washing me off the island. I flapped my wings to stay afloat.

The water settled.

Atlmaz, clothes burned and ripped, levitated in the air with his hands still aimed downward. There was a weird marking on his skin. They were dark purple zigzagged lines.

"What the hell is that?" I asked.

He smiled wickedly. "This is my demon skin. More like a shell purposely designed to raise my defense against energy and physical attacks."

"Demon skin…"

Astrae floated to the surface. I flew to him and picked him up into my arms.

"Why did you fight?" I asked. "You knew you couldn't win."

Astrae smiled with blood dripping out of his mouth. He looked at me and said, "I went into the fight with a plan, not to win."

I'll do what I can to slow him down, I remembered him saying.

"You risked your life just to slow him down? Are you nuts?"

He pointed at my sword. "It is now in your hands."

Atlmaz raised both of his hands into the air and gathered dark energy.

"I won't fail you."

"No more playing around! Now die!" Atlmaz yelled, launching the giant sphere of dark energy. I paid no attention to it as it slowly grinded downward against the walls of the basin.

The dark sphere engulfed us, creating a might explosion within the basin. I looked down at Astrae... he was dead.

My heart quaked with pain. I shook my head, trying my hardest to resist it.

I took my sword and slashed the energy from the explosion, opening up the blue sky. Atlmaz couldn't believe what he just saw.

A red flame encased itself around me. I raised my sword up at Atlmaz and said, "It's my turn." I pushed off of the water shooting up to Atlmaz. I went around his counter-attack then punched him powerfully in the face. He jerked downward into the mountainside.

He wasted no time getting back up here. He swung his scythe multiple times but I easily evaded. I hurled my sword in his direction and moved swiftly around him. He blocked my sword with his scythe, deflecting it downward. I delivered a fierce blow to his spine with my knee. He turned around with anger. I flipped backward, slamming both feet simultaneously against his chin. I landed fiercely onto his stomach, shooting him downward to the water.

He was on the move again. I can hear him flying from behind me. He raised his scythe, ready to strike. I pulled my sword upward with my mana and blocked his attack, this time resisting the force of his blow.

Atlmaz grinned, "Where did that all come from?"

I pushed off with my sword. "From right here!" I shouted, fiercely punching him in the heart. I moved behind him and punched him in the spine, then the stomach with an uppercut and finished with a spin kick to his face.

His demon skin cracked all over.

"You're the first person to have ever done this to me..." Atlmaz said. His skin was breaking apart.

"You'll get to see your blood today."

"How can you be faster than me... you couldn't even see me before..."

I thought about it. It was Astrae's attack that slowed him down.

"That's what he was trying to do."

Atlmaz growled, "Who? That little runt... What was he trying to do?"

"That blue ring that tied you up just didn't stop you from moving... it also drained some of your energy."

He growled, "Damn that Dracolyte."

Atlmaz went on the attack. I evaded most of his attacks easily, watching his slow movements with my Dragon Eyes. Our weapons sparked when they collided, lights racing passed us with every blow.

I grabbed hold of the handle of his scythe and pulled him forward, punching him fiercely in the jaw. Then I delivered a blow with my knee to his stomach, knocking the wind out of him. With a final attack, I clinched both of my fists together and slammed him deep into the mountainside.

A loud roar erupted from his direction.

"Damn you!" he cursed, breaking off boulders of rock from the mountainside with his power. He launched them after me. I hurled my sword in their direction slicing one straight down the middle then the second one. The four chunks flew by me and into the other side of the mountain.

"Seinaru Yoru!" I yelled. The barrage of energy balls exploded behind him.

The smoke cleared. He floated before me with his hands formed into a cup out in front of his chest. A strange force I couldn't resist pushed me backward up against the mountainside.

"I want to see you dodge this one!" he yelled. Atlmaz released a powerful dark energy along the mountains, making it crawl its way over to me like a snake. I couldn't move. The dark energy moved along the mountainside, rupturing it into pieces and down to the water.

"Damn it," I grunted, struggling to break free.

Atlmaz laughed, "Good game!"

"What did you do to me?" I asked.

"Those black dots from earlier are locking down your muscles!"

I gathered power from within, desperately trying to break free from the immobile effect. With a thrust in my muscles, I broke free just in time to avoid contact with Atlmaz's dark snake attacks. I plunged into the water.

The side of the mountains collapsed, creating an open area. I swam to the top slowly and pulled myself up onto a floating chunk of land. Numerous chunks of land floated to the top, creating a hard surface for me to stand on.

He floated in the air annoyed. I stared back while breathing heavily.

"You're really starting to annoy me," he said.

I called my sword with my mana. I bent my knees, ready to attack but someone stepped onto the land behind me.

"It's over for you…"

It was Corfits, all beaten up. Deadsong and Fearsong showed up shortly after he did... then Linwe... then Sithia... my friends were nowhere to be found.

"Where are they?" I asked.

He chuckled alongside his allies. "We defeated them, of course. No one can match our superior strength."

"The two were very energetic, displayed great teamwork," Deadsong said of Valen and Kirikah.

"Great teamwork, lack power though," Fearsong added.

Linwe pierced her lance into the ground, "That pest of a knight couldn't hold his own with his dumb tricks." She was talking about Aeric.

"And that loud boy ran his mouth endlessly so I had to shut up him," Sithia said of Mordakai.

"Game over for you, Ryushin," Corfits said.

"Where's Aida?" I asked.

"Oh, the little girl ran back to Draconia crying, like a baby. She was lucky I let her get away."

"Isn't this interesting?" Atlmaz asked. "Looks like the tables have turned for you, Ryushin. Now I will be able to gather power for Destati."

"Hurry up and start Destati!" Corfits yelled.

Atlmaz clasped his hands together with his elbows sticking out. He closed his eyes, concentrating his energy into place, creating a silver vibe around him. He was encased inside a bright purple flame once more.

I cupped my hands, gathering energy for one giant energy beam.

A dark wave raced passed me and into a chunk of land ahead of me. Corfits held his great sword with two hands. The others behind him held their weapons ready to attack.

"Here we come, loser!" Corfits yelled.

He slammed his great sword into the ground, creating a shockwave toward me. Deadsong and Fearsong ran along the waves and lunged at me. I evaded their attacks and kicked them away. Sithia poked at me with her spear on one side while Linwe did the same with her long blade on the other. Back and forth, I flipped and blocked their attacks, just watching their slow movements. Corfits jumped into the air with his sword raised above his head. I placed one hand on Sithia's stomach and the other on Linwe and blasted them away with an energy blast. I jumped onto my hands and into a handstand, nearly evading Corfits' deathblow by inches. I pumped my legs upward, ramming my right foot into his chin. I rotated on my palm and smacked him away with my left foot.

Point of View: Aida

"Thanks for coming back for us, Aida," Mordakai said, dusting off his shoulder.
"Yeah, we owe you big time," Valen said.
I helped Kirikah to her feet and said, "We have to help Ryushin. He needs us now more than ever."
Everyone nodded.
"Well, what are we waiting for?" Mordakai asked.
"Let's do this together?" I asked.
"Together," Aeric said.
I ran toward the broken mountain, the rest followed closely behind.
Mordakai lightly punched me in the arm and said, "I know you love the dude, he is a pretty awesome person."
"Look alive," Aeric said, drawing his sword, "Let's put an end to this."

Point of View: Ryushin

Corfits, Linwe, Sithia, Deadsong and Fearsong jumped into the air above me. I sprung quickly between all of them, gripped my sword tightly and let it fly. First was Deadsong, then I directed my sword across to Linwe, then to Fearsong on her left, across to Sithia and then finally Corfits to her left.

I landed onto the ground, catching my sword as it fell from the sky.

The five of them fell onto the ground, bodies roughly landing.

Atlmaz looked down at me, still concentrating his energy. His goons died on the ground in a circle around me.

He growled, "Now's the time!"

I flapped my wings and bolted toward Atlmaz as fast as I could. He pushed Destati out from his chest and blasted me back down to the water with its force. My sword was knocked loose out of my hands and into the water.

"Atlmaz, what are you doing!?"

"It's too late for you, Ryushin," he yelled. He raised his hands above his head and created a small silver and purple sphere. He pulled his arms way behind his head and then launched the Destati.

Here it came, the power of Destati burned through the sky, growing the closer it approached. The sky turned gray, the water turned gray, everything turned gray.

I was out of time, my sword was already deep within the water. I had no choice to gather energy for a counter energy attack.

"Kagayaku Hikari!" I yelled, blasted my energy out of my hands. The two powers collided, sending a shockwave all throughout the area.

The Destati's force was too powerful for me to push back but I didn't let up easily. The water underneath my feet began to part, pushing me further down toward the ground. I planted both feet into the ground with the water rising all around me, pushing back with everything I had.

"You can't win, Ryushin!" Atlmaz laughed loudly.

I saw the Trueblade sparkle in the water just off to the side. It was emitting its aura, helping me push Destati a little bit. I released one of my hands and tried desperately to move the sword closer with my mana. The Destati crushed the ground underneath my feet, further burying me.

I put my arm back into my attack.

"Ryushin!"

Aida and the others ran toward me slowly, jumping from pieces of land scattered throughout the water.

"Ryushin, we got your back!" Mordakai yelled. He hurled both of his axes toward Atlmaz with his Taka no Hane technique but the axes disintegrated midway through the air.

"You guys," I called, struggling to stay above the ground. "You gotta get the Trueblade! It's the only way to push back Destati."

"Where is it?" Aida asked.

"Over there, Aida!" Kirikah said.

They noticed the Trueblade sparkling in the water a little further ahead. Atlmaz blasted a dark wave downward, flinching them backward.

"Go, I'll protect you guys," Aeric said.

Aida and Kirikah scrambled toward the sword, diving into the wall of water. Atlmaz launched more dark waves of energy. Aeric used his Chokusha attack to explode the attacks in the air.

"Valen!" Mordakai called. They both jumped from the land above the water and down to the ditch I was in.

"Come on, Ryushin. Get out of there," Valen said.

"What can we do to help?" Mordakai asked.

Aida and Kirikah were taking way too long and the Destati was pushing me further into the ground.

"I don't know how long I can keep this up," I grunted. The energy supply in my power was low.

Aeric jumped down and joined Valen and Mordakai's side.

"He needs more energy," he said.

Mordakai looked at my energy beam and thought for a minute. Soon then, he placed his hands inside of the blue energy beam and closed his eyes.

"What the hell are you doing?" Valen asked.

"I'm giving up my mana, what does it look like I'm doing?" Mordakai answered.

Aeric did the same. Valen followed right after.

"Concentrate your mana into the energy blast," Aeric said. They all closed their eyes and stood perfectly still. The power of my Kagayaku Hikari increased. I flapped my wings and pushed forward, slowly climbing out of the ditch.

"Why you little ingrates!" Atlmaz yelled. He swiped his hands forward, causing the ground around us to explode. Everyone jerked onto their backs while I fought hard to stay in balance.

The Destati pushed me back into the ditch.

"Damn it!" Mordakai yelled, pulling slowly up to his feet. The three of them continued to lend me their mana.

"Ryushin!"

Aida splashed out of the water and onto the ground beside me. I gave a final push, just enough to pull myself out of the ditch. I grabbed hold of the Trueblade from Aida's hands, using one hand to push up with the Kagayaku Hikari.

"I hope you have insurance, Atlmaz!" I yelled.

The Trueblade flashed.

"Ryushin!" Atlmaz yelled.

"Shiden'issen!" I called.

The sword flashed brightly with power, then created four perfect replicas. I hurled the sword into the Destati with the replicas right behind it. The Trueblade flashed on impact, pushing slowly against the Destati. The replicas smashed into its surface, picking up speed on the reflection.

"No! This can't be!" Atlmaz cried.

He pushed his hands forward, trying desperately to regain control of the battle.

"Just a little further!" Aeric said.

I roared fiercely with every ounce of power I had in my body, blasting the Kagayaku Hikari right through Destati. The energy attack slammed up against Atlmaz and carried him up

into the stars. Destati's sphere shattered like glass, falling from the sky like a meteor shower.
    Everything returned to normal.
    I released my hands from the air and dangled sluggishly to the ground. The water filled in, flushing us with its flood. We all grabbed hold of each other and took the hit.

Chapter Nineteen
Far Worse than a Gisuru

The sun was shining brightly in the night sky, warming us with its power. Everyone sat in a circle around me with their hands laid upon my chest.

"He's alive," Kirikah said.

I sat up slowly. Everyone was fine, filled with smiles and happiness.

"You guys are okay?" I asked. "I thought Corfits and the others had beaten you guys."

"They sort of did," Mordakai chuckled, "Aida came back for all of us."

"Is it over?" Aeric asked.

Valen sighed, "I hope so."

Aida held my hand tightly with a smile. I gripped hers and smiled back. After all of that, we finally won. We succeeded in defeating Atlmaz and the Destati.

"Let's go home," she said.

"Home..." I remembered. With Astrae gone, there was no way of finding out where the gate was.

"Yea, let's go home. I could use a shower," Mordakai joked.

All of them stood up together.

"Hey, don't forget, you still owe me and Kirikah lunch," Valen said.

Mordakai staggered into the water and everyone laughed.

Aida and I walked slowly behind the others.

"Are you going home now?" she asked.

"What do you mean?" I asked.

"You know... like home, Home? Back to your world?"

I felt happy yet sad in my heart. I wanted to go back home to my family and my friends and my world but I didn't want to leave Aida.

I sucked it up and asked, "Will you come with me?"

The Adventures of Ryushin

"I don't know," she hesitated. She looked down into the water at her reflection. I could see Ayaka smiling next to her. "Okay, I will go back with you."

"Really?" I was excited.

She nodded.

Just then, I felt a sharp sense in the back of my mind, an evil one. For some reason, deep down in my heart, I could feel that Atlmaz was still alive. Aida continued to walk with the others, while I stayed behind.

She looked back and asked, "What's wrong?"

"Nothing," I said, trying not to alarm them. I came up with a lie and said, "Just looking for my sword."

"Oh, let me help you," she insisted.

"No no, it's okay," I smiled, "Stay with the others, I'll be right behind you guys."

I hurried across the broken pieces of land on top of the water, searching for that evil presence. He was around, I know it.

The water splashed up onto the tiny chunks, surprising me to death. The stars twinkled above ironically and the sun's light was a little colder than before.

A energy blast came from the side. A bubble wrapped around me and deflected the attack.

"Ryushin!" Kirikah called.

The others followed right behind her. Another one blasted toward her. Valen jumped out in front and took the hit. The force of the attack blasted both of them into the water, following with a powerful explosion.

"Valen! Kirikah!" Aeric yelled.

One more powerful energy attack ripped through the air toward me. Aida lowered her shoulder and rammed me out of the way, taking the hit to her chest. The energy attack exploded, jerking both of us into different directions.

The smoke cleared.

"Aida!" I cried out loud. I ran to her and knelt beside her, picking her up in my arms.

"Ryushin..." she faintly said.

Atlmaz emerged from the clear, but in an odd appearance. His upper body clothing was torn off, revealing his dark muscular chest with purple lines trailing all over it. Wings similar to bats flapped behind his back and half of his head was cover with a demon face. He was twice our size with giant claws and powerful legs.

"Dracolyte!" he roared, erupting the place with his power.

I paid no attention to him.

"Aida, are you okay?" I asked.

She said nothing and closed her eyes.

"Damn you, Dracolyte! Are you listening to me?" he yelled.

"Please, don't give up on me," I said. Tears started escaping my eyes. "Come on, let's go home. Please. I'll take you shopping and we can get you cute clothes ya know? We can go to dinner and everything... please... just don't leave me..." I couldn't help but let it all out. I cried on top of her.

She whispered, "Aishiteru..."

"No! Aida, don't go, I love you too... please..."

Point of View: Mordakai

Ryushin cried loudly. It was the saddest thing I've ever seen and it made me want to cry too. Aeric and I stood side by side watching the tragedy take place. Atlmaz was silent as well.

"Ryushin..." I whispered.

"Mordakai," Aeric called, "We have to stop Atlmaz. It doesn't look like Ryushin is gonna pull through this one."

Valen and Kirikah floated above water unconscious.

"Atlmaz!" I yelled. He turned and faced us.

"Ready?" Aeric asked. I nodded.

The two of us sprinted toward him ready to attack. I pulled my fist back and let it fly. Atlmaz countered and bashed me away with a hard backhand. He grabbed Aeric by the neck and flushed him downward into the water.

The Adventures of Ryushin

I pushed off the ground and slid across the ground, then continued my rush. Atlmaz easily blocked all my attacks and batted me away again. Aeric rose up out of the water and blasted his Chokusha attack. Atlmaz palmed his hand and countered with an energy blast of his own. Aeric wrenched backward onto the ground.

"You fools, you are no match for me," Atlmaz said.

I growled with my Shishiku technique, raising my attack power. I rushed head on but he was still too fast. He grabbed one of my punches and slammed his fist into my stomach like a ball on a string, pounding continuously.

Aeric wrapped his Kinbaku binding spell around his arm and held it tightly. Atlmaz pulled on the attack and snapped Aeric toward us. He brought me to his side, opened his wings and smashed both of us away in opposite directions.

Atlmaz exploded his power out of his body, pushing us back even further. He walked over to Ryushin slowly with his chest raised out front. Ryushin stood up slowly, knowing that Atlmaz was approaching.

Ryushin turned around with a distraught look on his face. His eyes were angry, his teeth were grinding up against one another and the tears from his eyes still watered down his cheeks.

Atlmaz threw a fierce punch but Ryushin countered with a punch of his own. Ryushin's punch collided with Atlmaz's knuckles. The force of Ryushin's attack jerked Atlmaz backward.

"I won't let you get away with this..." Ryushin said faintly, slowly walking forward. Atlmaz took steps back, frightened at Ryushin's words.

"Aeric!" I called. We both ran sluggishly over to the fallen Aida, watching Ryushin take charge.

"Dracolyte! What are you doing?" Atlmaz asked.

Ryushin yelled, "I WON'T LET YOU GET AWAY WITH THIS!" A large red flame encased around him, emitting a very powerful bright light. Ryushin raised his chest into the air and yelled at the top of his lungs.

His power wrenched Atlmaz backward, so he took off into the air.

"What is this power?" he asked.

Ryushin flashed once, then twice before exploding. The large red flame grew bigger every second, boiling the water underneath his feet. The tiny chunks of land shattered into tiny particles and started rotating around him. He still continued to yell loudly throughout the area.

"What's going on?" I asked Aeric.

"I don't know," he answered.

He flashed one more time and the area calmed down. Ryushin was different. His upper body gear was all blown off revealing a dark grayish skin color. Around his chest was pair of dragon wings and his arms was ripped with muscle. His face was completely black; no mouth no nose, similar to a Dracolyte. His hair spiked back sharply and his eyes were thin and angry. This must have been what Ragnorak and Kaisera were talking about, the true form of his Dracolyte.

"What the?" Atlmaz gasped. He was frightened.

The large flame continued to burn all around him with sparks of lightning crawling all over. Ryushin locked his eyes in on Atlmaz then disappeared in his place.

"No way? Where'd he go?" I asked.

All of us were looking all around the area, but he was nowhere to be found. Even Atlmaz couldn't find him. He looked side to side before looking down at us. Ryushin reappeared right in front of him and ripped a powerful punch against his face. Atlmaz flew across the sky with lightning wrapped all over him.

Ryushin appeared instantly in front of the unaware Atlmaz, and then threw kicks and punches quick yet sharply all over his body. Ryushin flipped into a somersault and slammed him down to the water with both of his feet. He pulled his fist back way behind him, creating a bright light within and tossed it down.

The lights flashed into the water with Atlmaz and exploded underneath. He flew out of the water and back up to Ryushin, who was missing again. Ryushin ended up behind him and ripped yet another punch into his face.

Atlmaz blasted through the sky once again and Ryushin continued his relentless assault.

"Dude, this is insane. Ryushin is way too fast for Atlmaz," I said.

"No kidding, I can't even keep up with his movements," Aeric responded. "I'm not so worried about Atlmaz but worried for ourselves. What if Ryushin comes after us? We have to find a way to bring him back."

"Oh yea, right," I nodded.

The Trueblade flashed just up ahead. I made a break for the sword while energy blasts came falling my way. I dove for the sword just barely avoiding contact with an explosion.

Atlmaz and Ryushin came to a stop. Atlmaz was in the air while Ryushin landed back onto the surface of the water.

"Damn you, whoever the hell you are!" Atlmaz yelled. Ryushin just stared back up at him. "I'll teach you!" He raised his hands above his head and blasted a barrage of shadow balls toward Ryushin.

I grabbed the sword and ran back to Aeric.

"Think this will work?" I asked, showing him the Trueblade.

"It has too," he nodded.

Atlmaz flew downward in front of the smoke and continued to fire shadow balls at a closer range. Ryushin deflected all of them easily.

He stepped into the attacks and delivered a breath taking punch into Atlmaz's stomach. He then wound up his arm and bashed him into the air with an uppercut to his chin.

I ran toward Ryushin with the Trueblade in both hands.

"Ryushin," I said. He didn't budge, just kept his focus on Atlmaz. "Ryushin, it's me, Mordakai." He raised his arm and batted me away. I dropped the sword next to him as I slid across the water.

"Mordakai," Aeric called. He grabbed hold of my arm and lifted me out of the water.

I gasped for air. "Freakin' that really hurt! I feel bad for Atlmaz."

Atlmaz screamed in the air.

"Where did you get all of this power!" he yelled. "This can't be happening!"

He clapped his hands together, and then opened them widely, creating a powerful giant shadow ball. He launched it downward to Ryushin, who stood there perfectly calm.

Ryushin tucked his hands down to his side in the form of a cup, ready to use the Kagayaku Hikari.

Just then, a golden heart shaped locket rose from his pocket and moved out in front of his eyes. He looked at it passionately while gathering energy into his hands. He reverted back to his normal form with a tear escaping his eye.

"Ryushin!" Aeric and I called.

"Tell me now!" Atlmaz yelled.

Ryushin triggered his Kagayaku Hikari attack forward and yelled, "You don't know what its like to fall in love!" The powerful energy blast burned right through Atlmaz's shadow ball with ease.

"Ryushin!" Atlmaz yelled one more time.

The Kagayaku Hikari attack plucked Atlmaz out of the sky and carried him beyond the distance. The force of Ryushin's attack jerked Aeric and me deep into the water. Aeric and I grabbed hold of each other's arms and held tightly onto Aida.

Chapter Twenty
Resigning of the Prince

Point of View: Ryushin

"*Do you still love her?*"

"I don't know what you're talking about," I answered pretty straight forward.

"*You don't remember her at all?*"

I stood along the railings of the airship, looking deep into the night sky. I was alone. There was no one around. But I can hear Her talking to me, talking to me in my heart.

"*When are you coming home?*"

"I don't know."

"*I'm still waiting for you.*"

Ayaka appeared next to the steering wheel of the airship. She was dressed in Aida's golden dress and her hair was held up by chopsticks.

"Ayaka...? What are you doing here?"

"You never came home, so I came looking for you."

She faded away.

I was alone once again on the airship. The scenery melted and molded into another one. This time I was in the Raigen's garden. A piano started playing a familiar melody I've heard somewhere before.

Ayaka sat near a rose bush, picking flowers for her bouquet. I walked over and knelt right beside her. She started humming along with the piano.

"You know this song?" I asked.

"Of course I do, silly." She smiled, continuing to pick the flowers.

"Can you sing it for me?" I asked.

She looked into my eyes. "My Japanese is a little off, so you'll have to bear with me."

I nodded and closed my eyes, listening to her beautiful voice.

First Love – Utada Hikaru

Saigo no kisu wa ka ba tabako no flavor ga shita
Nigakute setsunai kaori

Ashita no imagoro ni wa
Anata wa doko ni irun darou
Dare wo omotterun darou

You are always gonna be my love
Itsuka darekato mata koi ni ochitemo
I'll remember to love you taught me how
You are always gonna be the one
Ima wa mada kanashii love love songu
Atarashii uta utaeru made

Tachidomaru jikan ga
Ugoki dasouto shiteru
Wasuretakunai kotobakari

Ashita no imagoro niwa
Watashi wa kitto naite iru
Anatawo omotterun darou

You will always be inside my heart
Itsumo anata dake no basho ga aru kara
I hope that I have a place in your heart too
Now and forever you are still the one
Ima wa mada kanashii love love song
Atarashii uta utaeru made

The Adventures of Ryushin

**You are always gonna be my love
Itsuka darekato mata koi ni ochitemo
I'll remember to love you taught me how
You are always gonna be the one
Mada kanashii love love song
Now and forever**

I opened my eyes slowly to find myself lying in a bed in a bright room. Everyone were in beds next to me, sound asleep. Aida was the only one that wasn't around.

"I'm glad you're okay."

Gundita walked into the room.

"Gundita," I faintly said. I was too weak to get up. "Where's Aida?"

She looked down in dismay. I couldn't help but cry. A tear escaped Gundita's eye as well.

"I'm so sorry, Ryushin," she said. "She fought to stay alive but she just couldn't pull through. She was tired, you have to understand that."

"Gundita..." I cried. She and I hugged tightly, letting all of our tears out.

After a few days of lying in bed, all of us were able to make it to our feet. We were all in Draconia, helping rebuild the kingdom. Dracolytes, Humans and Kitsunes all worked together hand in hand.

Ragnorak and Kaisera stood in front of the throne as always, doing what commanders do best. He told me the whereabouts of the portal back to the other world but I didn't mind much about it. I wanted to stay here longer just to make sure things were okay, but I kept a side note just in case.

Lecia, Craft and Cildiari said their goodbyes and left back home for their kingdoms. They criticized my leadership of course but said, *"Not to worry, you will grow into a great leader in time to come."*

I stepped out into Garuda's Hexagon where the only cemetery laid rest. Astrae's tombstone rested in the middle of the rest with his hood covered the top of the stone. I knelt before him in honor of his death.

"Ryushin," Ragnorak called. "You have to do one more thing."

"What is that?" I said, strapping the Trueblade to my belt.

"Speech time," he said.

I balled my eyes and walked with him back to the top of the tower. I was fully restored back to normal, dressed in the armor that was given to me back at the crystal room.

The broken kingdom of the Dracolytes rested before me with workers, citizens and guests from the other kingdoms. Everyone was there again, all looking up at me from the bridge.

"Congratulations on a victory well fought," I said first. The crowd roared fiercely with pride all over. I smiled and then said, "But I have failed. I failed you and I have failed a close friend, more like a loved one." Their cheering went from loud to silent. "Until I can forgive myself for what I have done, I'm sorry, I cannot be your Prince." The crowd was stunned and a tear ran out of my eye.

"Ryushin," Ragnorak said.

"I'm sorry Ragnorak. I just can't go on living knowing that I let Aida down, but I want you to take care of this place for me. I'm going back to Raigen. If you need me, you know I'll be there."

He nodded.

The next morning, all of us- Mordakai, Valen, Kirikah, Aeric, Onry, Rheaa, Rhyona, Zandaris, Xamnesces, Ksama, Yoichi, Gundita, Nomak, Chrisa, Ragnorak and Kaisera- stood in Shiva's Hexagon, saluting Aida's casket before going our separate ways.

"You will always be inside my heart," I said.

Nomak and Chrisa lifted the casket onto Raigen's Airship. I looked at all of them and placed my hand in the middle. They all put their hand atop of mine.

"Together?" Aeric said.

I nodded. "Together."

We gave each other hugs and said our goodbyes before leaving. Gundita, Nomak, Chrisa and I flew back to Raigen, back to home.

The following day after our arrival back in Raigen, I stood before Aida's tombstone with her great sword drilled behind it. The tombstone read, Two Hearts. I placed the golden locket around the handle of her sword and knelt before her.

"So what will you do now?"

Gundita stood behind me with her hands behind her back.

"I've decided. I want to stay here," I said.

"You are always more than welcome, Ryushin," she nodded.

I kissed my fingers and planted it against the ground before Aida's tombstone.

"I love you..."

Dream of the Other Story

It has been over a year since my brother had disappeared. He warned us, my friends and me, that night we were eating at the Cheesecake Factory. My friends, Ralph and Jeice, sat around the dinner table but without him this time. I couldn't help but wonder where he was.

"Justin..."

I heard his voice echoing throughout the room. I got up and listened closely. It repeated over and over again further down the restaurant. He was there, standing next to the door. Derric looked up at me and smiled, then walked out the door.

"Derric!" I called but he couldn't hear me.

I ran through the door to find myself on a dark open field, the sky filled with the night and the moon showered its light all over. Up ahead was a dark mysterious figure with his back turned hosting two wings, one of a dragon and one of an angel.

Here came the rain, pounding fiercely into the grass below.

"Justin..."

I looked all over for him but he was nowhere around. The dark figure turned around slowly and glared at me with its dark eyes.

"Derric?" I asked.

It tucked its hands to his side in the formation of a cup and gathered a bright red light between them. A red flame grew from its feet and encased itself around the dark figure. A sword dropped from the sky and drilled into the ground in front of me. The name Trueblade was engraved on its edge.

The dark figure snapped its arms forward and fired a bright red energy beam toward me. Its power quaked all around the area, changed the color of the sky and flashed its blinding light into my eyes. The only thing that was visible was the sword.

"Justin..."

My brother, Derric, dressed in an awkward formal suit flew in from the sky and defended out in front of me with his arms spread out.

"Derric!" I called.

A cylinder of projections circled around us, showing us visions of another world. In the visions, Derric was fighting a giant spider, flying on top of colorful dragons and fighting a vast number of strange looking demonic creatures. Another projection showed a girl that looked just like Ayaka, holding onto him dearly in the rain.

"Justin, I need your help more than ever now," Derric said.

"What? What are you talking about?" I asked.

The Adventures of Ryushin

Another character that looked like Derric flew in beside him, defending him.

"Ryushin," Derric said. The two of them held joined hands and defended me. "Justin... the Dracolyte..."

I grabbed the sword and raced toward the dark figure, lowering my shoulder and moving under the red energy beam. With one push, I lunged into the air with the sword raised above my head.

"Leave my brother alone!" I yelled. I swung the sword downward and cut right through the dark figure. The figure exploded, jerking me onto my back.

I woke up in my bed, drenched in buckets of sweat. The moon glistened through the window of my room. In the corner of my eye, I could see him standing in the shadows. I turned on the light but no one was there.

"Justin..." he called.

There was a picture of me and him as kids at the foot of my bed.

"He's still alive..."

Maps

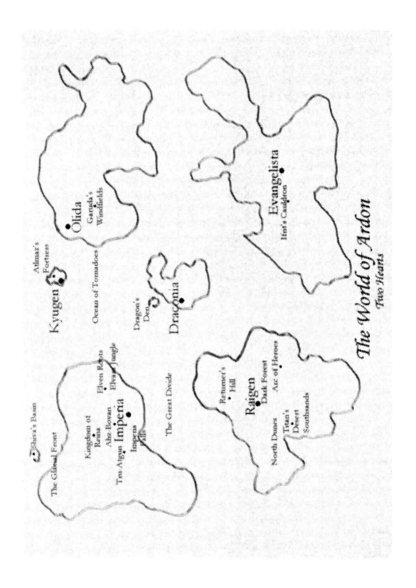

Maps

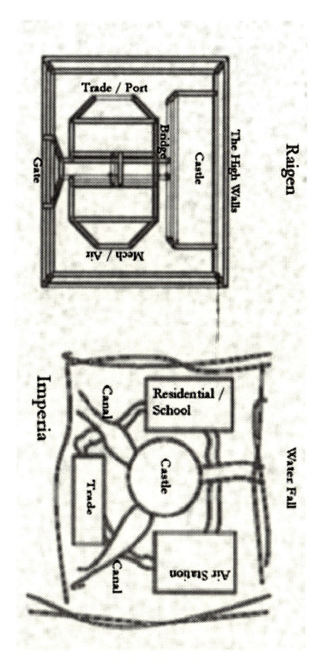

Maps

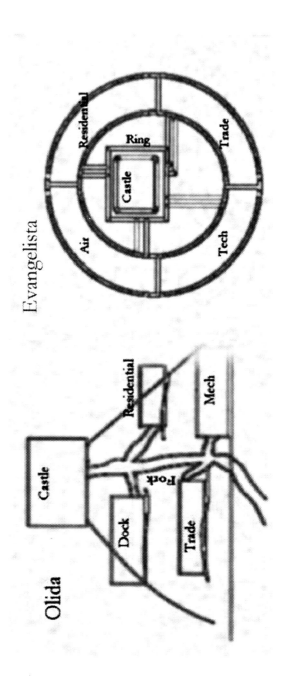

Maps

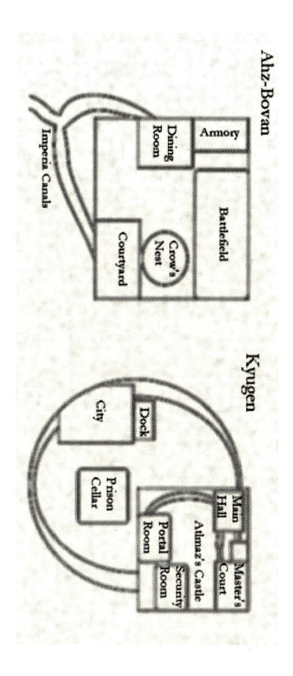

Maps

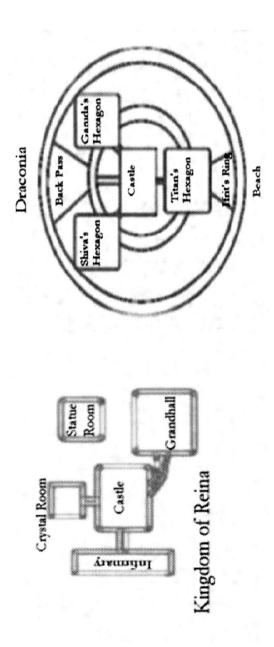

Maps

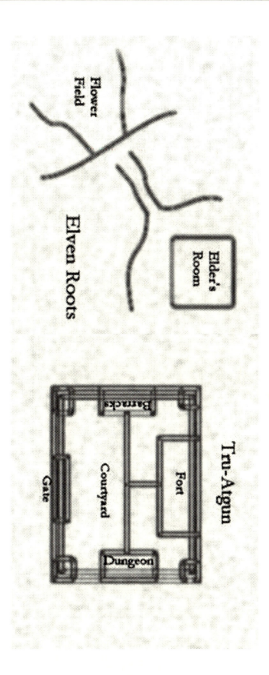

Maps

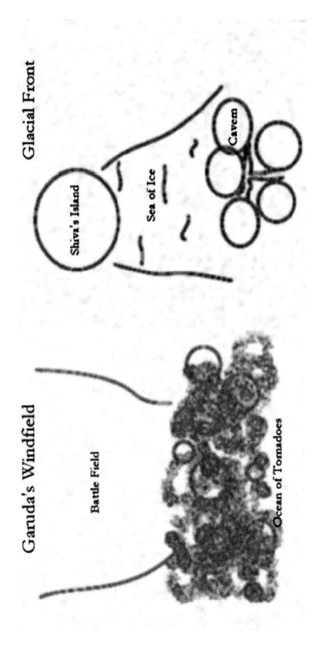

Maps

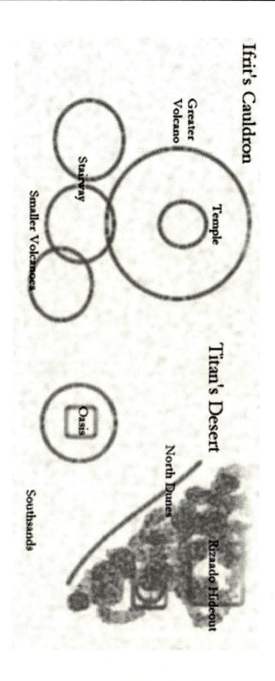

377

Attack Spell Technique Ability

Kagayaku Hikari	Shining Light
Tsukikage	Moon Shadow
Shimoyake	Frostbite
Sune-ku Kage	Shadow Snakes
Kurai-Shuuha	Dark Wave
Moetatsu	Burst
Chokusha	Direct Sunlight
Fuereasei	Flare Star
Kyoufuu	Raging Wind
Takuetsufuu	Prevailing Wind
Hibashira	Pillar of Fire
Kakeaimanzai	Rapid Fire
Kurosufaia	Cross Fire
Kyouheki	Ice Wall
Hyouhen	Ice Shard
Hyoushin	Ice Quake
Awaikae	Light Shadow
Kokuei	Silhouette
Moufubuki	Blizzard
Hidama	Falling Star
Kenboushou	Dark Amnesia
Gaikou	Beams of Light
Gyoukou	Light of Dawn
Shishiku	Lion's Roar
Taka no Hane	Falcon's Wing
Hekireki	Thunderclap
Denkouissen	Flash of Lightning
Rururai	Thunderbolt
Seinaru Yoru	Holy
Zenkai	Destruction
Kaimei	Darkness
Tsuikai	Reminiscence
Dokubari	Bee-Sting

Attack Spell Technique Ability

Shishou	Shadow of Death
Mekurumeku	Blind
Kinbaku	Bind
Motatsuku	Slow
Otoroeru	Weak
Hyoushou	Ice Lance
Ankokuseiun	Dark Nebula
Nakkura	Complete Dark
Shiden'issen	Flash of a Sword

Printed in the United States
76983LV00002B/45